A Dead Daughter

Jessica Huntington Desert Cities Mystery #3

Anna Celeste Burke

Books by USA Today Bestselling Author, Anna Celeste Burke

A Dead Husband Jessica Huntington Desert Cities Mystery #1
A Dead Sister Jessica Huntington Desert Cities Mystery #2
A Dead Daughter Jessica Huntington Desert Cities Mystery # 3
A Dead Mother Jessica Huntington Desert Cities Mystery #4 [2017]
Love A Foot Above the Ground Prequel to the Jessica Huntington
Desert Cities Mystery Series

Cowabunga Christmas! Corsario Cove Cozy Mystery #1
Gnarly New Year Corsario Cove Cozy Mystery #2
Heinous Habits, Corsario Cove Cozy Mystery #3
Radical Regatta, Corsario Cove Cozy Mystery #4 [2017]

Murder at Catmmando Mountain Georgie Shaw Cozy Mystery #1
Love Notes in the Key of Sea Georgie Shaw Cozy Mystery #2
All Hallows' Eve Heist Georgie Shaw Cozy Mystery #3
A Merry Christmas Wedding Mystery Georgie Shaw Cozy Mystery #4
Murder at Sea of Passenger X Georgie Shaw Cozy Mystery #5
Murder of the Maestro Georgie Shaw Cozy Mystery #6 [2017]

DEDICATION

To daughters everywhere, trying to do the right thing!
Keep at it—trying *is* what matters. You can do it!

.

CONTENTS

ANNA CELESTE BURKE

ACKNOWLEDGMENTS

This book is another product of love and patience on the part of my husband. I will never be able to express my gratitude for all he does, including reading every word I write and giving me feedback. He is also a great cheerleader and a vital support when the work bogs down. That's especially true when I'm lost in the lands of editing and marketing, places that challenge even the most intrepid authors. Thanks, Hubby!

My sister has also continued to hang in there with me on this book. Despite a life of her own, overflowing with work and other demands, she trudges on at my side reading and editing. Thanks, Sis!

Special thanks to Peggy Hyndman who has stepped in as the editor of record. She has re-edited the manuscript I continue to monkey around with the material even after I have published the book. I'm grateful for her willingness to tackle this book along with the others in the series. You've been a pleasure to work with, Peggy! Thanks so much.

PROLOGUE

Jessica used her bound hands to tug at the jacket she was wearing. Keeping it closed retained more of her body heat. With her hands under the edge of the jacket, she worked to loosen the rope wrapped around her wrists. Seated, with her back pressed against an outcropping of boulders near one of the scenic overlooks on the Desert View Trail, she could see much of the Coachella Valley. The spectacle below was breath-taking, a view she'd always loved, but not now. Overlaid by a grid-work of roadways and buildings, colorful patches stood out in contrast to swaths of white desert sand. The lights in the desert resort cities below sparkled as the day languished and evening approached. It got dark so early this time of year.

The air was crisp and fragrant with the smell of the pine trees that flourished in the Mt. San Jacinto wilderness at the top of the Palm Springs tramway. Jessica had come here, many times, while growing up in the valley below. She loved the short tram ride that carried you from palms to pines in minutes. This trip was her first visit since returning to the Palm Springs area after retreating to her childhood home in the wake of unfortunate events that had wreaked havoc on her well-planned life.

Despite her best efforts to take refuge behind the gates of the tony Mission Hills Country Club in Rancho Mirage, calamity prevailed. Jessica had soon fought, like a junkyard dog, to survive a series of shocking attacks. Not even an earthly paradise could keep murder and mayhem at bay. Now, here she was again. This time, in the company of another wealthy, pampered, thirty-something woman whose life was in tatters. Libby Van Der Woert had a gun and was in the midst of a full-blown manic episode.

1

"Please listen to me. It's getting cold and dark. Let's go inside where it's warm and talk this over. We'll get coffee and talk as long as you want."

The ties give as Jessica repeatedly picked at the knots and then stretched, clenched, and unclenched her bound wrists. She had been working on them since she sat down on the flat-topped boulder. Wiggle room meant she was making progress. An icy blast made her work harder. They'd followed the trail, away from the visitor center at the top of the tramway, after Libby stuck a gun in Jessica's ribs. When they arrived at the overlook, Libby had bound Jessica's hands and forced her to sit on the ground.

"No, you're trying to trick me. If I go back, the police will arrest me. My screwed-up life will get even worse. Do you think I want to spend what's left of it in prison?"

"I'll help you. Nobody wants you to spend the rest of your life locked up."

"Oh yeah? They think I killed Shannon. Why not, since I've lied to everyone, over and over? Now, thanks to you, they can add kidnapping to my rap sheet. I've had plenty of help from you, Jessica Huntington. If you had followed me when I asked you to, I wouldn't have had to use the gun."

Libby hopped from one huge boulder to another getting closer to where Jessica sat. A wave of vertigo swept over Jessica. It looked as though Libby hovered above a sheer drop into the valley. That image was deceptive. The land fell away at a slope not visible from where she sat. That didn't mean that falling from where the hyped-up young woman now stood, wouldn't hurt. It might even kill her.

"Untie my hands. Let's go back to the tram station while we still can without breaking our necks. It's going to get icy when the sun sets. If anyone asks, I'll explain that this was a big misunderstanding. There won't be any charges filed against you for kidnapping, I promise. We'll find someone else to help you if you don't want me to be involved."

"I've already got help. I've had help since I was twelve. Dr. Dick is just the latest in a long line of shrinks. He used me, but I let him do it. He believed me, Jessica. Anything I said, and the grimier, the better. It was such a rush, you know, making up all this sick stuff about people. I had it all worked out. With a little help from my respected shrink, I'd pay back the smug jerks for everything they had ever done to me."

As she spoke, Libby paced along the top of a row of boulders. She pretended to be walking on a tightrope, wobbling like she might lose her balance. That started another wave of vertigo, forcing Jessica to shut her eyes as she worked harder at the rope around her wrists.

"You should have seen how he worked me. He nodded with such concern in

2

his eyes and spoke with so much admiration for all I'd suffered. In fact, he was so sorry that I almost believed it myself. I even cried real tears! It was nothing but lies and more lies about my family. That's slander or libel or some crap like that, right?" She abruptly stopped pacing and almost lost her balance.

"Oh my God, Libby, no!" Jessica gasped. Libby steadied herself and picked up where she'd left off. A wistful note entered her voice for a moment.

"I thought he loved me. I figured that if I forced my parents to give me my inheritance early, I could run off with the love-of-my-life. Why not? If I waited until they died to get the money, I'd be too old to enjoy it anyway. That part was his idea—getting the money, I mean. I'm the one who tried to get it for him, though, so add extortion to slander and libel and kidnapping. Whatever." She shrugged and went back to her pretend high-wire act. That she had help from Dr. Richard Carr while hatching her scheme to harass her parents, was news to Jessica. Who knew how much of what Libby was saying bore any resemblance to truth rather than more lies or delusions?

"I'm not the first, but I will be the last psycho-tramp who falls for Dr. Dick. I pulled a 'Monica Lewinsky' on him, with enough of his DNA to make sure he never practices psychotherapy again. That's one thing I wanted to tell you when I asked you to meet me up here. It's all in a little blue bag, Jessica. Get it and use what's in it so I won't be a dead daughter for nothing!" She threw her head back and laughed, made a sudden turn like she was a gymnast reaching the end of a balance beam, and walked back. That dead daughter statement and the routine that followed sent a chill down Jessica's spine that had nothing to do with the temperature up there at eight thousand feet.

"Libby, I'm sorry Dr. Carr took advantage of you. Why wait? Let's go get him, now." DNA evidence was one way to sort fact from fiction. If he was taking advantage of his clients, perhaps the renowned psychiatrist had planted the seeds of false allegations in the confused woman's head, too.

"What's wrong with you? I broke my family! Don't you get it, or doesn't that mean anything to you?" With that, she stopped and hopped down closer to Jessica, with a menacing gleam in her eye.

"I care about my family," Jessica said. "I also understand how much trouble you can get into when you're angry and confused. Lots of us get in over our heads and hurt people, even the ones we love most." Jessica felt the ropes on her wrists give again as she spoke those words to Libby in a calm voice. Only a little more and she could slip free. What to do after that wasn't clear. The gun Libby held wasn't more than a few inches away.

"Shut up! You don't know what you're talking about, except the part about

being in over your head. It's over for me like it was for my so-called friend, Shannon Donnelly. I'm the one who told them what she was up to—Dr. Dick and that red devil, too. It's my fault she's gone. I'm going to pay for that one way or another. Here's an idea! Why don't I take you with me? I'll make you disappear too. Poof!" Libby waved the gun back and forth over Jessica as if it were a magic wand. Her face was pale, her dark eyes were wild, and her hair flowed in the cold mountain air. She was like a character from Harry Potter, a mad wizard-in-training. "You should have left me alone."

"You called me, remember? I'm here because you reached out for help. Please, no more dead daughters, okay? Get rid of that gun. Toss it down below, and nobody will know you even had a gun. You don't want to hurt me, yourself, or anyone else. I can help you. Paul can help you too."

Libby squatted down, fixing Jessica with a grimace on her lips. "Are you kidding me? Like he did when I had that car accident that killed Lela, you mean? Please don't tell me you believe that was an accident. I should have died, too, you moron. You aren't half as smart as you think you are." Libby stood up again and turned her back on Jessica.

"Paul Worthington was helpful, all right. All he did was let me get up to more mischief. That's what I've done, you know, caused a lot of mischief for Lela and Shannon and my oh so respectable family." Libby tossed her head back and cackled. The action caused her to wobble again. "My parents' lives are blown to bits. Such accomplished people with their rags to riches story and all that overcoming hardship garbage. No matter what else they ever do, they're losers as parents. If I haven't already made that clear, I will soon, won't I?"

"Come on, Libby. I can't believe you want that for them, or for you. There's always a chance to make things right. You just have to give it another try."

"Oh no, not that old 'try and try again' line. At a time like this? Is that all you've got? Woohoo, it's a long way down. Come, look." With that, Libby climbed back to the boulder she'd been using as a balance beam and took a couple of steps back without even looking.

"Stop! Don't back up anymore. You're so close to the edge already. You've got to believe me. These rocks get slippery."

"Come here now, or I'll shoot you!" Libby pointed the gun at Jessica.

"Then what? Who will help you make sure Carr pays for what he's done to you? Go ahead and shoot me because I'm not coming any closer."

"Do as she says, Ms. Huntington, or I'll do it."

Jessica's head snapped around, startled by the sound. There he was, on another of the nearby boulders, as if he had been conjured up out of thin air by

4

Libby's words. *The doctor's white hair gleamed in the afternoon sunlight. Dr. Richard Carr was waving a gun of his own.*

Jessica was about to warn him off when Carr, belying his age, moved toward her, in a flash. He hopped from the boulder he was on to another, and then down onto a flat rocky area near where Jessica sat. Grabbing her by the ropes, he jerked her to her feet.

"Libby has the right idea about you. You haven't been helpful to her at all. In fact, you've been a pain in the neck from day one. She'd be fine right now if you'd kept your mouth shut tight around that silver spoon in it. It is a pity you two couldn't help each other though. Under other circumstances, you might have been close friends. Two self-absorbed, poor little rich girls, with no real worries in your pointless little lives, you could have found plenty to whine about over manis and pedis. You and all the rest of the entitled children in my practice make me sick. What a bunch of naive, sheltered, self-centered monsters! Easy to manipulate, I will say that much for Libby, especially with the help of my liberal drug policy. She was doing fine until you stepped in. Now get up there, or I'll shoot her and then you." He motioned with the gun toward Libby.

"It won't work, Carr. They'll figure out you did it."

"How? Nobody even knows I'm up here. It'll be easy enough to believe you two psychos fought over the gun or something. Or maybe you decided you were Rodeo Drive's answer to Thelma and Louise and forged a murder-suicide pact. Who knows? There's ample evidence you're no more stable than Libby. You've been in treatment for years, with one therapist after another. Then a nasty divorce and all the other traumas you've been through in the last few months. It's enough to push anyone over the edge. Over the edge, get it?" Carr laughed at that last witty bit. His laugh was as unnerving as those that had issued from Libby earlier. Libby wasn't laughing now.

"How do you know I've been in treatment, or why?" Too wound up to answer, he continued to rant.

"I can't believe you had the gall to get Libby to turn on me. And you, Libby, are sicker and dumber than I ever dreamed. Why don't you do as Ms. Huntington suggested and toss the gun down below? Trust me. If you make even the slightest move, I'll shoot your meddlesome friend. I know you don't want another dead daughter on your conscience now that you seem to have found one."

Jessica stood, letting the new psychopath take his turn raging against the fates. His yank on the ropes had brought her to her feet but had also loosened them enough so that she could wriggle free as the madman spoke. In an instant, she reached over and shoved him. Caught by surprise, he went flailing backward.

He slipped off the boulder and fell flat on his back with an audible thud and a grunt of pain. The gun flew out of his hands and wedged into a nearby crevice. Jessica scrambled up onto the boulder where Libby stood, grabbed her by the hand, and yanked her toward the jumble of rocks they needed to cross to get to safety.

"Let's go. This ends now! We're going to tell the authorities all about your esteemed psychiatrist. He'll never hurt you, or anyone else, again."

As they moved past the spot where the doctor had fallen, he climbed on the rocks behind them. He reached for Libby, who teetered as she tried to evade his grasp. Libby shoved Jessica and then turned away as the man lunged for her. Dr. Carr grabbed hold of Libby's arm and pulled himself forward onto the boulder with her. She still had that gun in her hand as they all struggled to maintain their footing. Jessica heard two sounds—a gunshot and a blood-curdling scream. The scream was her own as she plunged into nothingness. Maybe it was a sheer drop to the valley below.

1 THE ICU

The room was cool and dark in the eerie twilight of the Intensive Care Unit where they had brought Jessica. It was quiet, except for a soft, rhythmic pinging and the whooshing sound of a machine hooked up to her. To her anxious mother, the room gave off a strange vibe, cocoon-like, everything suspended in time and place—a way station on the too thin line between this life and the next. What came next was unclear, but oblivion played a big part in Alexis' notions of the afterlife. Oblivion was a blessing when life asked too much, like now, when she was worried sick about her daughter. The wish for oblivion was for herself, not for Jessica, who had barely missed an early entry into the netherworld hours earlier.

Alexis sat in a chair next to the hospital bed. She'd been there all night. A rescue team had found Jessica alive and they lifted her off the ledge where she had fallen and transported her by helicopter for trauma care. She was in good shape, given her fall and hours of exposure to the elements near the peak of Mt. San Jacinto. It was below freezing by the time rescuers reached her. Her daughter wasn't out of the woods yet. Well, she was literally out of the woods, but hadn't received the "all clear" in terms of her prognosis.

She'd dropped twenty feet before hitting that ledge. Alexis tried not to think about what would have happened if that granite outcropping hadn't been there. Another member of Jessica's party missed the ledge and found oblivion. The room felt cold. Alexis rubbed her hands together to warm them and shake off the "what-if" chills.

Jessica was also fortunate to have landed in the piles of accumulated leaves, pine needles, and other debris that cushioned her fall. She'd sustained cuts and bruises in various places on her body, including scrapes on her face. The most serious cut, on the palm of her left hand, must have occurred when she grabbed something as she fell. That cut, a deep slice almost to the bone, had been cemented with medical grade superglue before bandaging. She had bruised, but not broken, ribs on the left side of her body, which absorbed most of the impact of the fall. Her left shoulder, slammed hard, was also bruised. The doctor described a broken bone in her left arm as a "clean break," whatever that meant.

"That part of your daughter's anatomy will soon be as good as new," the baby-faced doctor had assured Alexis, smiling as he spoke.

Alexis wanted to punch him. He was trying to be upbeat, but something about him grated her. Perhaps, his bedside manner bore a hint of condescension that the young too often displayed toward their elders, even filthy rich elders who could buy them several times over. She fiddled with the showy diamond ring on her finger. She still wore it even though she'd removed the matching wedding band Giovanni had given her.

Or, maybe it was just a doctor thing: a god complex running amok. In the last few months, she'd had more than her share of heart-to-hearts with doctors. So many well-regarded specialists in their fields, most of them were older men, women still far and few between. The young nerds, learning to ply their trade, weren't any better than the well-established older gents. Many couldn't even make eye contact if they had to ask sensitive questions or deliver bad news.

Where were the doctors like the one she knew in childhood? The Baldwin family doctor didn't have to ask what killed your grandmother because he already knew. All dead, and if not, a dying breed for sure, like their longtime family doctor, may he rest in peace. These days, it was a "McDoctor, can I take your order, please?" experience, without the please. Even the so-called "concierge medicine" she paid for helped little. Despite all the hype, it seemed more like a way to collect extra fees than a means to provide more exclusive, patient-oriented care, like good old Marcus Welby.

Marcus Welby! Right, Alexis thought, as the doctor next to her pored over Jessica's chart that was displayed on an electronic device.

You are showing your age, Alexis, my dear. That's most unbecoming of a lady and a Baldwin. Her mother's voice popped up on a tape in her head. Alexis needed to shut mum up to hear the doctor. It was already after midnight and she wanted to call Hank to tell him about their daughter's mishap. And she wanted to get back to Jessica. The Xanax she'd taken to calm her nerves wasn't doing any good. *How long before I can take another?* Alexis wondered as she struggled to focus on what this annoying little man said.

"We're still concerned about the nasty bump on her head. A scan revealed no evidence of any internal bruising or bleeding, but she was out cold when the EMTs got to her. She could talk to us when they first brought her in; knew who she was, what day it was, things like that. We needed to patch her up and set that bone in her arm, and she was in pain, so we sedated her. The plan is to keep her in the ICU overnight where we can control the pain and watch her to ensure we haven't missed anything." That smug smile appeared again! Peering from over the rim of his glasses, the resemblance to a nerdy twelve-year-old was even more pronounced.

If he reaches out to pat me on the head or calls me honey, he's getting an elbow or a foot in a place he'll not soon forget, Alexis thought, as she smiled and listened.

"Jessica's vital signs returned to normal once the EMTs reached her. If they stay that way, we'll move her out of the ICU in the morning. Unless a new problem pops up, she should be able to go home in another day or two." Relief swamped Alexis, hearing that optimistic punch line to the doctor's report.

Moments later, Alexis relayed what she'd learned to Henry "Hank" Huntington, her ex-husband, Jessica's father. She was sorry to have to call him so late, and with bad news. Still, she was grateful not to have to tell him he had a dead daughter.

That possibility had loomed large in her mind as she and Bernadette sped from Mission Hills to the hospital. It was a short drive with Bernadette at the wheel of the Escalade. Alexis, too shaken to drive, had already taken an Ambien. Not that one Ambien knocked her out, these days. But why chance driving when Bernadette was at the ready? And she'd taken several other pills as she prepared to retire for the night, so better safe than sorry.

"Why do you suppose no one called us earlier? It sounds like this began hours ago," Alexis wondered aloud.

"That's what I wanted to know when Don Fontana called us. I was ready to give him a chunk of my mind for not telling us right away that Jessica was in trouble. He said his department hadn't heard about it right away either, Alexis. At first, the rangers thought it was stranded hikers. You know, that happens all the time around here. Those mountains are crawling with people, even this time of year when it's cold up there."

"Sure, the tramway counts on holiday traffic to tide them over until the season gets underway."

"Don says the rescue team got on it right away. Then the rangers heard visitors saying somethin' about gunshots, so they notified the local police. Even at that point, Don's buddies didn't know it had anything to do with Jessica."

"Why would they? I didn't know she was up there, did you?"

"No, but Detective Hernandez said Jessica left him a message that she was meeting Libby Van Der Woert at the top of the tram. He's with the Cat City police department, so it took a while to put two and two together. When he heard something was going on up there, he called the Palm Springs Police Department and told them Jessica might be involved. Don said even after that, he waited to know for sure what was going on before he called us. People were falling and guns were shooting, so there was a lot of confusion. I guess it was all over the TV by then, but nobody else called me until they gave out Jessica's name while I was talking to Don. After that, the phone calls started, so I turned off the ringer. The answering machine will take the calls and I can listen to the voice mails later."

"What was she doing up there, Bernadette? How did she get into this mess?"

"She's good-hearted, but too easy to get in over her head with other people's troubles. This has to do with one of her cases, since she met Libby up there and called Detective Hernandez."

"How odd. At the dinner party we held for Nick and Nora, they seemed happy with their move to the desert, and glad to have Jessica handling their legal matters. Their daughter wasn't with them for dinner that night, so I didn't realize Jessica even knew her."

"There's a lot more going on. She was trying to figure it out even before Libby's friend went missing and Detective Hernandez got involved."

"You're talking about that Donnelly woman? That story was on the news, but I didn't pay much attention."

"Yes, Shannon Donnelly's car turned up in Cathedral City right after Thanksgiving. They found her car, but no Shannon, and nobody's seen her since. I'm betting whatever Jessica was trying to find out had something to do with that, but who knows? Libby's lucky to be alive; her doctor, not so lucky. What was he doing up there is my question? Who was shooting? Why? We can ask Jessica, I hope." They lapsed into silence at that point, as Bernadette sped up, driving as fast as she could to get to the hospital where the rescue squad had taken Jessica and Libby. At this point, they didn't know if Jessica could even answer anybody's questions.

Hank asked no questions when Alexis called him after the briefing from the trauma doctor. Now, he was making his way to the California desert as fast as he could. An architect by training and CEO of a real estate development company based in LA, he'd spent a lot of time in Asia after the Great Recession wrecked the California real estate market. His company contracted to complete several projects in Hong Kong, Shanghai, Beijing, and Singapore after the US real estate bubble burst.

He'd come home to LA at the end of July to attend the gala for a new exhibit honoring him and other well-known architects. Not just for the things that they built in Southern California, but for those "Never Built." Designs for projects that had never gotten off the ground, so to speak, were on display. Alongside those plans were magnificent photos and artists renderings of Hank's handiwork, featuring projects that *had* moved from paper to brick and mortar. That included their desert modern home in the Mission Hills Country Club. The "Never Built" exhibit had created quite a stir, bringing Hank well-deserved attention and prospects for new projects in California. He was currently on this side of the Pacific, making travel to the hospital in Rancho Mirage simpler.

Still, he was upstate, north of the Bay Area, when Alexis located him after midnight. Given the late hour, he would have to jump through a few hoops to get to Palm Springs. His corporate jet was at the airport in San Francisco. He was trying to rouse the flight crew and get them to file a flight plan. As soon as he could arrange it, a car would take him from Napa or Mendocino, or wherever he was, to the airport. No doubt, Hank had already rallied two or three colleagues or assistants to rearrange his schedule or fill in for him at events in an action-packed twelve to fourteen-hour day ahead. His stamina was legendary even though he was in his mid-sixties.

Alexis hoped he would arrive soon. Hank was better at handling crises than she'd ever been. She reached out and took her daughter's hand in her own. That hand was so small, cold, and thin. She tried not to cry or hang on too tightly as she sat at her daughter's side. As often happened, Alexis was fraught with doubt about the simplest act of mothering. The whole maternal instinct thing was a lot of hooey, as she well knew, having been reared by an icicle in a chignon and Chanel.

Jessica had been such a beautiful child, so inquisitive and full of life. Impulsive, too, and more energetic than Alexis ever dreamed a child could be. It had been exhausting trying to keep up with her daughter, and fulfill all the expectations as Hank's wife, both in LA and on the local charity circuit here in "the desert."

Tougher, still, was doing all that while fighting with her inner demons. She wondered if Hank had been alone at that hotel when she phoned. Not that it was any of her business. Alexis, of all people, had no right to be jealous if he found pleasure in another woman's arms. Besides, that was the least of her worries. It was all too, too much, then and now.

Not for a Baldwin! Her mother's voice chided. Emma Baldwin's stern face rose before her, lips pursed pencil thin. The woman stood, straight as an arrow, her perfect posture an angry reproach. Alexis felt her shoulders bow as she closed her eyes to make the image vanish. Her bent shoulders were, at once, concession and defiance.

"Thank God for Bernadette and Hank," Alexis sighed, not even realizing she had spoken those words aloud. Jessica stirred. Alexis squeezed her daughter's hand. The stalwart Bernadette was better at handling crises, too. She was off now, searching for coffee, and Alexis hoped she would return soon. Alexis let go of Jessica's hand to scoot back in her bedside chair.

"No, no, don't let go," Jessica called out. Alexis jumped to her feet and hung over the bed, drawing close to her daughter. A wave of dizziness flowed through her. She grabbed the rail on Jessica's bed to steady herself.

"It's okay. I'm here, Baby Girl. It's me, Mom. I'm right here." Alexis spoke in soothing tones as she reached again for her daughter's hand. Tears filled her eyes with gratitude at the sound of that plaintive voice, not just because Jessica was alive, but also because she was at her side and able to comfort her beloved daughter. Alexis had not always been there when Jessica needed her, but she was now. Here was her chance to do the right thing if only she could figure out how to do it.

2 SERENDIPITOUS EVENTS

Alexis sat as the minutes ticked by in the ICU, holding Jessica's hand. Her thoughts wavered between past and present. Sometimes, even in dire circumstances, you encounter serendipitous events. She might have been even farther away than Hank today. In July, Alexis had flown to LA from the Mediterranean to celebrate the "Never Built" event being held in Hank's honor, and had planned to leave soon after.

That all changed when a routine medical exam brought Alexis worrisome news and she headed to the Coachella Valley to get a second opinion from her previous doctor. There would be more tests before she knew what she was up against, but the doctors agreed that she had a problem. When Alexis shared what she'd learned, Bernadette was adamant that she stay put in Mission Hills. Not just until she learned more about her condition, but until she made a clear decision about what to do next. Here it was, December, and she still hadn't taken the next step, surgery. Nor had she shared the information about her condition with anyone other than Bernadette.

Hired as the housekeeper decades before, Bernadette became so much more. Not just in her official capacity as the household manager of the Mission Hills estate. Bernadette was a skilled coordinator of all the things it took to keep the estate running. Her skills had proved to be a lifesaver, even before Jessica's birth. The pregnancy was rough, and Alexis didn't bounce back, as everyone assured her she would, after giving birth. She tried to trudge on, but as a few years passed and Alexis' better nature yielded to the beasts within, she gave up even trying to keep up with the demands placed on her as a wife and mother. It still hurt to think about those last few years with Hank before they divorced.

Hank prodded and poked at her, wondering what was wrong, but a distraction, or something like it, had become preferable to dealing with him. When you have a lot of money, diversions are plentiful and easy to come by. There was always a gala or a getaway, somewhere. With all the shopping, primping, and jet-setting, sublime distractions from anything serious were within easy reach.

If distraction didn't work, there was blessed oblivion. Little by little, she relied less on distraction and more on oblivion. It was easy enough to pick a fight to drive Hank away, back to their house in Brentwood and his work in Los Angeles. She often used physical pain as a cover; tennis, horseback riding, and golf all took a toll. A headache, real or feigned, would give her an excuse to retreat to the master wing of the house and push everything away except solitude and oblivion.

Perhaps if she could have been more open about her struggles, things might have been different, but that would have meant going against the Baldwin stiff-upper-lip code, and it would have meant making herself vulnerable to others, including Hank. She chose not to do that. It wasn't Hank's fault. Alexis found it hard to be open to anyone, friend or family. The men in Alexis' life—a slew of them—shared her bed, but little else. That was even true for Hank, who had always wanted more from her than she could give. When he refused to settle for less, she made him leave. Bernadette was as close to a confidant as anyone in Alexis' life, but Alexis kept plenty from Bernadette.

Her main regret was that Jessica took it all so hard, especially, the divorce. On the verge of adolescence, Jessica had done what she could to make her anger and unhappiness clear. Wracked with insecurity, doubt, and guilt, Alexis couldn't rein in her acting out. Many times, when she should have set limits or sanctioned Jessica's behavior, that image of her own mother intruded. She didn't want to kill her daughter's spirit, so she backed off.

Jessica's anxious nature, the flip side of her out-of-control self, was just as hard to take. Rather than offering comfort and reassurance when Jessica was whiny and scared, Alexis felt her spine stiffen and her shoulders straighten. Her inner Emma emerged, chiding Jessica for her weakness. Occasionally, she fought her way through all the inner turmoil to connect with her daughter, but often, she withdrew. In time, Bernadette became her surrogate as a mother, too, stepping in to oversee Jessica's care as well as managing household affairs.

One by one, they all left Rancho Mirage, except for Bernadette. She stayed behind to manage the estate. In July, when Alexis arrived in Rancho Mirage, Bernadette helped her unpack the few things she'd brought with her. Bernadette had known that something was up. Their closeness was due to the fact it was so difficult to remain concealed in Bernadette's presence. She could read people like an open book, even a practiced deceiver like Alexis.

Once the truth was out about Alexis' health, she and Bernadette had talked at length about what to do. Still, Alexis hadn't arrived at a firm sense of resolve about whether to stay in the US or not. She could get the medical care she needed in Europe. Then, that afternoon in July, a few days before Hank's big event, Jessica had waltzed into the kitchen of the Rancho Mirage house. At that moment, Alexis knew she wasn't going anywhere for a while because a while might be all she had left, and she wanted to spend that time with her daughter.

She'd been tempted to tell Jessica the whole story, but the awkwardness of that moment in the kitchen had thrown her for a loop. It shook Alexis to see her daughter so apprehensive at the sight of her own mother, even though she pretended not to notice.

"Mom, what are you doing here?"

"Didn't you get my postcard? Hank's being honored and I wouldn't miss that for the world. Let's go have lunch on El Paseo and find something scrumptious to wear," Alexis gushed, as she so often did to hide her true feelings. It all came crashing down upon her and she rushed forward to embrace her daughter, nearly crushing Jessica.

"What is it? What's wrong?" She'd asked, a little worrywart expression spreading over her lovely face. Alexis chickened out and kept the bad news to herself.

"It's Giovanni. We're through. I'm not going back." That she wasn't returning to Giovanni was a truth revealed to her own heart when she blurted it out to Jessica. She would never let him see her sick. It wouldn't feel safe to be that weak around him. Nor would she allow him to remember her that way.

"Oh no, I'm so sorry," she'd said, hugging her. "It'll be okay. You said that about divorcing Jim, and now I know you were right. You want to talk about it?"

Blessed Bernadette had swept into the room then, saving Alexis from the war she was having with herself about how much to reveal to Jessica. Earlier that afternoon, she and Bernadette had decided Alexis would wait to tell others about her health scare. She needed the test results before she knew what she faced, and with the celebration for Hank only a few days away, it would be better to wait rather than put a damper on the joyous event. The docs all agreed she had time to consider her options, and could afford to wait.

There was Jessica to think about too. It had taken Jessica months to come to grips with the reality that her marriage was over and that was even after walking in on her faithless husband, caught in the act, with the toast of Tinsel Town. Alexis could have told her the guy had social climber written all over him, despite the boyish charm he used as cover. He had money of his own, and by the time he and Jessica wed, he'd acquired a position with a prestigious law firm, so he was no fortune hunter in any conventional sense. Still, it had done him no harm to insinuate himself into the circles in which the Huntingtons moved.

The polished, bespoke-suited man, who turned up at a high-profile social event a few years later, was no surprise at all to Alexis. James Harper was a smooth-talker and a skilled name-dropper. That wasn't the only thing she disliked about him; there was a slickness about him that made her wary, even earlier, in his tennis shoes and hoodie days. He scanned the room with skill while he spoke to you. There was no way was he going to miss a chance to mix or mingle if a more important figure ventured by. That night it had broken Alexis' heart, for her daughter, when Jim's wandering eye lingered on the women in the room—in particular a flashy-looking bit of arm candy from some former country of the Soviet Union.

Euro-trash, Alexis had thought. *It takes one to know one.* She wasn't sure what the equivalent label was for American women, but no doubt it applied to her when she joined the yachting crowd after fleeing her first marriage. From the beginning, Alexis had wanted to tell Jessica how she felt about Jim Harper, but Hank warned her off. Jim's ruthless betrayal wasn't a surprise when Jessica told her about it. Alexis hoped she hadn't seemed too cavalier about the whole thing, but she felt relieved that the slimy chameleon had shown his true colors while Jessica was still young enough to start over.

What Alexis learned from Bernadette was that the nasty circumstances leading to divorce hadn't been the only traumatic events in Jessica's life that year. She'd gone through a harrowing set of encounters with thugs hired by some nouveau riche mob boss trying to move up in the underworld. Alexis had never heard of the man, even though his name appeared in the LA papers on numerous occasions. Later, he was implicated in the murder of Jessica's best friend's husband, Roger Stone.

Even more recently, Jessica had fought for her life to evade minions dispatched by a twisted little prince of darkness who ruled over an entertainment empire. Alexis *had* heard of him. Poor Kelly Fontana, a frequent visitor at the Huntington house when Jessica was a teen, had the misfortune of getting mixed up with him and Jessica was dragged into the unsavory little man's realm while investigating Kelly's death. That ordeal was still fresh for Jessica when Alexis arrived in Rancho Mirage.

"Let's give her a breather for now, Bernadette," Alexis had said, deciding to wait before sharing more bad news.

When Bernadette charged into the kitchen that afternoon in July, she took command. She sat them all down in the morning room right off the spacious kitchen and changed the focus from Alexis' troubles, by asking Jessica to share the whole story about their adventures in sleuthing.

"Tell your mom what we did. We're like Cagney and Lacey," Bernadette said as she filled their glasses with ice-cold lemonade that had materialized out of nowhere.

"I'm not so sure about that. More like Lucy and Ethel."

"I bet that's what Detective Hernandez thinks. He gets mad like Ricky Ricardo. He was real polite when he called to thank me for my salsa recipe. I got him wrapped up under my thumb, now."

"You mean wrapped around your little finger, don't you?" Jessica asked.

"No, I said thumb. You're Lucy and I'm Ethel. I know the difference between a pinky and a thumb. I got the man right where I want him." That sent Jessica into a fit of the giggles as she tried to explain to Alexis who Bernadette was talking about.

"If you met this guy you'd understand why this is so funny. He's Ferdinand the Bull around Bernadette. This big blustery detective comes barging in here and the moment we see each other, it's like I've waved a red flag and he's snorting and pawing at the ground; but then Bernadette charms him with her sweet smile, salsa or some other goodie, and the guy is ready to flounce among the flowers. Though I will remind you, Bernadette, he threatened to arrest you for shooting that thug in the trasero."

"Yeah, but the last time he stopped by, he returned your dad's gun. More proof I got him right where I want him." Alexis had a bewildered look on her face as she spoke.

"Gun? Shot him in the trasero? Am I hearing this right, Bernadette? You shot someone in the behind with Hank's gun?" That set off another round of laughter.

"I shouldn't be laughing, but the stealthy maleantes who figured out how to get past the guard gate and into our backyard must have been shocked when Bernadette opened fire. The desperados were lucky that our beloved, pint-sized loose cannon here only grazed one of them," Jessica said. "Lucky for her that they didn't shoot back. She won't do that again, right Bernadette?" Then, Jessica started from the beginning and told the story of the whole dreadful ordeal surrounding Laura's dead husband, Roger.

Now, in the cool December twilight of the ICU, Alexis savored the memory of that sunny July afternoon. The warmth of the golden California sun had streamed in through the semi-circle of twenty-foot windows that defined the area of the morning room, which was one of the most beautiful spots in the house that Hank built. The glow emanating from inside Jessica had competed with the one descending upon her by the setting sun pouring through those cathedral-like windows.

In her thirties, Jessica was even more amazing than when she was younger. A lot of her youthful reticence vanquished, it seemed to Alexis, but what prevailed was the courage Jessica long possessed alongside the anxiety and self-doubt. Survival in the face of all the recent carnage must have made her stronger. Alexis wished she could have uttered those words that day and told Jessica how she felt. Instead, she'd said nothing. Worse than the inability to put her feelings into words was the fact that as she sat there, that old devil, envy, crept over her. Alexis was jealous of the easy manner and open affection that passed between the two women she cared most about in the world.

Envy passed, though, and the terror about being sick had fled too. They talked for hours. As if by magic, Bernadette whipped up a glorious black bean and sweet corn frittata while the stories unfolded. Jessica had pulled out a great bottle of Pinot Grigio and poured glasses for them as she continued telling harrowing tales about tracking down killers.

The story ended with her account of a rather tumultuous meeting earlier that day with the priest from St. Theresa's in Palm Springs. Jessica left that meeting perplexed by his advice. He concluded that all the shocking events in her life could be regarded as a "wake up call," one she needed to address.

"Heed the call. Look deeper into the mystery... huh? The more I try to figure things out, the more screwed up my life becomes. What does he want me to do—besides give up my black AMEX card? He was clear about that. Am I supposed to wander around in the desert for forty days and forty nights, like a penniless beggar or sit cross-legged in the sand like a Yogi contemplating my navel? Do you get it?"

"We've talked about putting that card away. Not that it means you need to be broke—just stop thinking that buying stuff will make everything better. You don't need more wandering around in the desert. That's what you've been doing since you got here. Most of the time, there's been some maleante chasing after you, and that's not your fault. Father Martin wants you to figure out a few things about your life, that's all. He gave you all those books to read, Jessica. I bet that's a good place to start. I'm not sure about the cross-legged yogurt thing, but I have a rosary you could use. That helps me be calm when I'm trying to figure out stuff." Bernadette had been so sincere, tender and concerned; still the whole priest bit rankled as Alexis listened.

There had been more, but Alexis' mind wandered. She was glad Jessica hadn't asked her what the priest meant. If she remembered him correctly, Father Martin looked more like your typical country club golf addict than a priest. There wasn't anything about him that struck her as enlightened or the least bit holy. She had little use for any priest or what he was selling. It wasn't just her Anglican bias against Catholicism, but a more general disregard for all things spiritual. She had long-since lost interest in the notion that there was any master plan at work in her life, or anyone else's. The world was too big a basket case to make that believable. Even as one of the "winners" in a game set out to favor the one percent, she knew better. Life was a mystery all right. Just not one worth pondering— life's a bitch and then you die. What else was there to know?

Devour life. Don't predigest it by ruminating like a beast lolling about in a pasture, or wander about in a desert. That would have been Alexis' best advice if Jessica had asked that day. If Jessica found consolation in what the priest said, so be it. Her conversion as a teen when she ended up at St. Theresa's, after being kicked out of two other private schools in the area, hadn't hurt her. Mass couldn't be any worse for her than enjoying a concert, or a good movie, or some other similar form of entertainment. So Alexis had kept her views to herself.

What she had shared with Jessica and Bernadette was news about her recent travels, and life on the Mediterranean, avoiding any references to Giovanni. She didn't want to be questioned about ending her fourth marriage. In a matter of seconds, like her little silver Porsche sitting in the garage, Alexis had shifted into high gear. In full-blown, jet-setting socialite mode, she gushed, sharing gossip about celebrities and royals that had crossed her path in the past year. The ruse worked, although she caught glimpses of concern from Bernadette.

Alexis sighed, remembering how time had passed that day. The whole afternoon and then, on into the evening, the three of them had talked. The chatter had allowed her to avoid thinking about the things she considered, now, as she gazed at her daughter. Her powerlessness over events weighed Alexis down. The thought of losing her daughter was far more disturbing than facing her own death.

It wasn't that she feared dying so much. Oblivion was a precious thing. A state she sought through physicians and friends with some powerful drugs at their fingertips. No, death didn't worry her. The terrifying part of being sick was the thought of having to give herself over to the care of others, to let them get close whenever they needed to be close. That prospect sickened her more than the disease itself.

That night in July, back in her room alone, after all that convivial chatter with Jessica and Bernadette, she'd sought escape, as she so often did, in oblivion. The doctors in her life did one thing right. They kept her well supplied with the best drugs that money could buy, making life so much easier to bear.

"Better living through chemistry," she had toasted aloud as she washed down a couple of sleeping pills with a swig of vodka. Managing all that good chemistry took some work. She didn't always do that so well. It also added a layer of complexity to the health issues she was facing—or not facing. She had time, they said. She would use it.

As Alexis sat, clasping her daughter's hand, her mind drifted to the other great love in her life, Hank Huntington. For several nights, back in July, she and Jessica stayed at the Brentwood Estate, to be close to where the celebration in Hank's honor was held. When they arrived, Hank was already there, and a flood of memories had enveloped Alexis as she and Jessica crossed the threshold of the Brentwood home. Once, she and Hank were so much in love, in that house with its lovely gardens overlooking the city of angels.

Hank's dark eyes sparkled with happiness at the sight of them both. The woman Henry Huntington reflected back to her was the woman Alexis had always wanted to be. Years earlier, that look had won her heart, and it had caused her to say yes when he asked her to marry him. If only it had been enough. Even when her problems and his business had come between them, that look in his eyes reached for her across the growing chasm in their marriage. There it was, still, decades and three husbands later.

She had almost broken down and told Hank about her illness. Then what? She wasn't any more prepared to depend on her ex-husband than she was to lean on Giovanni. There was so much more she didn't know about her condition. The word cancer had knocked the wind out of her even when followed by all the assurances about "early stage" and "high survivability" rates. She'd gone for that second opinion, right away, and had yet another consultation scheduled in August, once she returned to the desert. Then she would have a clearer picture about her options. Then she might ask Hank or Jessica for their input, so she put it off.

The whirlwind of shopping, hair, face and body treatments for the gala, left little time for subsequent bouts of weakness. *Even in darkness, light*, Alexis thought. For a few days, they were a family again and the celebration of Hank's accomplishments put them all in good spirits.

The evening was a gala one. As usual, the LA weather cooperated, and much of it was held out under the stars. The courtyard area in which the ceremony took place was awash in the twinkle of thousands of tiny lights strung above their heads. A gentle breeze caused the gauzy curtains, hung to define the space, to billow. A jazz combo played and the wailing of a sax set a cool urban vibe as the buzz of excited partygoers filled the surrounding space. Champagne flowed as a squadron of buffed and polished young servers hustled. Pretty people scurried to make sure all the other pretty people were well-tended.

In the darkness of the ICU, Alexis smiled, recalling how she'd been in her element that night. She and Jessica adorned in haute couture, with their hair and makeup flawless. Alexis floated through a sea of air kisses, and exchanged warm greetings with old friends and acquaintances. She promised to call, have lunch, or meet up at some subsequent event. Alexis had appeared at ease. A happy—no, make that an ecstatic—member of the one percent, untouched by life's travails. Superficial inquiries as to one's health and well-being met with superficial replies.

"Wonderful, darling, absolutely wonderful! So kind of you to ask and you?" Alexis was masterful, keeping the conversation light. Compliments flew if there was the slimmest possibility that a moment might turn serious. "You look fabulous, darling! Love your dress and your hair! Who did it?"

Here and there, a flirty glance or whispered comment suggested more might come of the evening for some. For the most part, there was no expectation of deeper truth, nothing exposed. All relationships, even the most amiable, adeptly controlled and kept at arms-length. The years had taken a steady toll on those with whom she'd shared banalities for decades. Some in her circle were gone, but those who remained sported valiant efforts to thwart aging. Many had become almost unrecognizable because of aging combined with so many nips and tucks. She admired their fighting spirit. *Do not go gentle—or un-remodeled—into that good night*, she'd thought.

23

The building itself blazed with lights as those invited to the gala wandered through the exhibits. Besides recognizing Hank, and half a dozen architects and designers, the event was also a fundraiser for the A+D Architecture and Design Museum. Dining, dancing, and a silent auction took place that night, along with the awards ceremony. It all went off without a hitch. Hank was beaming and Alexis performed her best "Nancy Reagan" version of the adoring wife—ex-wife in this case.

Jessica was aglow, stunning in Jovani couture. In the form-fitting slinky dress, made of a draped fabric that glimmered, she might have stepped from an old Hollywood film. Paul Worthington, the handsome lawyer who hired her to work in his firm's Palm Desert office, was a stunning companion. Dressed to the nines in a bespoke tuxedo, the tall, blond, blue-eyed man was dashing. Like Robert Redford in the Great Gatsby. Smitten with Jessica, he almost never left her side or took his eyes off her. Alexis was happy to see that Jessica enjoyed the man's company. There was a good-natured repartee between the two of them as though they had been friends for years. Jessica's divorce was still pending, according to California law, but Alexis hoped this man might bring new happiness into her daughter's life.

Alexis sighed once again at that vision of her daughter. As she stood in the half-light of the ICU, gazing upon her now, the contrast was startling. She felt a twist in the vicinity of her heart, perhaps the stirrings of something maternal.

"I should be in that hospital bed, not you," she murmured, reaching out to touch her daughter's pale face. Voices, and the sound of the door opening, caused Alexis to turn as Bernadette entered the room. Two steps behind, Hank Huntington strode into the room.

3 DISNEYLAND ANYONE?

"Look who I found," Bernadette announced, whispering, as she entered the hospital room. Alexis caught her breath at the sight of the tall, broad-shouldered man who was once her husband. His dark hair, now gray at the temples, sported a classic cut. His handsome, rugged face bore a worried expression that deepened the lines age had put there. Hank wore chinos and a buttoned-down shirt. No tie or blazer, but a bombardier jacket and sturdy, no nonsense shoes on his feet. These were the clothes he wore when he was at a work site. Even without the mustache, something about Henry Randolph Huntington always reminded Alexis of Clark Gable. Perhaps it was his lopsided grin or the glint in his dark eyes, but neither were evident at the moment.

"How's she doing?" He asked as he stepped toward Jessica's bedside.

"I think she's doing okay, but Nurse Andrews can tell us more after she's gone through her routine."

A nurse bustled into the room and stepped around Hank and Bernadette, reaching Jessica first. Her face was expressionless as she moved around the room checking equipment. She tugged here and there at a wire and read information displayed on machines that pinged, pulsed, and whirred. She wrote the information on a chart as she worked. Then she addressed Jessica in a clear, calm voice as she reached out and grasped her wrist.

"Ms. Huntington, Jessica, wake up. We need you to wake up, hon." Jessica's eyes fluttered open, but then closed again. "Jessica, I know you're sleepy. We need you to wake up for a few minutes. Look, you have visitors."

Roused, again, Jessica kept her eyes open longer and scanned the room. When her eyes landed on Hank, she smiled.

"Dad, what are you doing here? Are you okay? You're in a hospital."

"I'm fine, Jinx, but how about you?" He asked that lopsided grin on his face. Jinx was short for Jessica Alexis, a name given to her when, at age four, she demanded to have a nickname, like Hank. Later, in her 'tweens,' using that pet name could set off a drama queen episode. She deemed it humiliating and an effort to blame her for her parents' divorce. No one blamed her, but it was a way of taking responsibility for her parents' failed relationship. She told Alexis later that it was a childish effort to find control over a situation where she had none. Now, in her groggy state of mind, hearing that name caused her to smile, but also to express alarm.

"I am a jinx, Dad. Did you know I fell off a mountain? I guess I'm okay. Am I okay?" She asked the nurse, struggling to focus her eyes on the woman who was bustling around again. The nurse bent over her, checking the IV site where they were pumping Jessica full of who-knew-what, including some damn good pain meds.

"Yes, you're okay. Remarkably well, I'd say, considering you fell off a mountain." That comment broke through the nurse's clinical detachment and she smiled a real smile at Jessica.

"So, she's really okay?" Alexis asked.

"Yes, I think so. Dr. Welch will be here soon. It will be his call, but I bet we'll be taking this young woman out of here." She smiled again. Jessica's eyes widened.

"Yay, did you hear that Bernadette? We're all going home, isn't that good news?" She asked, with a loopy grin on her face. Then her face brightened. "Better tell the Cat Pack."

"You can't go home yet, Baby Girl," Alexis said, speaking in a calm voice. "Somebody needs to turn down that drip," she added. "We don't have a cat."

"I can 'splain that part. Let's hope it's not that bump on the head that's got her all loosey-goosey," Bernadette said as she handed Alexis a large cup of coffee.

"Ooh, coffee. Aw, that is soooo sweet. It's just what I need." Jessica struggled, raising an arm to make a grab for her mother's cup. "Ouch, oh ow," she winced, grabbing at her sore ribs.

"No coffee yet," the nurse interjected, moving to restrain Jessica. "Let's see what the doctor has to say. Stay put, and I'll raise the head of the bed a little." The nurse hit a button, changing the angle of the bed by a few inches.

"Dad, do something. You have coffee. I want... Wow, will you look at this?" She was staring at her arms. One was in a cast and the other hooked up to an IV. There were other wires attached to her, leading to the equipment in the room. "I'm Pinocchio." She moved one arm and then tried to move the other, pinned to her side. She sank down onto the pillow and yawned as though that small amount of effort wore her out. Then her eyes popped open again.

"Hey, that's a good idea, isn't it? Let's all get out of here and go to Disneyland. What a wonderful day to go to the happiest place on earth!" She pointed the one arm she could move in the general direction of her father. "Don't let me jinx myself again though. I better not fall off Sleeping Beauty's castle, or the Matterhern," she giggled, and then yawned again. "The Motorhorn, no, no, I mean the..." Jessica didn't even finish her sentence before drifting off. A loud snort left no doubt she was down for the count.

"Nurse Andrews, Alexis has a point. Can't you back off on the meds some?" Hank asked.

"Sure, I can adjust it a little. We're almost at the low end of what's left on order for her. I'm sure the doctor will make a change. He's on the floor, so it won't be long now." She twisted a knob on the apparatus holding the IV bag suspended above Jessica's bed.

Several hours later, they had whisked Jessica out of the ICU and into a private room elsewhere in the hospital. By noon, she was more lucid and able to have lunch if you can call a dish of gelatin and some soupy substance lunch. Jessica hadn't objected, but looked grim.

"If that stays down, Jessica, I can bring you some pudding or ice cream to hold you over until dinnertime. That will be a real meal, okay?" Jessica nodded in acquiescence to Nurse Andrews, still too drugged up to put up much of a fight.

Simple hospital fare would have to do. She sipped the broth and put away the gelatin, like a good patient. That got an approving smile from Nurse Andrews. But no coffee, now that was harder to take. She lusted after the large cups of coffee Bernadette and her parents each held, but said nothing. She didn't want to cause a ruckus. They looked worried enough. The pain meds dulled, but didn't quell, the guilt about being at the center of yet another calamity. She gave them a brief account of what had gone on, minimizing how bizarre the episode was.

"I'm sorry to worry you all. Please go home and get some rest. They'll take care of me. They'll probably just knock me out again for the afternoon."

"Okay, honey. I could sure use a shower and a shave," Hank had said, bending over his daughter to give her a kiss.

"Me, too," Bernadette said. "The shower, not the shave." She smiled and gave Jessica a little wink. She looked so tired. They all did. As they filled in the blanks about what happened after her tumble off the mountain, she learned they had been up all night.

"We'll come back tonight, Chica. I asked that nurse if we can bring you somethin' else to wear that doesn't hang open in the back. She says that's good as long as it's loose. They can help you put it on in the morning after they clean you up. I'm getting your muumuus from Maui, okay?" Bernadette brushed the hair back off Jessica's forehead then placed a tender kiss there. Jessica did her best to pat her back as she had done with her dad. That was hard to do with her right hand bandaged and still hooked up to the IV. Her left arm was in a cast and supported by a sling, snug against her body. An ice pack was strapped to her ribs to soothe the pain. She felt trapped by it all.

"Thanks, Bernadette that would be great. If they let me out of here tomorrow I could wear it home."

"Don't rush matters," Alexis said. "But I hope you get out of here soon, darling." She reached out to pat her daughter's bandaged hand and brushed her cheek with a kiss.

"Thanks. I'm so glad you were here last night. You've got to be exhausted. I'm sorry to do this..." The meds given to her with her meager lunch must have been kicking in. She was losing her train of thought. Her mother had tears in her eyes as Hank put an arm around her shoulders, escorting Alexis and Bernadette to the door. Jessica managed one last "Thanks," before dropping off for a nap.

Jessica dreamed of falling through empty space. At first, she was flailing about and falling fast. Then she slowed. Bodies fell—Roger Stone, her best friend's husband, cold and dead, his eyes closed. Poor Roger, his murder was solved, but his death still made no sense. She watched as Roger continued to fall into an abyss below. She was desperate for a way to stop her fall when her dead friend, Kelly, appeared. An angelic figure, her pale eyes shone. Her red hair and lustrous gown kept her suspended. Jessica reached out, but instead of grasping Kelly, she grabbed hold of a strap or rope. It sliced into the palm of her hand. She released it and the lovely image of Kelly vanished, leaving her dangling at the end of a rope wrapped around her waist.

Awakened in a state of sadness and disappointment, the loss of her childhood friend was fresh in her mind. Jessica's right hand throbbed, but that wasn't as painful as the ache in her heart from being reminded of Kelly's sad end. She took some comfort from that vision—so much like the image of Kelly alive, the one that had captivated and endeared her to Jessica. Despite the troubles that tormented Kelly and led to her untimely death at nineteen, Jessica loved her, as did so many others. They all still missed her. *Love isn't always enough*, she thought as she wept, not from the pain in the palm of her hand, but from terror and loss, played out over and over during the last few months.

Jessica's mind and body ached for sleep to avoid the perplexity aroused by those questions. That dream had made one thing clear. She wouldn't rest until she found out what was going on with Libby Van Der Woert. Not her friend, or a client, Libby was another miserable young woman, like Kelly, in serious trouble. What could that be? Could Jessica figure it out before Libby met Kelly's fate? *I can and I must, throw myself into the thick of human endeavor, and with no stopping for breath.* Those words from a book Father Martin had given her, Chardin's *Hymn of the Universe*, passed through her mind as she drifted back to sleep. She would try to save Libby.

4 THE SCOOP

"Oh my God, Jessica, you look like hell! Again!" Tommy rushed into the room and flew to Jessica's bedside. "You're broken!" Tommy's sweet pixie face was cast in a shadow of concern. Tommy was Kelly's younger brother and when she died, Jessica stepped into the role of big sister.

"Nothing permanent. One arm's the only thing that's broken and it'll heal. Careful, though, I haven't figured out, yet, where I hurt and don't hurt." Tommy slowed down as he leaned in to place a gentle kiss on Jessica's face, in a spot without a scratch or a bruise.

"These are for you," Jerry Reynolds said. Jerry was a PI with the law firm Jessica worked for and Tommy's smoking hot boyfriend. He was holding a vase loaded with a bouquet of jaunty yellow sunflowers and a small "get well" balloon.

"Those are gorgeous, you guys. Thanks." Jerry moved around Tommy to give Jessica a peck on the cheek. Then, he looked for a spot to place the flowers.

"Others beat us to it, I see," he said, eyeing a bouquet with dozens of huge roses in creamy pale colors. Several more vases sat on surfaces around the room. "Paul Worthington, right?"

"Yes, those are from Paul. I have a vague recollection that he dropped them off earlier today, soon after they moved me in here. I was in pain after all the moving, so they knocked me out. I've been out of it since then. My ribs are giving the most grief, but I hurt in plenty of other places, too. Unfortunately, I remember little of what went on with Paul. Hope I didn't embarrass myself. Mom and Dad said I was babbling about Disneyland, of all things, when the nurse woke me up at the crack of dawn. I find that hard to believe, but Bernadette swears I was about to burst into a chorus of Zip-a-dee-doo-dah right before I conked out again. Geez, I hope I didn't sing when Paul was here. The firm sent flowers, too." She gestured to yet another bouquet, red roses with baby's breath and greenery.

"And those amazing flowers are from the Van Der Woerts. Can you imagine that? They took time to send me flowers. They must be devastated about Libby. She's alive, but not in great shape. God knows what else they're dealing with now that word is out about their daughter being mixed up in yet another fiasco. The news sure seems to have spread fast."

"Not just fast, but relentlessly. They've replayed the rescue scene over and over. That started late yesterday afternoon when they first spotted you and Libby. It was still being rerun when we left the house today," Jerry explained.

"I hope I didn't scare the bejeebers out of you guys. Thank goodness, Mom and Bernadette didn't find out what was going on until the police called them much later. By then, at least they knew I was alive. They reached Dad before he could be terrorized by media accounts involving his daughter." She closed her eyes, wondering how all of this had happened.

"Bejeebers? You are a little loose, huh?" Tommy didn't wait for her to respond. "Anyway, we didn't know it was you at first, either, or I would have been totally freaked. We thought it was another hiker-gone-wrong situation. Then, we heard more was going on than a hiking mishap and knew they had rescued two women. Uncle Don called and told us it was you right before we heard it on the news. We came down here last night, but they wouldn't let us see you in the ICU. Bernadette told us that you really were okay and that we should come back today when they'd let you have visitors. Now, it's all over the news that you're a hero. Libby says you grabbed her by a strap on her shoulder bag or something. That didn't stop her from falling, but it might explain how she landed near you on that ledge so the fall didn't kill her."

"I guess they won't know how much damage she's sustained until they bring her out of the sedated state she's in," Jessica said, staring out the window at her gorgeous surroundings.

Not a cloud could be seen in the azure desert skies. Sunlight glittered, diamond-like, on palms that swayed in the breeze. The sight ought to have triggered a rush of endorphins and cause her to sigh "ah, paradise!" Instead, it struck a deeper chord, making her more aware that she had survived yet another brush with death.

It was late afternoon. She must have slept for hours after Bernadette and her parents left. Her head felt a lot clearer now that she was on less pain medication. Moving was uncomfortable, not just because of the sore ribs, but also from an assortment of bruises she was discovering one by one. Still, she was so lucky.

"Hey, Libby may be worse off than you, but at least she's alive. Not Dr. Carr—he might have been dead even if he hadn't fallen. He had a bullet hole in him before, you know, he took that dive off the mountain." Tommy did a little mock jump, like off the end of a diving board.

"Stop it. I doubt Jessica finds that funny," Jerry said.

"It's okay. I'm used to him. How did you hear about that gunshot?"

"The media reported a rescue was going on and got even more interested when the rumors started about a shootout. Hikers were talking to reporters after they got back down off the tramway. Some of them said they heard gunfire and saw a dead guy. Reporters were talking about a dead guy—even before the police knew his identity and notified his next of kin. That's one reason Tommy's Uncle Don called us. He was sure your name would get out, too, and didn't want us to hear about it on the news. He said his pals in the homicide division weren't happy that information got out about a shooting. By the time he called us, they had figured out the dead man was Dr. Carr, but they weren't saying what killed him—a gunshot or the fall."

"Yeah, they won't know that for sure until they do an autopsy." It made Jessica weary that she knew so much about how cops handled dead guys.

"I'll bet they have plenty of questions for you. What were you all doing up there, anyway?" Jerry asked.

"Yeah, what the hell happened before you fell off the mountain?" Tommy was about to do the nosedive again, but the look in Jerry's eyes stopped him.

"Shoved is more like it," Jessica said. "What did Libby say?"

"Not much. Uncle Don told us she came around long enough to say, 'Jessica did it.' At first, they thought she was talking about the shooting, or she was saying you caused the fall. Then she babbled on with 'Jessica grabbed my shoulder strap,' 'I was falling and an angel saved me.' Someone overheard her say that at the hospital or there's a leak among first responders. That started all the '*Huntington heiress, real-life guardian angel, saves troubled 90210 princess*' coverage that's going on now. It also didn't take long to figure out this isn't the first time Elizabeth Van Der Woert has been in trouble. The media got on that, digging up old information about Libby's past. That includes the drunk-driving accident and other incidents too," Tommy said.

"Did you know the police picked her up for shoplifting last year?" Jerry asked.

"No, her parents never mentioned it. It's possible they didn't know about it either since they didn't see her often. I told them to cut off contact after she began to accuse them of horrendous behavior. Libby's poor parents have been to hell and back with her, that's for sure." Jessica shook her head in sadness.

"Did you do what Libby said? Grab her?" Tommy asked.

"It all happened so fast, I'm not sure. I was grabbing for her before we fell. I was trying to get her to follow me when she pushed me away. Dr. Carr was yanking at her too. I know I had her for a minute. Then, that shove sent me flying backwards over the edge. If I snagged her again, it might explain how my hand got wrecked. It's more like a slice than a puncture wound. I could have grabbed a strap on the bag she was carrying or part of her clothing, who knows? So, I take it Libby has been too out of it to tell police what went on that afternoon?"

"Yeah, a few words on the way to the hospital is it. Soon after they got her here, they put her under. She's still in an induced coma to limit damage from a head injury that caused a brain bleed or swelling. I'm not sure what else is wrong with her, but she has internal injuries and broken bones. She must have hit something on the way down. From the video coverage, she landed at an angle that had to have done some damage. Another foot to the left, though, and she would have continued bouncing off things before landing closer to her dead doctor." It was Jerry's turn to shake his head. "So, what happened?" Jerry asked, taking a seat in a chair beside Jessica's hospital bed.

"Yeah, give us the scoop," Tommy added, perching on the edge of her bed.

"It's all still a little jumbled. Libby called me around noon. She sounded wound up and claimed she had information she needed to tell someone about Dr. Carr and Shannon Donnelly. If I wanted it, before there was another dead daughter, I needed to meet her, right away. When she told me she was at the top of the tramway, I agreed to go. It was a public place with lots of people around so it seemed safe to meet up there, but I thought the location was an odd choice. I was spooked by the tone in her voice, or I might have blown her off. She's tried to contact me a couple times in the past week, and I insisted she do it through her attorney. Anyway, I called Detective Hernandez to tell him where I was going and who I was meeting. Since he's been investigating Shannon Donnelly's disappearance, I relayed the claim Libby made that she had news about her missing friend. I never can get that guy on the phone. I left a voice mail message, that way I figured that at least he'd know where to look for my body. Guess I figured right."

Jessica gazed out the window again. She wished she were out in the breeze that caused the palms to shimmy. This time of year, desert breezes carried the fragrance of flowers, planted in and around places like the hospital. The temperatures were sublime, chasing away memories of the heat. Full of forgiveness for the torments of summer, fall offered new hope, like spring in most other places. Too bad that it wasn't as easy to let go of all the other memories from summer.

"The fall... I fell off a frigging mountain!' I'll just file that one away under 'N' for nightmares," she babbled. The 2013 file drawer in her head overflowed with one-of-a-kind photo ops straight out of Agatha Christie novels or an episode of CSI; except these were real and more graphic and brutal than the mystery tales she'd read or those TV shows. Tommy and Jerry glanced at each other and then back at Jessica.

"You okay?"

"Hell, no, where was I? Oh yeah, I hustled up to the top of the tramway. When I got to the visitor center, Libby was waiting for me. She insisted someone was following her and claimed we had very little time. When I wanted to go sit down and have cocoa or coffee, she refused. So, I followed her outside and down the ramp to the hiking paths. I kept prodding her to tell me what was going on, with no luck. When we reached the bottom of that ramp, I refused to go any farther. That's when she stuck a gun in my ribs and we set out on the Desert View Trail."

"She had a gun," Tommy gasped.

"She did. While we walked that trail, she ranted. I tried to pay attention, but that wasn't easy since I was scared she'd shoot me or some random stranger who looked at her the wrong way. Most of the rant was about 'nobody will ever believe me even if I tell the truth.' I couldn't argue with that. She was mumbling, 'it's your fault, Libby' and 'you've done this to yourself so shut up.' You know, talking to herself and I just happened to be there?" Jessica trembled at the thought of how loose Libby had been while holding a lethal weapon in her hands.

"When we got out on that overlook, she tied my hands and made me sit down while she continued to rant. At first, I said nothing while she continued to argue with herself. After a while, I wasn't even sure she remembered I was there. I worked on untying the ropes while she kept asking herself questions: 'how could I have been so stupid?' and 'how could there be another dead daughter because of me, like poor, pathetic Lela.' Remember? That's the name of her friend who was killed in that car accident with Libby at the wheel—drunk and stoned out of her mind?" Tommy and Jerry nodded yes.

"Anyway, at least part of that time, the argument she was having with herself was about me—whether I could be trusted or not. I kept working to get my hands free, figuring I might have to make a run for it. At some point, I became worried about what would happen if we were still out in the cold after sundown. I tried talking to her about that, but it did no good. She waved that gun around and almost danced on the boulders at the edge of the overlook." She paused and took a deep breath before reaching the end of her story.

"I was sitting on the ground, working to get my hands free, hoping someone would come along. I got my wish. Too bad our visitor turned out to be the late Dr. Carr. He had a gun, too. I'm not sure what Libby intended to do, since, at one point she talked about killing herself and me. Carr was clear, however. The monster planned to shoot one or both of us, then shove us off the edge of that overlook." Jessica shook all over.

"He ordered me to stand up. When I didn't do it, he gave a good yank on the rope around my wrists to get me on my feet. That did it—the rope came loose and I pushed him as hard as I could. His gun went flying. That's when I grabbed Libby by the hand and took off. Somehow, Carr got back up on the rock and yanked at Libby, who still had her gun. Either she shoved me or the momentum from their struggle sent me reeling. Anyway, we all went over the edge. I heard a shot, but I don't know who fired the gun."

"I'm so sorry," Jerry said.

"I thought I was dead this time for sure."

"You don't have to tell us any more if you don't want to," Tommy said, reaching out to put a hand over hers. His eyes were watery, dulling the sparkles of gold that usually twinkled in them.

"I want to talk about it. Carr is dead, but I don't think this is over." Jerry handed Jessica a tissue from a box at her bedside.

"What does that mean?" Jerry asked. His gorgeous brow furrowed, which made her feel guilty. Even under such unhappy circumstances, the man was beautiful to behold. His chiseled features sat in perfect symmetry upon his handsome face and a dazzling smile set off twinkling green eyes when not overcome with foreboding about one of Jessica's calamities.

"I'm not sure what it means. Libby was so out of it most of the time. But all that talk about Shannon Donnelly and 'another dead daughter' must mean something. Her friend may be dead, but I don't think Libby killed her. Not this friend, anyway. Lela, the one who died as a passenger in her car: yes. Libby admitted that car crash was her doing and even claimed it was on purpose. I'm not sure what that means either. Both girls were drunk as skunks that night and took turns driving the SUV on LA freeways, like speedway drivers, before the crash. Given she was making her last confession yesterday afternoon, I think Libby would have taken credit for killing Shannon if she had done it. She blamed herself for getting Shannon in trouble and with 'them.' That included Dr. Dick, but she also said something about that red devil too. When she was muttering to herself, she kept talking about that red devil, and at one point said he was behind it all. Red devil sounds crazy, I know."

"The whole situation qualifies as crazy. Given the state she was in for hours yesterday, it's not far-fetched to believe she killed her friend in a fit of rage. Who knows? What if Libby was in a delusional state and Shannon became that red devil? Delusional or in a fit of rage, either way she could have killed her friend. If the Donnelly woman's dead, my money is on Libby. Carr put himself in the running, too," Jerry said.

"Jerry makes a good point. That red devil stuff sounds like she's seeing things, don't you think?" Tommy added. His head tilted, his sweet face, with its spray of freckles and a little dimple, had an even more elfish cast to it than usual. Despite the dire circumstances, they were discussing, his love and admiration for Jerry made him doe eyed.

"I know what you're saying. She's a disturbed and disturbing young woman. There were times when it was almost as if she was acting out some immature teenage psychodrama. Like a scene from a soap opera or reenacting an episode of a crime show. She was in snotty mean girl mode most of the time, not a psycho killer like that cutthroat doctor. For some reason, the whole episode, starting with her phone call, felt like a test."

"Test or not, Libby is immature and out of control, a thirty-year-old, teenage drama queen. Who knows what impulse might have driven her to kill you, or anyone else, like Shannon Donnelly? And, I'm with Tommy that the red devil thing is more likely a part of her mental illness than anything to do with reality. A mania or drug-induced hallucination is more believable than Carr having a red devil as a co-conspirator."

"I know, Jerry. There's more, I'm sure. Other stuff she said about being betrayed and set up by Carr. Based on his words, not Libby's, it's clear we were right in suspecting that guy was up to no good. Carr admitted he was using screwed up young women for his own ends and Libby laid part of that out for me before he showed up. She claims they had a sexual relationship and she can prove it. And, at least some of the trouble she's caused for her parents was his doing. He put her up to extorting money from her parents in return for keeping her allegations about them to herself or something like that. My head hurts too much to sort this all out right now. I need another nap. Then, I need to get home—although that will be weird, with both Mom *and* Dad there, speaking of psychodramas. There's one underway in my family. I just can't figure out what it is yet."

"What does that mean?" Tommy asked, looking distraught.

"If I knew, I'd tell you. I've had the 'something's-up heebie-jeebies' ever since I came home back in July and found Mom standing in the kitchen. It's her kitchen, so she has every right in the world to be there, but why? At first, I thought it was strictly about reaching the end of the line with another man. Now I'm not so sure. Maybe it's the thought of Dad being back in the house, too, but I'm having this wave of déjà vu that just won't quit."

"Why not ask Bernadette? She'll tell you."

"Are you kidding? She's an impenetrable wall when it comes to answering questions about my parents. All I've ever gotten is her reassurance they love me, thank you very much, and vague statements that 'it's complicated.' You think? I was ready to corner Mom, but now I feel guilty about putting her through this terror at the top of the tram episode. They all looked terrible this morning after pulling all-nighters, thanks to me. Don't worry, Tommy, could be it's nothing more than my hyperactive something-bad-is-about-to-happen radar detection system."

"Jerry has that too. Good thing he does since I don't worry about half the things I should." Jerry reached out and gave Tommy's auburn locks a reassuring tousle that left them standing up on end. As Tommy smoothed his hair down, Jerry spoke.

"It's an occupational hazard. A PI, who can't imagine all the worst-case scenarios, misses out on a lot during an investigation. God knows, Tommy, you're working on becoming more vigilant. Stick with me, Kid, and I'll turn you into a professional caliber worrier in no time." Jerry's tone of voice was laced with a hint of Bogart. He beamed that dashing smile of his at Tommy, who went all goo-goo-eyed again.

"I'm not going anywhere. And you know what a fast learner I am." That little dimple reappeared in Tommy's cheek as he returned Jerry's smile with a wicked grin of his own. He winked, making Jerry blush. Jessica rolled her eyes, grateful to find parts of her anatomy that didn't hurt.

"Okay, you guys, enough of this sappy love banter. In my weakened condition, I can't handle so much sentimentality without bursting into tears or heaving my guts out. My plan is to stall if I can before I'm forced to give the police a formal statement. That's more for her parents' sake than for Libby's because they have plenty to worry about before more charges pile on. I'm talking about illegal possession of a weapon, kidnapping, assault, and manslaughter or murder, and who knows what else? There could be a law against using a public tramway for illicit purposes or defiling Mother Nature by dropping in on the pristine wilderness. All those rescue efforts you described couldn't have been good for that area and I can't imagine what a search and rescue effort like that cost. Ay yi yi." Her head hurt worse and worse.

"How can her parents go through this and stay sane themselves? I'm rambling, but my point is it's good Libby and I haven't spoken to the authorities. Before that slime ball Carr showed up, it occurred to me that Libby staged the whole stunt to get her parents to reengage with her. Odd that she confessed to me, her parents' lawyer, that she'd fabricated the allegations toward her father and uncle." Jessica leaned back against the pillow once again. Her mind and her body ached, making it hard to trust her judgment about anything.

"Anyway, let the investigators from the Palm Springs Police Department try to ask me whatever they want. I'm pleading confusion for the moment while I give myself a chance to sort out what Libby was saying. Detective Hernandez will be on my case, too, but I can deal with him. You two find out what you can about where they are, officially, with the police investigation into what occurred on Mt. San Jacinto. Did they find a gun—two guns? Was Carr already dead when he fell? If not, would the gunshot have killed him even if he hadn't fallen? Tommy, if you can, get a copy of the preliminary autopsy and police reports from Uncle Don, okay?"

"Sure." Tommy smiled, always so happy when Jessica depended on him to help.

"I won't dismiss your concern about Libby's use of the term 'them' regarding Shannon Donnelly's disappearance, even if I have my doubts," Jerry said.

"Okay, you keep digging, like you have been, into Carr's background, and see if a red devil turns up. Perhaps it's a reference to a bar or a club or something like that, rather than a person. Could you also chat with your friend in the Cat City police department about what's up with their investigation of Shannon Donnelly's whereabouts? I'm not ready to talk to Hernandez yet, or I'd do it myself. Somehow, it's my fault that Donnelly's abandoned car turned up in his jurisdiction. He about blew a gasket when he showed up to ask the Van Der Woerts questions about their daughter's relationship with Shannon Donnelly and found me there as legal counsel. He won't like my involvement in another incident involving his prime suspect in an ongoing investigation—even though I called *before* trouble started. That 'angel heiress' nonsense will irritate him, too." Jessica rubbed her temple with the exposed fingers on her bandaged hand. She was out of gas, her mind losing focus and her voice sagging.

"When I get home, I'll go back through the material about Libby and Carr that you already pulled together. You guys find out about this new report of a shoplifting incident. I'd also like to know more about her recent activities if you can track down anyone who knows what she's been doing out here in the desert. I know you have a lot to do, Jerry, since you're still splitting your time between the Los Angeles office and the one in Palm Desert. Get Tommy and Kim Reed to help you gather info. I'll run all of this by Paul, since only some of this relates to our clients, the Van Der Woerts. I'm also happy to pick up the tab, though, to get to the bottom of this mess. I presume once either the Cat City or the Palm Springs authorities bring criminal charges against Libby, she'll need a better lawyer than any of the bottom feeders she's been using to threaten her parents. It would be a sick irony if her poor parents ended up footing the bill to get her off a murder charge after all the allegations and threats she's made toward them. Life's too strange."

"You know I'm more than happy to do this. Tommy will be a big help and Kim, too. But please, you've been through an enormous shock. You've got to take it easy. For a few days, at least," he said, pleading in his voice and on his face.

"I couldn't have said it better myself." Jessica looked up at Detective Frank Fontana, who spoke those words as he walked into the room.

5 GAME ON!

"Are you kidding me? That Van Der Woert woman is still alive! How is that possible? Both women? Carr breaks his neck and the women up there with him survive! How is that possible?" Eric Conroy paced, back and forth, with his cell phone pressed to his ear. His face, flushed with exasperation, was almost as red as the hair on his head. He chewed on the end of an expensive cigar. The ember had gone out minutes before, but he hadn't noticed.

"Hang on a second, will you? The talking heads are at it again." As if on cue, one of the television screens in his office replayed a scene of the helicopter rescue for the umpteenth time. He turned up the volume to hear what the news reporter had to say. Media film crews had flocked to the area as soon as word got out that this was no ordinary rescue. Several hikers, finishing a late afternoon trek around the Desert View Trail, had heard or seen part of what happened. They were eager to share their stories about what went on, or what they thought went on, as soon as they disembarked the tram.

"This is film from the dramatic rescue of Jessica Huntington and Elizabeth Van Der Woert. As you can see, the rescue team faced quite a challenge once they found the women. That they're alive is nothing short of miraculous. This was no ordinary rescue from the Pacific Crest Trail or some other part of the Mt. San Jacinto wilderness. Hikers nearby reported a gunshot and heard screams as people fell. That sight, one horrified hiker says, is one he won't soon forget. Several hikers immediately went to the closest ranger station and reported trouble on the trail. Deploying helicopters and the rescue team while there was still a shred of

daylight, may have been the difference between life and death for these two very lucky women. Once rescuers located the women, they still had their work cut out for them as you can see from the careful way in which rescuers moved to the locations where they found the women. Getting them out of there was no small task either. A helicopter airlifted both women to a nearby trauma center. Doctors report they are stable, although Elizabeth Van Der Woert remains heavily sedated, with a serious head injury.

The third member of their party was not so lucky. His name was released late last night as Dr. Richard Carr. A well-regarded psychiatrist in the Los Angeles area, Dr. Carr was reportedly treating the Van Der Woert woman. It's not clear yet what happened or why the three of them were up there. Police have confirmed that Dr. Carr suffered a gunshot wound to the chest before he fell. They haven't determined the cause of death yet, however. Dr. Carr fell much farther than either of the women so other injuries may have led to his death.

We still have much more to learn about what went on up there near the peak of Mt. San Jacinto. Police are not saying, but there are reports that hikers heard shouting before that gunshot. We've also learned that Jessica Huntington may have saved the life of the other woman who fell. Dubbed the 'angel heiress,' supposedly Jessica Huntington grabbed Elizabeth Van Der Woert, pulling her close enough so she landed on the outcropping of rocks, not too far from where Ms. Huntington ended up. One thing's for certain, a couple feet in the other direction and both women might have shared the fate met by their companion, Dr. Carr. This is Angelina Collier reporting, live, from the top of the Palm Springs Aerial Tramway. Back to you, in the studio, Ed, Lisa."

"I'm back. There's nothing new—just the same story running over and over. I need to think about this. I'll call you back. Wait! Wait! If you hear anything new, call me immediately. Got it?" With that, Eric ended the phone call and sat down in the large leather chair behind his desk. He took a moment to relight his cigar and then pondered his options. He hated making decisions on the fly, but he was behind the curve on this event already. There was no choice but to figure out something quickly. What had that idiot Carr been up to? What on earth was he doing up there with those two women? Surely, he couldn't have imagined the place was private—not with the all holiday tourist traffic at sites like that.

"I told that jackass to cool it. We had things under control," he was mumbling, moving the cigar around in his mouth as he spoke to himself. He stood and moved to a small alcove where a mirrored wall supported glass shelves filled with bottles of expensive spirits. When he reached for the bottle of Louis XIII Black Pearl Cognac, his hand shook. The shaking was rage, tinged with fear.

"Damn it, Carr!" His voice bounced off the walls of his large, well-appointed office. Carr had been right that the Van Der Woert woman was coming unglued. They had an endgame for that—several of them, in fact. So, what had gone wrong? The only thing he hated more than being behind the curve on a dustup was being out of the loop altogether. True, they would have had to use finesse to handle Libby, given the Shannon Donnelly scenario was still a work in progress. Turning fantasy into reality was Carr's area of expertise, but selling stories was Eric's forte.

Once the police found Donnelly's body, it would have been a piece of cake to pin it on Elizabeth Van Der Woert. Nor would it have been a surprise to find that a looney tune like Libby had taken herself out of the picture after killing her friend. A drug overdose or a dive off that mountain up by the tram would have been an easy sell later. Jessica Huntington was another matter, but even if she continued to snoop, trying to stir up trouble; she wouldn't have anywhere to go once the Van Der Woert woman was dead. Had Carr been holding out on him? What could he have been hiding? His mind raced, and the shakes ramped up.

"Ah!" Eric sighed, audibly, as a sip of the expensive cognac sent a surge of warmth down the back of his throat after dazzling his palate and delighting his tongue. He felt his whole body relax as he gazed out of his twentieth-floor office at the gathering shadows on the streets below. The lights were shining on the street and in the surrounding buildings. La-La land was winding down, the inhabitants, like herds of sheep, heading for their concreted paths to pasture lands throughout the burbs. He relaxed further, sitting down in a comfy club chair facing the wall of windows. When the sheep slept, a wolf like Eric Conroy did his best work.

By the time he had finished his cigar and cognac, it was clear what had to happen next. Most likely, the police were already at Carr's office. They wouldn't find much, even if they knew what to look for, and they didn't. The same thing was true about anything Carr had at his home in Pacific Palisades, when the cops got around to checking that out, if they weren't already there, too. The most sensitive material having to do with the little enterprise he and Carr had going was in Eric's possession. That information was kept in his safe at home. He had insisted on that, trusting the top of the line vault and security system he'd installed at his Bel Air estate. He also had doubts about Carr's savvy for taking proper precautions. Still, there had to be files in his office or home related to Libby Van Der Woert and Shannon Donnelly. Who knew what seemingly innocent note or comment might trigger something in the mind of some Columbo wannabe? By moving swiftly, he could get a team to clean the place out before the police could get permission to go through the dead psychiatrist's client records. He might have no choice letting the police take an initial look around, but they wouldn't get a second chance. Sending in a cleanup team probably wasn't necessary, but Carr's office and house would get 'sanitized.' Break-ins at both places would raise suspicions, but the trail would be blocked. So check!

"And mate," he muttered, hitting the recall button on his cell phone. Not his personal cell phone, but the dedicated cell phone he used for the more surreptitious sidelines in which he engaged. A phone he tossed and replaced often. Maybe it was overkill, but that was another way to guarantee the police reached a dead end quickly. "Overkill, ha! Dead end, ha! That's even better than checkmate! Eric, my boy, you have a way with words," chuckling and speaking those words aloud as he waited for his call to be answered. He had to hand it to himself; if nothing else, he was thorough.

Just a few more days and he would have no further need for this whole operation anyway. When the board met one last time about the IPO, there would be no turning back. Not that he'd let that happen anyway. He'd be set, though, once even the most reluctant board members piled onto the good news bandwagon. In fact, all of this could work out well. It was a relief to have Carr out of the picture. A less splashy end would have been preferable, but this would do. Unfortunately, with Carr dead, there was no chance to find out what that little meeting at the top of the tram was about. Shouting and gunshots meant it wasn't a love fest. Libby Van Der Woert had been practically stalking Carr. Had she lured him up there to kill him? Why was Jessica Huntington there? No matter, he had moves to block her too.

"Yeah," barked a disembodied voice on the phone.

"The minute the cops have cleared out I want a team at Carr's office and his home. I want the places cleaned out—not a scrap of paper or electronic device is to be left behind. You know, take all the stuff he uses to communicate and keep records. Also, make sure that whack job, the Van Der Woert broad, never comes to. I don't want her telling squat to the cops. The Huntington busybody will be released from the hospital any minute now, so you may have to take care of her later. For now, keep tabs on her. I'll give you the 'go' signal on Huntington, depending on what happens after you take care of Libby Van Der Woert. You know the drill. It should look like she just didn't make it if you can do that, but do whatever it takes."

The decision made, Eric Conroy, Executive Vice President of Pinnacle Enterprises, Inc., relaxed. He could make a decision, even a tough one, and wouldn't stew about it or second guess himself and get on with the business at hand.

That's why he stood out as a leader. Well, it was one reason. He could stay cool and think strategically, even in a crisis. It had quickly moved him up the ranks as a purveyor of perception management. That's why he was much sought after as a so-called "spin doctor" when trouble erupted for their elite clients and the firms they represented. His ability to get out ahead of the other wolves he ran with was yet another sign of his capacity to lead the pack. That he had helped manufacture a few of the crises he was called in to manage was a measure of true genius. It's why they needed him at the helm of the flagship PR firm. The fact he wasn't already at the helm was their loss and they'd know that soon enough.

He was getting too old for this garbage, anyway. Soon the keys to the kingdom would be his and Eric knew exactly what he'd do with those keys, too. It had taken him more than five years to be named Executive Vice President, but without assurances that he was next in line for the CEO position. He could have forced that to happen anyway, but he decided instead to pursue his Personal Liberation Plan. He shook his head thinking about what a naïve shmuck he'd been when he stepped from college into his first job at CC&R—"Create Crap and Run," as he and other low level chumps referred to the firm behind the scenes. The job he landed at that small advertising firm in New Jersey was just a hop, skip, and jump from the Big Apple. That's where he planned to go after honing his craft through a lot of hard work, grit, and determination. Boy oh boy, had he been a fool. A Hoosier, from the Midwest, he was fodder for the gristmill that was the norm for advertising, public relations, marketing, and consulting firms when he entered the field.

They busted his chops while working him like an indentured servant. From day one, he was "nobody from nowhere" with his Hoosier-U marketing degree and his Hicksville, aw-shucks-demeanor. They had him cold-calling and hustling twenty-four/seven, trying to explain the value of marketing and media to half-witted, half-drunk prospects in charge of marketing and advertising at firms all over the country. He learned to call early before multi-martini power lunches put the jerks in a surly stupor.

The experience had opened his eyes. He was a quick study and had a penchant for innovation. As the first few years of his career unfolded, he saw the seemingly endless horizon that stretched ahead. Decades loomed. That's when he took matters into his own hands. He would apply the skills he'd learned to market his own life, orchestrating a public relations campaign that propelled him ahead before he entered the second decade of his career.

The third decade would be his last as a "spin doctor" and "mad man," not that there was much of the old Madison Avenue left. Despite all the Hoosier-bashing he had endured, you could do a lot of your masterminding from just about anywhere these days because so much of the action took place in cyberspace. A big splashy, brick and mortar presence, in one of the power centers like New York, LA, or DC still made a statement, though. Eric had decided to go west and try to strike gold on the "Left Coast," taking a job with a bigger firm than CC&R. By then, he'd learned one of the key secrets to success was leverage.

So much for honing your craft and working hard as the way to getting ahead, he'd decided. Turns out having a little something-something on somebody did so much more. It opened doors, cleared pathways, and removed obstacles. He sort of stumbled across that truth about business after running into one of the more egregious Hoosier-bashers at CC&R in a rather compromising situation. An old story, not the least bit original: he'd practically bumped into the man coming out of a posh hotel sucking face with a gorgeous woman. She wasn't his wife. Eric had merely winked at him in passing, not even stopping to say hello. After that, the grateful department head at his firm couldn't do enough to help him. As soon as he could, in fact, he'd helped Eric right out of CC&R and into another firm.

Somehow, he had a knack for being in the right place at the right time—the person on the other end of that situation might have considered it the *wrong* place at the *wrong* time. Oh well, that was no concern of his. Not all the situations could be kept hush-hush. Some of the unfortunate circumstances members of Eric's widening circle of hotshots found themselves in created opportunities for him to save the day with el primo crisis management, spin control, and a re-branding PR package. If he played his cards right—and he did—he could make hay from someone else's grand faux pas on both a personal and business level.

Thinking about how close he was to the brass ring now, he basked in reminiscences about how his greatest innovation in self-promotion had occurred. He was already in LA, mingling with a whole new crowd of potential clients. So many of the high-profile firms and individuals in Tinsel Town or the Silicon Valley were one tiny, precipitous step away from joining the ranks of the "reputation-impaired." One of his first big ideas was to sell "reputation insurance" to headline-makers. Kind of like insurance sold to protect against identity theft. Unfortunately, he couldn't find underwriters that could develop an algorithm to estimate the costs associated with a damaged reputation. Libel and slander courts had struggled with that issue in awarding reparations, and still thrashed it out, one case at a time.

From that failure, though, came the revelation that it wasn't much of a leap from *anticipating* hypothetical reputation-damaging situations to *documenting* them when they occurred. Much like that accidental meeting as his old boss strolled from the hotel, in the arms of his mistress, but being more organized and at the ready. The most susceptible clients were headed so clearly for a fall that, with the help of some well-placed gumshoe or shutterbug, all he did was capture the moment of indiscretion and make sure it got into the right hands. Heck, with cameras on cell phones, he could practically rely on the trend spotters he hired to do that work for him. It was as easy to capture an indiscreet moment, as it was to snap shots of hot ideas teeming the streets that could be marketed as the next big thing in fast fashion or fast food.

Taking that last step from documenting to *manufacturing* disreputable behavior had actually been the brainchild of Dr. Richard Carr. The man had been sitting on a gold mine when Eric stumbled upon the shrink's antics. That had come about as the result of one of those fortunate accidents Eric was poised to use to his advantage.

One of his biggest clients, who also held a seat on Pinnacle's board, had a weakness for young women. He had come to Eric's office, one night, in a drunken state.

"I need your help. Not for my firm, but for me, personally. My daughter has accused me of the most horrendous thing. I'm about to consult a lawyer, but will need all the help I can get if this gets out to the public. This is so impossibly disgusting. She says I molested her, years ago when she was a child. I admit I like younger women, who doesn't? But my own daughter, never! And never a child! Who could think of a child in a sexual way?"

The man had careened from Eric's office into the private bath nearby, retching violently. He was obviously overcome, not just by drunkenness, but disgust or worry about the damage this might do to his reputation. When he came back into the room, they sketched out a game plan. They would get ahead of this thing with some well-placed PR. That included donations to high-profile agencies known for saving babies, children, or animals, ending hunger, and preserving the wilderness. Word of Edwin 'Ned' Donnelly's good deeds would be leaked. That would include photos featuring the man donating blood, releasing rehabilitated animals back into the wilds, standing next to a doctor in scrubs and mask at a neo-natal unit featuring teeny, tiny babies. It was all pro forma, really.

"They'll be calling you Saint Ned by the time we're through with you. If your daughter goes after you publicly, it'll get you hailed as a martyr," Eric had assured the man, patting him on his slumped shoulders. The plan would be implemented, off the books, as a personal favor for a long-time agency client and a current member of the board.

"I consider you more than a client and colleague. You're a friend," he'd said in his most confident and reassuring tone. "Go home, get a good night's sleep, and let me get the ball rolling."

"How can I ever thank you?"

"Let's not worry about that now. Friends help friends when they need it. Who knows when I might need your help, right?"

As he spoke those words, he already knew exactly what help he needed and when. It wouldn't be long before Pinnacle's board would vote about taking the company public. An initial public offering, netting the company hundreds of millions of dollars, was a no-brainer to Eric but some of the founding fathers at Pinnacle had raised objections. "Dinosaurs, they deserve extinction," he'd growled under his breath, after battling with them at a board meeting.

Donnelly, however, was easily talked into supporting an IPO when Eric brought it up a short time later. In fact, you would have thought it was his idea, given his advocacy for an IPO at meetings of the board. His enthusiasm might have been related to the effectiveness of the campaign he was waging on Donnelly's behalf. He'd reassured Donnelly that regardless of any aspersions cast by his daughter, he would come out of it smelling like a rose.

Dr. Richard Carr was another matter. Eric smelled a rat. Questions put to Donnelly that night in his office set off his scam detector. Shannon Donnelly had seen a new shrink in the past year. Ned's daughter had become more distant, but they thought, maybe, that was a good thing.

"We took it as a sign of greater self-reliance. A new shrink, new meds, and she even had a major, finally. Now this..." Soberer after heaving his guts out and a few sips of coffee, he was still crestfallen. "Then out of the blue, she attacked me."

During her most recent tirade, she'd demanded money. Ned Donnelly had taken no notice of the money angle because he was so horrified by the accusations his daughter was making. Bailing his daughter out of trouble had been a regular event even though she was on an allowance from a trust fund set up by her grandma.

Like taking candy from a baby, Eric thought when he met with Dr. Richard Carr the next day. By that, Eric meant getting the guy to "fess up." Pretending to know more than he actually did, he wheedled and then threatened the doctor into disclosing his scheme. The old candy-from-a-baby adage also applied to the fools Carr was fleecing with the racket he had going. It was genius, in fact—the scheme, not the man who came up with it. Carr was a small-minded, petty criminal. He had to give Carr credit for having the imagination to find a new way to put the squeeze on the rich and famous. Extortion, wrapped in the trappings of psychiatry, lofty degrees, glossy brochures, fancy digs, and using a wasted daughter to deliver the demand for money was innovative. But that's where the doctor's imagination had reached its limit.

The esteemed doctor was mainly interested in funding his practice by manipulating spoiled princesses into getting money to support endless hours of therapy at three hundred bucks a pop and up, private pay. His setup not only got Daddy and Mommy to pay up for psychotherapy and med checks at his upscale office in the heart of Beverly Hills, but convinced them to fork over a sizeable concierge fee to ensure a place for their troubled daughters on his roster of elite clients.

Thinking of that first meeting now, Eric wondered about the doctor. Maybe the guy was already using too much of his own meds. It had been awfully simple to get to the bottom of matters. Chatting him up, with apple-polishing about his "genius," had prompted Carr to boast about his efforts. He even admitted he derived pleasure from ripping off the one-percent as he struggled to make ends meet on a meager two or three hundred thousand a year.

"Hey, you don't have to explain it," Eric had said. And he'd meant it. The upper middle class is still the middle class, squeezed from above and below. There was a twisted irony in Carr's projection of predation onto the parents of the young women while the doctor himself preyed upon them. His bottom line was utterly self-serving.

"In my mind, I'm not doing anything untoward, really. The girls who come to see me are so screwed up. They want to believe their parents did something so they can blame them for their wasted lives. Who am I to argue with that? I just help them give those sentiments shape and substance and make sure they get the resources they need to get help—from me."

Eric had later revealed to the sleazy psychiatrist the untapped potential his scheme offered. To be honest, he hadn't understood the full value of Carr's enterprising ways right away. It was only when Eric moved into the final stages of his own Personal Liberation Plan, that he'd put it all together. Now, as the endgame approached, with Carr's help that plan was about to be fully realized. He, not Carr, had figured out what could be done with the right leverage.

That idiot Carr hadn't bothered to reveal another secret until recently. There was more to his preying on the spoiled daughters of wealthy elites in Beverly Hills. When the Donnelly woman disappeared, Eric knew something was up and he confronted Carr, asking him point blank if he was behind the woman's disappearance. From the way Carr blanched when asked, he didn't need to know more.

"She gave me no choice, Eric. The self-centered dimwit lost it when she found out our romance wasn't exclusive. Her roommate, Libby, wasn't too happy about learning she wasn't the only sun in my personal solar system either. Shannon was planning to go to her dad about our business dealings. Libby claimed Shannon had seen us together, Eric, and had gotten her hands on some damning information. Shannon was hysterical that night, and I had to intervene. Libby's cool, too, now that she thinks she's won. I've convinced her to run off with me when she gets the payout from her parents. Like I'll need her money once we've hit the jackpot," Carr had said, laughing bitterly.

Eric's inclination had been to end the fool's life. Talk about dimwits, how could the man have been so stupid fooling around with both women? Dammit, they were roommates! Still, Carr had played a key role in convincing Ned Donnelly that he had plenty of reason to worry about his daughter's claims against him. The doctor stepped in and validated the girl's claims, saying that in his professional opinion, her recovered memories of abuse were credible. Carr had even put his opinion in writing, in an official looking document, delivered to Donnelly by his beloved daughter. Carr had performed a similar role in other situations, helping to leverage the backing or silence of individuals who could influence the outcome of Eric's Personal Liberation Plan, so he had let it slide.

Ned Donnelly had been shaken that night months ago when he had stumbled into Eric's office. Ned hadn't been much better during subsequent meetings, although the "Saint Donnelly" philanthropist and all-around good guy campaign was going well. His daughter's subsequent disappearance might actually have been a relief to the old guy, except that Carr's affidavit kept the old gent cornered.

When his daughter went missing, it was headline news. Eric had Donnelly's back there, too. In a brief televised interview, Ned Donnelly emphasized that he was fully cooperating with police in their investigation into his daughter's disappearance. At his urging, Donnelly offered a substantial reward for information about her whereabouts.

Donnelly was devastated by the whole ordeal, having aged ten years right before Eric's eyes since that first drunken appeal for help. Eric tried to reassure Ned, even going so far as to explain how Shannon's disappearance worked to his advantage, making him more sympathetic in the public eye. Donnelly had taken that the wrong way. Dazed and confused, he'd left their last meeting without even thanking Eric for the work he was doing. That was okay. Eric didn't need his thanks; his continued cooperation was all that mattered.

Score! Eric mentally sank a three-pointer from mid-court, recalling the exhilaration he'd felt when the votes were in, including Donnelly's thumbs up on the IPO. More jubilation when the lead underwriter was unleashed to preach the good news. Evangelists of greed, they eagerly hit the road to sell, sell, sell, public shares of Pinnacle!

"My kind of guys," Eric chortled to himself in the empty office.

If only he could hold it all together. It was a matter of days at this point. Maybe he should have done more when that arrogant bastard, Carr, went into take-charge-doctor mode before the latest mess in Palm Springs.

"I've got this covered, Eric. No one will find Donnelly before we want her to be found. Libby's gloating about the fact that with Shannon gone, she's got no competition. That's what she thinks anyway," he folded his arms and chuffed.

"What do you mean, 'that's what she thinks?' She'd better not have any competition. Nix the Romeo thing until this is over and you're sitting on some beach somewhere. You'll have all the time and money in the world to chase as many women as you want. Until then, cool it—even with that Van Der Woert woman. Got it?"

"There's no reason to get worked up about this, Eric. What harm can there be in stringing Libby along at this point? Besides, I'm too old to be Romeo—Casanova, maybe," Dick Carr had said erupting into guffaws at his cleverness. He had leaned back and put his clasped hands behind his head before going on.

Eric had wanted to wipe that grin off his face, but he could wait. Learning there might be other clients-with-benefits, besides Shannon and Libby, was infuriating. Still, Carr might have been right about having it all under control, except for Jessica Huntington's meddling. Carr had only mentioned Jessica's name in passing. The name rang a bell, but he'd mistakenly figured she was just another young woman with all the right neuroses and connections to make her a candidate for daddy-bashing. He hadn't given her much thought until Carr brought up her name again. As he was about to leave Carr's office, the psychiatrist had finally responded to the admonition about cooling it with Libby.

"I suppose you're right about Libby, Eric. Jessica Huntington is playing mind games with her. Thanks to that Huntington woman, Libby's having a bout of 'buyer's remorse.' After all I've done for her, too, the ungrateful little minx. She bought into the scheme to take down Daddy and claim what was rightfully hers, so what is her problem?"

He sensed there was more to the story than Carr revealed. When Eric checked Jessica Huntington out for himself, what he found set his teeth on edge. He knew her name because the woman was a lawyer from a prominent family. Not just any lawyer, but a member of Canady, Holmes, Winston and Klein. Who was one of her clients? The Van Der Woerts! It was all too cozy to be coincidental. When he confronted Carr, the joker admitted he knew about the connection between Jessica Huntington and Libby's parents. He had made it quite clear to Libby that Jessica Huntington was working for the other side after Libby had gone to her law office in Palm Desert— right before the sudden surge of conscience.

"I questioned Libby about that meeting. It was brief and uneventful, so maybe she's just still ticked about Shannon. Women! Who can ever understand them?"

True, Eric had thought. Carr's eyes were rolling around in his head, so he guessed Carr had been dipping into the samples of pharmaceutical-grade, mind-altering substances kept in a bowl in his office. He'd left Carr's office grateful that the end game was underway. Soon, he'd never have to deal with Dr. Richard Carr or his ilk again.

New questions nagged at Eric now. If Donnelly was taken care of, and the 'fix' was in on Libby Van Der Woert, too, what had happened after that? There had to be some reason for that meeting of loose minds up there at the top of the tram, but what? He could feel his blood pressure rising.

Let it go, he thought, stretching his neck and shoulders. Another week, two at the most, and it would all be over. No way would the board do anything to disrupt the IPO process. A change in course at this point would shake Pinnacle to its foundations. Maybe, knock it down altogether. That would happen, anyway, but not until after the IPO.

The rest of his plan was already in place, too. A simple one: take the money and run. The jerry-rigging he and the CFO had done to get their S1 past those desk jockeys at the SEC might not stand up to another round of scrutiny, but it shouldn't have to. The Pinnacle Enterprise financial documents, backing up the S1, were a skillfully written work of fiction. Pinnacle was the mother of all holiday turkeys. A turkey all right, but one they could sell, raising a billion dollars almost overnight. It was lights, camera, and action, as the road show rolled out before the IPO. Game on!

"Yes! Game, set, and match," Eric said. He slammed his fist down on the desk again. This time it was an act of triumph.

6 TIRAMISU

Frank Fontana had more flowers. A bouquet of bright orange daylilies mixed with sprays of deep blue columbine and other wildflowers. Wild, like the man, himself. As usual, his dark brown hair was a little too long. He needed a haircut, but money and time were scarce for the hard-working single father of two. As he dashed into the room, he never took his dark eyes off Jessica, even while giving his cousin, Tommy, a pat on the back. He nodded to Jerry Reynolds as he leaned in and placed the flowers next to Jessica before bussing her cheek with a kiss.

Jessica's heart did a little flip-flop as Frank bent close enough for her to catch a whiff of the outdoors that hung about him. Detective Frank Fontana, with the Riverside County Sheriff's homicide division, had no official business with Jessica Huntington. There was plenty of unfinished personal business between them though.

She had sworn there would be no new men in her life for at least a year after divorcing her two-timing ex-husband. The most traumatic aspect of the split was betrayal by a man she'd trusted and pledged to love for a lifetime. For several months, now, her mind could stumble upon the ghastly image of Jim's betrayal without wanting to vomit or stomp the man into the ground while wearing five-inch Jimmy Choos. *An awful thing to do to those shoes*, she thought.

Before Frank retreated, she placed a kiss on the ruggedly handsome detective's cheek. *He could use a shave*, she thought as he squeezed her hand. Not that she minded his being a little rough around the edges. In fact, she liked it.

An image of her ex floated before her. James Harper, in tennis shoes and a t-shirt, sitting on the floor of their apartment in Palo Alto, his hair shaggy and in need of a shave as they studied together for the bar exam. That image vanished as a more polished, but less wholesome, version of Jim appeared. This one, clean-shaven and sporting a three-hundred-dollar haircut, was naked, running for his life as Jessica hurled objects at him from their bedroom. The shrieking, silicon-enhanced Hollywood 'Barbie,' his partner in crime, was dashing ahead of him.

That image of Jim was sobering. It put a damper on yearnings to find out just what it was about Frank Fontana that smelled so great. In addition to that, she was lying in a hospital bed, with a body too banged up to do anything about it even if she discovered the secret of his allure.

"How's she doing?" Frank asked. "I'd ask her, but she'd give me the invulnerable Wonder Woman version and I want the real scoop." He had a rueful grin on his face and Jessica stuck her tongue out at him as Jerry answered his question.

"Well, I'm sure she thinks she's doing better than she is. It's too soon to know how good a shape she's in. That's why they still have her trapped in here, but I can tell it won't work much longer. She's chomping at the bit to get out of here. Wait until she tells you how she fought off Carr, with both hands tied, before he and Libby Van Der Woert tossed her off a boulder overlook." That worried look was back on Jerry's face.

"I had my hands untied by then. I don't get it, you guys. Miss Marple investigated dozens of heinous crimes, and about the worst thing that ever happened was that she dropped a few stitches in her knitting. Hercule Poirot, the punctilious little detective, almost never had more to complain about than sore feet or getting his spats dirty. Me, I've been punched in the face, thrown to the ground in a parking lot, accosted by gangbangers on the side of the road, kidnapped, drugged, and shot at! Now, to top it all off, I get shoved off a mountain. What am I doing wrong?"

"Do you really want me to answer that?" Frank asked with a glint in his eye, interrupting her rant. She was sure he was about to remind her of the many times he and his counterparts in other homicide units had urged her not to chase cutthroats and let the pros do the dirty work. She had to admit that she'd been ill-prepared to face the onslaught of ugliness vented upon her as she plunged into sleuthing. She'd thought that was all behind her until this latest incident caught her off balance.

"Hey, I kept my promise not to go after Dr. Carr on my own. That was not my intention when I headed up there to talk to Libby. I also called Detective Hernandez and told him where I was going. Another promise kept, Frank Fontana." He was getting her stirred up as he often did. The grin on his face said he knew what he was doing.

"Ooh, here we go again," Tommy said, shifting his weight on the foot of her bed. It was like he was settling into his seat at the theater. "You realize a lot of this is just sexual tension, right?" Frank laughed, but Jessica and Jerry both shot Tommy a dirty look. Tommy didn't care as he took full advantage of the special place he held in Jessica's heart. He took delight in taunting her, like a mischievous younger brother, especially about Frank.

"What? I can't help it if you heterosexual types require so much foreplay before you..."

"Tommy, knock it off," Jerry interrupted, shaking his head. That made Frank laugh louder and his laughter made Jessica angrier.

"Lack of foreplay has nothing to do with it," Jessica blurted. "Wait, that's not what I meant."

As they had promised Frank's dad, Jessica and Frank were taking things slow. Since their initial entanglement during the investigation into his cousin, Kelly's, murder back in June, they'd seen each other regularly and there had been a few knee-buckling hugs and several tantalizing kisses, but not what you could call foreplay. Okay, so maybe there was some sexual tension between them. What stressed her out more than that were the mixed feelings she had for Frank. The attraction she felt was undeniable. Still, he was a man and like most men, he could irritate—some of that was the cop thing. "Serve and protect" often seemed more like "command and control!" Then there was the issue of money. It didn't bother her that she had a lot more than he did, but it irked him. Misbegotten male pride or another aspect of the machismo cop culture. When word got around that they were seeing each other, his cop buddies ribbed him. The classy lady lawyer who clobbered bad guys with expensive smart phones and high heels was renowned county-wide among police personnel. That wasn't likely to get any better with all the *"angel heiress"* news coverage.

"There's too much testosterone in this room. I haven't decided if I even like men very much anymore, gay or straight!"

"Does that mean you're thinking about switching teams?" Tommy had a wicked look on his face. He was blinking and ducking his head like someone might take a swat at him any second.

"You know that's not funny, right?" Jerry was growing red in the face with anger, or embarrassment, or both. Even though they were mad about each other, Tommy often pushed Jerry to the brink with his outlandish statements. That Frank's wife had left him for another woman was the reason for Jerry's distress. "It's not very PC of you either," he added.

"Thomas, you are a brat and you're getting on my nerves. I just fell off a mountain, for goodness sake. Give me a break. Frank and I are friends. We've made a promise to keep it that way until I can figure out whether I can ever trust anyone, including myself. Maybe it's the last vestiges of the Catholic schoolgirl in me, but I intend to keep that promise."

Jessica made a quick little sign of the cross as she spoke that vow aloud. She stole a look at Frank who had quit laughing but still had a smirk on his face. She couldn't decide who she wanted to smack more, him or Tommy. Tommy had gone into "what me?" choirboy mode, playing the innocent as he did so often after he'd stirred things up. The ability to feign a seraphic demeanor was a trait he had shared with his sister, Kelly. She'd kept so much hidden from them all using that ploy. It didn't work so well for Tommy. Deploying her Jessica Huntington version of the Vulcan mind probe, she penetrated his veil of feigned innocence, and his face drooped.

"I'm sorry. You've been through a lot. It's just that I don't handle the tension..." He must have caught another look from Jerry because he didn't finish the sentence. "Sorry Jessica, sorry Frank, no offense."

"None taken. It's been over three years since Mary 'switched teams,' as you put it. I'm over it. But I keep my promises, too. You might have to put up with more tension since Jessica and I still have a lot of things to sort out. At least for a few more years, I have kids at home, so it's not just me that I have to think about before getting involved with a woman. Especially one as stubborn, uppity, and exasperating as our friend here, no matter how lovely and beguiling she can be." He leaned over and tousled Tommy's hair as Jerry had done earlier. Jessica felt herself go all mushy inside. They did have a lot of things to sort out, but, damn, the man knew how to make it seem worthwhile.

"It's okay. I'm not the only one in this room who's stubborn and exasperating. In fact, I believe that *our friend* here was about to tell me, once again, to cool it. Do I look like I could get into trouble like *this*?" She asked, holding up her arm with the bandaged hand. Free, for the moment at least, from an IV. The other was still in that sling made to support her arm and shoulder and allowed little movement.

"If it were anyone else but you, I'd say not. Your inner Joan of Arc has you ready to believe you can take out bad guys with both hands tied so why not with one in a sling?"

"That's just not true!" She thought about that moment when she went toe-to-toe with the gun-toting psychiatrist. "Okay, I shoved him first. The scumbag had a gun pointing right at me."

"Sheesh, that's what I'm talking about! Look, this is getting us nowhere. Besides checking on your well-being, I stopped by hoping to get the low down from you about what happened up there. Pop and his guys will be here, in an official capacity, to ask for a statement any time now. I'd like to hear it myself, off the record since I have no role in the police investigation. It's more than idle curiosity, though, since you've had me playing 'consultant' on your investigation into Libby Van Der Woert's trouble with her parents."

"Consultant, woohoo," Tommy hooted. "That's a fancy term for our Cat Pack snooping activities. I like that!" The Cat Pack was the name she and her friends had adopted for themselves when, like a herd of cats, they had wandered about during their first murder investigation. Less glitz and glam than the sixties "Rat Pack" that hung out in the Palm Springs area, their strange little band had forged a bond about as strong as that between Sinatra and his chums. They even had a Frank of their own.

"I should remind you, about the risk of being too nosy—you know that old saying about curiosity and dead cats. And please don't paw the air or hiss. It just makes me feel worse about anything I do that encourages you to go on with this amateur sleuthing."

"Well, we're not all amateurs," Jerry said. "I'm a card-carrying PI, and it's the way I make a living."

"I'll remind you that Jerry works for me, at the firm... most of the time. Okay, often anyway. *And*, I might add, Tommy's on the payroll along with Kim Reed, as Jerry's assistants. So, I suppose that leaves Bernadette and Laura as the amateurs because Peter's a pro too."

"Don't forget about Brien. Are you going to make a case that his barroom bouncer training qualifies him as a pro? He thinks he's 'muscle,' but I sure hope, for his sake, he doesn't give up his day job."

"Now, don't pick on my poor pool boy. He's not even here to defend himself. For your information, Peter has taken the guy under his wing, hoping to give him a little security training to go with that well-intentioned brawn of his." Frank's mouth popped open, but no words came out.

"Brien and Peter? Are you sure about that?" Frank still seemed incredulous when he finally spoke.

"Yep! Brien has been doing ride-alongs, and he's taking a course to get the basic training he needs for a California Guard Card. I guess Peter's company does that thing—offers training certified by the Bureau of Security and Investigative Services." Now Jerry wore a befuddled expression, too.

"*What?*" Jessica asked. "That's it, isn't it, Jerry—BSIS?"

"Oh yeah, you've got that right. It's just that I'm about as surprised as Frank about the ride-alongs. Brien gets on Peter's nerves. I can't imagine them in the same car together for long without an incident."

"Brien gets on everyone's nerves. Even our sweet, patient St. Bernadette gets pushed to the point where I think she'll take a rolled up newspaper to him. He's like a big, hyperactive dog underfoot. But he means well, and Peter's of the opinion that discipline and training will do him a world of good."

"Woof, woof!" Jerry and Frank both glared at Tommy. "Nothing wrong with discipline—in the right hands."

"Oh, stop it. These guys will sign you up for obedience school, too, if you keep that up, Tommy."

"Promise? Do I get to wear a collar?" Tommy asked, panting like a dog. Jerry blushed and rolled his eyes at Tommy's antics. It was Jessica's turn to be puzzled.

"Now *I'm* lost, Tommy. What are you babbling about?"

"Shades of Grey, Jessica, what planet are you on?"

"Oh yuck, you too? We've spent the last fifty years trying to get women out of bondage, way over fifty shades of it, and one hyped up book makes it chic to put them back in it. Not to mention all the effort that's gone on to try to help people sort out the boundaries between sex and power. There is nothing sexy about being bound. I know what I'm saying—my wrists are still sore from my latest stint in ropes, see?"

"Speak for yourself. You know for me, it has nothing to do with women. But, point taken. Maybe you need to stop with all the whipped puppy stuff." Tommy stared at the floor with a sad look on his face—feeling sorry for himself most likely after having been scolded. Ten seconds later, he made whiny puppy sounds, grinning as he settled into a nearby chair. Jessica felt her embattled nervous system getting riled up.

"Don't make me tattle to Bernadette about you." That shut him up. He believed that the saintly Bernadette possessed special powers. "She'll call forth the hounds of hell. Then what will you do, Smarty Pants?" Jessica asked, as she turned her attention back to the matter at hand.

"Gentlemen, I've had about all I can take for one afternoon, speaking of tension and getting on people's nerves. I love you all. I mean that in the truest sense of the word—Cat Pack esprit de corps and all of that. As you can see, Frank, I am doing fine. If you will all shut up for a few minutes, I'll give you the rundown on what happened with Libby. After that you can all go, so I can get my beauty sleep. Since Bernadette isn't here, I'll call Nurse Andrews and we'll see what an empowered woman can do without any props."

Jessica spent the next twenty minutes going over, once again, what happened the day before at the top of the tramway. Frank asked several clarifying questions, but otherwise, the men in the room kept silent. Jessica told the story in a more coherent way this time, but that didn't mean it made more sense.

"So, here's the big picture: Carr was treating both Libby and Shannon and he was up to no good," Jessica said, concluding her account. "What kind of 'no good' still isn't clear, although at least some of it involved an inappropriate sexual relationship with Libby. Even if Libby has evidence of an affair, I find it hard to believe he'd kill her because of it. That means there's more going on. Given Libby's rambling, it could be related to Shannon Donnelly's disappearance. I don't have a good feeling about that. Libby also said all Carr wanted was the money she was trying to extort from her parents by making false allegations against them. Maybe Libby wasn't the only client scamming her parents. While sexual indiscretion isn't a crime, blackmail is. If he was using his clients to get a share of their ill-gotten gains, and Libby or Shannon had proof, it might be a motive for murder. Libby seems to know what happened to Shannon, so maybe that's why Carr planned to kill her, and me too, if he thought Libby had told me about Shannon. I'm not sure where the red devil fits into all of this. Argh! You guys are right. I'm too worn out to figure this all out. I need to back off."

"You're fortunate to have survived that ordeal. If I can believe that what you intend to do is take it easy, I'll rest easier too, and I won't go waving my badge at you. What's the point of having this crack team of Cat Pack consultants if you don't use them? What I propose is that you let us pick up the trail from here for a few days while you recover. I'll run interference for you with Dad and his colleagues at the Palm Springs Police Department, to give you another day or two before they interrogate you. That also means that when they question you, they get the whole story. No shielding Libby out of an over-developed sense of loyalty to her parents. If you care about them, you'll give the police every shred of information you have, even if it raises suspicions about their daughter."

"It's a deal! Thanks for giving me a little more breathing room. I sure would like to know whether that blue bag or suitcase exists and what's in it. Maybe the Cat City police have enough on Libby as a suspect in Donnelly's disappearance and they can get a warrant to search her place in Los Angeles."

"If you tell Hernandez what you've learned, it might make that happen. That's presuming they haven't already done it. Or maybe Pop and his guys can get someone to do it. It's likely Libby's involvement in Carr's death, whether they charge her with murder or involuntary manslaughter, will give them a reason to do a thorough investigation."

"Unless they decide she acted in self-defense."

"Okay, so maybe voluntary manslaughter then. That still means a formal police investigation. My point is here's another chance to let the process run its course while you get back on your feet."

"I hear you. There are all these little snippets of conversation with Libby that pop into my head at odd moments. Little details that nag at me. Like, how did the press get hold of the idea that Carr was treating Libby? That's confidential information, so how did it get into the hands of the press?"

"That's a good question." Jerry took out the small notebook he always carried with him and made a notation in it. "We'll track down the reporters and ask where that information came from. Don't hold your breath about getting a clear answer though." She leaned back against the pillow and closed her eyes.

"Did I tell you it hurts to talk, you guys? If I suck in air the wrong way, I pay a penalty. My body is telling me to back off, too."

"Good! Not because you're in pain, but because you're paying attention to the messages your body is sending you. It's a lovely one, and worth the attention. I can vouch for that." He smiled, affection softening his dark brown eyes—and shyness stealing over him at the words he had just spoken. This more vulnerable version of Frank Fontana was the one she found irresistible. Kind and thoughtful, he often expressed care and tenderness toward his children and parents, displaying a depth she couldn't remember ever having seen in her ex-husband. How odd she hadn't noticed, until too late, that Jim's relationships with others were shallow and self-serving.

"Well, it's the only one I've got," she said as their eyes met.

"Get some rest." Visibly relieved when she nodded in agreement, Frank moved closer. He picked up the flowers he'd set on the bed next to her and dropped them into the water pitcher on a tray beside her bed. Jessica must have looked askance.

"Don't worry. I'll take full responsibility with Nurse Andrews. I'll ask her to bring you a new pitcher and more water on my way out, promise." With that, he leaned over and kissed her lightly on the lips. The sensation provoked a different set of messages from her body. Not one of them told her to back off.

Jessica watched the man leave the room, swagger in his step as he went off to battle with Nurse Andrews. Jerry and Tommy left, too, after planting friendly smooches on her face. They said something as they left, but her mind was too full of Frank Fontana to process it.

"Don't tell me that's not foreplay!" Tommy hollered from the doorway, a devilish grin back on his face.

Jessica drifted into a dreamy state. Nurse Andrews entered the room with a fresh pitcher of water. She poured a cup of water and offered it to Jessica along with some pills.

"Your friend said you're feeling some pain. It's time for your afternoon meds, so this should do the trick. If not, let me know and I'll call the doctor for you. He made me promise to take good care of you." She smiled for a moment before the sight of those flowers in the water pitcher wiped it away. Picking up the old pitcher, she put the new one in its place. Jessica thought she heard the nurse utter a quiet harrumph as she found a spot in the room for Frank's flowers. That Frank kept his promises was another striking difference between him and the well-heeled heel she had married. As she drifted toward sleep, she reveled in pleasant memories of another promise Frank had kept.

In August, Frank cooked Jessica one of the best Italian dinners she'd ever eaten. A peacekeeper in the family, he had been at his Irish mother's side when his Italian grandmother and aunts taught her to cook all the Fontana family favorites. Not the kind of meals they had eaten in Italy, but the meals that had become customary in Italian immigrant households. The centerpiece of the meal was pasta. Spaghetti, cooked al dente, and then covered with salsa di pomodoro simmered to add depth to the rich tomato flavor. Garlic, and fresh herbs, enriched the sauce. Frank served small meatballs on the side. They were made from a mixture of ground beef, veal, and pork, and flavored with a hint of nutmeg, parsley, garlic, and parmesan cheese.

Frank called the appetizer that began their meal bagna cauda. It was like the crudité featured with many restaurant meals. Crusty chunks of bread, blanched asparagus, cauliflower, and carrots set out with a warm dip. A luscious concoction of salty anchovies, garlic, and olive oil, blended and then warmed. Not a fan of the anchovy, Jessica had been dubious when he described the ingredients as he placed the fare in front of her.

"My effort to keep up with trends in Italian cooking," Frank had offered, as he set a tiny bowl of mixed olives beside the bagna cauda. The olives were warm, and laced with sprigs of rosemary, crushed red pepper, and lemon zest.

"Oh my God, Frank! This is to die for!" Jessica had exclaimed after tasting the bagna cauda.

"I won't tell Bernadette you said that. I want her to continue to like me."

"Frank, what are you saying? The only thing you have to worry about is getting recruited to step in and help feed our little Cat Pack." Their group had added new members during that awful summer. Not just Frank Fontana, but Kim Reed, had joined their ranks. When Jessica met Kim Reed, she was the office manager for a prime suspect in their investigation into Kelly Fontana's death. Kim had been helpful in determining who killed her dear friend, Tommy's sister and Frank's cousin.

"This is an experiment for both of us," Frank had said, breaking into Jessica's reverie. A note of anxiety was in his voice as he placed a side dish of Artichoke Gratinata, next to the hand-painted earthenware pasta bowl containing her spaghetti. His face lit up with delight when Jessica let out a little sigh after tasting a bite.

"This is amazing, too, Frank. Keep on experimenting!" she said before stuffing another bite of the delicious food into her mouth. *Not very demure, but what the heck*, she'd thought as she savored the crispy bread crumbs atop warm artichoke hearts. The dish melted in her mouth.

"You know the way to a woman's heart." She mumbled between bites.

"I sure hope so," he said, a flirty grin on his face. "Can I ply you with more of this obscenely delicious wine you brought to share?" She nodded as she continued to shove food into her mouth.

Thinking about that night now, it wasn't just the food that had captivated her. True, the meal added a sensual quality to the evening. As did the 2001 Corison Kronos Vineyard Cabernet that Jessica had brought to the table. A perfect addition, the wine was vividly aromatic, cassis-scented, and had dramatic color and legs in the glass. It rolled over the tongue with grace, bursting with flavors of dark cherry and oak. One of the last bottles she and her ex-husband had bought as a couple, her enjoyment was more evidence that Jim Harper was becoming a less painful part of her past.

The companionship was welcome. Not all their get-togethers were fraught with tension and disagreement. Their meal had been a leisurely one, uninterrupted by Frank's kids, Evie and Frankie. They were with their two moms for the weekend. Mary, Frank's ex, had remarried. Her new wife was a cop and his former co-worker in the Sheriff's department. He had his own healing to do from a marriage that had come undone when he discovered his wife and his colleague were having an affair.

The thing that Jessica found most touching about that whole evening was the care that Frank had taken with the meal. The man worked endless hours as a homicide detective with the Riverside County Sheriff's department and had two kids underfoot much of the time. He and his ex-wife shared custody, but they spent most of their time with him while school was in session. That he had planned and shopped and cooked such a splendid dinner had called that adage to mind about the connection between food and love.

They had taken their dessert, vanilla gelato covered in a light, lemony sauce, out to the back patio at his home in Perris. Sixty miles east of Rancho Mirage, the evening was cool by desert standards, and offered a welcome change. So did Frank. His eagerness to please, and apparent openness, was a pleasant change from her ex, who had grown more self-absorbed and remote before their marriage ended.

Jim Harper had seemed so right. He had money of his own when they married, so she believed money would not come between them. Wrong! Jim wanted more. At some point, his insatiable lust for more had become an overwhelming drive, almost obsessive. As she learned the hard way, that lust had extended beyond money, to encompass other prerogatives of a master of the universe—including a trophy wife straight from the big screen. The second Mrs. James Harper was a double-D pinup girl to adolescent males everywhere, many disguised as adult men. All of that weighed down upon her as she sat with Frank that night, and as she thought about it again after he sauntered out of the hospital room. It was still too soon to take their relationship further.

There was also the little matter of a gentleman by the name of Paul Worthington. Despite her best efforts to stay away from men in the wake of Jim's betrayal, there were two intriguing men in her life.

Paul Worthington, a cool blue-eyed blond on the verge of middle age was, in some ways, Jim all grown up, but in a good way. Born to money, he was mature and intelligent. His good traits were many, a stand-up guy, unspoiled by the wealth and power he commanded as a senior associate with a Vault 100 law firm.

So handsome, too. The fragrance of bergamot and amber hung about him. That scent, Jessica had discovered, was a Casswell-Massey product he always wore. Not cologne, but shampoo, soap, gel, or something like that. A light citrusy fragrance with an undercurrent of something richer, "like lemon meringue pie," Jessica muttered as she slid toward sleep. Frank Fontana was a different story, "warm apple pie or maybe tiramisu." Jessica giggled at the thought of characterizing the two men as delectable desserts. *I'd better see about getting those meds cut back!* That was her last thought before she drifted off for a nap until Nurse Andrews brought her dinner and dessert stood at the foot of the bed with his blue eyes sparkling.

7 LEMON MERINGE PIE

Jessica struggled to focus and drive ideas about men as desserts out of her mind. What to do about their relationship was troublesome enough when it came to Paul Worthington. Drooling over him as he sat there would not be helpful. Money issues were not a problem since Paul could hold his own with her on that front. No one would mock him for taking up with a wealthy woman as some of Frank's buddies did. She and Paul had a lot more in common than their wealth. Not just the law. They shared a love of theater and cinema; in particular, film noir classics. There was their love of opera, art, architecture, and travel, too. They both enjoyed many of the good things that money could buy, and with none of the awkwardness or embarrassment, she sometimes felt around Frank. Not that Paul shared her spendthrift tendencies—he didn't enjoy shopping, as she and her ex had, and as Jessica continued to do, despite vows to stop.

Paul was kind, generous, and full of surprises. The dashing lawyer could dance. Jessica loved to dance, and early in their marriage, had forced Jim to go dancing with her. But Paul didn't need to be forced into anything. Light on his feet and great in the clinches, he could keep up with her at the foxtrot, waltz, samba, and tango. Like Jessica, he'd taken dance year after year, along with etiquette classes. Unlike many males in that situation, Paul had loved it. As Jessica soon learned, in dance, the reticent side of the man gave himself over to the moment.

Those moments enthralled Jessica. Like that first night, dancing under the stars at the celebration for Hank, she found herself swept up in an exhilaration she hadn't experienced while dancing with Jim, or anyone else. There was more to Paul than met the eye, although that was plenty. As he gazed at her, his blue eyes filled with concern, she tried not to think about lemon meringue pie, or those moments spent in his arms. The two of them pressed together, moving in sync to the rhythms of whatever music was playing. Two things kept her from abandoning herself to those moments—the slashes of betrayal left by James Harper, and the fact that Paul Worthington was her boss. She also felt a little guilty about Frank.

"Hey, sleepy-head," Paul said as she shook off the remnants of her nap. "How are you doing?"

"Okay, considering I fell off a mountain," she said, still trying to make herself believe it. Jessica struggled to put up as much of a professional front as she could from a hospital bed, despite wearing bandages and a cast.

"You're so lucky to be alive," he said using almost the exact words Frank had used earlier and using the same worried, chiding tone in his voice. "Not just the fall, but also because Libby had a gun. It sounds like she finally went off the deep end if you'll pardon the expression under the circumstances. Her parents have been telling her for years she would eventually get herself into trouble they couldn't help her fix. From what I've heard, this just might be it."

"I know. Not just Libby. Her charming shrink had a gun too. I can see how Dr. Carr might have 'passed' as sane to get his mitts on a handgun, but Libby? I find it hard to believe she'd get through a background check." She shook her head. Then she spent the next few minutes telling the story, once again. She ended up back at the point Paul had made about a gun. "Who knew she was packing heat—that must be a probation violation. What was she thinking?"

"Her probation ended a little while ago. She didn't wait long before getting into more trouble, did she? The gun isn't her only problem now, with kidnapping and maybe murder charges looming—that gun will put her on the fast track for maximum prison time if she's convicted."

"Using it to kidnap me was a spur of the moment thing. She was scared and convinced someone was following her, so I presume she brought it with her as protection. Until Carr showed up armed with a gun, I thought she was delusional, paranoid, or attention-seeking. Kidnapping and murder never entered my mind... at least not my conscious mind when I agreed to meet her up there. On some level, I thought it was a good idea to tell Detective Hernandez where I was going and who I was meeting, so maybe I sensed she was dangerous. The odd thing—one of them anyway—is how surprised Libby was to see Carr when he turned up. Who did she imagine was stalking her if Carr's presence was a surprise?"

"That's an excellent question. I'm sure the police will ask if she recovers enough for them to question her. She could have been surprised by the fact that he had that gun. Especially if she had lured Carr up there to kill him. Jealousy is an all too common reason to kill. It could be she was angry enough about not being the only 'psycho-tramp' in the man's life to kill him. That's a new one—psycho-tramp's a term I haven't heard before. Maybe she planned a murder-suicide until Carr showed up with that gun. If it turns out the gunshot *is* what killed him, there's a case to be made for self-defense with the two of them wrestling over that gun as you described it." The defense attorney wheels in his head were turning.

"Libby's fear appeared genuine, but there's no way to rule out the possibility that her paranoia about being followed was delusional. Maybe part of a bigger delusion about a conspiracy behind Shannon Donnelly's disappearance involving a red devil."

"It sounds crazy. That's for sure. She didn't conjure up Dr. Carr, though."

"True, and I can vouch for the fact that he had murder on his mind, so the self-defense issue is legitimate. I think that surprised her, too. He wasn't just armed, but intent on killing her. In those moments, her reactions seemed more unguarded than they had been in the hours before Dr. Demento stepped out of the shadows. Why tattle on Carr, and tell me she had evidence to nail him for malpractice, if she was just going to kill him anyway?"

"I hear what you're saying. If she didn't lure him up there, how did he know where to find her?" He asked. A chill passed between them, perhaps both thinking about that red devil comment Libby had made.

"I'm not sold on the idea he was in league with a devil, but I suppose Carr could have had a partner who was following Libby and keeping tabs on her. If she had spotted the person tailing her, that would explain her paranoia. That doesn't tell us why Carr was after her, himself, and with a gun. Another possibility Jerry and I talked about earlier today is that Libby does know something that implicated Carr in Shannon Donnelly's disappearance. That's what she said she wanted to talk about when she called me, but she never got around to telling me very much."

"It's too bad she wasn't more forthcoming with specific information about what kind of trouble she caused for Shannon with Carr and his red devil sidekick. I wish we had news for Shannon's father. I saw Ned Donnelly at a holiday charity event for the LA Philharmonic this week. He looked grim. I wouldn't be the least bit surprised to learn that he's gone through as much with his daughter as the Van Der Woerts have with Libby. It's enough to make you never want to have children. Can there be that many deranged daughters roaming around?"

"You know the answer to that better than I do. I'm sure you've seen more than most, given your experience as a defense attorney for the rich and famous. Not just their daughters, either. Look at those Menendez brothers. Who knows if they're deranged, spoiled, or bad seeds? You raise an interesting point though about Ned Donnelly. If Libby's telling the truth, both she and Shannon were seeing Dr. Carr—at his office and in more intimate settings. Carr bragged that his 90210 princesses were easy to manipulate. Maybe that applied to Shannon Donnelly, and he was using her to extort money from her parents, too. I don't suppose her father would have disclosed that to the police investigating her disappearance. When Hernandez met with the Van Der Woerts and me, he was focused on finding out what he could about Libby's relationship with Shannon and her whereabouts when Shannon went missing. He didn't ask about the relationship between Libby and her parents, so the Van Der Woerts and I were tight-lipped about Libby's accusations. It seemed unrelated. If Shannon Donnelly was Libby Van Der Woert's psychic doppelganger, maybe her parents have been going through the same nightmare."

"'Psychic doppelganger!' Okay, that's a new one, too. You're right. It's not the kind of trouble the Donnellys would volunteer if the police didn't pry. Both Shannon and Libby are grown women in their thirties, not minors who might have run away from home. You could ask Detective Hernandez to go back to Ned Donnelly and do a follow up, but then you'd have to reveal more about what's going on between Libby and her parents to interest him in the idea. Given Libby's confession to you about making false allegations, and the tie-in to Carr, you should include that in your statement to the police, anyway. Withholding that kind of information could impede the investigations involving both Libby and Shannon. You don't have to go into the grimy details, but you need to say something about the allegations and extortion efforts by Libby and lover-boy-Carr. I'll touch base with Nick and Nora and fill them in on what you've told me. That will save you the stress of telling your story all over again to them—although at some point they may have questions for you. I'll explain that your statement to the police will include basic information about the latest round of trouble with their daughter." The level of emotion evident in Paul's remarks baffled Jessica.

"Sorry, I know you feel bad for them. This is another fine mess I've gotten us into, isn't it? Not that I'm sure how I instigated a change of heart on Libby's part as Carr claimed. I didn't deliberately try to trigger a bout of the scruples."

"You don't need to apologize. This isn't about anything you've done. A woman as mercurial as Libby might have had a change of heart for many reasons. Maybe she got up one morning, heard a particular song on the radio, and missed her parents. Or, more likely, experienced a bout of self-pity about being alienated from the parents she drove off, you know? Since when is remorse a bad thing? Good for you if you gave Libby a good jolt and evoked a shred of decency. I'm just glad you don't blame me for putting you in the path of that psycho-tramp, or whatever label she prefers. You're right that I've seen more, unprincipled and ungrateful children than I care to think about. Most of the time, they wait until the parents are older, on their deathbeds or in the grave, before they make their grab for the gold, which doesn't make it any less diabolical."

"Not to worry, Paul. My heart goes out to the Van Der Woerts, and I'm glad to be in their court—let's hope it's not a real court, though. Maybe it is diabolical and Libby is possessed. That makes about as much sense as any other explanation for her behavior. There were times when she was hissing like a snake, in between howling and other antics. No vomiting up green slime, or head spinning around backwards, like the girl in that old Exorcist movie." Jessica shuddered, recalling the glint in Libby's eyes as she waved that gun around with her hair blowing out around her, Medusa-like. Paul frowned as he let Jessica ramble on. *This is getting to him,* she thought, wondering if there was something personal about it.

"Paul, I'm kidding about the whole Exorcist thing. I feel awful that you have to follow up with the Van Der Woerts—adding that to your 'to do' list. This has been a setback, just when I was hoping I might make a run at matching your pace as a lawyer."

"Don't worry. You've already exceeded my expectations since we opened that office. I just got a call from Lesley Windsor. She was worried about you. She loves the house you helped her purchase out here, and the community it's in, so much that she helped her mother move out here into another country club. That hasn't worked as well for Mom, and she's in the middle of a brouhaha with members of her own homeowner's association. Anyway, Lesley has referred her mother to you. So your hard work is still paying off even while you're in here."

"I'm just sorry she had to call you about the brouhaha... I..." Jessica struggled to hang on to a professional demeanor. Paul reached out and put a reassuring hand over hers. The tingle that ran through her didn't help her feel more professional. Nor did the softness that had filled those blue eyes, the tender smile on the man's sensuous lips, the curve of his chin, the wave in his hair, or the way his tie needed adjusting... *Down girl!* She commanded herself. There must be a disinhibiting effect of the drugs she was on that had her emotions rampaging, especially when there was a deliciously handsome man nearby.

"Everyone faces setbacks—more likely from the flu than a shove off a mountain, I'll give you that. It's the holidays and everyone's preoccupied with the season. Our offices are scheduled to be closed for a few days. When you're feeling better, you'll have time to get caught up. You have about the best bad luck I've ever seen," he said shaking his head. "Trust me, I've seen plenty of wrong-place-wrong-time scenarios, and you are so fortunate to have landed where you did, when you did." He smiled. That smile was reassuring and helped her regain her composure.

"Don't let Detective Hernandez hear you say that. He'll lecture me on the dark side of kismet. I once made the mistake of using that term around him and he hasn't let me forget it. I'm sure I'll get another visit from him any minute now, too." Paul gave her hand a squeeze, sending her into lemon meringue pie territory again.

"My point is that things at the office will be just fine. Amy's got your back. She's already rescheduled your meetings. You two make a crack team, and Kim Reed has turned out to be a Phenom, according to Amy. Kim will keep working on the routine things you've assigned her to do. If you're not out of here in another day or two, Amy will stop by and go over everything with you here. Do as you're told so you can get back on your feet quickly. We've got more dancing to do, you know? Much more, I hope."

"Okay, boss," she said, gulping as she spoke.

"I won't always be your, boss. In fact, as soon as this office is up and running, in another year or so, my plan is to step out of the role." She must have looked alarmed or shocked.

"What? I'm not leaving the firm. I just won't be your boss anymore. Heck, by then, you could be running the place. It will be up to the firm to decide who to put in my place though. It's part of my overall plan to bring balance into my life. I want more room for other things—for people." The blue in his eyes deepened, pulling her into them. She realized how sad it would be not to have him around. Granted, he wasn't at the office every day, but at least two or three times each week. The place came alive with the force of his presence. Jessica fought a teary sensation as Paul spoke again.

"It's too soon to retire, but not too soon to dream about it and plan for it. I'm thinking of buying something out here in the desert. And that's another reason for you to get back up on your feet. After the holidays are over, I want to check out places. I could use your help if you don't mind. You know so much more about the area and have some idea of my taste in architecture and style. Will you give me a hand?" His hand was still resting on her free hand and Jessica's fingers, almost of their own accord, linked with his, but she let go as soon as she realized what she'd done.

"Of course, I will," she said as the man stood up to leave.

"Here's looking at you, kid." He chucked her on the chin as he uttered that line from Casablanca, one of their favorite old films they had watched together. So, lemon meringue pie or tiramisu, what was it going to be? *Whoa, baby, I'd better figure this out before someone gets hurt,* she thought as Paul shut the door behind him.

8 A CRUTCH

Alexis lay on her bed in the glamorous master bedroom that had once been the room she shared with Hank Huntington. It was a strange, but familiar sensation being back in this house with him in a guest room nearby. They had relied on such an arrangement before, many times. Then, as now, it had been the way they coped with shared parenting duties as their marriage deteriorated, and then dissolved. And, here they were again, reunited under one roof, because of Jessica.

Her head still hurt, even after taking Xanax to relax and Oxycontin to kill the pain. She should cut back and had vowed she would. The doctors wanted to schedule surgery for a hysterectomy and had put it off several times when her blood work came back loaded with the kind of drugs that make a general anesthetic risky. Especially for a woman in her sixties as her gynecologist pointed out.

"You're not a young woman anymore. The drugs are taking a toll: weight loss, elevated blood pressure, and an irregular heartbeat. Your liver's not looking so good, either." Her gynecologist, the one female in the portfolio of doctors managing Alexis' health care, had been gently reproachful. She was one of the first doctors Alexis consulted after the routine pap exam in LA revealed trouble. In August, Dr. Kate Mendel confirmed the diagnosis of early stage cervical cancer. Then, like the physician in Beverly Hills, she reassured Alexis it was a cancer that could be contained. Her gynecologist recommended surgery and set up consults with local surgeons and an oncologist.

Despite the trouble with Jessica, Alexis had kept her follow up appointment this morning. Now, over three months later and still in limbo about what do next, her gynecologist made another suggestion. Perhaps, if she couldn't wean herself off all the tranquilizers and pain meds alone, it was time to get some help. She knew what she meant before the woman could say "Betty Ford." She'd been down that road before and sobriety was a bitch. Given all that was going on in her life, she hesitated to face it without chemical enhancements. Nor was she in any position to do a stint at Betty Ford, not that she needed that kind of help anyway. She just needed her life to settle down.

"You can't put this off much longer. While the cancer is at an early stage and treatable, it's still cancer. This isn't the first time we've talked about a hysterectomy. You've had problems with fibroids for years and the surgery would give you relief. I don't want to be too dramatic, but major surgery is never free of risk. With all the drugs you're on..." Alexis had quit listening at that point.

Pay attention, you wretched girl, her mother's voice had chided. Alexis had mumbled something signifying acquiescence. All she wanted to do was get out of there, go home and take a few pills. The thought of giving up the pills just made her want to take more while she could. Like binging before going on a diet—she had done that a few times, too, before pills mattered more than food.

When she returned home from her doctor appointment, she checked with Hank and Bernadette, who were still waiting for news from the hospital about Jessica's release. The previous night, when they had returned to the hospital after dinner, it had been a relief to find Jessica much improved. Their spirits had soared at the sight of her, propped up in bed, speaking with a handsome visitor.

Paul Worthington greeted them as he left the hospital room. He shook hands with Hank and chatted for a moment about the projects Hank had underway. Paul was familiar with Hank's work and had helped to support the gala honoring him. As the two men spoke, Alexis realized why she held Paul in such high regard. He was a lot like Hank—amiable, intelligent, direct, and hard-working. Perhaps, too hard-working, which might explain how the tall, rich, good-looking blond was still unmarried at forty. A catch for her daughter, but more than that, a real chance at happiness with a man as forthright as Hank.

Jessica was watching the two men, her head cocked to one side, as Alexis sat down beside her. Alexis was glad that Jessica didn't see she had wobbled as she sat, not quite hitting the seat as planned. She chided herself for having that last glass of wine before leaving home and hoped she could keep it together, for Jessica's sake. She stifled a giggle at the thought of hitting the floor instead of that chair. It wouldn't be good if another Huntington woman—well, ex-Huntington woman—took a fall. When she looked up, Bernadette was eyeing her.

Oops, Alexis thought. *Nabbed, damn it.* When she felt like giggling again, she knew for sure she shouldn't have had that last glass—number two or three or four. What the hell, it had been a long and difficult day. Who wouldn't drink a little too much wine? She'd let Bernadette and Hank take the lead speaking with Jessica. Animated and more coherent than when they left her at lunchtime, she had soon grown tired. They were all still exhausted, too, so they kept the visit brief. The best news was that Jessica would be sent home soon. Perhaps the next day.

Today they were all busy taking care of errands while awaiting word from the hospital. Hank was trying to keep his business ventures afloat, and Bernadette was catching up on a backlog of tasks related to the management of the Rancho Mirage estate. They agreed to drive to the hospital in the late afternoon, even if they hadn't heard anything. That way, at least they could spend a little time with Jessica. Alexis grabbed a bite to eat and then used the headache that was overtaking her as an excuse to take a nap. Bernadette didn't pursue the matter, perhaps distracted by chores.

Back in her room, Alexis mulled over that morning meeting with her doctor. She had to do something and she would, too, when things were back to normal—soon, but not now. Not today. Once Jessica was home and up on her feet again, and Hank moved back to Brentwood, then she could think more about taking care of herself. There was also the little matter of filing for separation from Giovanni. She'd been making excuses to account for the delay in her return to the Mediterranean. Twice, she'd stopped Giovanni from coming to the desert. She wasn't sure she could resist him, face-to-face. Nor could she stall him much longer.

"Surely, no one expects me to face all of this alone. Everyone relies on others occasionally. Who doesn't need a crutch, now and then?" She whispered. She wasn't talking about people, but the pills. People she could do without—pills, maybe not.

She sat on the side of the bed and reached into the drawer of the elegant nightstand. The pill bottles rattled as the drawer opened and she grabbed one, almost at random. Relaxation, mood enhancement, pain reduction, it was all much the same thing. At night, there was the extra oomph she needed to sleep. She had a couple of things for that since Ambien didn't always do the trick.

Popping a lid off the bottle, she glanced at the label. "Good enough," she said, as she put not one, but two pills in her mouth. She tried to count how many pills she'd taken that day. Tracking was a difficult problem when using alcohol and pills. Rules about what, when, and how much she would consume worked well for dieting, but not so well for substances that altered memory and resolve.

"Oh, what the hell," she said. Once the pills worked and she'd had a nap, she'd figure it out. She had skipped the wine Hank opened for lunch, keeping her promise to herself not to drink until dinnertime. Later, she would get up to check on her daughter. Until then, there wasn't much she could do anyway. Besides, Bernadette could do whatever needed to be done. She and Hank were so much better suited to those tasks and Alexis wouldn't have to see them watching her. Hank with that vision of her as the woman he imagined her to be, and Bernadette hovering, waiting for Alexis to do the right thing. Both believed she was an adult, a mother, and a woman of substance.

What she was and what she was content to be if the world would leave her alone was a hollow, empty shell of a person. That's what she'd always been. "Just like you, Emma Baldwin. You couldn't fool me. Not even with all that straight posture, stiff upper-lip, and clean living. You were as much a manikin as I am. More so, all form and no substance. You should have worn shades, Mummy, to hide that empty look in your eyes. If you'd ever let your hair down, for even a minute, you would have dissolved into thin air." Alexis spoke the words aloud to the large, empty master bedroom as she drifted toward oblivion.

9 CODE SILVER

Nurse Andrews bustled about the room. Was this only Jessica's second day in the hospital? No, technically, it was her third. She remembered little of that first night spent in the ICU. Despite threatening to sic the nurse on Tommy and the guys yesterday, she couldn't take much more of the well-meaning, but officious, Nurse Andrews. It would be so wonderful to go home—well, the closest thing she had to a home, these days, given she was squatting in her parents' estate in Rancho Mirage where she'd grown up. It still wasn't clear if she'd be released today, but she was too tired to fight about it.

"Jessica, do you feel up to some company?" Laura Stone popped her head in the door as she spoke, and then swept into the room without waiting for an answer. Laura had recently returned to work following the murder of her husband, Roger Stone. An operating room nurse here at the hospital, she wore scrubs. The shoulder-length bob she had worn since high school framed her sweet, caring face.

"Yes, come on in, I'm so glad to see you." Jessica glanced at Nurse Andrews, expecting a signal she and Laura were breaking a rule fraternizing or something like that. Laura hugged Jessica and then sat down in the chair nearest the bed. Nurse Andrews gave Laura an officious nod of acknowledgement as she zipped out of the room. "Where have you been?" She asked, relaxing as Nurse Andrews exited.

"I stopped by several times and even sneaked in once while you were in the ICU—just to make sure they were taking proper care of you." As she spoke those words, she dropped the level of her voice a little, as though she might be overheard. "You've been sleeping a lot girl! A deep sleep, too. I tried to get through to you, but with no luck, even after they moved you out of intensive care yesterday. I ran into Tommy and Jerry who said you were doing great. By the time I got in here, you were out cold. I heard you had a visit from Frank, too." She smiled and then glanced at the door to make sure Nurse Andrews had shut it when she left the room.

"This is for you," she said as she handed Jessica the large cup of coffee she'd brought into the room with her. "This'll wake you up, for sure."

"I love you soooo much! You're an angel sent from heaven." She sipped greedily at the cup, even though the coffee was hot.

"Not me. I hear that's *your* title these days. It's all over the news. Even Diane Sawyer featured a clip of the rescue and said a few words about Jessica Huntington, the *'angel heiress.'* I wouldn't be surprised if you have the paparazzi after you."

"Great, just what I need. With any luck, Jim's beloved will do the right thing and pitch another fit in some highly visible location. That baby has got to be here any minute."

"She looks like she's about to pop," Laura said.

"You are so right." Cassie-the-worm-hearted-Harper was about twice the size she'd been the day Jessica caught her with Jim in flagrante. "Not that impending motherhood has triggered anything maternal. I suppose you caught her latest tantrum." Jessica winced as she spoke with the recollection of yet another embarrassing and very public meltdown by the new Mrs. James Harper. Laura nodded, in solemn affirmation.

"Wasn't that hideous?" Jessica leaned her head back on the pillow, closing her eyes. The whole scene ran over in her head, like a bad b-movie. The latest altercation had occurred outside a local luncheon hot spot in Beverly Hills. The flavor-of-the-month film star had stopped on the street to sign an autograph, all bubbles and smiles as she left the restaurant. When a server ran out to return her purse, she thanked the server with air kisses to both cheeks. Then she'd turned to her assistant and flown into a rage. Tourists that had already been snapping pics and recording clips of the bloated film star caught the whole scene.

"You stupid, stupid cow! What do I pay you for? How could you have let me walk out without my bag?" Spit flew as Cassie yelled. The stunned young woman, reportedly, *"the fifth personal assistant in as many months,"* just stood there. Something bovine had overcome her as she endured that loud, mortifying, tongue-lashing. Her placid stance further enraged the engorged star of stage and screen. The newly minted Mrs. Harper pummeled her cowed assistant about the head and shoulders with the purse returned to her by that server.

Horrified onlookers gawked as the young personal assistant, covering her head to ward off the blows, sort of slid down the wall near the entrance to the restaurant. Diners sitting near the windows inside the restaurant stood, craning their necks to see what was happening outside.

"What are you looking at?" the People's Choice Award nominee wailed. She flashed her middle finger at the diners indoors. Then she lunged at bystanders outside, her long red nails taking swipes at them. "Get the hell out of here! This is between me and my so-called assistant."

"But that's assault. You can't hit someone like that. I'm calling 911," a bystander sputtered.

"I can't? Who says I can't? You will not call anyone." Cassie was shrieking at the top of her lungs and took a couple steps toward the man using his cell phone. He turned sideways just in time to avoid being hit by the Gucci bag she was wielding like a medieval flail.

Another onlooker, closest to the dazed personal assistant, took advantage of the momentary distraction to swoop down and yank the assistant to her feet. The irate actress spotted them as they bolted, and took off in pursuit, belly-first, buttons and zippers popping. She had advanced a few paces when she realized the futility of her actions. Stopping, she kicked off her shoes, picked one up and hurled it at the fleeing women. When she reached down for the second shoe, her pants split. At that moment, her fans got to see way more of the real deal than they might ever have expected to see, given that a body double had been used in her films of dubious acclaim. A *"Hollywood diva moons Beverly Hills fans"* headline went viral, along with photos sent out on Instagram.

The media circus, never far from the she-beast, had caught up with her by then. Most of the debacle was recorded on video in hi-def. The good news for Jim, if there was any, was that he wasn't there to get caught on film, too. Nor did cameras catch him bailing the banshee out of jail. Taken into custody, the family lawyer, not Jim, secured her release. However, when the media replayed the incident, ad nauseam, an older image of Jim was plastered on the TV screen, alongside his beloved.

"I bet she's not at all happy that the ex-Mrs. Harper is getting more attention than the current one. You're stealing her limelight, you know. Some entertainment news show has connected the two of you. So she's been getting exposure out of this too."

"Oh no, please, not that. All I need is to be linked to that ding-dong in a tabloid love triangle. Is that what they're doing?" Jessica was almost afraid to ask.

"Well, I didn't actually see it. You should ask Bernadette. I'm sure she has all the details. What I heard is, since you're dubbed the *angel heiress,* they've set her up as the *devil temptress* or something like that—a halo on you and horns on her," Laura giggled.

"I have to admit, that is kind of funny," she said and laughed. "Maybe she'll go into labor and have that baby at Tiffany's or another favorite spot on her stomping grounds. And I do mean stomping. You just have to hope you're not the one on the ground being stomped." Jessica had trouble getting the words out she was laughing so hard. "Oh, ouch, that hurts," she said, grabbing her side as her laughter jarred her ribs.

"If that happens, I bet they put little devil horns on that poor baby, too." The momentary look of pity on Laura's face was more than Jessica could bear and set off more laughter. "I can see the headline now, *'Succubus gives birth to Satan's baby on Rodeo Drive.'* Jim should ask for a paternity test to make sure Satan's not Daddy, don't you think?"

"Stop, have mercy, please. Ow, ow, ow!" She got another jolt of pain from her ribs. Tears were streaming from her eyes.

"At least you'll be back behind the gates in Mission Hills soon. You can hide out until the media circus moves on."

"That's true, but it will be stranger than ever going home, now. Not only is Mom back, but Dad's there, too. Mom is being so weird.

This breakup with Giovanni is harder on her than I ever dreamed it would be. She's usually so cavalier about things like that. At least that's what I've always thought."

"We both know that it's not so easy losing a husband."

"That's true, but she's had more practice at it than we have," she said, pausing for another sip of coffee.

"What's she doing that's so weird?"

"I don't know. She's distant, evasive—hides out in her room a lot. If she was in there buying things, online, I'd get that, but she doesn't even own a computer. No binge shopping trips or spa days anymore, either. There were a few of those when she first got to the desert back in July. I have these déjà vu moments about her disappearing act—like what went on when she was divorcing Dad. It was almost like I lost her too when Dad moved out. I've tried to get her to talk about it, but she brushes me off and runs away. It strikes me as odd, but then, I've never thought of her as normal. Isn't that awful?"

"Well, I don't know what you mean by normal. I've never thought of her as weird. Over the top, definitely! I thought it was how all rich moms behaved, you know? She seems a lot like those women on that Beverly Hills Housewives show."

"Yeah, well, some of them are plenty weird, in my book. They have *so* many problems—terminal shallowness being one of them. Then, who doesn't, huh? Here before you sits a woman who just told you she could understand it if her mother was running away to her bedroom to jump on a computer and shop! I'm griping about Mom after she sat up all night with me while I was in the ICU, speaking to me. Even though I couldn't make out most of what she was saying, it was comforting. I *love* her even if I don't *get* her, you know?"

"Sure, maybe with some people, that's the best you can hope for—to love them no questions asked." She and Laura looked at each other. They both must have been thinking about their lost husbands, unknown and unknowable even before they disappeared from their lives. Then, they cleared their throats, almost in sync.

"No, forget that. I'll keep asking questions—even if it turns me into a nag."

"I agree. Ask all the questions you can while you can. You never know when someone will slip away." Laura's voice was almost prayerful as she uttered those last few words.

She sipped more coffee, wondering how much of the headache dogging her for the past couple of days was caffeine withdrawal. The orderly had brought her a dark brown watery substance that morning. She had downed the six-ounce cup in a couple of gulps. The cup in her hand wasn't her usual "high-test," brewed in a French press, but it was good. The coffee, the laughter, or maybe Laura's companionship had eased the headache. Jessica stopped sucking at the coffee long enough to inspect her friend.

"How are you doing? You look wonderful."

"I'm okay. It's still hard to be back at work. I don't have my working woman mojo in high gear, yet."

"Tell me about it. Things were taking on the semblance of a routine, and then I have to fall off a frigging mountain. It's always something, I suppose." That struck Laura as funny and she snorted.

"Yeah, falling off a mountain will not help fine tune your mojo! I don't plan to do that soon. Nor am I starting a new job, like you. I haven't tangoed with as many lowlifes as you have in the past year. Even if you count one or two of the realtors I ran across during my condo search, you're at least half a dozen creeps ahead of me." Laura shuddered a little, but laughed again.

"You've had more than your fair share, too. I will definitely have to add creep attractor to my super powers. It's right up there with calamity magnet. If there's a fiasco out there somewhere, you can bet I'll find it, especially if there's a creep at the center of the melee. My specialty is attracting well-heeled heels, I might add—starting with James Harper, Esquire. I'm amazed, though, at how well you're doing. You're one tough woman." Laura smiled, but a more somber demeanor had settled upon her lovely countenance.

"I still have nightmares about finding Roger like I did, but I'm sleeping better. I almost never cry myself to sleep anymore. There are fewer moments when I think I see him out of the corner of my eye, or catch myself thinking I'd better remember to tell Roger this or ask Roger that."

"I understand a little of what you're going through. You have your own post-trauma calendar running, like the one I started in

March after walking in on Hollywood 'Barbie' and two-timer 'Ken.' Let's hope there's some truth in the notion that a year makes loss easier to bear."

"I hope so too. The women in my grief group keep reassuring me things will get better. And they are. At least the money stuff is better, thanks to that double indemnity payout. Who knows how many more creeps I would have had to deal with, though, if you hadn't helped get me that check. You've been my angel, too."

"Aw, stop it. You're making me blush."

"Speaking of calamities and creeps, what's going on with the missing and misguided girls of 90210? We haven't had a Cat Pack get-together since you all came to my housewarming party, so I need updating. I guess Dr. Carr is the latest well-heeled creep at the center of an ongoing calamity. You thought he was up to no good."

"That's for sure," she said, and gave Laura a brief rundown of what had occurred up on Mt. San Jacinto.

"So, what happens now?" Laura asked.

"If I'm out of here by Friday, we'll have a cookout. Bernadette's already planning the feast. Consider this an invitation. In the meantime, Jerry, Tommy, and Kim are all tracking down a few things while I'm being held captive here. Paul is running interference for me at the office and will touch base with Libby's parents, so I don't have to face them yet. Frank's holding off Uncle Don and his buddies at the Palm Springs police department while I sort out a few things that are still hazy in my mind. I guess I'm safe as long as I'm in the hospital. Sooner or later, though, I'll have to run the gauntlet of stern-faced police officers, and spill my guts. While the police figure out what killed Carr, I want to get a better handle on what he and Libby were ranting about. Part of what he was 'up to' was getting Libby to extort money from her parents. When I chat with Detective Hernandez, I'll see if he can ask Shannon's father a few more questions and see if he was being extorted by his daughter. The other thing I want to pursue is Libby's claim that she was being screwed by her shrink, literally, as well as figuratively."

"No! She was sleeping with the man? Isn't that illegal?" Laura was aghast.

"It's not illegal, but it is actionable—a breach of ethics. Most likely, it would have meant a slap on the wrist unless he'd been sanctioned before. Carr came up clean the first time they ran a check, but Tommy and Jerry are taking another look. He could have challenged her claim, unless she has evidence of a tryst, as she also claims."

"Oh, ick, ick, ick! What on earth does that mean?"

"I'm not sure since we didn't get that far along in the discussion before the man of her dreams turned up, gun in hand."

"I'm sorry to keep asking so many questions. That had to be terrifying."

"I wish I could say no, but, alas, I'm still a wimp when facing gun-toting maniacs. Anyway, Libby mentioned Monica Lewinsky, so I assume she has one or more touching mementos of cozy moments spent with Dr. Dick, as she so lovingly referred to him at one point."

"That also means she must have had doubts about his being Mr. Right—or Dr. Right, in this case."

"Yes, and she also said that evidence is stashed in a little blue bag—a suitcase, maybe, a tote, or an overnight bag. Who knows what, or where, it is? My thinking wasn't too clear or I would have asked more questions before taking that leap into the abyss."

"Falling like that must have been awful."

"It was. I don't remember landing, thank goodness. I wouldn't be worrying about any of this now if I'd missed that ledge and hadn't landed in a nice cushy spot. Libby wasn't as lucky."

"Luckier than Dr. Dick! I'm sorry about Libby. Even though you got pulled into this because of your relationship with her parents, I know you had hope for Libby. I'm sure that's why she's continued to contact you, like that day she spoke to you while we were eating lunch. She sure didn't hide much from me. You were so kind to her. I bet that's why she called you, thinking you'd relay her confession to her parents in a sympathetic way."

"It could be, I guess. She did seem vulnerable, but I was mainly focused on sending her back to her own lawyer and keeping the contact to a minimum. Until this latest incident, anyway. At least I have a better understanding of how those allegations toward her father and her uncle came about—mix one part malicious Libby with a conniving shrink, throw in a bunch of drugs, and you get a toxic cocktail."

"No one would have taken her seriously, given her history as you've described it." Laura had such a serious look on her face.

"That's true. She risked creating more trouble for herself, too. Depending on what she said, how, and to whom, she could have opened herself up to charges of libel or slander. She used those terms during her rant. Carr must have cautioned her against spreading the story around."

"I suppose extortion doesn't work all that well if the allegations are already out there. What's the point of threatening to make them public if you've already leaked them?"

"True. Maybe, one of the bottom feeders in my profession she hired to sue her parents, warned her early on to shut up."

"Sue her parents?" Dread arose on Laura's face.

"Yeah, that's another threat she's made, with the shrink backing her up. She's on her third lowlife lawyer aiming to use the courts to extort money. They could have been the ones who told her that you can't sue for your inheritance early, in exchange for signing a nondisclosure clause, if you've already blabbed to everyone you know, or broadcast your story of woe on Facebook. Kim's checking into that—she's a whiz on the computer. If Libby's left a trail on the Internet, that could mean more trouble for her when she comes out of the coma. It might also provide more clues about Libby's relationship with Dr. Dick, Shannon, or another daughter of woe in Carr's harem."

"More women..." she murmured as Jessica drifted away.

Jessica had to stop herself from plunging into the pit that this case had opened for her, again. What was wrong with people like Libby and Jim, or those fiends responsible for murdering Roger and Kelly? She felt her anxiety rev up. Both her shrink and the priest had told her to stop it when her mind crawled too close to that well of darkness.

"Let go, let God," Father Martin had said when she lamented about the unfathomable nature of depravity. "You can't right every wrong in the world. You've got your hands full getting your own life back on track."

"Duh," was what she'd wanted to say in reply to the well-meaning cleric; "true," was what she said instead. Then he had shifted the focus back to pondering her failed marriage and her shopping compulsion. She'd put that black AMEX card away, but the numbers on that card were flashing through her mind even now. Shopping sounded enticing as she snapped back into the moment, draining the last of the coffee to bring her into the present and away from the urge to shop.

"Nothing Libby said would have stood up in a court of law. Not these days anyway. In the eighties, there was a rash of court cases based on recovered memory of alleged abuse. A lot of those allegations later proved to be false because the accuser retracted them or some bit of evidence cleared the poor shmuck targeted by them. Police and courts have backed off pursuing charges based solely on recovered memories, some of them involving paying out hefty settlements to those who wrongfully accused others. Memory is tricky. Even eyewitness testimony has been proven unreliable. Throw in mind-warping wonder drugs and the line between lying, and believing the lie, gets thinner, I suppose. Anyway, if I can get out of here soon, I intend to keep a date with an old friend. Do you remember Betsy Stark?"

"I do. Who could forget Betsy Stark? She used to help around your house when we were in high school. I remember her tagging along and towering over Bernadette."

"I was younger when Betsy turned up at the house one day. She must have been about sixteen then. She was already closing in on six feet tall and big, too. I was afraid of her, at first."

"I could see how you might be wary of the woman. Model tall, but not model thin, she made quite an impression. That's not all I remember though. You also seemed more than a little jealous, as I recall." She had an amused look on her face. "You were a snotty little beast around her on more than one occasion."

"Stop it, please. I'm horrified thinking about that now. Let's blame it on the divorce and all the chaos that went on before that—right about the time Betsy showed up. I was through most of the trauma-drama when I met you, but I hadn't gotten over my feelings of insecurity. It bothered me to share Bernadette with Betsy—sibling rivalry between two strays adopted by Bernadette."

"I'm sorry you felt like a stray. Betsy was smart though, right? She enrolled in community college while we were at St. Theresa's. What has she got to do with any of this?"

"She's a social worker, licensed and with a master's degree. According to Bernadette, Betsy has training in behavioral health from UCLA or USC or somewhere like that. She's also had case management experience with people who have serious mental health problems, and she knows the ins and outs of the disability system. I'm hoping she can help me get a better handle on what was going on with Libby and Carr. I'll apologize to her too."

"Gosh, I haven't thought about her in years, but who could forget Betsy Stark, the titan?" Laura paused as the door to the hospital room burst open. "Speaking of giants, look who's here."

"Yo, we brought you lunch," Brien, the pool-boy-cum-bodyguard, announced as he entered the room carrying bags of take-out food in both hands.

"Did Nurse Andrews say this was okay?" Jessica asked as he set the food down on the windowsill.

Behind him was the giant Laura had referred to. Peter March was carrying drinks. Both Brien and Peter were muscular, but Peter was huge. At six-six, he resembled one of those guys striking a pose on the cover of a bodybuilding magazine, even when standing at ease. Brien, at five-eight, was Peter's 'mini-me,' a shorter, more compact version of the man. An alter ego, too, Brien's loquaciousness counterpoint to Peter's reticence. Both men had come to Jessica's aid as members, in good standing, of the Cat Pack.

"Hey, who will stop them? Brien has that '*don't mess with me, it's feeding time,*' look on his face." Brien beamed, taking Laura's statement as a compliment.

"I suppose you're right. I doubt anybody in this wing of the hospital would get in your way, eh Peter?"

"Let them try to stop me! I'm a man on a mission." Peter laughed. The head of a high-profile security firm in the desert area, he was more than capable of finishing any mission he set upon. That broad smile he wore never quite seemed right on his face shaped by years of special ops training and life experience Jessica didn't want to know about.

Jessica looked down for a few seconds, digging into a bin of French fries Brien had handed her. When she looked up again, Kim Reed was standing at the foot of the bed. The young woman had appeared out of nowhere as she so often did. She was no longer wearing an outfit befitting a member of the secretarial pool on an episode of Mad Men. Her previous employer had insisted she dress that way to please him.

Kim had an edge about her, though, and it was more than the vibrant tattoo of the Hindu goddess Saraswati that ran shoulder to elbow. Kim now wore her jet-black hair in a short, asymmetrical bob. Her coal black eyes were dramatic, with thick lashes and dark eyeliner adding to the drama. The dark hair and eyes sat in contrast to pale skin and bright red lips.

She wore a simple, straight black skirt and a gray chunky cardigan with cap sleeves and small, ribbed pockets. A high collar and offset panels gave it flare that had qualified it to go into the "buy" pile when Jessica had fitted Kim out with a wardrobe for work. There was an interior stillness about her that went with the silent movements—a cloak of invisibility cultivated to enhance her survival while working for a very bad man.

"I brought dessert," Kim added, expressionless, "cookies."

"Not just any cookies," Peter announced. "Those are vegan, peanut butter, chocolate chip, oatmeal cookies." Peter-the-giant was an enthusiastic vegan.

"Don't worry; I tested them on the way here. They're righteous, even if they are good for you," Brien said while stuffing French fries into his mouth.

"That's why I'm holding the bag. Brien's testing was getting out of hand. We wanted to make sure there would be some for the rest of us when we got here." Kim's lips twitched upward for a split second—the hint of a smile.

"I made them stop and get Double-Doubles for us, Jessica. Bringing you a fake burger didn't seem right with all the bogus stuff that's been going on around you. That's what *they're* eating." He jerked his head toward Peter and Kim who were pulling burgers out of a different bag. A lock of surfer-boy, bleached blond hair fell back into place with that jerk of his head. "You can thank me for getting you real food."

"What about me?" Laura asked.

"I'll share mine with you," Jessica offered.

"No sweat. We've got you covered. Brien here got three Double-Doubles for himself. He won't mind giving you one, right?" Peter locked eyes with Brien as he spoke.

"Dude..." Brien said as though he might protest. Then, digging into a bag, he pulled out two burgers, handing one to Jessica and another to Laura. He reached across Jessica, rather than walking around the bed where Laura sat in one of two chairs in the room. "That's cool. I can stop for something on the way home. I need to score some basics, like beer and chips, before I go home anyway."

"Thanks." When Laura smiled at him, Brien-the-eating-machine paused a moment before diving back into the fries he had been demolishing three or four at a time.

"No problem," he said, pausing again, with a big grin on his face.

"Kim, do you want to sit over here next to me?" Laura asked.

"Sure," Kim responded. She smiled a genuine smile, fleeting though it was, as she took a seat near Laura. Kim Reed was a puzzle. Smart as a whip and a hard worker, she was distant and skittish, yet vulnerable despite the sharp edges. The rest of the Cat Pack members had recognized that, welcoming her into their quirky little group with open arms, but still giving her space. Kim was the most feral cat among them. It was real progress that she often appeared at ease, content to be in the same room with them, even if long spells went by with little comment from her.

It was the same way at the law office on El Paseo, where she kept to herself unless she felt she had something worthwhile to contribute. Amy Klein, the office manager, was a quiet soul, too. Jessica often felt like the odd duck as the most gregarious member of her work group. That was true unless the charming Attorney Worthington was in the building.

"This is wonderful, you guys. Real coffee and real food! Do I know how to pick my friends or what? I can't believe Nurse Andrews is letting us get away with this." She was talking with her mouth half-full. Who knew when Nurse Andrews might pop in and spoil their little party? Jessica took another big bite of the scrumptious burger, not wanting to risk giving it up if there was a raid.

"What's that," Peter asked moments later. Their heads swiveled in Laura's direction. In the distance, a wailing sound could be heard.

"Maybe Nurse Andrews is on to us," Jessica murmured, before taking another bite of what was left of her Double-Double from In-N-Out Burger.

"It sounds like a fire alarm. But it must be in another wing or building on the medical campus. Don't worry; if it had anything to do with us, we'd get a code or I'd have a text message." Laura pulled her cell phone out of her pocket and checked it, just in case.

"Nothing," she said, setting the phone down on the bedside table next to where she sat. She went back to devouring her burger, too.

Several minutes passed before a calm, but insistent, voice sent out a message over the loud speakers.

Code Silver, ICU. Repeat. Code Silver, ICU.
Shelter In Place. Repeat. Shelter In Place.
Code Silver, ICU. Repeat. Code Silver, ICU.

Laura and Peter both stopped eating and went into action. Laura moved to turn the lights off in the room. Then she opened the door, pulled out a key and locked it from the outside before shutting the door again. Peter closed the drapes and went to work securing the door from the inside. He made a wedge of magazines and jammed it into the corner of the door. He moved the chair Laura had been sitting in and adjusted the angle to add another wedge, this one under the door handle.

"What is it? What's going on?" Brien asked. He didn't stop eating that second burger he was working on, but he had slowed down.

"Code Silver means there's an emergency in the building—the ICU in this case, according to that announcement." Laura answered as she checked her phone for text messages sent out with emergency codes. "It says the same thing here, Code Silver, shelter in place until further notice."

The eerie voice repeated the warning in the same unemotional, detached tone.

"ICU, do you think it's Libby?" Jessica asked. "I don't mean Libby, but you know, someone trying to get to her?"

"I was down there earlier today. There was one other patient in the ICU, an older man who had suffered a serious heart attack. So, yes, my guess is this has something to do with Libby and the mess she's mixed up in." She spoke softly as she sat on the foot of Jessica's bed.

"The mess we're all mixed up in, don't you mean?" Jessica asked, her stomach souring from stress, or from eating so fast, or some combination of the two. Her heart pounded.

"It can't be too bad or they would have issued an evacuation order. Most likely, we're not talking about multiple intruders or a bomb. They said stay put, so that's what we'll do." Peter spoke resolutely as he went back to eating his lunch. A gun had appeared from somewhere in response to the alarm. It now sat within easy reach as he faced the door, standing no more than a step or two from Jessica. Jessica rested her head on the pillow and tried to calm down.

He thinks someone might be coming for me, she thought. She kept the words to herself. Speaking them aloud would make things worse, adding to the suspense they already felt.

"No bomb? Okay, that's cool," Brien said as he moved back into high speed eating.

"Cool isn't the word I would have chosen. It sounds like we have no choice but to wait this out. We're not in any immediate danger. No one's pounding on the door, or trying to get in." That was the most words Kim had spoken since walking into the room. During the brief whirlwind of activity from Laura and Peter she had sat, frozen like a statue, taking it all in. When Peter went back to eating, she did too.

They sat in silence for several minutes, waiting for an update. The minutes passed like hours. At the sound of a little ping, they all startled. Even Peter tensed up. It was Laura's phone. She read the text message aloud:

Lone gunman. Shots fired. No injuries. Gunman's location, unknown. Continue to shelter in place.

Before anyone could comment or react, a sudden flurry of commotion began outside the door to Jessica's room. Peter grabbed the gun and moved closer to Jessica. "Do you know how to unhook this stuff, Laura?" He asked in a low voice, nodding toward the IV connected to Jessica.

"Sure. No problem."

"Get her unhooked and help her into the bathroom. Brien, Kim you get in there, too, with Laura and Jessica." As he spoke, someone jiggled the door handle. "Move it, you guys. Stand off to the side, not in the direct line of the doorway, got that?"

"Got it," Laura said as she freed up the pole on which the IV bag hung so it could move with Jessica.

Brien did not hesitate. Not even long enough to take the last of his food with him. Neither did Kim, who also headed toward the bathroom. She paused for a moment to help untangle a cord that Laura was trying to free.

Without the use of her left arm, and her right hand connected to the IV, Jessica's exit from the bed was awkward. She had on one of the muumuus Bernadette had brought to the hospital, so she didn't have to worry about an exposed backside. Laura slid the rails all the way down on the side of the bed nearest the bathroom. She and Kim helped Jessica scoot to the edge of the bed and then waited as, with their support, she eased her way to the floor. Jessica winced as her ribs protested.

The door handle jiggled again and someone was pounding on the door now. Jessica and the rest of the crew hustled inside the bathroom, crammed into the tiny space. Brien stepped into the shower stall to make more room for the others. They heard another ping on Laura's phone as they shut and locked the door.

"Shoot!" Laura said. She'd left the phone on the foot of the bed where she had put it down to assist Jessica. From inside the bathroom, they could hear more pinging, ringing, and pounding. It sounded like it was a long way off. Deceptive, since danger wasn't more than a few yards away.

10 CAR CHASE

Eric was about to have a stroke. He couldn't believe what he was watching on television. Reporters filmed a man running at top speed from the hospital. Hospital security and a uniformed police officer weren't far behind him. First responders flocked to the scene along with reporters from the local news outlets in the Palm Springs area. A police helicopter followed the man as he hijacked a car that had been waiting with the engine running in the patient pickup area. He yanked the driver out of the car, threw him on the ground, and fired two shots toward the officers chasing him on foot. Bystanders fled for cover. The officers he shot at ducked, giving him time to get into the car and take off. As he sped away, he turned onto the main street in front of the hospital complex and headed toward the I-10 freeway. A nearby police patrol car was after him in a split second. Not long after, two others joined the pursuit.

"Shades of OJ Simpson," Eric said as he slammed his fist on the desk. "Damn it, when I get my hands on that son-of-a-bitch, I will give *him* the OJ treatment. Oh hell, let him clean up his own messes." He pulled the burner phone from his pocket and called Kirk, who answered on the first ring. Eric didn't need to introduce himself.

"This is unbelievable. What is going on? You were supposed to keep this simple. A quiet operation is what I asked for. What the hell happened?"

"Jack says there was a cop at the hospital—some yokel with the County Sheriff's department. He busted in on him, even with our distraction scenario in play. Jack had no choice but to get out of there. I'm not sure if he took care of the girl or not before that hero got into the act."

"I don't get it. Your guys can't pick out a cop?"

95

"He wasn't in uniform and didn't look like a cop. He wasn't even wearing one of those crappy detective suits. Besides that, he had some old guy with him. Jack thought they were family members paying the girl a visit. He waited for them to leave the room before he ran down the steps, lit the fire in the basement, threw the alarm, and sprinted back up there. It was all working just fine. Jack's mic was on, so I heard the whole thing. When Jack slipped back into that room, I could hear people yelling for everyone to exit the building. Not two minutes after they left the girl's room, the two guys came back. That's when one of them identified himself as a cop, and I told Jack to get the hell out of there. What kind of idiot heads back into the room when everybody's telling him to leave? He and the old man with him had him cornered. Jack had no choice but to wave a gun around. In fact, it was smart thinking and quick action that allowed him to get out of there at all."

"I don't want to hear anymore. This is a disaster and I want it stopped! Now! Where are you?"

"I'm in my SUV, on a route to intercept Jack. I know what I've got to do. It makes me sick to lose a guy like that, but I'm on it."

"You better be. Clean this up or I'll give you something to feel sorry about." Eric ended the call. What was up with the Van Der Woert woman? Had that loser finished that part of the job, at least, before creating such a stink? He hoped so. With luck, Jack wasn't about to die for nothing.

He continued to watch, fascinated as the helicopter feed of the car chase in the desert was broadcast live on LA networks. Californians loved their car chases. The stolen car was moving at high speed on a road heading toward the I-10 freeway onramp.

"What an idiot," Eric muttered. Even if he could get to the freeway, where was he going to go? West would take him to LA and massive traffic jams in no time. East led to nothing but a lot of highway and desert before reaching Blythe and the border with Arizona. Maybe that's what he was trying to do. No way would it work. Even if the car he stole had enough gas, the cops would be waiting at the state line. East or West, the police would have roadblocks up in no time. The good guys had him in the crosshairs, but so did his team leader.

Police vehicles were in hot pursuit, sirens blaring. Other vehicles on the road tried like mad to get out of the way, as the convoy hurtled down the thoroughfare. The car had to be traveling at close to a hundred miles per hour, according to newscasters. As the car neared the last major intersection before reaching the freeway ramp, a tire blew. The car spun out of control. In the next instant, it hit a curb, flew up into the air, and then flipped over and over. After skidding a hundred yards, the car came to rest, still upside down. Then the wrecked vehicle burst into flames.

"Sorry, Jack, you poor schmuck, whoever you are. That's what you get when you don't do your job right." He picked up his cell phone and redialed the number, breathing easier than when he had made the previous call.

"Good job. Lucky for you."

"Luck had nothing to do with it. Now what?"

"What do you mean, 'now what?' You finish the job, that's what. Find out what's up with the Van Der Woert girl, ASAP. If Jack didn't get it done, you do it."

"There's no way I'm getting another crack at her today."

"Okay, so lie low for now, until we get a report on Van Der Woert's status and things settle down. Keep tabs on that Huntington woman, too. She won't be in the hospital much longer. I want to know where she is until my business is concluded. Got that? The countdown is on, dammit. Shut up Libby Van Der Woert and don't let Jessica Huntington out of your sight. Do you think you can handle that?"

"Sure thing." The tone in Kirk's voice was irritating.

"Don't get snippy with me. In fact, if you don't want trouble from me, you get your butt back over to the hospital now. You're a pro, Kirk, so don't tell me you can't at least figure out whether you need to clean up after Jack or not. If Libby Van Der Woert is still alive, I want to hear that from you. One more thing, if I find out that nut job is talking, I promise I'll take matters into my own hands. That won't do your reputation any good, now will it, Kierkegaard?" Eric knew he disliked being called that even though it was his real name. So what? If this screw up got in Eric Conroy's way, Kirk wouldn't need to worry about his reputation, being called Kierkegaard, or anything else for that matter. Eric would bring in another company to fix this mess and Kierkegaard Kunzel would be one of the loose ends that were tied up. Eric wished he could slam the phone down, like he used to do with a real phone.

As the media replayed the whole chase scene, Eric stood there and watched. Rather than feeling horror or sadness when that car burst into flames, Eric felt relieved, once again. The coverage went back live, to the crash site. Not just the police, but fire and rescue had converged on the location. Dark black smoke billowed. He had the sound turned down low, but could hear the excited babble of talking heads doing voice overs to go with the scenes being broadcast.

"Their ratings just went through the roof as I get a kick in the pants. This can't go on." With the IPO scheduled to launch on the twentieth, all he needed was a few more days. The board would meet this Friday to hear from the joint book runners. He presumed the boys at "Golden Slacks" and the other major investment firms honchoing the IPO would have good news to report. That assumption was based on snippets of info coming in about the road show that was underway.

Eric didn't expect he'd have much to do to keep all his ducks in a row, no matter what happened, but he didn't like surprises and was taking no chances. Getting the votes to support the IPO had taken some doing. Even the CEO had required more convincing than Eric imagined it would take. No matter. Their fearless leader was on board now. The CEO was doing fine, too, as that dog and pony show made the rounds. If he were the CEO and Chairman of the Board, as he should have been, those meetings would be smoking. Pinnacle needed him at the helm—well, *had* needed him, but it was too late for that now.

"Too little, too late," Eric muttered in anger. "A few more days and it'll be clear what too little too late gets you, too. You should have put me in charge and the future of Pinnacle might have gone in a different direction." Eric spoke those words as if the board members were sitting in front of him. Then he sat down and started a countdown in his head as he marked off the days on a desk calendar: ten, nine, eight… In a matter of days now, Pinnacle would rise, attaining great heights, before crashing back to earth like a misguided missile. By then, he and a quarter of a billion dollars, or more, would be long gone.

11 THE SHOOTER

The phone in Jessica's hospital room rang. Laura's cell phone was ringing too. The pounding on the door continued and Jessica thought she heard someone shouting her name.

"Somebody's calling my name, Peter. What's going on?" Jessica asked. "No bad guy would shout at me like that, right?"

"They haven't given us the 'all clear' yet over the loudspeakers," Laura responded. "We should stay put until that call goes out."

"You guys do that. I'll go check the phones," Peter said. He had been fiddling with his own phone from the moment they entered the bathroom. "I can't get a signal in here or I'd call somebody and ask. Lock the door behind me," Peter said as he opened the bathroom door and stepped back into the hospital room.

The pounding and shouting stopped a minute or two later. Peter returned and instructed them to unlock the door to the bathroom. When Jessica stepped from the bathroom back into the hospital room, it was full of people. Nurse Andrews was standing there with her arms folded across her chest. Behind her stood Jessica's doctor, another nurse, and a man in a suit who must have been a hospital administrator since he didn't have that surly cop look on his face. Next to them stood Frank Fontana, with Detective Hernandez on one side of him and Uncle Don on the other. Two men in hospital security uniforms stood nearby, too. Eyes widened when Jessica stepped out of the bathroom, followed by Laura, then Kim, and, last but not least, Brien.

"It's like one of those little clown cars at the circus," Detective Hernandez said shaking his head. "Why am I not surprised?" He commented to everyone in the room.

"I take it everyone's okay," Don Fontana commented with a note of sarcasm in his voice. "Hope we didn't disturb you."

"No problema, Man. We were just sheltering in place. A small place, but hey, that's cool!" Brien said, before he turned around and went back into the bathroom. "Excuse me, uh, I gotta *go*," he said as he closed the door, peeking around the edge until he closed it.

"Yes, we're fine. So kind of you to ask," Jessica sniffed. She didn't like the way this was going. Wisecracks from Detective Hernandez signaled trouble, as did snide comments from Uncle Don. Nurse Andrews had donned a nasty "Nurse Ratchet" look as she moved to help Jessica get back into bed. The nurse stopped to remove the container that had held Jessica's French fries, which had turned upside down, scattering fries and crumbs.

"One moment, Ms. Huntington," she said, a coldness in her voice, as she cleaned up the scraps and brushed crumbs from the bed. Jessica glanced around the room. In their hurry to respond to the alarm, they had left uneaten food and wrappers scattered about.

So it's back to Ms. Huntington, is it? She thought as the nurse guided her back into bed. Aloud she asked, "Are you all going to just stand there and gawk, or is somebody going to tell us what all this ruckus is about? Don't you dare try to pin anything on me, Detective Hernandez! I was lying here, minding my own business, having lunch with my friends, okay?"

Before anyone could say another word, Tommy and Jerry bounded into the room from the hallway. Tommy stopped, coming up quick to avoid bumping into his Cousin Frank and Uncle Don. That caused Jerry to career into him, shoving Tommy into Frank anyway. It was like a row of dominoes as Tommy jostled Frank, who nudged Detective Hernandez, who bumped into Uncle Don. Don stepped on the toes of one of the security guards, who knocked into a bedside tray sending items flying in several directions. The nurses in the room scurried to clean up the new mess.

"How did you two get up here? Carter, Carter!" the gentleman in the suit bellowed, donning a surly look now, too. He was a hospital administrator with authority over the security guys, judging by the commanding tone he used and the way the men in security outfits flinched.

"Yes, Sir?" asked another member of the uniformed security team who stepped into the room in response to that command.

"I thought we had this whole floor sealed off, including the elevator and stairs."

"Yes, Sir, it was until we got the all clear minutes ago on our cell phones." Before he could say another word, the same disembodied voice that had sent out the code silver announced the all clear.

The supervisor pulled his cell phone out and examined it. "He's right. Someone went ahead and sent out the all clear without contacting me first. Must have come from higher ups." He sounded chagrined as he spoke to the group in the room.

Jessica was about to speak again when there was more commotion outside the door. Bernadette dashed into the room, stunned for a moment because there were now about twenty people in the small hospital room. Jessica's parents stopped in the doorway, taking in the scene.

"Talk about your tiny clown cars," Jessica mumbled. The door to the bathroom opened and Brien stepped out to rejoin the throng.

"Hey, Mrs. B! Yo, dudes, 'sup?" Brien said as if it was the most natural thing in the world to find them all there.

"Mom, Dad, squeeze on in. A gathering is being held in my honor, although no one has told me what we're celebrating."

"What we heard was that a gunman was on the loose, and that they had shut the whole place down. We got here as fast as we could—we were so afraid..." Alexis said as she pushed her way through the crowd to reach her daughter's bedside.

"Yeah, we got here as soon as we could, too," Tommy said. "We sat in traffic for a while because they had closed streets and then we had to wait to get into the lot once the streets opened up again."

"I'm hungry," Brien said out of the blue. A wave of puzzled looks sped around the room as they made a stab at processing that non-sequitur.

"Hang on a minute, will you Brien?" Jessica asked. "We knew someone was here at the hospital with a gun or other weapon. Laura filled us in on what a Code Silver means. What makes you think that has anything to do with me?" Jessica asked.

"Well, that's because the 'ruckus,' as you called it, involved your friend in the ICU, Ms. Huntington." *So, it's back to "Ms. Huntington" with Detective Hernandez, too.*

"Libby is, um, not a friend, Detective Hernandez," Jessica said, correcting the man. She tried for a second to figure out what she was—not a client, not a friend, what? She gave up. "Is she okay?"

"She is, but it was a close call," Frank said, answering the question before Detective Hernandez could respond.

"We were on our way to see how you were doing, when we dropped by the ICU. We thought you might have some questions about Libby's condition, so we stopped in there first," Uncle Don said, pausing for a second, perhaps not sure how much he should say with so many people in the room. Detective Hernandez nodded, urging him to go on.

"The nurse on the ward said Libby was doing okay and let us see for ourselves. When we stepped back out into the hallway from her room, a fire alarm went off."

"We heard that, but it didn't sound close enough to be concerned about," Laura said.

"A diversion, I imagine," Frank said.

"Frank and I didn't know that then," Don added. "We took a quick look around trying to figure out if the problem was nearby. The alarm sounded like it was in the same wing, but we didn't smell smoke or see a fire. People were rushing to the central nurses' station to ask what was going on. We headed that way, too. Out of the corner of my eye, I saw somebody go into Libby Van Der Woert's room. I just glimpsed him. He was in scrubs, but something about him struck me as odd. Maybe the way he looked around before he stepped into the room. Something about him was just 'off.'"

"When Dad said he saw someone go into Libby's room, I figured it was a member of the medical staff making the rounds. You know, checking on patients in the ICU disturbed by the sound of that alarm? Or maybe someone charged with getting Libby out of the building in an emergency situation like a fire. Dad's got good instincts, though, so when he said he was suspicious, we went back in there. When we entered the room, he was about to add something to the IV bag with a syringe and startled when he spotted us. I knew that wasn't good. I told him to step away from the bag. Before I could get to my gun, he pulled out one of his own. I wasn't sure if he was trying to scare us off or if he intended to shoot Libby. I gave the nurse's cart a shove and that banged into him. He fired a shot. I grabbed for him as I pushed Dad to the floor. I was off balance and went down, too, when the jerk slammed that table into me."

"Thanks a lot for knocking me to the floor like that, Son." Don didn't sound thankful. "We'd left the door to the room open behind us, so the perp scooted past us and out the door. He still had that gun, I guess, although he dropped the syringe. Someone called in the incident and that Code Silver went out right away."

"We sent a nurse to check on Libby," Frank said, picking up the story. "Then we took off in pursuit of the gunman. Security was after him, too, by that point. Your guys either spotted that gun or were responding to the report of shots fired," Frank said, speaking to their supervisor. "They were on the ball." He must have been relieved to hear Frank say that because he let out a big breath.

"That guy with the gun was fast. He was down the stairs and out an emergency exit. The code was sounding and more alarms were going off. Detective Hernandez, or someone else, can better describe what happened outside the hospital. We weren't far behind him, but by the time we got out the door, the perp had grabbed a car and taken off in it. There was already a police presence, I guess responding to the fire alarm. A couple patrol cars sped off after the shooter."

"That's right, and a helicopter picked up the chase after that," Detective Hernandez said. "More police headed to the hospital as soon as the call went out that shots were fired. I talked to Fire and Rescue and it was two or three minutes after the fire alarm went off that the first patrol cars arrived. The ones you saw, Frank. I got here a few minutes after that. I was already on the move when I got word that the trouble had started in the ICU and Ms. Huntington might be in danger. Several patrol cars gave chase, but the guy was moving fast. With the helicopter up, no way was he going to get away. The plan was to cut him off before he could get on the freeway. Then he blew a tire or hit something in the road and lost control. The car flipped over two or three times and then burst into flames, close to the intersection with Ramon Road."

"It all happened fast, Chica. The news got out lickety-splickety..." Bernadette said, scooting closer to Jessica's bedside. "My phone was ringin' and pingin'. I knew it was too much of a coincidence there was a fire at the hospital while you were here. I called Detective Hernandez and told him not to let some maleante get to you."

"Bernadette knows all about my super powerful calamity magnetism," Jessica said to those in the room.

"I didn't need Bernadette to tell me you might be in danger," Hernandez growled. "As soon as Frank and Don Fontana realized the guy was after Libby, they called it in. When I called to check on you I found out that the staff had seen two suspicious-looking guys—one over-sized—in the corridor near your room, accompanied by a woman covered with strange tattoos."

"One tattoo and it's not strange," Kim said, despite her usual shyness, especially in a crowd. They were the first words she had uttered since they had all taken refuge in the bathroom. Hernandez ignored the comment.

"I prefer to think of myself as right-sized, and Kim's tattoo is a work of art," Peter growled.

"Yeah, that tattoo is righteous," Brien added, to the annoyance of Detective Hernandez.

"I guess I should have realized you were in no danger when they said one guy was eating. What kind of bad guys eat on their way to take out a target?" Detective Hernandez asked.

"Speaking of eating, I'm hungry. You guys hungry?" Brien asked.

"Not now, Brien, *please*," Jessica implored.

"Anyway, when Frank and Don couldn't get you to answer the door, we all made a beeline for you. Since none of the members of your entourage wasted any time getting this place locked down, what do they know that we don't?"

"Hey, wait a second. We were just following hospital procedure," Laura responded. It was her turn to get annoyed.

"And is it hospital procedure for Ms. Huntington to be throwing a party in her hospital room?" He asked, glowering at them.

"It wasn't a party, or they would have invited Jerry and me," Tommy said. "Isn't that true?"

"Yes, that's true." Jessica smiled feebly. Her head hurt again as well as her ribs. She felt exhausted by all the turmoil and distressed by that attempt on Libby's life.

"Look, I'd be happy to answer your questions, Detective Hernandez. I don't know what's going on any better than you do, but let's talk things over. Not now, but soon. I don't feel so well, right now. I..." Nurse Andrews cut her off.

"You don't feel well? How could you? There's a reason we haven't been feeding you greasy burgers and fries... and coffee," she tsked-tsked as she bent down and picked up the empty Styrofoam coffee cup that had landed on the floor near Jessica's bed.

"As soon as I get home and settled, I'll be happy to listen to all your questions. I'll even try to answer them. If you can figure out what's going on, in the meantime, that's great. I'm not the least bit happy about the idea that somebody wants Libby dead. It can't be Carr because he's already dead. My head hurts too much to think straight, much less figure any of this out. Nurse Andrews, Doc, you all will send me home soon, right?" Nurse Andrews had that pressed lip thing going on. No way could any words escape the slash that passed for a mouth on her face. Jessica's doctor, who was still in the room, spoke up.

"Barring any unforeseen developments, I expect to release you tomorrow, Jessica." He spoke those words with a tone of relief, glad to be rid of her, no doubt. She found that irksome, but at least her attending physician addressed her by her first name.

"Oh, that's wonderful news," Bernadette said, glaring at Nurse Andrews. "We can take good care of you, and you won't have to starve. Peter and his guards will get back on the job so no guy can sneak in and shoot at you."

"Yes, I agree. It is unacceptable that a gunman roaming the halls puts my daughter at risk and you chew her out for eating a burger. Maybe we should take her out of here now, and move her to another hospital while she's still alive. You realize she's a lawyer, right? If she sues you for the trauma she's gone through today, I wouldn't blame her." Jessica's mouth fell open as her mother spoke. Alexis was furious, her shoulders back, arms tight against her body, and fists clenched. Her mother's whole body shook.

You go, Mom, Jessica wanted to say, but didn't. Instead, she reached out and grasped her mother's hand. Alexis startled, for a second, at Jessica's touch. Recovering, she laced her fingers through her daughter's and returned Jessica's smile.

"I don't think we need to do anything rash," Hank said. The twinkle in his eyes betrayed the fact he was thoroughly enjoying Alexis' outburst. "However, Jessica's mother has made very good points. The Van Der Woerts must have a lot of questions about how this happened, too, and I'm sure you'll have answers for all of us once you've completed a formal investigation. Why don't we clear out of here and let Jessica get some rest? It sounds like she will go home tomorrow, Alexis. I'm sure Nurse Andrews and the rest of the hospital staff are deeply embarrassed by the breach that occurred today, and will have someone apologize before they send her on her way. As for you, Detective Hernandez, I must ask you to use a more professional tone with my daughter." Detective Hernandez, taken aback, was speechless. Another first for the day.

"Aw, he doesn't mean nothing by it, Hank. That's just his tough cop talk. He likes Jessica—a lot. He's not so good at showing it, right Detective?" Bernadette asked. Hernandez wasn't just speechless, but he flushed bright red. Jessica couldn't tell whether that was from embarrassment or anger.

"You'll hear from me day after tomorrow, Ms. Huntington. Get settled in, because we need to have a long talk." With that, he turned on his heels and marched out of the room. The rest of the crowd drifted away, with a "sorry" tossed in here and there.

Jessica doubted she would get anything like an official apology for the scare. At least not until the hospital's legal team had come up with wording that acknowledged the inconvenience without assuming responsibility for the incident. Nurse Andrews, the last of the staff members to leave, didn't say another word.

"Frank, Uncle Don, thank you both. If you hadn't acted as you did, who knows what might have happened—to Libby or me." Uncle Don moved close enough to Jessica to speak in a quiet voice.

"We can't let anything happen to you. It would break this old man's heart and I'd hate to think what it would do to my boy here."

Both father and son stood with matching expressions on their sweet faces. She could see where Frank had inherited the tenderness that gave his brown eyes such depth.

"I won't break your hearts, promise." As she spoke, Jessica prayed she could keep that promise.

12 AN INTERVENTION

It wasn't clear who was happier about Jessica being released from the hospital: Jessica herself, her friends and family, or the hospital staff. After that incident with the gunman in the ICU, they beefed up security. The hospital authorities posted guards round the clock outside the rooms occupied by Jessica and Libby. That cost a bundle and couldn't have been reassuring to visitors who had family members or friends in nearby rooms. They let her go home Wednesday afternoon.

Once she was home, Jessica felt much better. The beauty of the desert worked its magic as she reclined on a patio chaise. A gentle breeze swirled around her, carrying with it the sweet scent of jasmine. A light snow on the surrounding mountains glistened as the sun settled on their peaks, bathing the golf course in a golden, late afternoon glow.

Paradise beckoned, although something was up and nobody was talking. Jessica wished she had Bernadette's gift for picking up stray thoughts, or making sense out of body language. There were more people in the house than there had been in months and yet the silence was deafening. Bernadette scurried about, her Dad had a lap full of papers, and Alexis sat pretending to read a magazine.

Her mother was thin and drawn, showing her age in a way Jessica hadn't noticed before. Alexis was distant, too, maybe preoccupied with the events of the past few days. *Her fourth marriage is on the rocks and her daughter has escaped death twice in the past week, what did I expect?* She mused as she eyed her mother who smiled warmly.

"I'm so glad you're okay," Alexis said, looking for a moment like she might cry. Then she seemed to fade away into her own world. Not long after, she excused herself and retreated to her wing of the estate. She left the magazine on the chair as though she was coming right back.

It was another déjà vu moment as Jessica, Bernadette, and her father watched the woman drift off to the patio entrance that led back into her suite. Jessica caught a glance that passed between Bernadette and her father. *Just like old times*, Jessica thought, recalling how often a scene like this one had played out before her parents divorced. Perhaps it was the way her mother coped—divorcing everyone in her life for a time when she got rid of a husband. Jessica didn't understand or like it now any more than she had at twelve.

"I better check on dinner," Bernadette said. She gave a nervous glance at the retreating figure of Jessica's mother before heading for the doors leading into the kitchen. The sound of the screen doors closing as Bernadette ducked inside echoed the sound made as her mother entered her suite.

Hank stayed put. Their conversation was amiable even though he remained distracted. That could have something to do with the number of projects he had going and the backlog of tasks amassing, despite efforts to stay on top of the work from a distance. Jessica asked him to bring her up to date on his work. His enthusiasm grew as he spoke. Sitting with her father, talking about his work as an architect and developer, set off another round of "been-there-done-that" moments. As her mother withdrew, her father worked harder. Was that the pattern setting off eerie twilight zone music in her head?

"I'm glad you're home, safe and sound, Jinx. Think you'll be okay if I head back to work tomorrow?"

"Sure! I've got Bernadette and Mom to help me. If they can't handle it, I can always call Laura or Tommy. So, don't worry."

"I am worried. What about that trouble at the hospital?"

"Peter's on top of it. We're covered round-the-clock. They won't let anyone get near me even if they get through the gate. The police are on it, too. Detective Hernandez and his counterparts at the Palm Springs police department are as eager as we are to sort this out."

"I'm sure you're right. I couldn't quite get what's up with that Hernandez guy."

"Bernadette's got his number. He's a marshmallow covered in a crusty coating of grumpy cop. Sort of like Uncle Don, you know? We don't always see eye-to-eye, and I don't always like the way he expresses himself, but he's gruff because he cares. My track record for knowing when to cool it isn't that great. And, I'm a sucker for incremental commitment—in for a penny, in for a pound. Before you know it, I'm in way over my head. The cops in my life keep me on a short leash, Dad."

"I guess that's part of what I'm concerned about. You sure have had some close calls. Maybe I should call and thank them for harping at you. I'm with them about cooling it."

"Yeah, I know. But I hate it when something's going on and I can't figure out what it is. It's like an itch and I get this compulsion to get to the bottom of it. I admit it. I stirred things up trying to find out who killed Roger Stone and Kelly Fontana."

"Going after Libby in the hospital seems daring and desperate. Your detective friend implied you know more about this than you've said. Is that true? Are you keeping things from him?"

"Detective Hernandez always assumes the worst. The short answer is no, at least I don't think so. I can't tell you all that's going on because I just don't know. We have been doing some investigating—just routine checks on Libby Van Der Woert and her shrink. She's in trouble that's somehow tied to her dead psychiatrist and a friend of hers who's missing. That's how Detective Hernandez got mixed up in this—he's looking for her missing friend. Maybe it *will* all make more sense after I've spoken to him. I owe statements to the Palm Springs police, too, but I've told Frank Fontana the whole story. I'm sure if he thought I had vital information that could solve the case—*cases*—in Cathedral City or Palm Springs, his colleagues would have been at me already. For now, I'm out to sea with a boatload of puzzle pieces and no clear idea of the picture I'm trying to assemble. I'm not even sure I know what mysteries need to be solved. Why is everything always so complicated?"

"Hey, if I knew the answer to that I'd be a lot richer than I am! You need to be careful until they figure this out. Libby's in deep trouble if someone wants her dead bad enough to go after her in the hospital in broad daylight. You may have some boundary issues dealing with other people's problems." He wore that lopsided grin of his. A twinkle in his eye told her he was trying to make light of his concern.

"Oh my God, have you been watching Dr. Phil? Can't be Oprah, she's not on TV anymore."

"What makes you think I haven't spent a little time of my own with a shrink? I'll have you know I've spent big bucks, just like you, to get better boundaries." Even though he seemed to be taking what she said in stride, Jessica recognized worry when she saw it.

"Look, I'm working on it. Not just the boundary issue, but also a lot of other things. I'm always glad to see you, and love hearing about your work, but you don't have to babysit me if you need to get back."

"I still need more help to set limits—you get the incremental commitment problem from me, I'm afraid." Hank let out a loud sigh. "Don't wait until you're as old as me to figure it out. When you're my age, it's not so easy to get caught up when things are backed up. I love you and if you need me, I'll be here—work be hanged. It will always take second place to you."

"I know that. Thanks. Paul Worthington and Amy Klein have my back, but I'm dealing with the same issues about work, on a much smaller scale. So, I totally get it. The holidays are coming and I'm on the mend, let's do something fun together, okay?"

"That's a great idea. Let's go to the Nutcracker or the symphony for a Christmas concert, or something here at the McCallum. I'll look for some dates for us. In the meantime, you promise to recover and stay out of trouble, okay?" Before she could answer, his cell phone rang. He took a quick look at the number, "I've got to take this and I need some files I brought with me. Sorry," he said as he stood up, planted a kiss on the top of her head, and moved inside the house.

Their conversation had set off a surge of anxiety about her workload. Her job with the firm had taken off in the fall, almost as soon as the doors opened at the Palm Desert office. On Labor Day weekend, she and her mother had held a dinner party for the Van Der Woerts. With her mother at the helm, the evening had been a delightful one. Cocktails and a dinner party had become a more elaborate affair than Jessica had envisioned since there were several mutual friends and acquaintances in the area who knew both the Huntingtons and the Van Der Woerts. Before she knew it, an intimate dinner had grown to include over twenty people. After that, Jessica's new practice had expanded fast, though. Most likely at her mother's urging, several dinner party guests had contacted or referred someone to Jessica for legal advice.

Jessica fought off an image of her inbox overflowing with files stamped "URGENT" in bright red letters. She should take that advice repeated by caring and concerned men in her life and have "COOL IT" emblazoned on a paperweight. Where *were* the boundaries on her work as a lawyer, or between her problems and those that belonged to friends and family? What was the name of that shrink her father had seen?

"Jessica," Bernadette called out, "Go tell your mom it's time to eat."

"Okay."

"I can do it," her dad said, as he stepped to the patio door, with an empty plate in his hand.

"No problem. My behind is falling asleep from all the time spent in a near-prone position. Get your food. I'll get Mom," Jessica said, easing herself out of the chaise, which was much harder to do without the use of both arms.

"Mom," Jessica called out, tapping on the glass door. "Dinner's ready." Jessica peered into the shadowy room. Her mother lay stretched out on her enormous bed. She looked so tiny. Was she struggling after finding herself sleeping alone, again since her separation from Giovanni? After Jessica's own split with her husband, there had been a lot of sleepless nights. Online shopping binges with her black AMEX card had been one strategy for filling the empty hours provoked by the empty space in her bed.

"Thanks. I'll be right there." Another failed marriage couldn't be easy to handle. Giovanni had called, but her mother hadn't said a word about their conversation, or why their marriage was over. Jessica wanted to ask, but felt constrained by her mother evasiveness. Their relationship was often circumscribed by bonding rituals around shopping and spa visits, sharing food and wine, or a round of golf. She knew so little about her mother as a person, or her experiences as a woman. Why was that?

Maybe, tomorrow, I'll ask her, point blank, about Giovanni, Jessica thought as she shuffled back to her seat on the patio, taking care not to jar her still sensitive ribs. Dinner was delicious. They ate red snapper, "Vera Cruz style," according to Bernadette, accompanied by tiny roasted potatoes served alongside baby carrots tossed in a mango salsa. Alexis joined them, but said nothing as she picked at her food. She ate little, but refilled her wine glass several times.

On the outside, quiet prevailed, although this dinner was supposed to be a homecoming, of sorts. Inside, Jessica was growing more and more upset. It was good to be back in the lap of luxury and behind the gates at Mission Hills. With Peter and his guys back on duty sitting out in front of the house, she was safe for now, but not happy. What was getting to her was the undercurrent of a too-familiar, yet mysterious, family dynamic.

Her mother sat, tired, withdrawn, and a little shaky. Her father, worn out, but also wary and on edge, stole worried glances at Alexis. Even Bernadette grew quiet after a few attempts at conversation went nowhere.

Another old feeling swept over her—guilt. *How much of all that worry and weariness is my fault?* Jessica wondered. This time, it was no debacle ending in expulsion from private school—two, in a matter of months—or a world-class tantrum that weighed them down. Instead, she'd been tossed off a mountain in a fracas with maniacs, and might have been next in line for attack by that guy who shot his way out of the hospital. Were they sad, angry, or too just exhausted to speak? Her mind raced as the guilt hammered at her. The difference between the thirty-four-year-old Jessica and the fourteen-year-old one was that she now knew she was no mind reader. Nor was she willing to ignore the feelings that something was wrong.

"Okay, you guys. What *is* going on? Are you all ticked at me?"

Alexis looked up. If she was aiming to meet Jessica's gaze as she tried to feign wide-eyed innocence, it didn't work. She had to correct, mid-course, to make eye contact. As she did that, she slopped the contents of her wine glass on her white linen pants. She looked down and swiped at the damp spots on her lap.

"Good thing it's a white wine, huh?" She asked, and then giggled. Jessica could see Alexis the society-darling-Mom struggling to kick into gear. But with less skill than normal, or she might have missed it. It dawned on her how often her shape-shifter mother went from sullen social isolate to social butterfly when prodded or provoked.

"No one's upset with you, Jessica. I'm not sure what's going on either. My guess is your mother is drinking too much—again. I'd say she's well past tipsy." Alexis tried to look offended, but once again, her gaze missed the mark. She had to readjust her line of sight to send daggers at Hank.

"Mom, are you loaded?" Alexis did that morphing thing and the anger toward Hank dissolved into society-girl giggles. That stopped when Hank spoke again.

"I figure she's had a head start on the rest of us or there's something extra in the mix. Am I right, Lexi?" His use of that pet name softened what was otherwise a harsh question.

Jessica flashed on a glimpse she'd caught of the bedside table next to her mother. Pill bottles, several of them were on that table, one with the lid off. She hadn't thought twice about it. Her mother *always* had pills around—lots of them. Alexis had long been a hypochondriac, concerned about her own health and quick to run Jessica to a doctor, too. It had never occurred to her that all the pills might mean something else.

"Besides boundaries, therapy has given me a better appreciation for directness. Consider this an intervention, Lexi. Not a well-planned one and the timing may suck, given Jessica's latest troubles, but enough is enough." Bernadette spoke next, in a soft, firm tone.

"The jig is out here, Alexis, don't you agree? The goose is out of the barn, too, and you better spit out the beans." No more tender voice had ever uttered such a garbled string of idioms. A pointed silence followed. Finally, Alexis spoke, misery on her face and in her voice.

"Yes, I have a problem. More than one, in fact." Alexis tried to steady her voice. Her eyes had filled with tears and her lips trembled. "I'm sick.

13 FRENCH TOAST DEBRIEF

The next morning, Jessica took her time climbing out of bed. She was raw, mentally and physically. The impromptu "intervention" with her mother the night before had been revealing, but unnerving. Not only was her mother dealing with cancer, but alcohol and drug abuse. Learning that her mother had cervical cancer was bad. That she was putting off surgery because she didn't want to give up her pills and alcohol was terrifying and infuriating.

She'd fought off the urge to take her mother by the shoulders and shake her. She wanted to shake her father, too, and even Bernadette for keeping so much hidden from her for so long. But with one arm in a sling and the other arm with a bandaged hand, she wasn't in any condition to shake anybody. What good would that have done anyway? She struggled to make sense of the new reality unveiled to her. Life as she knew it had changed in a matter of moments on that patio at dusk.

Her mother had been forthcoming about the problems she faced, but her thinking was far from clear. Alexis knew she was in trouble. Still, she stunned Jessica when she hesitated about getting into treatment after admitting she needed it. She didn't balk, but wheedled and attempted to stall.

"I can't go... I, uh, what about Giovanni?" Alexis asked.

"What about him?" Bernadette countered. "He's not going anywhere and you don't know for sure what you want to do about him, or you would have done it. Get yourself cleaned up and what to do about Giovanni will become clear, too." Alexis nodded, sniffling.

"Jessica needs my help," was another tack she had taken, to which Jessica had replied as fast as she could get the words out.

"Mom, if you want to help—if you care about me, you'll get treatment now!" She'd tried to keep the anger out of her voice, without diminishing the urgency she intended to convey. Not just anger, but panic had set in. The panic she so often felt when forced to reason with the unreasonable.

With a little more coaxing, Alexis agreed to get into treatment. Hank was on the phone immediately and found her a spot. Nothing was available at Betty Ford, so Alexis agreed to go to another classy rehab center—this one in Malibu. Jessica sat in silence, a stunned twelve-year-old again, as the three adults acted. More than falling off a mountain, this long held secret had knocked her flat on her back. Once her mother had gone to pack, it had taken Jessica half an hour to speak without anger; first to her father, then to Bernadette.

"I don't understand. Why did you keep this part of our family life from me for so long?"

"There are so many reasons. I spent years in denial about your Mom's problems. She was such a delight to have in my life so much of the time. Alexis was enchanting to be around, so full of energy and life. Then, this other side of her emerged soon after our marriage. She became moody and withdrawn at times, but who doesn't? At first, even that didn't set off any alerts. In time, things got worse. Still, she was such a good actress that if I said anything to her, she'd pull it together for a few days and I'd think I was crazy."

"Did she have problems growing up? Grandma Emma always seemed happy to see us when we visited. Mom was a little quieter around her, but they seemed to get along."

"Emma and your mother were opposites. Emma was stern, and so much more rigid and uptight than Alexis. She was critical of your mom, too. Her criticism seemed to be typical 'generation gap' things—disputes about clothes and makeup, etiquette, all rather superficial. Maybe your mother took it to heart. I don't know. Did your mother ever complain about being whipped with hangers or other 'mommy dearest' type moments? No. And Emma stayed out of our affairs once we married. We didn't visit often, but when we did it was always tolerable."

"What about her father?" Jessica was almost afraid to ask, given the horrid things that Libby and her doctor had cooked up to torment and extort her parents. It felt wrong to be asking such questions, like she was trying to pin the blame for her mother's problems on her grandparents.

"He was an affable guy. He drank a lot, but I never saw him drunk, if that's what you mean. The man always held a responsible position at work, and the community held him in high-regard, so if he had a problem, he kept it hidden. I never asked Alexis any of these questions, so I don't know if there's a family history of alcohol or mental health problems. At some point, I became concerned about her mood swings and how much she was drinking, plus all the pills. When the news about Betty Ford's problems came out, and she announced she was opening her clinic, I made a stab at getting Alexis to do something. She went into treatment and gave it all up right before she became pregnant with you. After your birth, she hung on for a while, but then slipped back into all the old patterns. She had an injury or two, or so she claimed, and the pills showed up again. I asked, but she told me to back off. She argued that doctors wouldn't give pills to her if she didn't need them. I'm not sure she ever stopped long enough to figure out if the booze and pills were the source of her problems, or if something else was going on. I felt confused and blamed myself. It was hard for me to gauge how much my work was impeding our relationship. At some point, my harping no longer seemed effective. I wasn't sure what to do, much less what to tell you. You were so young."

"Did you know about this, Bernadette?"

"Sì, some of it. I did what I could to get Alexis to get help. It was hard to get the complete picture. I wondered about all the medicine she was taking, but like Hank says, she always had a reason—headaches or back pain from falling off a horse or pulling something playing golf or tennis. It was always somethin'." Bernadette shook her head, looking every bit her age.

"I'm sorry I left," Hank added, "but this went on for years and I'd reached the end of my rope. The tension between us was causing you harm, and I figured that outweighed any good I could do. It's like I had become part of the problem rather than the solution. We separated for a while and I hoped she'd come to her senses. You know, figure out which problems were because of me, and which were her own? That didn't happen, so I gave up and agreed to a divorce. Eventually, she went into rehab again somewhere in Switzerland—soon after you went off to college in Irvine, right Bernadette?"

"Yeah, that helped some, too. She got herself cleaned up and was sober for a while, but the drogado wasn't the only devil in her life. I don't think she's faced up to all of them yet."

"Isn't Switzerland where she met that Cranston guy?" Jessica asked.

"That's right. She was feeling better after the treatment. Then she met Cranston, fell in love, and married him in no time at all. Too fast, I thought, but what could I do?" Bernadette said.

"We had lived apart for years, but I was heartbroken. But when I saw her again after that, it was a relief to see her happy, so I hoped he'd succeed where I had failed."

"He turned out not to be so good for her. Soon she was back on the party-wagon. On the wagon, off the wagon, I forget which is which when it means she's doing good or not-so-good. When she wasn't around much, it was even harder to tell what was going on. One day, Cranston's gone and another guy's there. Was that a good sign or bad? I didn't know for sure."

"I hated being kept in the dark. The undercurrents made me crazy! I thought it was *my* fault that our family fell apart."

"When you were young, we all told you it wasn't your fault. Later, when you became an adult, you were so busy making a life for yourself—college and law school and Jim and the bar test. With a job and a wedding and the house-fixing, what could you do about your mother's life?"

"Bernadette's right. By that point, your mother was my ex-wife. What she did wasn't my business anymore—unless it had to do with you."

"It was so confusing. I knew things weren't right. There was so much I didn't understand."

"You were a child then. I wasn't sure what was going on with your mom either. We did what we could to reassure you we both loved you even if we couldn't work things out between us. That wasn't always easy given the way you acted out, I might add."

"I know, Dad, I feel guilty about that too!"

"I don't want you to feel guilty. All I'm saying is that we all did the best we could. Now that you've divorced Jim, it must have crossed your mind that if you had kids, things would be even more complicated than they are. You'd have difficult choices to make, deciding how much to say to your child about Jim's behavior and the problems in your marriage. I didn't want my disappointment to turn you against your mother. It wasn't Bernadette's place to tell you more than I did. I just kept most of what was going on, or what I assumed was going on, to myself. All I could do was to tell you, repeatedly, that your mother and I never stopped loving you even when we couldn't be together anymore."

"I am grateful for that. You're right. I have given a lot of thought to how much more difficult divorce would have been if Jim and I had a child. Having to be in the same room with him still seems like more than I can bear. So, thanks for figuring out how to make that work with Mom."

"It was hard at first, but my relationship with your mother improved, especially when she was sober. I can't tell you for sure how I know that. There's just something different about her when she's sober and when she's not. It's clear she hasn't won whatever fight she's been waging to achieve sobriety. Given the way all the old patterns reappear, I'm with Bernadette that Alexis hasn't faced down the demons that bedevil and beguile her." Jessica was curious and wanted to hear more about those demons, but an interruption ended their conversation.

"Well, if you all are through psychoanalyzing me, I'm packed, demons and all." Her mother stood in the doorway, lit from behind. A strange halo illuminated her as she spoke. A rush of emotions overtook Jessica. Anger and fear, supplanted by sorrow, and even pity, for this woman she loved. All those years of her mother's life spent in turmoil. Jessica felt crushed by the waste of it all—the loss of what might have been.

Now, Alexis was sick with cancer, too. At least there was still time for her mother to sort things out. In a split second, Jessica was at her mother's side, pulling her as close as a one-armed woman with battered, sore ribs could. Her mother clung to her as best she could without causing Jessica more pain. They wept for several minutes.

"I love you. Please do what they tell you to do so we can be a family. I'll try not to expect perfect. Even if it's a little screwed up, that's okay. I'll take what I can get—you, Dad, Bernadette, and me. But, please Mom, you've got to keep fighting to stay alive. Get clean enough to have that surgery soon. Okay?"

Alexis nodded her head yes, "I'll try, Baby Girl. Promise!" Jessica didn't object to the "Baby Girl" name that so often chafed when her mother used it. She would answer to any name her mother called her if it meant they could have a future together. Jessica covered her mother's face with kisses before releasing her.

Hank put his arm around Alexis' shoulders, picked up the bag she had with her, and escorted her to a car that was waiting for them. The car would take them to Jackie Cochran airport, a few miles away, where Hank had arranged for a helicopter service to pick them up. They were taking her straight to the facility in Malibu and admitting her that night, leaving no chance for Alexis to change her mind.

It would be at least a couple days before Alexis would be allowed to have contact with family. Jessica planned to make her way to Malibu to see her mother in a few days. Check on her, or maybe, check *up* on her. She wouldn't be remiss again and would wield her powers of hypervigilance, at least until her mother got that surgery. They'd have to run more tests at that point to figure out if Alexis would need chemo and she'd stand watch then, too.

By the time she and Bernadette said good night, a little while later, Jessica felt exhausted. She wanted to indulge in a bout of anxiety-driven-information-gathering and read everything she could find on the web about early stage cervical cancer. Instead, she had fallen asleep.

As she slouched her way down the hall, the next morning, the house felt too big. Empty, now that both her mother and father had left. She could hear noises coming from the kitchen and as she got closer, smelled delightful aromas too.

"Coffee, I smell coffee. It's making me dizzy."

"Sit down and I'll bring you... Jessica, you're still in your clothes from last night!" Bernadette stopped, dead in her tracks, with a large mug of coffee in her hand. Jessica's mouth watered at the sight.

"I know. I meant to change. I climbed into my bed with my laptop and passed out. Trust me; it wasn't because of any drugs either. I took one of the co-Tylenol they prescribed, but I am spooked about taking anything more than a couple of aspirin, today. A little pain seems a small price to pay for keeping your wits about you. I don't care what Dad says, drug and alcohol problems run in families. And speaking of drugs, once I get caffeine into my system, I'll go clean myself up and put on different clothes." She winced as she sat down at the table in the morning room off the kitchen. Even ordinary movements jarred her ribs.

"Not taking drugs is a good idea, but I heard them tell you not to let the pain get so bad you breathe funny and get your lungs in a mess. You made a face when you sat down. I saw that."

"I am sore, but so far I can take it. The aspirin should help soon." Bernadette set the mug of coffee down in front of Jessica. The bandage on her hand was smaller than the first one put on in the ER, but she still found it awkward. One-handed, she had to be careful with hot coffee, despite her eagerness to scarf it down.

"You ask the doctor about it when you go for your checkup, this afternoon, okay?"

"Sure, if you think I should. I'll take an ice pack and use it when I go back in my room. That helps, too. Oh my God, this coffee is wonderful. I love you."

"Aw, I'm glad you're not still mad at me about not telling you more about what was going on with your parents. Gracias a Dios, this is all out now, though." Bernadette crossed herself as she spoke those last words.

"I was more shocked than angry. If I'm angry with anyone, it's Mom! Not just because she's been hiding a drug problem from me for years, but she's also chosen her drugs over getting treatment for cancer. I'm sure she's telling us the truth that her prognosis is good, but not if she keeps putting off surgery. I'm going to read about it today, but I'm pretty sure if she can get through detox, she can go ahead with surgery. Now there's a sentence coming out of my mouth that I never expected to utter. You never know what's coming next, do you?"

"Another cup of coffee is what's next for you, Chica. I fixed it just the way you like it—in the French press, steeping for ten minutes, after grinding the beans. I like that part of it now, too. They smell so good. I get that 'connect high' like the drug takers talk about."

"Do you mean a 'contact high?' Where on earth did you hear that?"

"One of those true crime shows. Or maybe it was in a story about Charlie Sheen or Robert Downey Jr. They've been to rehab too, you know? I hope it works better for your mom than it has for Charlie." Bernadette turned around, shaking her head as she headed back into the kitchen.

"Well, Robert Downey Jr. seems to have pulled out of the tailspin his life was in. I thought he was a goner after they found him in a stranger's house out here in the desert."

"I think he spent some time at the same place Hank took your mom. It must be a good place."

"Yeah, and I suppose it takes more than one try at treatment for addicts to recover." Jessica caught her breath again, from the pain in her heart, not her ribs. Her beautiful, vivacious mother was an addict. How impossible was that to believe?

"The world has gone mad. My husband, a cheating fool, marries a crazed, out of control, massively pregnant exhibitionist. Laura's husband gets himself murdered and Kelly Fontana, too. She was pumped full of drugs but *wasn't* an addict and Mom *is*! Go figure."

"It'll be okay. You'll see. You fell off a mountain and you're okay. Maybe that was the shakeup your mother needed to make her face her troubles. The whole family here, together, at once was a good thing. You and your Dad speaking up at the same time was a good thing too."

"Yeah, that's all true. You didn't back down, either, even when she tried to use Giovanni and me as reasons to put off treatment. A lot of things that went on when I was a kid make so much more sense now. I hear what you're saying—good things can come from bad situations."

"Speaking of good things..." Bernadette hustled into the kitchen and came right back.

"French toast—you made me French toast—my favorite! Did I already say I love you?" The luscious scent of maple and cinnamon reached her even before Bernadette set the plate down in front of her. She dug in, one-arm style, savoring the ambrosial, melt-in-your-mouth, blend of flavors. Bernadette sat down across from her with a plate of her own. Then she slid a card toward Jessica. Pausing for a moment, Jessica put the fork down and picked up the card.

"Oh my God, it's your recipe!" Shock must have been on her face. "You're not sick too, are you?"

"No, but now you're grown and around here all the time, you need to figure out how to fix your *favorites*." Bernadette chuckled. "Close your mouth and finish your breakfast." She shook her head, still smiling.

"Well, I can't shut my mouth *and* eat, can I?" Jessica paused, torn between devouring the food on her plate and reading the secret ingredients revealed in that recipe. French toast, accompanied by thin slices of a salty Spanish ham and fresh raspberries, won out.

They spent a blissful half hour eating and drinking coffee. She read the ingredients, and the instructions for preparing *St. Bernadette's Divine French Toast*, as Jessica had named it. Bernadette provided a step-by-step commentary as Jessica read the list of ingredients. Thick slices of brioche soaked in eggs, sugar and cream, spiked with brandy and fresh squeezed orange juice, Mexican cinnamon, and Mexican vanilla. No wonder Jessica's previous attempts had fallen short. The last instruction on the card was the most touching, another of Bernadette's secrets revealed.

"Never forget to prepare and serve with love. Ay que Bueno!" How could so much goodness be packed into that small, precious being sitting across from her at the table? Bernadette, as Jessica knew, had experienced her share of hardship and loss.

"I don't know what I would have done without you all these years—still don't. Mom and I wouldn't have gotten this far. I am so grateful."

"Aw, that's just the French toast talkin'," Bernadette said with a big grin on her face. Her eyes were a little misty, though. "It's been a blessing for me too. Families always have troubles, and taking care of each other is just what they ought to do."

"Most aren't as lucky as I am, though, and I never want to take the good in my life for granted."

"That's a good practice—to be grateful. Let me know when you want to get ready so you won't be late for your doctor appointment this afternoon. I'll drive you."

"Okay, I'm not up to driving yet, that's for sure. Who knows what other hurdles I'll face trying to get around in my current condition. I'm slow, but I'm getting the hang of doing some things with one arm. Keeping my cast and bandages dry with a plastic bag is a trick I learned when I sprained my wrist, so I can manage a shower. Ah, the things I've added to my skill set this past year! I can get the sling off, but I might need your help putting it back on."

"Just holler when you're ready to do that. How about your hair? It's grown out a lot. I can at least give you a hand with the blow dryer when you get that far."

"I'm sure the doctor won't care if I show up with my hair hanging in my face. Maybe I should get it cut again—even shorter this time. I appreciate your going with me. I could have one of Peter's men do that, but I'd rather have you with me. We still don't know what's going on with that attack on Libby in the hospital. I don't know if I'm a target, too, and I'm in no shape to find out the hard way."

"Have one of those guys go with us, too. I can drive, but you should have someone come along behind us to keep an eye out for maleantes."

"You're right. That's the first thing I'll do when I get back to my room—give Peter a call. I should also call my office and check in with Amy. There's plenty more to do if I can get myself organized."

"Don't put too much on that 'to do' list of yours. You're a tough nut to crumble, but not Superwoman."

"Cookie, Bernadette—I think you mean I'm a tough cookie or a tough nut to crack, that's the way the cookie crumbles..." Correcting Bernadette's misuse of idioms was a habit she needed to break. It wasn't necessary, nor would it work. It annoyed most people when she corrected their misstatements, her perfectionism oozing out like a leaky faucet, even when she thought she had it shut off.

"Cookie—that too, Jessica. You don't crumble easy. You get my drift, right?"

"Sure, I get your drift." Bernadette was smiling and Jessica wondered if Bernadette was toying with her, playing with words to lighten things up. She downed the last sip of coffee and stood up, carefully, waiting for the pain to register. "Not bad. The aspirin must have kicked in. If I get stuck trying to get ready, I'll yell for help, promise."

"Okay, mi dulce princessa," Bernadette said.

Hopped up on caffeine and loaded on a breakfast made in heaven, by an angel here on earth, Jessica felt almost normal. Well, as normal as possible, in the current context. She basked in the glow of secrets revealed. It wasn't just that recipe from Bernadette. As tough as it was to face her mother's situation, it was better than not knowing, knowing half-truths, or believing lies. Having it all out in the open satisfied some inner longing. Truth revealed, a mystery solved, or at least on the way to being solved.

She'd know more after she read up, not just about cervical cancer, but also alcohol and drug problems. She'd call Laura later, too, and drill her about both kinds of health problems. Given her nurse's training, she'd know how best to support her mother. Maybe she would quiz Betsy Stark about the drug issue, too, when she came by the house tomorrow. That she was meeting with Betsy reminded her that she had a huge set of issues to deal with, besides those having to do with her own family. There were all those other mysteries hanging out there for another family. She felt more keenly aware of how much damage family members could to each other, accidentally or on purpose. What was going on with Libby? Where was her friend Shannon Donnelly? With Dr. Richard Carr dead, who was after Libby? Was Jessica's life on the line? Why?

14 FIRST CONTACT

When Jessica returned to her room, the first item of business was where to sit to get work done. Those ribs were still giving her grief, so she opted to get back into bed. That could be risky, given her general state of exhaustion, warring with the caffeine and sugar she'd just consumed. In bed, she propped herself up at the best angle to work with the least amount of pain, surrounded by things she needed: her phone, laptop, and several file folders with photos, police reports, and printed copies of information Tommy and Jerry had produced for her about Libby Van Der Woert and Dr. Richard Carr.

Jessica picked up the Van Der Woert's folder. It seemed like years, instead of months, had passed since they hired her to put their estate plans in order. Retirement loomed, and they had wanted a plan in place for the long haul. That included a modest allowance for their daughter who seemed unable to provide for herself. But by the time Jessica got down to the business of figuring out how much of their assets to put into trust for Libby, the ground had shifted. They moved up their retirement date, and took Paul's advice to set up a trust to *protect* their assets from their daughter's aberrant behavior, rather than simply making provisions for her.

She picked up Libby's file next. The sordid details of the young woman's life, spelled out in the pages of that file, pushed Jessica toward that pit of despair she felt about wasted lives. Libby's youth seemed spent using every advantage she possessed to destroy herself and others. Jessica's first face-to-face, encounter with Libby had occurred when the young woman showed up one day at the Palm Desert law office. Libby waltzed in without an appointment and demanded to see Jessica. Jessica agreed to meet with the rude, noisy young woman, from both curiosity and the need to preserve decorum. Kim Reed had spoken up as Libby Van Der Woert followed Jessica down the hall to her office.

"I'll be right with you as soon as I get what I need to record the interview." Libby stopped, as if to balk, and turned to confront Kim. Much to her surprise, Kim was close. So close, Libby almost bumped into her. The steely determination in Kim's dark eyes, her edgy dress, and no-nonsense demeanor, must have convinced Libby to abort any form of protest she was considering.

"Whatever!" Libby shrugged and moved to the door Jessica had just walked through. Jessica's office was roomy, with large windows that overlooked the parking lot that served their building and the nearby shops. Beyond the parking lot and busy streets was a view of the mountains, towering palm trees, and those blazing blue skies that dominated the Coachella Valley. Jessica had seated them at a small conference table and then took control of the conversation.

"Okay, Ms. Van Der Woert, how may I help you?"

"Oh my God, you are exactly what I expected. I heard my parents hired a gorgeous, young female lawyer. You'll make Dad look less like scum standing next to him, if I have to take him to court." She smiled in a crooked way, tilting her head to one side, like a hawk sizing up its prey. Jessica had seen that look before. A tingle of recognition danced its way down her spine, as she remembered her encounters with the diabolical Margarit during the investigation into Roger Stone's murder.

"My shrink says you have a soft spot for the bastard—anybody who sides with my dad must have a daddy thing going. He's right, *Ms*. Huntington, you look like a daddy's girl."

"You must know I can't talk to you about your father, or my role as his lawyer, so how may I help you?"

"Help me? You're the last person in the world who can help me. I don't get it. How can you all be representing Dad? You used to be my lawyer. Isn't that a conflict of interest or something like that?" The predatory look on her face had vanished and in its place was a pouty ten-year-old. Her bottom lip poked out and she twisted a strand of hair around her finger, as her eyes grew misty.

"I've never been your lawyer, Ms. Van Der Woert. I..." Before Jessica could finish, the disturbed young woman interrupted.

"Cut the *Ms. Van Der Woert* routine already. It makes me feel ancient—like you're talking to my mother. It's Libby okay?" Pouting had morphed into surliness.

"Sure, Libby, but as I was saying, I have never been your lawyer. Just because the firm in LA defended you in a previous case, doesn't mean I'm under any obligation to represent you or to turn down your parents' request for help. From what I hear, you have your own lawyer with another firm. You need to take up whatever concerns you have with him."

Paul Worthington, Jessica's boss, had honchoed the case in which the firm defended Libby from charges related to a drunk-driving incident that killed Libby's friend, Lela. Lela Vasquez had been as drunk and stoned as Libby was that night. Libby was at the wheel at the time of the accident, in part because the police had stopped them earlier that night when Lela was driving recklessly. Rather than taking them both into custody, the officer had given them a warning and let them go. When the crash occurred later, Libby was at the wheel. It wasn't her first incident involving drunk driving, but the law firm was able to keep records of earlier incidents out of court because she was underage when they occurred.

She took a deep breath, waiting for Libby to reply. She didn't break eye contact and took her own turn sizing up the adversary in her midst. On the surface, the woman looked credible, but she'd learned that was not at all unusual for your garden variety sociopath. They were often good at faking it, passing as a normal person with a conscience, for short periods anyway.

Libby had garnered a host of diagnoses over the years, having been in and out of treatment since the age of twelve: conduct disorder, ADHD, and depression as a teen. Borderline and bipolar disorders were added to the list, along with substance abuse problems when she was a young adult. She struggled to remember if Libby's parents had mentioned sociopath—antisocial something-or-other, maybe. Libby had been in treatment since the deadly auto accident, as mandated by a probation agreement, and she'd changed shrinks several times. Treatment included an assortment of prescribed drugs, but those weren't the only substances she used. Her history of drug use revealed during the investigation into that late-night single-car crash was distressing; that she hadn't died from an overdose, remarkable. Jessica wondered how many of the drugs on that list were used by her mother. Why hadn't she asked?

Jessica refocused on Libby's file. The most recent communications about Libby's mental health status involved a new diagnosis: PTSD from sexual abuse, allegedly, experienced at the hands of her father and uncle. That information had been conveyed to her parents by Libby, by Dr. Carr, and in sloppy, typewritten threats on letterhead from a series of schlock lawyers Libby had hired. She threatened to sue her parents if they didn't fork over her inheritance.

"That new diagnosis must have meant new drugs, too," she muttered, poring over the file again for information about prescribed drugs. Some familiar names popped up, others were new: Adderall, Zoloft, Celexa, Prozac, Lamictal, Valium, Xanax, Seroquel, Abilify, and Ambien. The list of drugs doled out over the course of twenty years was astonishing, and didn't include the street drugs Libby added to the mix. She suspected Libby was on something the day she'd shown up at her office. Libby's behavior hadn't been as coherent as her attire. By all appearances, Libby was an attractive, well-groomed young woman, dressed in a simple, pricey ensemble. She wore a gorgeous abstract printed long-sleeved silk wrap shirt. The wrap featured more cleavage than she would have chosen for herself, but it fit Libby well, and didn't gape open when she bent forward. With black tapered-leg ankle pants and a gorgeous pair of black, Manolo Blahnik point-toe pumps, sporting four-inch heels, she was appropriately dressed. Jessica did the math in her head—*fifteen hundred dollars for that outfit, easy.* The young woman lived well without ever having held a job for long.

"So, you know all about my accident, don't you?" Libby had asked with her mood on the move again. "Do you know what I've been through with my father and uncle?" Simpering won out as the mood of the moment.

She won't be able to buy clothes like that much longer, Jessica thought. Libby's parents had set up a trust for her as part of a probation agreement. Charges for "gross vehicular manslaughter while intoxicated," reduced to vehicular manslaughter, resulted in a conviction for a misdemeanor rather than a felony. The court suspended Libby's license and she, or more accurately, her parents paid a substantial fine. The trust was there to support Libby while she got back on her feet. Fast-forward five years later and Libby was on her feet all right, in a stunning pair of heels. One of many pairs she wore as she walked all over her parents. That trust ended when Libby turned thirty in 2013.

"Reason enough for many young predators to spring into action, Jessica." Paul Worthington, who had seen it all before, had told her.

Jessica used two fingers from her bandaged hand to scratch up under the cast, recalling how her palm had itched that day to do some shopping. Both Father Martin and her new shrink had challenged Jessica to handle her stress over frustrating situations in some other way. She had tried to do that by ending the conversation. Jessica hoped Libby had come there with a specific purpose. The snarky remarks and moody shifts in tone confirmed that Libby had trouble taking responsibility for her own behavior and wore a big chip on her shoulder as an accessory to that designer outfit. There was nothing Jessica could do about that.

"Look, Ms. Van Der... Libby, I'll ask you one more time, and then we're done. Why are you here?"

"I just wanted to meet Attorney Huntington, that's all. See if you were the bloodthirsty type. Will you rip me to shreds on the witness stand?" She growled and flexed fingers with long manicured nails that were painted a dark red burgundy. The usually imperturbable Kim reacted by rolling her eyes. A couple more minutes of this, and Libby Van Der Woert might not have to wait until she took the witness stand to get ripped to shreds. Kim, wound up, was ready to do some predatory pouncing of her own.

"Well then, I guess that means we're done. It's better for both of us if, in the future, any communication you have for me comes from your new attorney. I haven't met him yet, but I'm open to such a meeting." Jessica stood, signaling that the meeting was over. Kim followed her lead. Libby Van Der Woert did not.

"I'm in a world of trouble, aren't I? I bet you never get in too deep, do you? So deep that it's like you're at the bottom of a dark, empty well with no way up or out?" For an instant that day, it was as if all the fragments of Libby's flighty persona had coalesced and an adult version spoke. There was no whining or petulance in her tone or on her countenance, as she made eye contact with her shields down. Jessica felt moved by the rush of potential oozing from Libby at that moment and she struggled for words to speak that might offer hope. Before she could respond, Kim spoke.

"Of course she does, Ms. Van Der Woert. I was down in that well with her, so I know what you're talking about too. You need someone to throw you a rope—offer you a lifeline, right?" Libby stared at Kim, her eyes lingered on the colorful tattoo that extended beyond the short-sleeved blouse she wore, reaching all the way to the crick in Kim's arm at her elbow.

"They've given me plenty of rope—enough to hang myself, in fact. It's too late for me," she said, giving an imaginary rope around her neck a yank. Jessica went on alert, concerned about the threat that gesture implied.

"I'm sorry, but you're scaring me. Kim's right that there's always a way out. It's never too late to turn your life around. Is there someone I should call to come get you? I don't think you should be alone." That moment of reflection was gone, and a wicked grin stole across Libby's face.

"Who? My friends are few—the ones I haven't killed yet, like poor Lela. Or maybe you mean my parents or another family member? Do you think you can find someone who will have anything to do with me at this point? I'm toxic to three generations of family. My parents have made sure of that. I thought they'd keep this all quiet, like they did with the trouble I've had in the past, but oh no, the word is out. I'm poison."

"How about your lawyer or your therapist—can I call one of them to come and get you?"

"That's unnecessary since I'm on my way to meet with my shrink. Dr. Carr drives all the way out here for appointments with me. How's that for service?"

"I'd like to be sure of that before I let you go." Libby rolled her eyes.

"Oh my God, you have got to be kidding! Why do you care? You want to talk to him? Hang on a second." Libby hit a speed dial button. "Hi, Di... uh, hey Doc, it's me, Libby. Someone wants to talk to you." With that, she shoved the phone into Jessica's hand.

"Uh, hello, Dr. Carr?" Jessica asked. Libby was smiling at her obvious discomfort.

"Yes, this is he. Who's this?"

"It's Jessica Huntington. As you know, I'm the lawyer handling legal matters for Libby's parents."

"Okay, well what can *I* do for *you*, Ms. Huntington?"

"Nothing, Dr. Carr. Not for me, anyway, it's Libby. She seems upset, and I wanted to make sure she had someone to talk to before I let her walk out of here. Libby says you're expecting her. I wanted to make sure that was true."

"Yes, that's true. But, I don't understand. What is she doing with you?"

"Well, I'm still not sure, to be honest. She stopped in here to meet me, she says. Checking me out, isn't that right, Libby? I suppose she'll tell you all about it when she meets with you." Libby nodded in agreement. Jessica felt ridiculous for having been so concerned about the young woman.

"It wasn't a wise idea to meet with Libby alone," the psychiatrist said, sniffing with disregard as he spoke.

Okay, this is odd, Jessica thought. The big red needle on her creep-o-meter was moving. She had imagined the conversation would start with questions about Libby and the reason for Jessica's concern. Had she missed something?

"It's not every day I get legal advice from a psychiatrist, Dr. Carr. Libby and I are *not* alone." There had been a hint of something unpleasant in that admonition from the doctor.

"Oh, is her attorney there? I don't think she mentioned that." Libby hadn't mentioned anything before shoving the phone into Jessica's hands. Jessica was getting annoyed as that red needle bounced around again. She had also tried to decide which was closer, Saks or Escada. It would be simple to get them to call AMEX and get her card number. As the image of that card flashed before her, all the numbers on it stood out. The urge to shop had gone from itch to burn in a moment. *Warning! Time to end this*, Jessica remembered thinking.

"No, her attorney is not here, but my assistant is, and she's recorded the conversation. If you think it would be helpful, clinically, to hear what Libby had to say, I'd be happy to send you a transcript.

Libby would have to sign a release, of course. Look, I don't think we need to go into this further. I presume that you'll follow up if Libby doesn't show up for her scheduled appointment. I'm not sure what Libby had in mind by calling you, but ensuring her well-being was my intent." Libby was twisting a strand of hair again and had that "cat that swallowed the canary" look of satisfaction on her face. Jessica had expected a little yellow feather to pop out of Libby's mouth any second.

"Of course. It's not every day I get clinical advice from a lawyer, but follow up is what I would do for any client who misses an appointment. I appreciate your concern for Libby and I'm sure she does too. Put her back on the phone, please." Dr. Carr had not attempted to hide the sarcasm in his voice when he spat out those words. The red needle on the creep-o-meter was in the warning zone and the alarms in Jessica's head were wailing.

"Yeah, it's me. Uh-huh, sure. Really? Oh, okay. I'll see you in twenty minutes. Bye." Libby ended the call. "Dr. Carr wants me to apologize for scaring you. I didn't mean to. Sorry." She tried, but couldn't quite hide the self-satisfied smirk that tugged at her lips as she issued that apology.

"An apology is unnecessary. But I'll accept it in the spirit in which it you made it," Jessica said, fixing her with a direct gaze. Surprise swept the smirk off Libby's face. Her little bubble of "duper's delight" pierced, Libby went back to indifference.

"Whatever," she said, shrugging her shoulders again as she had done earlier. Her behavior was more like a twelve-year-old than a thirty-year-old, and Jessica flashed for a moment on her poor, disturbed childhood friend, Kelly. At thirty, Libby had managed to outlive Kelly, but she'd left a trail of carnage in her wake.

"I am hoping you'll be okay. Remember, it's never too late to start over. Kim and I have both had to do that. If we can help you figure out how to do it too, we'll try. Come on. We'll walk you out." Jessica was eager to conclude their meeting without further incident. Her heart had skipped a beat and then raced. She hadn't had a full-blown panic attack in weeks. What was it about Libby Van Der Woert that had set off all the alarms? Or were the alarms set off by that slick sounding creep paid to help Libby stay out of trouble?

That afternoon, as soon as the door shut behind Libby, Jessica's head had spun with images of silky, shimmery items for her bedroom she didn't need. She yearned to be surrounded by soft, pure white sheets with sky-high thread counts, and thick, fluffy towels made of Egyptian cotton. The clean fragrance of soaps and sachets would restore hope that there was more to the world than troubled women, destroying themselves and those who loved them.

Between the Sheets, a luxury linen shop, had called to her from two blocks away. Remembering that moment, Jessica reached out with the fingertips on her bandaged hand to touch the duvet cover, plunder from that afternoon when she'd caved in and yielded to the urge to shop. She didn't break her promise to Father Martin. She didn't use her black AMEX card. She used another card, instead.

"Let's go, I need to gaze upon exquisite things. What colors do you use in your boudoir, you two? Don't be shy? It's time for a little retail therapy, Jessica Huntington style." That afternoon, both Kim and Amy had gone along, curious about what Jessica had in mind.

The store did not disappoint. Jessica's heart rate settled down as her eyes roamed the walls lined with colorful folded linens tucked into cubbies that reached for the ceiling. Her breathing came easier as she inhaled the mix of fragrances that filled the scented air. Dazzled by the sparkle and sheen of silks and satins, a glow enveloped her. Then she'd spotted her first "find," a sale sign hovering over the display. Cashmere throws, soft and beguiling, in an array of colors. They would be wonderful as fall slipped into winter. The plush fabric would appeal to her beloved Bernadette, and to her mother; they would make great Christmas gifts. Jessica picked out one in a tawny neutral for her mother, a deep purple for Bernadette, and a copper-colored one for herself. Then she got one for Laura in a sage green.

Amy and Kim had drifted away, roaming among the narrow aisles of the store crammed full of merchandise. Jessica moved to join them as a clerk rushed to her side.

"Can I put these aside for you?" A well-dressed attendant asked.

"Thanks. That would be great!" Jessica said as she let go of the stack of throws, a little reluctant to release them.

"They'll be at the register when you're ready to checkout. Let me know if I can help you with anything else."

"Will do," she replied. Then she went to work.

Jessica joined Kim, who was eyeing a gorgeous duvet in a woven jacquard peacock design. At that point, Kim almost had a heart attack when she glimpsed the price tag.

"Oh no, are you kidding me?" Kim might have been a tad dizzy.

"Do you like it?" Jessica asked. "In a queen-size, right?"

"Yes, that's right! What's not to like? My entire bedroom set cost less than this!"

"But do you like it? It's scrumptious. Would it look good in your room?"

"It would look good in any room. The price is obscene and I..." Jessica interrupted before Kim could finish.

"Then we'll take it. Consider it an early Christmas present," she said as the alert clerk snatched up a packaged version of the comforter. Kim objected, but gave in after Jessica persisted, arguing that this was better than putting her in a position to buy a gift Kim might not like, so she was actually doing Jessica a favor. When the helpful sales woman returned, Jessica made sure she also included sheets and other items designed to coordinate with the duvet. Kim tried to protest again, but to no avail.

"Please, let me do this for you. I owe you my life."

"But you've done so much for me already. I, I..." Kim's eyes had flashed with emotion before she turned away. Jessica reached out and touched her on the shoulder.

"It's about time someone did. You did that nice thing for Libby. Okay?" Kim turned back around and smiled. A real smile, her eyes widening with childlike delight, as the stack of items grew. Jessica continued making her way through items on the shelves and tables in the store, finding more gifts for friends and sumptuous pieces for herself. Each item was a testament to the fact that beauty trumped all the sad squalor she'd just witnessed in the person of Libby Van Der Woert.

"Talk about delusional thinking," Jessica muttered to herself, recalling the logic that had motivated that shopping spree and so many others. "I'm sick, I know it." Still, she had such good feelings about that time spent with Kim and Amy.

Amy, hard at work on her own shopping that day, didn't know Jessica intended to pick up the tab for her items, too. The woman had paid a dear price, already, for getting pulled into Jessica's gravitational field. They hadn't known each other long when Amy became an unwitting victim of the calamity magnet Jessica had become. Libby's intrusion had triggered memories of a previous office invasion that didn't end well. Amy had bounced back right away, but not without a trip to the hospital. They'd even laughed a little, later, about what had gone on that afternoon in July. Jessica had been waiting for an opportunity to acknowledge Amy's pluck and resilience. Still, Amy had protested.

"What on earth are you thinking?"

"Hey, we're sisters in crime at this point. All three of us, in fact," Jessica said. "It's either this, or 'I survived Mr. P.' t-shirts. Bonding over goodies seems better than having to explain that t-shirt to everyone we meet."

"Yeah, what would clients think?" Kim asked. They all had a good laugh at that point.

"You are one-of-a-kind. All I can say is thanks, sister! I didn't have one growing up, so this could be fun."

"Let's hope so. Maybe we should hang a sign on the door, 'mischief free zone' or something like that so we keep the Libby Van Der Woerts of the world out of there from now on. I don't know about you two, but I'm sick and tired of mischief makers."

"I hear you, but we'd also lose at least some of our clients."

"True, mischief or the threat of mischief keeps us in business, doesn't it?"

"And a little mischief isn't always bad." That was Kim putting in her two cents' worth.

"That's a good point. How about we put the loot into our cars and let's go make a little mischief at a happy hour somewhere nearby?"

"On one condition," Amy said. "It's my turn to pick up the tab."

"Deal," Jessica replied.

"Okay, since my capacity for mischief far exceeds my cash reserves," Kim offered, as close to jovial as Jessica had seen her. "I like the sister thing, too," she added shyly. "I don't have a sister, either. With my luck, I would have ended up with one like Libby Van Der Woert. This is much better." Jessica had to agree. Happy families sure seemed to be scarce. She thought about her mother and father,

her own failed marriage, and Bernadette's story about the love of her life lost to a family rift.

"Libby's parents have tried to make their family a happy one. What does it take?" Jessica now asked aloud as she scrawled a few new notes in Libby's file. She still couldn't see how the things that passed between them that day could account for Libby's subsequent change of heart as Carr claimed before shoving them off the mountain. Could Kim's sincerity have touched Libby somehow? How had her shrink settled on murder as the solution to whatever problem Libby posed? He wasn't the only one with Libby's murder on his mind, given that nightmare in the ICU. What is going on? A quiet knock on the door was enough to cause Jessica to jump.

"Are you decent?" Bernadette asked.

"Sure, come on in." The door opened and Bernadette stepped into the room and shut the door behind her.

"Detective Hernandez is here. He wants to talk to you. You want him to go away?"

"Yes, I want him to go away. I'm sure all he wants to do is rant at me, but I'll talk to him."

"He wanted me to tell you that there's stuff you need to know about the guy that tried to get to Libby at the hospital. And, Jessica, they found a body."

15 BISCOCHITO INTERROGATION

"Okay, tell him yes. But can you help me dress so I don't have to meet with him in my bathrobe? I could do it on my own, but that would take me half an hour." Jessica felt her body rev up and prepared for that moment when her heart would leap from her chest. Panic Disorder had been the diagnosis after a series of tests had ruled out other reasons for her symptoms. It wasn't just heart palpitations, but also sweaty palms, trouble breathing, and difficulty swallowing. Today, her body must be low on adrenaline. She regained control before Bernadette exited the room. Jessica needed information from the detective more than she dreaded his scolding or what she might hear.

"I thought you'd need a hand—give me a second. I'll put him in the great room with a cold drink. If we all sit in there, we can prop you up on a couch. With your feet up, it'll be a lot more comfortable. I'll be right back." Bernadette scooted out of the room, hollering as she went.

"Detective..." Jessica didn't even try to hear what followed as Bernadette shut the bedroom door behind her. Jessica climbed out of bed, stood, and removed the sling. As she did that, the chilled pad she had been using on her bruised ribcage dropped to the floor. She shuffled into her enormous walk-in closet, where everything was laid out in perfect order. Gleaming wood drawers with brushed nickel pulls occupied the center of the room. Clothes hung from rods that lined both sides of the room. Shelves held items, like sweaters, that didn't hang well. At the opposite end of the room was a door leading into her bathroom, and a wall of shelves. Those shelves contained shoes and handbags in a sea of neutrals with occasional splashes of color.

Her inner neat-freak basked in the order displayed in that room as her eyes roamed the rows of clothing. As she stepped into her own private cathedral to couture, the cut and color, warp and weave of the fabrics called to her senses. All the polished surfaces and glittery doodads in the room exuded comfort and promise—the world is a silky, satiny, glorious place to be. There were also all the memories that clung to items hanging in that room, like the gorgeous dress worn to that celebration in her father's honor.

Jessica had tried to explain her feelings to Father Martin in yet another of their "to shop or not to shop" discussions. Shopping was an activity she did for fun, alone or with her mother or her friends. It had become an ingrained way to enjoy the world and cope with life.

"People talk a lot about that 'new car smell,' but there's a new clothes smell, too." That hit her now as she luxuriated in that room. "I get a rush from shopping, Father, a pleasant sensation of well-being. I feel alive, and like I have a future, even when it's bleak. I'm in control. Have a baby or stop my husband from lusting after mega-deals and Hollywood blonds, no. Buy a gorgeous duvet, in a slinky imported Italian fabric with a divine cinnamon hue, yes! And on sale, oh my God, that's even better!"

"Oh, come on, you know that's a fleeting effort to find what you're looking for. Well-being? Control? I can't believe an intelligent woman like you is convinced you can have any of that by simply swiping your black AMEX card and walking away with a shopping bag full of stuff. That's just an empty ritual. Nor am I convinced you need physical props to feel better about your life or to recall important events."

"You of all people should understand the value of ritual. Beautiful rituals marking important occasions, are everywhere in the Church. The Mass is largely that, and from what I remember of my Catholic school experience, we celebrated some saint almost every day. What about all the music, art and icons, crucifixes and rosaries? Aren't those props?"

"Yes, all of that's true. In your case, it's a cart before the horse kind of problem. Or maybe it's a cart without a horse problem. You can't put objects ahead of the concepts they should represent. You need a horse—a force to pull you forward or you go nowhere in that cart loaded with stuff. What's the force behind your shopping binges? What do all those objects represent beyond illusions of well-being and control—flashes of life imagined in objects devoid of life? Even more important, you need a direction—a destination and a path to set the horse and the cart upon. As you've learned again and again this year, it's all a lie. The things you buy may give you pleasure, but they don't give you control over your life, nor do they offer you true comfort or safety. That duvet doesn't make you a better person, a truer friend, or bring you closer to understanding the mystery of life. You can't allow rituals, religious or otherwise, to divert you from those larger tasks we face as humans."

She let out a huge sigh, releasing the tension and confusion she always felt after speaking with Father Martin. On some level, she grasped what he was saying—his words spoke to the part of her that kept her going back to see the exasperating priest. On another level, she just didn't get it, or maybe she didn't want to get it. It made her happy to shop—not just for herself, but also for others. She had the money. What was the big deal?

As she dropped the robe, she glimpsed herself in the full-length mirror. A battered wreck stared back at her, in boxer briefs and a sports bra. Her hair in disarray, there were scrapes on her left cheek and a bruise hovered above her left eye. One arm in a cast, the hand on the other arm bandaged, it was easy to believe the unbelievable—that she'd fallen off a mountain and lived to tell about it.

"No shiner, at least," she said aloud, recalling a previous injury courtesy of a lowlife wearing pantyhose on his head. Her left shoulder bore bruises above the cast on her arm, front and back. The worst bruising was around her ribs, dark and ugly. "You are lucky, Chica, just to be alive," she said, pointing at that image in the mirror. Father Martin was correct about the whole control thing being illusory.

"Dios mìo, you can say that again!" Bernadette said as she stepped into the room beside Jessica. "I've got Detective Hernandez all set up in the great room. Let's get you dressed and I'll brush your hair for you. I gave him some lemonade and one of my magazines to read. We have time to do this."

"What to wear with bandages, bruises, and a cast as your accessories? Now that's a fashion challenge, isn't it?" They settled on a loose-fitting pair of yoga pants in a soft knit that didn't bind at the waist. Jessica pulled them on with care, hoping not to jar the ribs too much. Bernadette helped slip a sleeveless tank top over her head without getting it caught on her cast or bandages, and without having her raise her arms too high. Still, she winced as a surge of pain moved from her shoulders to the area around her ribs.

"Thanks," she said as the dear woman helped her put the sling back on without much more pain. "This outfit doesn't hide the bruising. Maybe the detective will figure I've already taken my lumps and will go easy on me. I'm not up for a serious duel with him yet."

"I'm softening him up for you. I gave him cookies to go with his lemonade. Plus, I set a plate out for him to take home along with my recipe for the biscochitos. He ought to be mellow by now. You want me to warn him that if he's mean to you he won't get out of here with those cookies?" She'd put her hands on her hips in a bantam rooster fighting stance.

"Nah, that's okay." She leaned in and gave the woman a peck on the cheek. "Let's go get him." With Bernadette on her side, Jessica felt like she could handle the bull of a man waiting for her.

Great room was the right term for the room in which the detective sat. The heart of the desert modern home in Rancho Mirage, it was a spectacle to behold. Twenty-foot ceilings, with a stacked stone fireplace at one end that ran floor to ceiling. The outer wall of the room was made of glass pocket doors, which could be slid away, opening the entire room to the outdoors. A beautiful patio area off the great room could host large parties, doubling or tripling the capacity that the room itself offered. In front of one set of windows was a well-stocked, step down wet bar, with buttery leather swivel chairs in front of the granite bar that allowed you to gaze out at the beautiful landscape and drink in comfort.

The proportions of the room made the detective look smaller than he was. He also seemed tame, munching cookies and drinking lemonade. Hernandez did a double-take when he saw Jessica.

"How are you, Detective Hernandez?" She asked as she sat down on a plush sofa, bolstered by pillows. Bernadette helped her get as comfortable as she could.

"I'm fine, but I should ask *you* that question. Holy cow, you are a mess."

"Words every woman longs to hear, thanks very much. I've been better. Then again, I could be a lot worse, so I won't complain."

"That's the truth. You are one lucky woman as I have pointed out on other occasions."

Oh no, he's winding up for I told you so mode, Jessica thought. "Hey, I'm being brave, here. Don't I get any pity points for what I've been through?" Before he could say a thing, Bernadette interceded.

"Jessica, I'll go get you some cookies and lemonade. Can I bring you more, Detective?" The petite woman bore down on him with a beatific smile more disarming than her offer of cookies. "We have milk, too, if you'd rather have milk. Or can I bring you fresh coffee to go with the cookies?" Bernadette seemed to float, her feet barely touching the ground, as she radiated good will.

The burly detective, who had leaned forward in his windup with Jessica, sank back into the oversized armchair in which he sat. The rugged, angular features of the detective's face revealed the native Cahuilla in his ancestry, despite his Spanish surname. They softened as the comfortable contours of the chair cradled him. The clever Bernadette had seated Detective Hernandez with a dazzling view of the outdoors from that wall of windows that reached for the blue sky they framed.

"Sure, if you don't mind. Coffee and more cookies would be great."

"I'll go with milk, Bernadette. What's better than milk and cookies when you've got trouble on your plate, already? Am I right, Detective Hernandez?" Jessica asked.

"You're right. I need the coffee so I can keep moving after we're done here. But, in principle, I agree. There's nothing better than milk and cookies. Special cookies, too, like the ones I remember as a kid—and it's not even biscochito season yet. This is a treat."

"I'm glad you like them, Detective. This is my practice batch before I bake for our Cat Pack Christmas party. I have to get to work, soon, if I want to have enough on hand for them. That little group keeps getting bigger. And then there's Brien."

"Brien, you mean your surfer pool boy? He's the one at the hospital that kept asking if he could go eat, right? As I recall, we were still trying to figure out if a bad guy is gunning for you, and he's hungry."

"That would be him, Detective. His mouth is legendary around here. Not just because of the unusual things he utters, at odd, inappropriate times, but also because of the volume of food he can put away."

"Sí, Brien Anthony Williams es un boca grande. Just like a baby bird, 'feed me, cheep-cheep-cheep, feed me, *dude.*' That surfer talk sounds plain loco, half the time. Excuse me, you two. All this talk about milk and cookies makes me want some too. I'll be right back, but wait 'til I get back before you get to the part about the dead body, okay?"

"That part will be quick. We've found the body of a young woman not far from a hiking trail in Cathedral Canyon. The body has been out there for more than a week now, and the coyotes got to her, so to I.D. her we've got to run a DNA check or use dental records. It could be Shannon Donnelly, but we won't know for another day or two." With that, Bernadette crossed herself and then bustled out of the room, muttering. Jessica thought she heard her saying Dios mìo and something about maleantes as she fled. She had heard all she wanted to hear about dead bodies.

"So, before you start the third degree, I should tell you I'm not a hundred percent yet. It's been four days since I fell off a damn mountain. Not only did that scare the bejeebers out of me, it jarred my senses, so I don't know if all my wires are connected like they should be."

"Okay, so what does that mean?" The detective leaned forward a little, scrutinizing her. They had more respect for each other after tangling during two prior murder investigations. Still, they would never be BFFs or anything like that. Jessica feared the detective would pull rank, or start chest-thumping if he didn't like what he heard.

"I guess it means I'd prefer, first, that we keep this low-keyed, if possible, and second, off the record for now. I'm happy to talk to you, but I'm in no shape to swear to anything."

"That's no problem. I'm not here to interrogate you. What *I* want is, *first,* for you to tell me what went on with Libby Van Der Woert, and *second,* any new information she gave you about Shannon

Donnelly. I don't want you to be all dodgy with me—holding your cards close to your chest..."

"Oh, but Detective, she has to keep her arm in the sling," Bernadette said as she scurried back into the room with a tray of refreshments. The air filled with the heavenly aroma of cookies, spices, and fresh brewed coffee, as she set the tray down on the coffee table. Bernadette poured a mug of coffee from the press pot, handing it to the detective. Then she refilled his plate with cookies cut into small fleur-de-lis, star, Christmas tree, and angel shapes.

"What he means, is that he wants me to lay all my cards on the table—tell him everything I know about Libby Van Der Woert, Dr. Richard Carr, and Shannon Donnelly."

"But you told him you don't have a full deck, right?" Detective Hernandez, who was scarfing down cookies still warm from the oven, about did a spit take. He took a swig of coffee to wash down the cookies and then smiled.

"That didn't come out so good, did it?" Bernadette asked as she held out a plate of cookies so Jessica could grab one. She put a little plate of cookies on a folding table next to Jessica, along with a glass of milk. Then Bernadette sat down nearby with her own cookies and milk.

"No, it did not. My deck is full, I'm just not sure, yet, what hand I'm holding. Since I'm rattled, and still can't think straight, I don't know how smart it is to make a play at this point. I have clients to protect, too—not Libby, but her parents. So, it's a little tricky, Detective Hernandez."

"Tricky is the way most cases go. Let's try doing this your way—low-keyed and off the record and see what that gets us." Bernadette's cookies and fresh coffee were working their magic. The man was almost jovial. "I'll go first and put my cards out there, off the record, too."

"Sounds good," she agreed, while Bernadette nodded, assuming she was along for the ride.

"As you already know, Shannon Donnelly's car was found in a parking lot near the IMAX in Cathedral City. A security patrol called it in Sunday morning, Thanksgiving weekend. Nobody was sure how long it had been there, but those patrols are done regularly. The guard thought he'd seen it the day before, in the same spot. That's what caught his attention. When he got out of his car and looked closer, he thought he saw streaks of blood on the front seat so he called us. The responding officers confirmed it was blood and cordoned off the area until we could get CSIs out there. By the time I got to the scene, they'd run the plates and determined that the car belonged to Shannon Donnelly. It was a late model Lexus sedan without a mark on its exterior, so no sign that anyone had tried to break into the car. The investigators did a preliminary search of the car. They bagged and tagged several items scattered about on the floor of the car on the passenger side. There was blood on the steering wheel, driver's seat, armrest, and several other areas. Not a huge amount, but enough to suspect that something might have happened to the driver. I had the car towed back to the lab in Indio so the CSIs could work it over. The CSIs found little else at the scene except for several small drops of blood leading away from the car, and an earring, later identified as one belonging to Shannon Donnelly." The detective paused for a moment to have another swig of coffee. "I told you most of this already."

"Yes, you did, when you came to ask Libby's parents about their daughter. You left out the technical details about the evidence you collected. I presume that's how you connected Libby to Shannon and the car. You found her fingerprints and DNA in the car, correct?"

"Yes, that's true. We also found a receipt and other items that belonged to Libby. According to a theater attendant, they had been to a movie Friday night. The two women were a 'couple of hotties,' in the words of the teenaged lothario I spoke to. Memorable later at the restaurant too, not just for their good looks, but because they polished off two bottles of expensive wine and tipped everybody well that night. The time stamp on that receipt says they left the restaurant after midnight when the place closed. If they walked back to Donnelly's car, still parked near the theater, that wouldn't have taken more than a few minutes. No one reported hearing or seeing anything of concern that night, so it doesn't sound like there was a big brawl or noisy confrontation. The last show at the theater was over a little *before* midnight, so most theater goers would have left before our hotties got back to that Lexus. We know they got that far because that receipt was *inside* the car. After that, our story ends and the trail goes cold." Detective Hernandez paused, staring off into space for a moment while he chomped on another cookie, wiping his hands on the napkin Bernadette had provided. "You know what I remember about that meeting with you and Libby's parents?"

"No. What?" Jessica was savoring the crisp cookies laced with cinnamon and anise, countering the apprehension she felt as he asked that question. So far, this was about the least painful episode of interrogation she had ever undergone.

"Besides my surprise at finding you tied to what might be another homicide in my jurisdiction—that would be three for three in 2013, I should add. What I remember most is a sinking look on all your faces. Still, you all hardly flinched at the idea that Libby Van Der Woert was a person of interest, witness, or suspect, to a possible kidnapping, murder, or some other heinous crime."

"Well, that's presuming that Shannon Donnelly is dead, or a victim of foul play, rather than missing because she's a flake like her friend, Libby. Let's wait until you're sure you have her body before you tell me I'm batting a thousand for murders in Cathedral City."

"Fair enough. Maybe it'll turn out that the body we found belongs to some other woman. Could be Donnelly was snatched in Cat City and isn't dead yet, or she's dead and her body's been dumped somewhere else. Not that you haven't stumbled into homicides elsewhere in our fair valley. In any case, if Donnelly's on the run, she's keeping a low profile. There's been no word from her since that night. No activity on her credit card, no ATM withdrawals, no phone calls, nothing. I don't get her, or Libby Van Der Woert."

"Neither do I, Detective. I can't go into all the problems their daughter has presented for the Van Der Woerts, but there have been many. That's besides the incidents on record that explain why you found her fingerprints and DNA already on file. I'm not a shrink, so I can't put this in technical terms, but I think it's safe to say that neither woman is too tightly-wrapped. That her friend, Shannon, has run off isn't too far-fetched, given she may not be in much better psychological shape than Libby is."

"That means *alrededor de la curva*," Bernadette added, making the little circular motions you might expect to go with the "round the bend" pronouncement she'd made.

"Yes, I understand. That Libby's parents have been round the bend with her was clear from that meeting with them. The Donnelly woman's parents reacted much the same way—upset, but almost too weary and worn out to get worked up about the fact that their daughter is missing, maybe injured or dead. What is it about these 90210 Beverly Hills rich girls? Why can't they at least keep it in their own zip code?" Detective Hernandez stared out the window, unable to hide his dismay.

"I can understand your frustration. Their lives make no sense. You must know more about what was going on with Shannon Donnelly than I do. With Libby, it's been one thing after another since she was a teenager. What did Libby tell you about that night when you caught up with her?"

"Friends told us the two roomies had left town together, for a vacation in the desert. So even if we hadn't found those items from Libby's purse in Donnelly's car, we would have picked her up for questioning. It took a day to track Libby down. The credit card number on that receipt led us to one of your favorite haunts, Jessica—the La Quinta Resort. When we located Libby, poolside, she said she hadn't seen Donnelly since their dinner ended Friday night. We asked her why she hadn't reported her missing when she failed to return to the bungalow they shared and Libby said she figured Shannon had met someone. At first, Libby claimed she and Donnelly had parted ways outside the restaurant. Libby wanted to go back to her bungalow and call it a night, but Donnelly wanted to go clubbing downtown. When they couldn't agree, Donnelly stomped off to her car and Libby Van Der Woert called a cab. We asked her what cab company she called so we could confirm her story. Libby couldn't remember, nor could she remember if she'd paid with cash or a credit card. She admitted they were tipsy that night as she started down the 'I don't recall' road. The tipsy part I find easy to believe. Drunk enough to have memory loss, I doubt it. At that point, we decided it was time to move our discussion to a more formal setting." The detective shook his head, draining his cup of coffee. Bernadette popped up, as if she was on springs, and refilled the detective's cup from the press pot.

"Thanks, fantastic coffee. You're spoiling me." Bernadette put more cookies on his plate even though he still had a couple left. She gave Jessica a little wink when she turned away from the detective. Jessica shoveled the last of her cookies into her mouth, then held out her empty plate, using her best Oliver Twist begging waif look.

"More please," she said in a voice muffled by the cookies in her mouth. Bernadette, not taken in by the waif bit, shook her head. She distributed the last of the cookies on the tray, dividing them between Jessica and herself. *Who needs Brien,* Jessica thought as she grabbed for another cookie. The detective must have thought she'd directed that "more please" at him. He put down the cookie he was about to shove into his mouth and picked up his story.

"At that point, we made Libby go to her bungalow and get dressed. I thought a ride in the back of a police car, and hanging out with us for a while, might help jar her memory. Our clientele and accommodations are a far cry from those at the resort. But she was more than just nonchalant about it all. In fact, she vamped it up, cooing and flirting with the officers on duty, acting like she was enjoying it! Loco sounds about right, Bernadette. She reminded me of the younger sister in that Big Sleep film, starring Bogey and Bacall. You know the blond with a demented smile who threw herself at Philip Marlowe?"

"I know who you mean," said Jessica. "The Raymond Chandler story is a favorite. That is an apt comparison to Libby, who is mercurial and inappropriate much of the time."

"That's for sure. When we showed her that receipt, and the lipstick and other items we had retrieved from the floor of Donnelly's car on the passenger side, she snapped out of it and lawyered up." He ate another cookie as he pondered what he had seen.

"We put her in a holding tank while she waited. I couldn't have been more shocked when her LA lawyer showed up. The guy was unkempt, like he'd been on a weekend bender or was sleeping in his car. He wore a cheap, wrinkled suit over a rumpled shirt. His tie was crooked, he hadn't shaved, and he had an old pair of Nikes on his feet. Not the wing-tip, Brooks Brothers, manicured attorney I expected. I remember wondering at the time: *what is Miss Gucci two shoes doing with this guy?*" He looked at Jessica, perhaps concerned that his next remarks might offend.

"He's the epitome of an ambulance chaser, in my mind anyway. Hell, I wasn't even convinced he was a lawyer, so I ran a check. Ambulance chaser is right! He handles accident claims: fender-benders, slip and falls at grocery stores and mega-malls, claims about ugly things found in your soup, and other things like that. From what

I can tell, he's not even good at that. A lot of complaints are on file about the guy, and there's a citation against him for letting his malpractice insurance lapse. You know, a scraping the bottom-of-the-barrel kind of lawyer, in my book, anyway?"

"That sounds about right. The woman has run through several like him during the past few months. They take their fee, have a look at the suit she keeps threatening to file against her parents, and then run for the hills. Did you get a name?"

"Harvey Burgess or something like that. I'm not sure now."

"That's a familiar name. I've had a communique or two from him. Nothing to do with Donnelly, but I'll tell you more when it's my turn. So, what happened when he showed up?"

"After conferring with Burgess, she gave us a formal statement. She and Donnelly were two girlfriends on vacation. They had gone out to a movie and dinner that night. Outside the restaurant on the way back to the car, they had a dispute about who would drive the car. Libby said she's had enough trouble and would not risk a DUI. She suggested they call a cab, but Shannon didn't want to leave her fancy car there overnight. So, Libby claims she called a cab for herself. She spilled the contents of her purse when she dug out a credit card to pay for the ride back to La Quinta. We've verified that she did that about half an hour after they paid for dinner. The cab driver said the two women were in the middle of a dispute when he arrived a while later to pick Libby up. He confirmed that he dropped Libby back at her bungalow a little before two a.m. and that her companion was sitting in the driver's seat, very much alive when he drove away from that parking lot."

"Okay, so you're wondering why she lied to you about what they quarreled about that night, right?"

"Yeah, that's one thing that bothers me. It seems odd, too, that she wasn't more worried when her friend didn't come home later. She didn't want to ride in the same car with her because she'd had too much to drink. Don't you think she might have worried Shannon had an accident when she didn't show up the next day? Not that I should be surprised. When I spoke to Libby's parents, I was trying to get a handle on what kind of person she might be. You all said little. You didn't have to. Between the tension in the room, and the public information about her, it's clear that the woman is capable of wrongdoing, maybe even murdering her friend."

"I have no doubt she lied to you. Who knows why, since she lies even when she doesn't even have to. I won't disagree with your conclusion about her propensity for wrongdoing, but I'm not sure that includes murder. Besides, the cab driver saw the woman alive so Donnelly couldn't have been injured at that point, at least not too bad, right?"

"Yes, that's true."

"Did you ask Libby about the blood?"

"We did. She had a story for that, too. According to Libby, her friend took a spill on the way back to the car. Donnelly took a misstep and fell off the curb in six-inch gold snake heels whatever those are. She gave us some Italian designer name."

"Ooh, yeah, Detective. Giuseppe Zanotti—they're gorgeous, but I'm getting dizzy just thinking about wearing them. If she'd had a lot to drink, that could have happened."

"Well, I don't know why you women like to walk around on stilts. That can't be comfortable or safe under the best conditions, much less when you're drinking. Not only that, but paying a couple hundred bucks for the privilege."

"Don't look at me. I'm short, and I'm fine with it. Who wants to spend that much money just to have farther to fall?" Bernadette asked.

"Sorry, you two, but it's more like a couple grand, if you're talking about the shoes I think you're describing."

"Whew, now I'm getting dizzy. It's good to have a trust fund, I guess."

"I suppose Shannon Donnelly's parents told you she has a trust fund? Or did you find that out some other way?"

"We did both—asked the stressed-out parents how their daughter was making a go of it, *and* we ran a check. The woman was sitting pretty, that's for sure. When she turned thirty, she came into a big chunk of change put away for her by her grandmother and held in trust by her parents. That wasn't more than a few months ago. Kind of surprising that her parents hadn't heard from her in weeks, given they had doled out a legacy like that. You'd think she'd feel an obligation to stay in touch, wouldn't you?"

"What did her parents say about that?"

"Not much. 'You don't know our daughter.' I've never seen two more despondent parents, except maybe your clients. Okay, so at this point I'm still inclined to believe that one Beverly Hills mean girl did something nasty to the other Beverly Hills mean girl."

"You can tell from the encounters you've had with Libby that her thinking is disorganized. Given what you know about events that night, it doesn't seem likely she went back to kill her friend. There's nothing on Libby's credit card about another cab ride that night, true?"

"True."

"I take it Libby claims the blood at the scene was from an injury Shannon sustained when she fell."

"Yeah, Libby says Donnelly banged up her knee, and cut her hand."

"If that's what happened, there should have been blood near the restaurant and drops leading back to the car."

"Also, true. All we found were those smears inside the car and drops leading away from the car, toward the IMAX theater. To another car, perhaps, since there were only a few drops before they stopped."

"Okay, so it sounds like Libby was lying about the blood. I'm sure you checked the phone records by now. Did Shannon call a cab? Did she or Libby make any other phone calls that night?"

"As a matter of fact, they did. No more cabs. You'll love this, though. Both women called the late Dr. Carr."

"No way!" Bernadette gasped. "Why would they call him?"

"Here's the deal, he was treating both women," he said, waiting for Jessica to respond.

"I found that out from Libby and Dr. Carr," Jessica said. "Please go on."

"When we interviewed Carr a few days ago, he was cool about it. He said it's not unusual for his clients to call when they're in crisis. Libby and Shannon had a fight that night. It got them riled up, and they both called him. I asked what the fight was about, but he said that was a privileged communication."

"Dios mìo, it was after midnight, sì?"

"Yep. I thought that was fishy, too. Both women called him minutes apart, using his private cell phone number. He made light of it, claimed that kind of access is what the 90210 crowd expects. Don't shrinks have a service to screen their calls, or an emergency number for clients to call after a certain time?"

"That is correct. I thought it was odd Libby direct-dialed the guy when she came to my office back in November, not long before her friend disappeared. She had the guy on speed dial and he picked up right away then, too. I think I know why."

"Okay, it's your turn."

16 A TANGLED WEB

More than an hour with Detective Hernandez had left Jessica wrung out. It could have been so much worse if Bernadette hadn't put the guy into a cookie stupor. At least it was over, for the time being. He'd listened as she described what went on that afternoon at the tramway. Not involved in that investigation, his main interest was in hearing what Jessica had learned from Libby about Shannon Donnelly.

"Okay, I will try to put this latest episode with Libby in context, from my point of view. I'll summarize my involvement and intentions as best I can. What I'm about to tell you may lead you to a very different conclusion about what's happened to Shannon Donnelly."

"Sure, Counselor, sounds like I'm about to hear your opening argument."

"My bottom line, anyway. My team and I have been investigating Libby over the past several months because of recent problems with her parents. There is a tie-in between those troubles and Dr. Richard Carr. We ran a check on him, like you did on Libby's lawyer, to make sure he was legit. Turns out, he's for real. Not a stellar background, he's a diploma mill grad, old school training from decades ago. He is credentialed, though, and his license and insurance were up-to-date. His private practice in Beverly Hills is at a pricey location and he charges a three-hundred-dollar hourly rate to make ends meet. He's got a fancy car, almost new, and an expensive house he bought years ago in Pacific Palisades. Like a lot of psychiatrists, he has a hand in places all over So-Cal—hospitals, clinics, schools, even some private corporations where he provides training and consultation."

"I get the hospital and clinics, schools even, but what's the tie-in to corporations?"

"He has a certification in crisis intervention—like schools, corporations keep guys like him in the wings to step in if there's an incident. Everybody's on alert about workplace violence, so he's paid to consult. You know, how to identify and deal with disgruntled employees? He provides formal psychiatric screening through an Employee Assistance Program or as executive development or something like that, for upper management."

"Got it, the same supports are available for first responders. So, did you find anything that made you think he's a crook?"

"Not a thing. Except that all that extra work stopped not long ago," she said.

"Geez, then what was all that big wind up about?" The detective leaned forward, his eyes moving from Jessica to Bernadette and back to Jessica.

"Why give up a steady income unless he has a more lucrative source? I'm convinced Libby Van Der Woert is caught up in some scam involving Carr. Not all the features of the scam are clear yet, but Carr despised the spoiled, not-too-tightly-wrapped, rich girls in his practice, like Libby Van Der Woert *and* Shannon Donnelly. In his sermon on the mountain, Carr claimed they were easy to manipulate."

"Okay, what does that mean?"

"Manipulate is an interesting choice of words for a psychiatrist to use don't you think?" Before he could answer, she moved on.

"When Libby Van Der Woert popped into my office, for no apparent reason other than to check me out, she got riled up by the time our meeting was over. I wanted to call somebody to come get her. Who does she suggest? Her shrink! She had Carr on speed dial and he picked up right away. Like he did that night when both women called him from Cat City after midnight. I don't know about you, but I don't get that kind of service from anyone except Peter and that's because he's a friend, not just a service provider. That's how I have a direct dial number for his cell."

"Yeah, and your friend Peter knows a call on his direct line means you're up to your nosy neck in trouble so he'd better pick up, quick."

"Not true; okay, well, sometimes true. But mostly when I call Peter on his cell, I'm inviting him over here for dinner, or something like that—personal, not business. Jerry and Tommy checked, and Carr doesn't have an office here in the desert, so meeting Libby for therapy in the desert, as she claimed, was odd."

"Okay, okay, are you saying Carr and the Van Der Woert woman had something going on besides therapy?"

"That's what Libby said at the top of the tram. A client-with-benefits arrangement, although Libby thought it was love. And, she may not have been the only one."

"Does that mean Shannon Donnelly, too?"

"Could be. That would explain the late-night calls to Carr from both women, right before Donnelly went missing. Libby was all over the place up there, loose and paranoid. She swore someone was after her. I wrote it off to disordered thinking until Carr showed up toting a gun."

"Why the gun? Was she was threatening to rat him out about the affair? How bad could that get for the guy?"

"Libby may well have been threatening him. I don't like dwelling on what it might be, but Libby says she can prove she and Carr knew each other in the Biblical sense. Somebody needs to get a warrant to search Libby's condo for a little blue bag or suitcase where she's got the evidence stashed away. I agree that an affair doesn't warrant murder. If there was more than one indiscretion on Carr's part—and with Donnelly too—that might make the licensure board's sanctions more serious. But a reason to kill Libby? I'm dubious."

"I've seen dumber reasons to kill somebody, I guess," the detective commented.

"You might try talking to that skanky lawyer of hers. He'll hide behind lawyer-client privilege, but it's possible Libby was threatening to take Carr to court. Perhaps sue him for damages because of his breach of professionalism. That's pure speculation, but it could have caused more of a stink than filing a complaint against him with some board. Heck, Carr's malpractice insurance fees might even have gone up if they had to defend him in court. Still, it's hard to believe that would drive him to commit murder and why would Carr want to kill me?"

"Could be you were in the wrong place at the wrong time, courtesy of the kismet you love so much."

"I knew you'd get around to the curse of kismet somehow. What if Libby and Shannon were on to Carr's scheme and planning to 'out' him?"

"What kind of scheme?"

"Extortion, wrapped in a layer of psychobabble about abuse. I'll remind you that this is off the record, and I won't go into all the disgusting details. With her psychiatrist's backing, Libby went after family members with allegations of childhood sexual abuse. Then she tried to shake down her parents for hush money. At the top of the tram, Libby admitted the allegations were false, and claimed the good doctor came up with the idea to demand money. Murder makes more sense if he was trying to avoid criminal charges."

"It does," Detective Hernandez said.

"Worse for Carr if he was behind Shannon's disappearance. Too bad Libby wasn't more direct. She took responsibility, claiming Shannon's gone because she told Carr her friend planned to squeal on him. Tell what to whom? I don't know. More important now is that Libby said she told '*them*' about Shannon's plans. A conspiracy sounded like paranoia until that incident in the ICU. It might have been more believable, too, if Libby hadn't raved about a 'red devil' being behind it all."

"Ay, Dios mìo," Bernadette gasped, making the sign of the cross as Jessica uttered those words.

"That sounds out there, all right. A blue suitcase and a red devil, okay." He was shaking his head.

"But there must be more going on, Detective. The head-shrinker is dead, so who is trying to make sure Libby gets to meet up with him so soon? It must be important, too, to be stampeding the hospital *como un elefante en una cristaleria*," Bernadette said, making stomping motions with her feet.

"Libby's given us plenty of reason not to believe a word she says, but Bernadette's asking the right question," Jessica said. Bernadette nodded in solemn agreement.

"More than you know," the detective said. He was leaning forward, staring into the cup of coffee he held in both hands. "It turns out the guy who came after Libby was a pro. The Palm Springs PD identified him right away after that crash and burn incident on Ramon road. Don't ask me how, but they got prints off the guy. He popped up in the system, with half a dozen aliases and wanted for questioning in a homicide-for-hire case. With a resume like his, it's reasonable to assume someone paid him to take out Libby Van Der Woert. She must know something someone doesn't want her to share. It's got to be more than the contents of that little blue suitcase, because the guy she could hurt with that evidence is dead. So, yes, who wants Libby dead is the right question, Bernadette."

"Right question, but not a good one, is it?" Bernadette asked with apprehension.

"No. Not a good one at all. There's more. The 'accident' that took out Libby's would-be assassin wasn't an accident at all. They've gone over the footage from the chase and there's a flash, as someone took a shot at the speeding car. Some shot, too! It hit a tire that triggered the wreck."

"No!" Jessica and Bernadette cried out in tandem.

"Yes! It's clear Libby's in way over her head. Whatever was going on with Carr and Donnelly and an unknown co-conspirator— more likely human than a devil—does not get the woman off the hook. If even part of what you're saying turns out to be true, it points to a motive for Libby to be a murderer. In her twisted mind, she had plenty of reason to kill Donnelly *and* Carr if the doctor was fooling around with her friend. I'll go back to Donnelly's poor parents and ask if their precious daughter was extorting them. Who wants Libby dead is another matter. Whatever the motive, you're right, too, that he's in a hurry to get the job done. He's got money to hire a pro, too. Could be, if he was Carr's partner in that extortion racket, it has paid well. Anyway, it's time to sit back and count your blessings, Jessica. You're still alive. That could be more miraculous than we know, depending on what Libby's mixed up in. Oh, what a tangled web we weave..." he said as he sauntered out the door, a plate of biscochitos and the recipe in hand.

"He's right about a tangled web." Jessica said, dragging herself off the couch. It was time to shower and dress for her doctor's appointment.

"Maybe for Libby, but it's not like you were her lawyer. I don't see why anyone would have it in for you."

"Except that my name is splashed all over the media right along with hers. Carr blamed me for some change of heart on Libby's part. Maybe his colleagues do too. Or maybe Carr thought Libby told me too much about whatever the hell is going on, including Shannon's murder." Jessica had wandered down the hallway to her bedroom, with Bernadette at her heels.

"Un momento," Bernadette ordered, taking charge. She pulled out a small pair of scissors from a pocket, clipped the tape and removed the bandage on Jessica's right hand. "Mira, Chica, mejor, si?"

"Sí, mucho mejor," Jessica agreed. Her palm was much better. The slash, closed with surgical glue, was a tidy line. Darker than the original lifeline on her palm it crossed, a reminder of how close she had come to ending her life altogether.

"Here," Bernadette said, shoving a plastic bag into Jessica's hand for her cast. Then Jessica slipped out of the sling, with Bernadette's help. "You'll feel better after you shower. Holler if you get stuck," she said as she dashed from the room.

"I'm just going to climb back into bed and forget about all of this," Jessica said taking a step toward her unmade bed. The soft sheets and silky duvet called to her.

"Oh no you don't," Bernadette hollered from down the hall. "Get crackling!"

"Cracking, Bernadette, get cracking," she hollered to her.

"That's what I said. Call Peter and get a shower! I'm fixing us a salad." Full of biscochitos, Jessica didn't see how she could eat a salad, but Bernadette was too far away to hear her objections and she wouldn't have listened anyway. Jessica pulled out her cell phone and confirmed that she had an escort for the short jaunt to the medical center. It was reassuring to talk to Peter. He and his crew had skills, too. If anyone could keep a sniper from shooting out the tires on the huge Escalade that the petite Bernadette would drive, it would be Peter and his team.

The shower was wonderful, except the part where she had to raise an arm over her head to shampoo her hair. Her ribs objected, so she did the minimum to mix the shampoo through her hair. Bending over to scrub her legs and feet was out too. She just stood there letting the water blast away from all eight sprayers set on gentle, aiming at her from different points in the enormous shower. It cleared her head. While she was at the medical center, she would pay a visit to the ICU. Maybe Libby was coming around and had more to say that might help make sense out of this mess. At the least, she could find out when, and if, Libby would ever have more to say about anything.

17 THOR AND UBER-THOR

Jessica's trip to the medical center brought good news and bad news. A quick x-ray revealed her broken arm was on the mend. The swelling around her shoulder joint was almost gone, and the bruising around her ribs was better too. She left with a new sling, a small band aid on the injured right hand, and a prescription for more pain pills.

"As long as I'm careful, Dr. Ziegler, I can get through the day with aspirin and use the pain pills to sleep at night."

"That's great. You're young and a fast healer, but there's no reason to play the martyr. If you need the pills use them."

"I hear you," was what she said. "*No way in hell*," was what she thought. That set off a flurry of worry about her mother. How was she doing in that Malibu treatment facility? Could they help her? How uncomfortable was she in detox, given the mix of drugs and alcohol she'd given up? It would be another day before Jessica could call or visit. Good news from her doctor meant a road trip was in her future. Saturday or Sunday she was Malibu bound!

The first bout of bad news came even before Jessica could report the good news about her checkup to Bernadette. When Jessica returned to the waiting room where Bernadette sat, a woman approached.

"Hey, aren't you the one who fell off Mt. San Jacinto? Earl, get over here, quick," she said to an older man sitting in the corner staring at the television. He didn't look like he was going anywhere.

"Earl, it's her I told you. It's the angel heiress. Can I get your autograph? Hang on a minute. Let me get a pen and paper." Jessica didn't know what to say. Two women sitting in another corner of the waiting room whispered to each other.

"Can you give me a hand here, Earl? I need a pen." Earl took his eyes off the TV for a second and clapped a few times. "That's not funny, Earl." Then, with a burst of speed, she took off and knocked on the nurse's window. "Can I borrow a pen, please? It's the angel heiress. I want her to sign something for me. Thanks!" She grabbed the pen and dashed back over to where Jessica had stepped closer to the exit, motioning for Bernadette to follow. Bernadette stood up, but couldn't hide her amusement at Jessica's plight.

"It is you, isn't it?" The woman asked. *How on earth did you respond to a question like that?* Jessica wondered as she decided the simplest thing was to keep mum and oblige the request. Jessica accepted the pen the woman offered her. Writing would be no problem now without the cumbersome bandage on her hand. What the heck was she supposed to do? Sign it, like it was a receipt? Jessica must have looked as flummoxed as she felt.

"Just say, 'To Ellie, with blessings,' E-L-L-I-E, and sign your name. Your full name," she said. "Oh, and add, 'angel heiress,' okay?" Jessica did as she asked. Ellie ripped the top page from the notepad.

"This one is for Earl," Ellie said. "That's E-A-R-L." While Jessica scrawled, *To Earl with blessings, Jessica Huntington,* on a new sheet of paper, Ellie perused Jessica's handiwork on the first. Writing with that pen had been harder than Jessica expected.

"You're not good at this, are you?" She asked. "You sure you're you?"

"Oh, I'm me," Jessica responded. *Who else could get into a situation like this in the playground of presidents, moguls, and movie stars?* At the moment, the Coachella Valley, known for being rather nonchalant about celebrities, was not living up to its reputation. Bernadette looked at the floor. Jessica hoped she was looking for a place where the carpet was loose enough that Jessica could crawl under it. That wasn't likely, since Bernadette was laughing.

"Well, I could get more on eBay for it if it was neater. Oh well, let me see the one for Earl," Ellie clucked as she looked at Jessica's second attempt. She pushed it back toward Jessica and shook her head in disdain.

"You forgot 'angel heiress.' That's the best part! Just put it in right there," she said, pointing to the spot where she wanted it. Earl had stirred. The guy had to be in his eighties, and was making his way to Ellie's side, using his walker.

The two whispering women in the corner rose to their feet. One held a magazine she'd picked up off the table near her seat. The other was digging through her purse and came out with a notepad of her own. They headed Jessica's way, pens at the ready.

A flash went off. Another patient-in-waiting must have decided a photo would be a better memento of the occasion than an autograph. Several others, still seated in the crowded room, whipped out smart phones and took photos or video.

"Are you really an heiress?" someone asked from behind Jessica. She jumped out of her skin. Her ribs made her pay. Her heart raced as the person behind her reached out and rubbed her cast as if it was a genie's lamp. A line had formed. No, it was more a ring than a line, and they were closing in on her, walkers and all. *They don't call Palm Springs God's waiting room for nothing*, she thought, as a horde of octogenarians descended upon her. An orthopedics waiting room in the Palms Springs area was a foyer to the pearly gates.

Jessica glanced again at Bernadette. Her eyes were still downcast, and her shoulders shimmied with laughter! Jessica tried to sign the things being shoved her way. There had to be a dozen people around her now, and another half dozen ambling her way.

"She saved that other girl. She's an heiress, all right, and *an angel*," someone else said, reaching out. This one did a little knock-knock on Jessica's cast. "That's for luck," the smiling cast-knocker said. "It's a miracle she's alive," the cast-knocker asserted. "You're lucky you're not dead, aren't you?" Jessica had no time to reply.

"You're right, she has to be an angel," another member of the crowd added as she moved a step closer to Jessica. The entire crowd was closing in around her, the circle growing smaller.

"If she's an angel, she's an awful foxy one. Sign this, baby," a young man said, as he approached her with his shirt raised and his abs exposed. Not bad, but no way was she going to sign his exposed six pack.

"Bernadette, we have an appointment elsewhere, do we not?" Jessica asked.

"*Do we not?* Will you listen to that? That's rich woman talk if I ever heard it," someone hooted.

"That proves the *heiress* part," another said, "that's the money talking."

"Cordelia Watson," a nurse announced, calling the next person to the back for her appointment. "What is going on out here?" The nurse asked, as she stepped into the fray. Answers came in a jumble as the level of noise increased. Jessica used the momentary distraction, by the nurse, to slip through an opening and step toward the door. That drew fire from the crowd.

"Hey, she's trying to leave without giving us her autograph," one member complained.

"She has an *appointment elsewhere*," another mocked. Bernadette had stopped laughing.

"And is there a problem with that?" The crowd went silent as that question boomed above the hubbub. Peter stood in the doorway, hands on his hips. Like the jolly green giant, only not green and not jolly. That flash went off again, along with the clicks of smart phones snapping photos.

"Are you ready to go, Ms. Huntington? We're running behind schedule," he said, glaring at the crowd as he stepped aside so she could pass.

"It's Thor and Uber-Thor," someone in the crowd snickered. Right behind Peter was Brien, his shock of surfer-boy blond hair a striking contrast to the black t-shirt he wore, plastered over bulging muscles. He and Peter were quite the pair in their look-alike security-company clothing.

"Shut up, you idiot. Either one of them could snap your scrawny neck like a toothpick." Murmurs of "bodyguards" passed through the crowd as they all left.

"Ready to get out of here?" Peter inquired as they headed down the hall leading away from the waiting room crowd. She could hear the cry of the nurse trying to restore order.

"Hope this doesn't get back to Nurse Andrews," Jessica sniffed with indignation. "I am *so* ready, Peter, but I'd like to stop by the ICU. Just for a moment. Is there a quick way to get there from here?"

"Follow me. Put your sunglasses on. Maybe that'll keep people from recognizing you. No more of that fan club stuff today," Bernadette said as she made a right turn toward a bank of elevators.

"More like angry villagers who've got the monster cornered— smart phones instead of torches," Jessica sputtered as she put on a pair of sunglasses she found in a pocket of her purse. "I have to give Cassie credit for putting up with that all the time."

"Here, use this, too," Peter added, handing her his baseball cap to put on.

"How did you know I was in trouble?" Peter held up fingers, one at a time.

"One, the body count of dead and wounded has climbed. Two, you've added bandages to your attire, and three, there are bad guys running around with guns and we're back at the scene of a crime. I wouldn't leave you alone for long." He did that smiling thing that never worked for him. The grin faded and grim-faced Peter returned. Jessica relaxed.

"After what went on in this hospital, I never should have let you two come up here alone. At least not without checking it out first. If Brien hadn't been running his mouth, that might have dawned on me sooner."

"What do you mean?" Brien asked as they sped off after Bernadette, who was on the move.

"What I mean is that it's been 'dude' this and 'dude' that since you got in the car this morning. That's in between the pleas for food, every hour on the hour, like a baby. At least when you're shoving food in your mouth, I get a few minutes of quiet. Except for the slurping and the smacking, that is. Something happens to my brain. To tune you out, I've got to shut down critical faculties. Not good."

"Tune me out? Why?" Brien did a little quick step to keep up with Peter's longer stride. It was like watching a Chester and Spike cartoon, with Brien the little dog moving from one side to the other of the big dog, Peter. Jessica expected big dog to reach out and smack little dog at any second. Brien was going on and on about how he was doing everything Peter asked, and he couldn't help it if he got hungry, and they had to go get coffee anyway. "You drink a lot of coffee, even for a humongous guy, Dude," he said.

"Not that much, *Dude*. Anyway, I've got to have a lot of caffeine to keep up with your mouth." The ping of the elevator stopped the conversation for a moment as they all filed in.

"That's bogus. I feel all this pressure, Man, to keep up the conversation. You go all dodgy on me. Like, 'ooh, I'm a secret agent. I know plenty, but I'm not talking,' or something like that."

"Yeah, so what's your point?"

"How am I going to learn all that secret stuff if you don't teach me?"

"You're in training to do security, not spy work."

"What's the difference if you don't teach me any of it anyway?"

"Lesson one: look and listen," Peter said, pointing two fingers at his eyes then at Brien, and then tugging at his ear. Lesson two: "Zip it," he said making a zipping motion across his lips.

Jessica coughed a time or two to stifle her laughter. That hurt, but laughing at the interaction between the two men would have hurt more than the little fake cough. She wasn't sure she should encourage the sniping anyway.

"Bastante! Is this what you two do in the car all day? You seem to have plenty to say, Peter. Just what are you trying to teach Brien? How to talk the bad guys into giving themselves up? Take them on one of those ride-alongs and I'll bet they'll confess to anything in no time. Ay yi yi," Bernadette said, staring up at the two men and shaking her head.

Brien and Peter stopped speaking at her command. They both looked at her with the same quizzical expression on their faces.

"What do you mean?" Thor and Uber-Thor asked, almost in unison. That was it! Jessica lost it and burst out laughing.

"Oh ow, ow. Stop it, all of you before I've got to check myself back in here. The nursing staff won't like that one bit. Please, I can't breathe and it hurts. Oh, stop, please." Jessica fought to get her breath back even though all three of her companions were now looking at her like she was the one being ridiculous. She had to hustle once they got off that elevator. Bernadette flew down a hallway, made a couple quick turns down more hallways and they were in the ICU.

"Wow, Bernadette, you sure do know your way around," Jessica observed as she caught up, out of breath.

"Hey, I made a few coffee runs that first night we were here, waiting to find out you would be okay. I figured out the quickest way back and forth to the cafeteria and coffee bar."

"Cafeteria?" Brien asked, on high alert.

"Coffee bar?" Peter asked, with almost as much eagerness in his voice.

Jessica tried to shush them all as she approached the nurse's station. They were getting scrutiny from a nurse on duty. A police officer still posted close to what must be Libby's room, stood and walked toward them.

"Can I help you?" The nurse asked.

"Yes, I'd like to see Libby Van Der Woert. Is she permitted visitors?" Jessica inquired.

"You can't all be family."

"No, we're, um, well..."

"Jessica, is that you?" a soft voice asked from behind them. When Jessica turned, Nora Van Der Woert rushed forward to greet them. She had just stepped out of one of the rooms they'd passed. The woman had been crying.

"Nora, what's happened?"

"Libby's taken a turn for the worse. I, uh, we don't know what's going on. The doctors are with her now. I'm doing what I do best in situations like this—sit and wait. What are you doing here?"

"I hoped to look in on Libby while I was here for a checkup. Do you want me to sit with you while you wait? Bernadette and my friends were just talking about going for coffee. Can they bring you some?"

"That would be great. If you don't mind, I'd appreciate it. I don't think we've met," she said, holding out her hand and introducing herself to Peter and Brien.

Peter did a quick check of the area. The nurse gave him dirty looks and was about to chide him, but the police officer gave her a reassuring nod as he and Peter had a chat. Jessica followed Nora into the waiting area. "It looks okay, Jessica. None of your autograph seekers will get past that nurse or the police officer. We'll give you two a few minutes of privacy, but stay put, okay?"

"Sure, thanks." The two men hurried off after Bernadette, who was already increasing the distance between them. "Let's have a seat and you can tell me what's happened." Nora sank into a nearby chair. Jessica followed, easing her way into a seat next to her.

"I'm not sure what happened or what it means. I came down here to visit, and I was in there for a few minutes when she stirred. Then she opened her eyes." She looked as though she was still trying to process the moment that followed.

"I felt stunned after that when she spoke. I was so excited that I couldn't breathe. Do you know what my daughter's first words were?"

"No," Jessica replied, feeling her body stiffen in anticipation.

"Libby opened her eyes and said, *'Where is that bastard? He's going to pay!'* or something to that affect. It was such a relief to see her awake. But then she uttered those words in this awful vicious tone."

"What did you do?"

"I wasn't sure if I should keep her talking or urge her to be quiet, so I hit the call button for the nurse. Then I said, *'Libby, it's okay. It's Mom.'* She had closed her eyes again, but opened them when I called her by name. She stared at me with cold, hard eyes. *'Where is that son-of-a-bitch Carr, Mom?'* I didn't want to tell her he's dead. All I said was, *'It's okay, Libby, he's not here, you're safe.'* The nurse came into the room right then and checked all the readings on the equipment. Libby was getting more and more upset, even trying to sit up. *'Tell Jessica to get him. All she needs is in that blue case at my house. She has to get the rosary, too'* and something about a key or *'it's a key.'* She was growling in between curses, and spitting like a rabid dog. Then she just seized up, spewed foam, and her body convulsed. The nurse sent out a code, and a team rushed in to work on her. They shoved me out of there when they wheeled in the cart with the resuscitation equipment on it. That was over an hour ago. She's stable again, but nobody can tell me what happened or why, much less what any of it means for her recovery. I went back in there, for a moment, but I can't tell anything by looking at her. The doctors are checking on her now."

"I am so sorry."

"It's the story of my life with Libby. I feel exhilaration one minute, terror and disappointment the next, followed by confusion that never goes away. I thought you should know she had a message for you. I don't get that either. Does it have something to do with why she called you to meet at the top of the tram? Have you got any idea what that was all about?"

"I know Paul already told you about the admission she made to me that the allegations toward Nick and his brother were false, and that Carr put her up to trying to get money from you and Nick. I don't quite know what else is going on, but I am trying to piece it together. That day at my office, she got it right away that the good doctor and I didn't hit it off. I thought that amused her. In fact, later, I wondered if she'd engineered it that way."

"That would be like her."

"It bothered me enough to have our investigators at the firm inspect the guy again. We had done the background check on him you asked us to do. Carr had come up clean, although he's bounced around from place to place. Lots of his affiliations didn't last long. That's a little odd, given most places need a psychiatrist of record on their team and there's a shortage. What we encountered when we dug deeper the second time around were several 'can't talk about it' or 'no comment' responses. Open hostility, even, at the mention of his name. That tells me he did not leave on good terms and there may have been a confidentiality clause resulting from legal proceedings. We haven't found any public records about legal problems, so whatever went on must have happened outside of a courtroom. At least part of the problem, according to what Libby told me up on Mt. San Jacinto, could be that Carr didn't always keep his interest in his clients strictly professional."

"That doesn't surprise me. I was almost certain that's what Libby was trying to tell me months ago when she was gushing about him like he was a rock star."

"If he made a habit of crossing the line, it would explain his sudden departures under unpleasant circumstances. Even though it's behavior that ought to be reported, agencies don't want bad news to get out, so they handle it themselves. Often, guys like Carr move on, continue to practice and do it again elsewhere. That's part of what she was trying to say today, about making him pay, could be about feeling betrayed, or because he was hell-bent on getting rid of her. I'm still trying to figure out why." A wave of sadness hit Jessica. "I'm so sorry I couldn't have done more before this all got out of hand. When Libby tried to contact me after that unexpected meeting in my office, I told her to go through her attorney. Maybe she'll pull through."

"Good Lord, she almost killed you and you're sorry. You had to behave in a professional way with Libby or you'd have an ethics mess on your hands, too. Besides that, she's still alive, thanks to you, from what I've heard. This isn't the first time I've had to face the prospect of losing Libby. I've mourned her loss for a long time. I have memories of her like any mother does—cherished ones, mine to keep. Libby as the infant I cuddled, and as the toddler, I taught to walk and talk. Images of sweet little Libby at Christmases, birthday parties, trick or treating, and her first day of school, are all stored away in my mind and heart. I tried to keep that girl alive as long as I could, even as she slipped away. When she came after her father and her uncle, I knew that girl was gone. Nor would she ever be the woman I hoped she might become." Tears fell as Nora whispered those last few words.

"I can't imagine what that must feel like. I'm sorry." Jessica wished she could offer something more tangible in the way of support.

"It is what it is, as they say. I don't have to like it. I just need to face it. Lord knows, I'm not alone. Parents of seriously mentally ill children have to come to grips with what they can expect of their children as adults. Mental illness is as devastating as any physical illness, more so maybe, because it's so hard to know what's a sickness and what's not. You'd think I'd be better at figuring that out, having grown up with a mother who was disturbed, but I don't get it."

"That she's stable again is a good sign."

"Could be, but nothing will ever be the way it was before this latest mess. Even if she recovers, I won't trust her, or have the same hope for her ever again."

"You don't know that. Where there's life, there's hope—that sounds trite, but it's true." Jessica caught an image of her mother, leaving the house with Hank at her side. Would things ever be the same for her relationship with her mother? Change might be good. Nora must have read Jessica's thoughts.

"Maybe it's a good thing not to go back to the way things were. I'll place my hope in that. It's all over for Carr, now, at least. Are you still investigating him?"

"Yes. What's happened to Shannon Donnelly is still up in the air, and he may have had something to do with that. According to Libby, Shannon was having a fling with Carr, too. So, he may turn out to be the linchpin in all this, dead or not. What about that little blue suitcase or a bag she mentioned? Do you know what that is, or where?"

"No, I've never seen a blue suitcase. It might be at her condo. Her car is in a parking garage there, too. You're welcome to take a look around yourself—or send Jerry. Keys to her condo and car are on my key ring if you want them."

"Sure, that would be great, if you don't mind."

"Mind, no. If Libby survives, and her psyche is at all intact—if that's something you can ever say about Libby—she'll be facing a lot of questions. It will help her if you can figure out what's going on. I have been so out of it, I haven't even had time to process what it means that someone tried to kill her, here, in the ICU. The police asked me about it. How do I know who my daughter's enemies might be? I didn't even know Nick and I were on that list until recently. Sometimes I still wonder where I went wrong as a mom. It's so hard not to blame yourself—everyone else still blames moms when their kids go wrong." Nora handed keys to Jessica, one an electronic key that belonged to the car, another for the door to the condo, and a smaller key. "That little key is for a mailbox."

"That someone is still after Libby is the scariest part of this. The police are making progress. I'm sure they'll share what they've learned with you if you call Palm Springs PD. In the meantime, I'll get someone to go look for that bag. Does what she had to say about a rosary mean anything to you? Is she a Catholic?"

"We raised her as a Catholic, dragged her kicking and screaming through all the CCD classes. She took me to task more than once for putting her through it, loading her up with guilt, blah, blah, blah. If she goes to Mass or owns a rosary, it would surprise me, so I have no clue what she's talking about or what that has to do with a key. Could be none of it means a thing. With Libby, you never know."

They sat in silence for several more minutes before Jessica's trio of friends returned with coffee. Peter passed a large cup to Nora. Jessica was ready for a cup, too, after that sad conversation. Blessed Bernadette had brought her one even though she hadn't asked for it. Peter was guzzling coffee and Brien was stuffing his face, so no more banter. She was about to say goodbye when the doctors came into the waiting room and told Nora she could go back to Libby's bedside. They had little to report about what had happened to Libby or her prognosis.

On the ride home, Jessica was quiet. Nora had spoken from the heart when she said daughters don't always become the women their parents hope they will become. Mothers aren't always what you hope for either. She was deep in thought when Bernadette spoke.

"Mira, Jessica. Something's going on."

"What does that mean?" Jessica asked, as her heart leapt into her throat. A huge, dark-colored SUV pulled in behind them—in between their Escalade and the SUV that Peter and Brien occupied.

"You want me to step on it? This car is big, but it can move when I want it to." Jessica looked around at the afternoon traffic. It wasn't bad yet, but there wasn't much room in which to maneuver.

"Where are you going to go?"

"Back to Mission Hills, fast, and get us behind the guard gate," she responded, speeding up as she spoke.

"You're going fast enough, already, to do that." It hurt to turn around, but Jessica managed and saw that the SUV was staying right with them, not far from their bumper as Bernadette sped up.

"Okay, so maybe you've got the right idea. Step on it!" As she spoke those words, a second dark-colored SUV moved in beside them. The tinted windows were so dark that she couldn't see who was driving. She and Bernadette were in the far left lane and had passed the last possible turnaround. There wasn't anywhere for them to go now except forward. At least no one was taking pot shots at them.

"Geez," Jessica muttered. "We're sitting ducks."

"Not quite. I've got us covered." Bernadette reached into a pocket between the driver's seat and the door and pulled out a gun. She set it on her lap so she could return to driving with both hands.

"Oh my God, Bernadette. What are you doing with Dad's gun?"

"Take it, Jessica. Don't use it unless you have to. I gotta concentrate on drivin'. That light up ahead is about to change. I can beat it." Jessica reached over and took the gun. Twisting got her a round of protests from her ribs. No matter, her heart was pounding against her ribcage so hard that she couldn't catch her breath anyway.

Another jolt ran through her when her phone rang. She whisked it out of her purse and answered.

"Hello."

"Uh, Jessica, it's Peter. We've got a situation on our hands. A bogey on your tail, about three cars back."

"Three cars back? What are you talking about? There's one almost in our back seat, and another in the lane next to us." In that instant, a third SUV appeared out of nowhere. This one swerved across two lanes of traffic to get in front of them. Cars honked as it cut them off. That third car hemmed them in. Bernadette honked and sped up, getting as close as she could to the bumper of the SUV in front of her.

"We're surrounded. Do you think these are kidnappers? Should I run the light if I can get around the guy in front of us?"

"Run the light? What are you talking about?" Jessica asked.

"I didn't say anything about running the light," Peter said.

"Not you. Bernadette's lost her mind, she's talking crazy."

"The Mission Hills gate's just up ahead beyond that light. Let's see these guys go up against the guard house. They will have some 'splainin' to do if they follow us in there. This guy wants to cut me off. I'll show him that's not polite." With that, she sped up again and almost tapped the bumper of the SUV in front of them. The driver ahead sped up, and the others did too.

"You got that gun handy?" As she spoke, Bernadette leaned on the horn. The SUVs around them honked too.

"Yeah, I've got the gun."

"Gun, what gun?" Peter shouted into the phone.

"Me, Peter, I've got the gun."

"Jessica, you don't need it. Don't shoot. Stay with my guys. I've got to go get that bogey."

"Stay with 'your guys'... 'bogey'... what are you saying?" She asked.

In her side mirror, about three cars back, Jessica saw a pizza delivery car cut to the right, across two lanes of traffic, and make a right turn. Not far behind was Peter's SUV. Behind him, another SUV did the same. As she strained to watch what was going on behind them, Bernadette honked again. They all reached that intersection and went barreling on through it, honking like a flock of geese. Jessica prayed not to clobber or be clobbered, as they ran the light just as it changed. Peter's words finally registered in Jessica's mind.

"It's okay. These are Peter's guys. We're safe; you can slow down. But not too suddenly, mind you. We must all be doing eighty." The SUV in front of them tapped the brakes; taillights flashed, and a left turn signal started. Bernadette eased back on the pedal, and tapped her brakes, too, as the entrance to Mission Hills Country Club came into view two hundred yards ahead.

"That's what I figured after you said, 'your guys.'" They slowed down even more as they reached the turn into Mission Hills. The SUV on their right continued in traffic, tooting its horn as it sped off. With the two remaining SUVs, front and back, they all turned into the gates together. The driver of the SUV in front spoke to a guard, who let all three vehicles pass through right away.

When they were through the gates, the SUV in front of them used the turnaround and headed back out to the road. The escort in the SUV behind them tracked them all the way back to the house. Bernadette hit the garage door opener and pulled in. By the time they shut off the engine, their escort in the SUV had vanished. The security guard who was already at the house joined them in the garage, speaking to Bernadette through the passenger window.

"Message from Peter," he said in a gruff, no nonsense voice. *"Got the bogey, asking him questions."*

Jessica's phone pinged. A text message from Peter appeared, saying the same thing.

"Thanks, Doug," Bernadette said, with a sweet smile on her face. Doug's gruffness evaporated.

"No problem, heard you had a little trouble. Glad you're both okay. Stay put until Peter contacts you again, please," he added, returning Bernadette's smile. A smile sat no better on Doug's face than it did on Peter's.

"Am I allowed to bring you a cold drink or something?" Bernadette asked, as she hopped out of the SUV, to the floor of the garage. Doug, another of Peter's men recruited from the land of giants, held the door for her. She looked up at the well-muscled, black man with a buzz cut. He had to be at least twice her size unless the adrenaline still surging through Jessica's mind and body was altering her perceptions. Bernadette was as cool as a cucumber and had already shifted from getaway driver into hostess mode.

"That would be nice, thanks," he said, backing up a little.

"Doug, go give Jessica a hand getting down out of the car. The doctor says she's doing better, but she's still got some injuries. Bring her inside, will you, and I'll fix us a cold drink, okay?" Doug shut Bernadette's door and headed around to the passenger side of the car.

Jessica realized she was still holding the gun. She shoved it into her handbag before tackling what seemed to be a monumental task of moving out of the Escalade and into the house. Doug was a big help once she scooted to the edge of her seat. He lifted her out of the car and placed her on the ground. As he escorted her into the house, Jessica stewed. *What a frigging stupid, scary day. How close was I to having my head blown off by a sniper, or getting ripped apart by a rowdy crowd of autograph-seekers? Argh! This all has to stop—even if I have to go get that damn blue bag myself.*

18 MALIBU BLUES

Alexis paced from one side of her bedroom to the other. Accommodations at the clinic were elegant and comfortable. The crisp, clean decor captured the spectacle of the white-tipped waves of the blue Pacific Ocean. A wall of sliders opened to a patio and a view of the ocean that pounded against the cliffs. Her lavish bath, slathered in marble, offered a steam shower and a Jacuzzi tub. The bed and bath were part of a suite that included a living room with a fireplace. The patio could be accessed from the living room, too. A small kitchen area allowed you to stash yogurt and other items for snacks. Five-star dining was steps away, though, featuring healthy haute cuisine. Other accouterments you might expect to find at a high-end resort included a large pool, hot tubs, tennis courts, a spa, and a fitness center with an assortment of workout classes.

Tall stone fences surrounding the facility were believable as structures to ensure privacy rather than to keep you inside. During the day, you could pass through gates and walk down flights of stairs to the beach below. Once you reached the beach, there was nowhere to go. The small strip of sand was bordered by rocky encroachments that made escape from the beach dicey. The setting also made it tough for paparazzi to scale those rocks, even if they could get close enough to the rocky area by boat. Alexis had already caught glimpses of several Hollywood favorites, so keeping the paparazzi out was a good thing. In principle, she could sign herself out without the "escape-from-Alcatraz" drama. Down there on that beach, though, she felt the urge to run for it.

Since Hank dropped her off Wednesday night, she'd given up alcohol and her drugs. They didn't expect her to go cold turkey and had her on a regimen of medications intended to prevent severe withdrawals, and make detox more tolerable. There had been rough patches in the last two days, but the physical symptoms on day three were mild. She experienced lightheadedness, antsy feelings, mild nausea, sweating, and intermittent headaches. They were at their worst when it came close to time for the clinic to administer the next dose of Suboxone.

A knock at the door stopped her from pacing. Was it that time already? Alexis moved to answer the door and let the therapist into the living room. They made "house calls," so-to-speak, in this luxurious facility by the sea catering to the rich and famous. Perhaps, the house call was also another way to take stock—observe you in a more natural setting. *Like a zoo animal or a lab rat*, she thought.

"Come on in, Angela," she said, moving away from the door. Her shrink shut the door behind her and waited for Alexis to pick a seat. When she chose a comfortable club chair, with a view out to the horizon Angela sat down opposite. She made sure not to block the view.

"How's it going Alexis?"

"How do you think it's going? I'm into day three without my goodies. The physical withdrawals aren't too bad, but everything is so much sharper."

"Is that bad?"

"Are you kidding me? The whole point of taking Oxy or Xanax and a drink or two is to smooth out the sharp edges of the world." That was putting it mildly. How could she tell this woman how much she hated the intrusiveness of the external world? All Alexis wanted was to be oblivious to her surroundings and the truth of her situation.

"I think I get it, but can you tell me what you mean by that?"

"Everything is so bright and shiny. I see edges, angles, and corners, everywhere, like out there on the horizon. It should be sky blending into the sea, smooth and silky like an impressionist painting. Instead, it's this slash, with flickering points of water below and a bright blue sky above. There's too much blue and all that light bouncing off the water hurts. It's hyper real like HDTV, but intense and painful." Talking about it made it worse. She shifted in her seat to block the view, making eye contact with the gray-haired woman sitting across from her. Dr. Angela Graham had to be about her age. There was nothing sharp or edgy about her gray on gray appearance.

Why doesn't she do something about that awful gray hair and why no makeup? She's not an unattractive woman, but wrapped in a haze of gray, who could tell? Alexis shifted back the other way to get a view of the outdoors. She blinked as though blinded by the sun beating down on the Pacific Ocean.

"Is there anything that seems to help?"

"Yeah, but you won't let me use those," she snorted, half in anger, half in laughter. "Just kidding," Alexis said as she stretched to reach a pair of sunglasses on the opposite side of the end table near where she sat. "These help." She put the dark glasses on.

"Okay. Some of what you're experiencing is withdrawals. Even with the Suboxone, that's not uncommon. I'm sure things around you were dimmer before—they had to be. You were up to six or more Oxycontin a day and maybe about that many Xanax, in addition to Ambien and alcohol. That's bound to blur the edges for anyone. It sounds like you feel that support has been taken from you, right?"

Duh, was what Alexis wanted to say, but the etiquette of psycho speak demanded better. "I've told you that's why I use them. I also know you haven't taken them away from me. That's my choice, even though I made it after getting some prodding."

"By your family you mean?"

"Yes, and by my doctor."

"So why do you suppose you've been getting all the prodding?"

"I *suppose* because I was letting things get out of hand." She didn't keep the sarcasm out of her voice. This talk therapy dance was painful too. You're detoxing, and still they want you to talk and talk and talk. Individual sessions, group sessions, and lectures on drug and alcohol use. Her itinerary hadn't started bad, but it was getting more packed each day. Like joining a cult—soon, there wouldn't be a moment left for solitude.

"What does that mean?"

"Getting sloppy, mixing booze with the pills, things I should have been managing better."

"So how do you do that; manage better?"

"Well, no alcohol until dinnertime is one thing. Then, two or three drinks, and keeping better track of when I took the last pill. Resting more, things like that."

"Resting more, at night or during the day?"

"Both. During the day, if I get a headache or am stressed out, it helps to go to my room and rest."

"Okay, so you go to your room. But, isn't that where the pills are?"

"Yes. I don't have to take them."

"Do you?"

"Yes, but I don't make a scene, at least."

"What kind of scene?"

"I don't know... breaking down or getting all needy, I guess."

"Is there something wrong with breaking down or being needy? Does that bother Giovanni, or your other family members?"

"It doesn't happen with Giovanni. I just keep moving when I'm around him—one party or activity after another. I'm like a shark that has to keep swimming or it'll drown." She laughed as she said that. "He likes bubbly, so I give him bubbly."

"Are you sure about that?"

"No, but does it make sense that Giovanni, or any man, would want to be around a clingy, needy, drag?"

"And that's the alternative to nonstop bubbly: clingy, needy, and a drag? That's the person you're afraid will make a scene, the one you hide away behind with pills and a bedroom door?"

"Yes, I guess so."

"It must exhaust you to keep up that front—stay bubbly all the time. What about coming up with an alternative to bubbly that's not clingy or needy, so you don't have to put on like that all the time, or escape to get a break from it? Do you think we could work on that?" Alexis was silent for a long time before answering.

"Maybe, but do you think we could work on taking the edge off, inside my head, too? My thoughts are like darts being thrown at me, a hail of pin pricks. I can't think straight half the time. Sometimes, with just the right amount of buzz, I can—think straight, I mean. As long as that's going on, I don't think I can figure out how to be another way."

"Okay, so what are the thoughts about?"

"Does it matter?"

"I don't know. Let's find out, okay?"

"I'm scared to death about the cancer. I'm so tired of bubbly and I can't always keep it up, even when I should be able to do it. Like after my daughter, Jessica's birth. I was a mom with a beautiful new baby daughter. I had money, clothes, houses, services and supports, and a man in my life that cared for me. Plus, this amazing woman who started out as our housekeeper and ended up doing a lot more. Everyone told me, over and over, how lucky I was to have it all. Do you have any idea what that feels like, to have it all and still not be able to get out of bed in the morning?" She searched the therapist's gray, deadpan face. She didn't wait for her shrink to answer. "I'll tell you how it feels, like you're nothing. Like you should be nothing, want nothing. So I looked for it—a lot of nothing; ways to push it all away." The words spilled out, like water over a dam; tears too. The shrink popped up, grabbed a box of tissues on a nearby side table and passed them to her.

"Thanks," she said, dabbing at her eyes. "Here I am again. At the drop of a hat, Giovanni would be on a plane from Zurich or Paris, London, Rome or wherever he is. He'd be here, at my side. If I told him the truth about all that's going on, he'd insist, in fact. But I don't want him here. I don't want him to see me like this."

"Like what, Alexis? You seem raw and genuine. I'd say authentic. We all need support from others, that's part of what makes us human. Why is that so bad?"

"It's not, I guess. My daughter's had her own problems and I've added to them. She's standing there all banged up, having been through hell, and she's worried about me."

"Yes, I saw that story. I'm sorry that you've had that shock to deal with, too. She is one fortunate young woman."

"Tell me about it. She's more worried about me than she is about herself. She's angry too, but she wants to support me. Hank, my ex, and Bernadette, too, are in my court. So, I have family—

people who care about me. I don't feel good about myself, or safe, when I break down. It's unseemly for a Baldwin woman."

"That sounds like another clue, maybe, about how you view yourself and how you handle challenges, big or small, in your life. Like a new baby or a health problem. You've got a lot going for you, Alexis. It's good you can acknowledge the people in your life who care about you."

"Too bad I'm not one of them," she laughed hoarsely. There was a harsh edge to the words she spoke next. "I know what I've become. I'm an addict. Talk about weak and needy. I detest the booze and the pills, and all the managing it takes to be a functional addict, but I'm too worn out to find a new way to live this late in life."

"Well, it's hard to know how much of that is the booze and pills talking and how much of what you're describing is another problem. Is there a history of depression or anxiety in the Baldwin family?"

"My mother never talked about anything like that. Mom kept to herself, proud and haughty. I can tell you she did not approve of needy, so it's hard to imagine she ever felt that way, depressed or not. I'm not sure she ever felt much of anything. She was cold and distant, so who knows?"

"Okay, so, your mother didn't approve of needy, but it doesn't sound like you felt better when she withdrew or withheld herself from you. Does haughty, cold, and distant sound better to you than needy?"

"No. She didn't like bubbly either. I'm not sure how it came down to a choice between bubbly or needy, with hiding out as the solution." Alexis looked at Angela, like she might have the answer.

"What I can see is that it doesn't seem to be working all that well for you. This is a tough time. I'll grant you that. That doctor who's prodding you to get surgery says you have time to sort things out. And, you're here. Sixty-two isn't too old to learn some new tricks. Hiding out is not the way to deal with cancer. How about we take stock as you leave the drugs and alcohol out of the picture? Let's try to sort out how much of what you're thinking and feeling is the sly tricks an addict's mind learns to play and how much is you—the real you? Then we can figure out which parts you want to hang on to, change, or discard."

"That could take a while."

"Sure, but it beats holing up in your room and poisoning yourself with drugs and alcohol, while you get sicker from cancer."

"I suppose not all the work has to be done here?"

"No, and you don't have to wait until all the work is done to get that surgery. That could happen soon, in fact. What you do here, and in outpatient treatment, will help you get through the surgery and whatever comes after surgery. In the meantime, let's talk about how we can get and keep the important people in your life where they are for now. No more hiding or dumping people before you even give them a chance to see you as you are. Agreed?"

"Agreed, but it might take me a few more days before I can come clean to Giovanni. It's a lot to talk about on the phone."

"You don't have to do it all at once."

"He knows I've had issues with pills and with alcohol, so that won't be new to him. Who hasn't? Maybe I'll start there. Going to rehab isn't more onerous these days than visiting a fat farm. Less even. Rehab often gets used as a cover for nips and tucks—twenty-eight days in *rehab* and you come back with a new face. I'll call Giovanni when it's a decent hour there." She let out a long, deep breath. A breath it felt like she had been holding for months.

"Good, that's a step forward. We can process that call, if you want to, when we talk tomorrow. Or if you need to talk before that, find me. I don't mind needy, Alexis—that's why I'm here."

"Thanks, Angela." They spent another half hour together, most of it reviewing inventories and social history forms Alexis had completed on her first day. From all that background, they began to form a few treatment goals, giving focus to her therapy. That background included information about Alexis' drug use. In the beginning, alcohol and drugs had fueled bubbly, her social butterfly routine an affectation of teenaged rebellion. That had been such a long time ago. So much time had passed.

All that talk about her past caused Alexis to glance in the mirror when she accompanied Angela to the door. Age was taking a toll on the one thing she had always felt good about, her beauty. She still looked good, *for her age*. Gone was the luster of youth even with hormone replacement and skin and hair treatments. The alcohol and drugs had added to the destruction wrought by sixty years of gravity, ultraviolet radiation, and oxidative stress. She could lecture on the subject of aging, but she couldn't do anything to stop it.

What good was it to be rich, loved, and beautiful if it was all going to end in dust anyway? The harder she fought to keep the harbingers of age at bay, the more she yearned for oblivion. The more she sought oblivion, the more she hastened the destructiveness of nature. It was a vicious cycle that was made worse by the new battle she faced with cancer. Bette Davis had said it all: *Growing old isn't for sissies!* Surgery, chemo what was the point? Where were the compensations to those who aged—wisdom, self-acceptance, and peace?

How many pills did she have stuffed into the lining of her overnight bag? She'd brought them along as insurance, in case they were lying about being able to control her withdrawals. The long nights without sleep were the worst. *How on earth did I end up here?* She wondered as she looked out to the horizon. A favorite line by Ralph Waldo Emerson popped into her head: *The years teach much which the days never knew.*

"Let it be true," Alexis whispered as she turned from the door to look at the schedule for the rest of the day. Next to that schedule was a gift from Bernadette. "She's no sissy, that's for sure," Alexis said, as she picked up the sparkling crystal rosary. Could she find the courage that Bernadette had displayed in her own life? Tackle the mess she was in, yes, and find some way to be more available as a mother to Jessica. Perhaps by focusing less on her fear of being needy, and more on being needed. She didn't know what her daughter needed, but she would try to find out.

19 DEGREES OF SEPARATION

"The line between bad therapy and out-and-out fraud is thin, Jessica. Too many therapists do things that make me wonder about my chosen profession. They're not all social workers. There's plenty of bad practice by psychologists and psychiatrists too. Some of it's a lack of professionalism, like not keeping up to date on what works and doesn't work. There are those who stretch the ethical boundaries. They manipulate insurance to get more treatment sessions, switching from one client to another in a family to extend treatment or use it all up! Psychotherapists will tell you they're trying to make the most of meager mental health coverage to get work done with clients, and often that's true. Some let their do-gooder tendencies foster dependency. My colleagues who practice brief term, problem-focused work somehow figure out how to get a lot done in six to ten sessions. It's a tough job, Jessica, so I shouldn't be so judgmental."

Betsy Stark sat at the table in the morning room as she had often done since the early nineties when Bernadette had brought her home. She wasn't eating like a starved creature, as she had been when Jessica first caught sight of her years ago. Jessica had walked in on the enormous teenager eating slice after slice of Bernadette's French toast. Betsy's jet-black hair had been long and curly, out of control, even pulled back with a scrunchie. She had worn baggy sweat pants and a loose t-shirt in a gray color.

How does any girl that big find clothes that baggy? Her snide younger self had wondered.

Jessica had said nothing snooty out loud, at least. When Bernadette introduced them, Jessica sat down across from Betsy, with her own plate of French toast. They had eyed each other with wariness as Bernadette bustled around them. Bernadette sat down and attempted to engage them in conversation, but Jessica and Betsy had been monosyllabic in response that day.

What a little snot I was, Jessica thought as the two of them sat across from each other, now, two decades later. Jessica had been a wimpy little thing, full of fear about anything new or different. It wasn't just Betsy's hair, her size, or the way she attacked that plate of food that had seemed so fierce. There was a tension in the way Betsy sat—like a rattler, coiled, and ready to strike.

More likely on springs and ready to bolt, Jessica figured, thinking about it now. From the snippets of background she had wrung out of Bernadette, Betsy Stark's life was a hellish one. She had much more reason than Jessica did to be a scared rabbit. True, at ten, Jessica's parents' marriage had begun to crumble around her. Still, Jessica had a home, parents who loved her, and Bernadette, too. Betsy had nothing. Worse than nothing, because the people in her life were more like blood-sucking vampires than caregivers. As far as she could tell, wolves had raised Betsy Stark.

What Jessica remembered most was the awe she had felt as the teen rose from the table. Betsy stood and stood and stood... It seemed like it took several minutes for her to rise to her full height. She was close to six feet tall, at fifteen or sixteen-years-old.

The woman who sat there today appeared transformed. Even taller, she was big, too. She had a solid build without an ounce of fat anywhere. She wore an inexpensive suit, in a dark blue pinstripe, with a pale blue cotton blouse—business attire on a budget. Pumps, with a low heel, and dark stockings completed the outfit, creating a no-nonsense, professional air.

Betsy's hair was not the least bit unkempt. Dark as coal, it was pulled back into a tight bun at the nape of her neck and not a strand was out of place. She wore a hint of makeup on her broad oval face, with its high cheek bones and arched brows. Her dark eyes sparkled with intelligence, confidence, and good humor. None of those were the words she would have applied to Betsy Stark during the years she had shown up several times a week to help around the house. The adult Betsy Stark was an attractive, albeit unconventional, woman with a daunting presence.

"Some of them step way over the line, in my book, 'advocating' for clients, which includes signing off on what I suspect are false claims for disability. Often referred by members of your profession who aren't any more ethical, I might add. Over-prescribing medication is one of my biggest gripes. Too many of the clients that end up in my office have a problem with drugs prescribed by a doctor or psychiatrist. A few, like Dr. Carr, cross the line by having romantic or sexual encounters with clients. There are more subtle flags that ought to set off warnings about wounded healers that haven't tended to their own wounds. We're not so great, yet, about policing our ranks or getting the word out about unscrupulous or impaired professionals. A lot of clients have little choice about treatment providers and don't know their rights as clients." Betsy took a breath and slugged down coffee. "Sorry, you've hit a sore point and triggered a rant."

"I get it. As you mentioned, we have similar problems among practitioners of the law. So how does any of this relate to false allegations, False Memory Syndrome, or whatever it's called?"

She regarded Betsy with the respect she afforded professionals she consulted, from time to time, in her work as a lawyer. It was more than that though. Betsy was a marvel, a walking miracle, given all she had lived through. *The woman had spent time in 'the slabs' as a child*, she recalled. Slab City takes its name from the concrete slabs left behind when Camp Dunlap was shut down. Not far from Salton Sea, the area had become an ad hoc off the grid community. Temporary and permanent residents included homeless in makeshift campsites, snowbirds, retirees living in RVs, and an assortment of others in unconventional abodes. The most famous dwelling, dubbed Salvation Mountain, marked the entrance into the slabs.

When Betsy turned up again in Rancho Mirage in August, Jessica had registered surprise. Bernadette didn't. She and Betsy had remained in contact even after Betsy went away to college. While Jessica was off pursuing her own education, marriage, and law career, Betsy returned to the Coachella Valley. Back in the community where she had grown up, Betsy had visited her old friend and mentor often.

In August, Betsy and Jessica spoke briefly, exchanging polite greetings. That's when Jessica discovered that Betsy's career had involved case management with severely mentally ill adults. Smart, hard-working, and with that master's degree in social work, Betsy had moved up the ranks and into administration. She was now in an administrative role at one of the local disability offices.

Even before the incident at the top of the tram, it had dawned on Jessica that Betsy might be a resource to help her better understand the chaos and confusion surrounding Libby Van Der Woert's life. Nora and Nick Van Der Woert had been more than willing to give Jessica permission to consult the woman about Libby.

"I'm dubious about the notion that there's a False Memory Syndrome, per se. Syndrome is too structured a way of characterizing false claims of molestation or rape based on recovered memory. False allegations occur, in or out of the therapeutic context in many ways. You must have encountered that in your profession."

"True. My knee-jerk response has always been to take women at face value when they make claims against their spouses, fathers, or other men in their lives. We learned that rape and abuse are scary and humiliating, and under reported. My limited experience with pro bono work in community agencies and clinics says that's true. I saw several situations in which women were unwilling, out of fear or shame, to report or file charges after an assault. Still, there are endless stories about couples making false allegations in the course of a bad divorce or a custody dispute. In those situations, the lawyers are pretty convinced the charges are trumped up out of spite, not delusion or mental illness."

"Yes, spite is one reason why people 'bear false witness against thy neighbor.' Anger, greed, revenge, too, can be reasons a sane person might cook up a story aimed at taking down a partner or family member, even a perfect stranger for that matter. That's what keeps libel and slander attorneys in business, right?"

"True," Jessica replied. It was amazing how quickly Betsy was getting to the heart of the matter.

"Okay, so it's not just divorce proceedings in which false allegations are made."

"Yes, threats to spread nasty stories unless money is paid out, is old-school extortion. In Libby's case, money *is* involved, so extortion is on the list of charges that might be brought against her. That presumes she's well enough to be taken to court."

"That doesn't sound the least bit crazy. Morally corrupt, but not anything that would get a clinical diagnosis. Well, I take that back—it could get you a personality disorder label. In this case, without talking to the woman, it's hard to know."

"At some point, she's had just about every diagnosis in the book. Until recently, they had settled on bipolar disorder. Nora, her mother, thought Libby had prescriptions for a mood stabilizer and an antipsychotic medication, but she wouldn't always take them. Libby was agitated most of the time while we were at the top of the tram— pacing and talking a mile a minute. Not all of it made sense, so I thought maybe it was a manic episode."

"There could be a delusional component to the allegations. Delusions can be expressed during both the manic and depressive episodes of bipolar disorder. It sounds like Libby's had problems being truthful for a long time."

"Yes, she's a practiced liar, according to her mother. This isn't the first time Libby's come up with strange claims about the people in her life, often directed at her mother. Nora's never known, for sure, if her daughter was just being histrionic, trying to get her goat, or if she believed the things she said. Was Libby wondering aloud about the scary, chaotic thoughts stewing in her troubled mind; or continuing to play the part of a teen well into her twenties by being nasty; or flat out accusing her mother of infidelity or possessing witchlike powers because she actually believed it?"

"Who knows for sure? It sounds like Libby's been on a lot of drugs since adolescence. That has to have damaged her ability to think straight."

"Dr. Carr didn't make that any better. My conversation with him at the top of the tram was a brief one. But one of the points he made, during a pompous rant, was how skilled he was at manipulating his clients. He implied that the drugs helped him do that. The gentleman held me at gunpoint while he ranted, so I could have some memory problems of my own. Too bad I'm not better at that repressed memory bit. I could do with fewer memories, thank you very much."

"I'm sure you could. But a more typical response is intrusive memories and recurring images of the traumatic event, Jessica. Documented cases of trauma-induced amnesia are few unless there's a head injury. It's far more common to think about the event over and over, and replay it, rather than forget it. That can be disturbing. If it's a problem, you could see someone..."

"Thanks. I've got a therapist who's been helping me. She's focused on getting me to expand my repertoire of coping skills beyond binge shopping at Saks. I'm hoping I can manage the flashbacks until I forget the latest brouhaha. Maybe my skills at repression will get better."

"You won't forget, but making the memories more manageable is a reasonable goal. Putting improbable events in proper perspective helps. I'm not sure how you do that when it comes to taking a tumble off a cliff. I suppose it helps to realize it won't happen again. That's a low probability event, to begin with, so what are the odds of it ever happening again?" Jessica nodded, resting her weary head in the palm of her hand, closing her eyes for a moment as she considered Betsy's point.

"Slim, I'm sure. I spend an inordinate amount of time in the land of low probability events, however."

"Well, that's what you get for being a member of the one percent."

"No! Do you think that has something to do with it?" She looked up to see a smirk on Betsy's face.

"Of course not, I'm kidding. I've spent plenty of time in that zone myself and I'm no one-percenter. Shopping won't help any better than drowning your sorrows in alcohol or drugs, so it's good you're working on developing other strategies to cope with stressful events—rare or not. Getting back to your original point, though, drugs might have been useful to the doctor, adding to Libby's confusion, making her more dependent or more easily influenced by him. He wouldn't be the first psychiatrist to over prescribe medications to his clients. The FDA just ordered docs to lower the doses of Ambien being doled out to women. That's a zombie drug as far as I can tell."

"That's what I think, too," Bernadette said, appearing out of nowhere. "I keep reading about sleep-dramas because of that Ambien. Zombie drug problems cause serious trouble for celebrities," she said, as she swept on by, headed out to the back patio with a covered tray.

"Carr's manipulation of Libby is like the circumstances in the nineties that set off the False Memory Syndrome backlash against recovered memories of abuse. Several techniques used by therapists came under scrutiny, including hypnosis and the use of high doses of medication. Planting a false memory using leading questions isn't hard to do. Have you seen that study about manipulating memories of encounters with Disney characters—telling stories to study participants, some of them creepy and some of them fun? The ones who heard creepy stories later remembered bad experiences with characters at Disney. I'll bet Disney is thrilled."

"I saw that when I was doing background research about Libby's parents' situation. Libby used the recovered memory lingo when her parents first asked her where the allegations came from. She told me that she made it all up and then began to believe it. She was all over the place about where those allegations came from. The Disney company execs must have been shocked to learn how easy it is to turn someone against Mickey with the mere hint that Mickey is a creep."

"Yes, it's unnerving to learn how easy it is to create memories, even in brains that aren't already struggling with delusions or doped up."

"Once the legal system started winning malpractice cases, I understand therapists backed off using hypnosis, asking leading questions, and relying on the idea that even if you have no memories of an event, your body can remember, or something like that."

"You're talking about body memories. Sometimes the shrinks are more disturbed than their clients. I had to take a case manager to task for talking to one of her clients about entities—some pseudo-religious belief she picked up from reading a book. Body memories," Betsy muttered to herself, shaking her head.

"Body memories, thank God I don't have those," Bernadette said as she whooshed by them again. Standing at the fridge in the kitchen, she turned around and asked. "Is that what zombies have left after they turn into zombies?"

"Sorry, zombies and body memories are both figments of the imagination," Betsy chuckled. "It's a chore to get psychotherapists to rely on evidence based practices. The numbers who do are growing, but there's still way too much voodoo in my business."

"Oh no, voodoo, too? What have you got mixed up in this time, Jessica?" Bernadette asked, crossing herself before she whisked another load of items out of the fridge and through the sliding doors to the patio.

"I wish I knew." Jessica had a worried look on her face.

"It sounds like you figured out that what turned the tide on the recovered memory debacle was a spate of cases brought against therapists. Clients who felt led astray by their therapists sued and won malpractice claims. When insurance providers had to pay out money, the professional boards took action."

"I saw something about that—a task force set up that issued guidelines warning about the dangers with 'if you feel abused you were abused,' so let's dig until we find the repressed memory."

"That's not helpful to someone like Libby, who's already having trouble sorting out which of the nightmares in her head are real. Given Libby's long history of troubles, as you've described it, she seems to have a serious mental disorder. That her problems worsened in late adolescence and early adulthood, is typical for many serious disorders, too. Anyway, it's not surprising she can't hang onto the truth for long, or that her stories about being persecutor or persecuted keep changing."

"Carr claimed her previous mental health issues were reactions to the underlying trauma of childhood sexual abuse. He diagnosed her with PTSD."

"With as much time as she's spent in treatment, if her father or uncle had done such a thing, she would have reported it earlier. I hate to disappoint you in your quest to become more adept at repression, Jessica, but the concept of repression hasn't been validated. It's a holdover from the mid-century infatuation with Freudian psychoanalysis. Psychodynamic practice got a well-deserved kick in the pants in the sixties and seventies, but made a comeback in the eighties and nineties. To borrow a concept from early psychiatry, though, I'm afraid PTSD has become the hysteria of our day."

"That's among the growing list of diagnoses in my own case file, I'm sure. After the last year, it could be true. Does anyone get through life without trauma? The rates of PTSD have skyrocketed. Not all of that has to do with returning vets, either, although rates are up for them, too."

"This might shock you, but PTSD is one of the easiest diagnoses to fake. That makes it a useful tool for unscrupulous malingerers to get onto permanent disability, making it tougher to serve vets or others who have a legitimate claim for help. Not to mention using PTSD to explain away heinous behavior. Most people with a mental health disorder don't hurt other people."

"In legal circles, it's called the 'abuse excuse.' It's almost pro forma for defense attorneys to play the abused-kid card when they've got a client nabbed for doing something monstrous."

"Sad to say, but some people will sell out a father or an uncle for a lot less than what Libby stood to gain if she collected on her inheritance. It might have worked, too, if her parents had just rolled over and played dead. There's a whole subculture out there who regard *putting one over on the man* as a family tradition. I can say that because I grew up in a culture like that. In my case, it was the byproduct of desperation and ignorance, but drugs and mental illness were in the mix too. None of that's an excuse." She stopped to stare into the glass of iced tea she was drinking.

"Well, for the late Dr. Carr, money was part of the motive. From what he said, he also found gratification in manipulating his privileged clients. That included exploiting them sexually, too, according to Libby. She says she has evidence to support her claims against her psychiatrist—if it exists and I can locate it."

"Setting aside the validity of Libby's claims against him, there's no denying he was intent on killing you and Libby. He had a reason; one he shared with whoever tried to kill Libby after Carr was dead." Betsy went blank, staring off into space; her eyes widened and her mouth gaped.

"I need to find that suitcase. That's one way to start sorting this out," Jessica mumbled to herself, wondering what was up with Betsy. She had a vague recollection of a similar moment when Betsy was younger. Jessica was about to say something when Betsy began to speak again, as though nothing had happened.

"Pros don't come cheap. That's not surprising, is it? Libby and her missing friend moved in the same circles of wealth and power— that's how Carr found them both. So, would it surprise you to learn she's being hunted by someone else from that circle of high rollers?"

"Not in the least. I have a knack for getting tangled up with le crème de la crud. I even married one of them. Okay, so I need to be working the six degrees of separation angle in Beverly Hills. Who, besides Carr, might have had an interest in shaking down the moneyed parents of poor little rich girls? One thing about being a member of the one percent is that there aren't that many of us. Our paths cross since we share the same habitat."

"Then I'd say Carr's co-conspirator may be closer than you think—you won't even need to use all six degrees of separation to find him. Staying close to the circles in which all three—Carr, Libby Van Der Woert, and Shannon Donnelly moved—along with their wealthy parents, is the place to start." A chill ran down Jessica's spine as she thought about previous encounters with high living lowlifes and their murderous thugs for hire.

"I presume that's what the detective assigned to investigate Donnelly's disappearance is doing. I'm not sure what files the police have gone through at Carr's office, but I'll see if we can get that information or send Jerry in there to look. Carr's the odd man out in that trio. He had nowhere near the kind of money Libby and Shannon's parents possess. I wonder who referred whom to the doctor for care. Maybe there are records like that in his files—if we can jump through all the hoops to get a look at them."

"It seems like that network would have been the lifeblood of Carr's practice. It's possible there's a referral database that's separate from the case records. Records like that are easier to access than case files, even without a release from Libby or a court order."

"Well, given her current condition, her parents can act on Libby's behalf. They want to sort this out. Maybe they can help us get access to Libby's records, including whatever's on file about how she found Carr. I'll see if we can get a look at the doctor's contact list, at least. Thanks, Betsy these are great ideas."

"Glad I could help a little. You never know what will turn up when you're dealing with disturbed people in trouble and at the hands of ruthless men like Carr. No one has pushed me off a mountain, but I have had to deal with some dicey situations. Balancing a client's rights with the need to protect them or others is always tricky." Jessica was so impressed by the thoughtful woman sitting across from her. Another wave of guilt washed over her about the dismissive way she had treated this remarkable person in the past.

"Do you want to stay for dinner? I'm having a few friends over. We'll talk about the investigation. That might give you more background, and a clearer picture of what's going on than I just gave you. You've met Laura Stone and Tommy Fontana when we were all much younger. He was Kelly Fontana's younger brother. You must remember his sister, Kelly."

"Kelly is the gorgeous redhead who turned up dead in the parking lot, downtown, near the casino, right?"

"Yes, that's her." A jolt of sadness shot through her. *Speaking of disturbed people who were in trouble*, she thought as she fought off the rush of emotion that engulfed her.

"She's hard to forget. So is that pixie-faced brother of hers. I used to see all of you carrying on out there while I helped Bernadette."

"About all that, I'm sorry that I was such a witch back then. I was so insecure."

"I recognized fear when I saw it. It was easy to understand why you were afraid of losing what you had. You had more to lose than anyone I had ever known before. It surprised me that you saw me as someone who mattered enough to worry you. That was validating in an odd way. Bernadette explained that it was a hard time for you. I could tell your mother was in bad shape." Jessica sucked in a little gulp of air.

"You could see that? I was so oblivious to other people's pain, even my mother's. You are amazing, Betsy Stark."

"Thanks for saying that. Maternal dysfunction was a familiar problem, too. One that reaches across the wealth divide, I should add, and recognizable when you've lived through it yourself. I couldn't have put that into words back then."

"Then I guess it won't surprise you to know she's having trouble again. That's why she's not here. The good news is that she's working on it—she's gone back into treatment with the folks at Transformations in Malibu." Betsy let out a little whistle.

"That's a great place, but it's pricey. You get that gorgeous setting, though, as part of the package."

"Yes, it would have been good if she could have gotten into Betty Ford's here in town, but they didn't have a bed, and we were taking no chances that she might back out."

"Let's hope it helps her turn her life around." Betsy said.

"It has to. Alexis has to get cleaned up enough for surgery to take care of another problem in her life," Bernadette offered, a tender tone in her voice. "I'm praying, and doing a novena for her, too."

"You are a good woman. Talk about kids in need of an attitude change. I was a piece of work back then. She's the best thing that ever happened to me." Betsy directed her last comment to Jessica. "Bernadette changed my life."

"St. Bernadette changed all our lives."

"Oh, stop it, you two. I'm standing right here, you know." The two women turned their heads, in tandem, toward the tiny woman who stood with her hands on her hips and a sweet smile on her face.

"We know," Betsy replied, and gave Jessica a little wink.

"Bernadette has her less than saintly moments, however. One thing we'll be debriefing about over dinner is an incident that occurred yesterday. Bernadette was at the wheel, honking like a mad woman, as we hurtled down the road."

"We had an escort. They were honking too. It was scary at first, but also exciting." Bernadette's eyes sparkled.

"See what I mean? She isn't the least bit remorseful that she broke several laws, speeding, running a light, as it turned red, and carrying a loaded firearm, without a permit, *again*..."

"A gun, no way! Bernadette, is this true?" At that moment, the doorbell rang.

"Saved by the bell," Bernadette said, as she made a move to answer the door. Before she could get far, someone hollered from the front entry.

"Yo, don't worry, it's just us." That was Brien's voice. It was hard to know who 'us' included. Trampling sounds came toward them.

Peter marched in, as his name and demeanor gave him license to do. He wore a dark suede bomber jacket with his company logo on it. Brien, in an identical bomber jacket, was on Peter's heels and carrying a case of beer. Behind them, Kim, Tommy, and Jerry were also part of the parade.

"Jessica, Brien let himself in—you all should keep that door locked even with my guys out in..." Peter came to an abrupt stop.

He'd entered the kitchen just as Betsy stood up to leave. His eyes followed her as she rose. At first stunned, his expression changed, registering appreciation on his face. She wasn't a woman you ran into every day, for sure. Brien swerved to avoid a collision with Peter and continued around him to the beverage cooler with his beer. Everyone else came to a halt, too, clustered together in the kitchen.

"Peter, meet Betsy," Jessica said. "Tommy, you know Betsy. Betsy, these other two friends are Kim and Jerry."

"Nice to meet you," Peter said, as he took a step forward and grasped Betsy's outstretched hand. Her eyes made their way up to meet his—not something the statuesque Betsy had to do often when introduced to anyone, male or female, Jessica imagined. Betsy didn't wince when the giant shook her hand several times, with vigor. He had the biggest, goofiest grin on his face that she'd ever seen him wear. Betsy smiled back.

"The guy with the beer is Brien," Jessica said, continuing with introductions.

"A beer sounds good. Maybe I'll take you up on that offer to stay for dinner." Betsy spoke without taking her eyes off Peter's still-smiling face.

"Wow," Brien said, stepping forward to hand her a beer. "How tall are you?"

"Six-two," she answered, in a matter-of-fact way.

"Can you believe that?" Brien commented and went back to filling the beverage cooler with beer. Then his head popped up.

"How much do you weigh?" The opposite of a gasp went around the room—as everyone sucked in air. Nobody let it out, waiting to see what a woman of Betsy's stature might do in response to a question like that.

"One-eighty is my fighting weight, but if I drink too much beer, I can top out at over two hundred pounds, easy. Right now, I'm working out a lot, so I'm close to where I like to be, and ready to rumble. How about you? I'm guessing you're about five-seven and around one-eighty, too, right?"

"Whoa, absolutamente! You better watch it, Bernadette. She's got special powers, like you. It's like she just read my mind." Jessica looked at Bernadette, with a good guess at what Bernadette was thinking even before she spoke.

"If she read your mind, Brien, she wouldn't have much to say. Maybe something like heinous this or bogus that, but nothing that makes any sense." Bernadette was shaking her head, muttering in Spanish, something involving the word casquivano—scatterbrained.

"She's got powers, not to twist you into a pretzel shape after asking such a rude question," Peter admonished. Brien's face was blank, that *no entiendo* sign flashing over his head. English or Spanish, he wasn't getting it. He handed out more beers.

"Brien, for future reference, Peter's right. It's considered rude, so don't ask people how much they weigh, how much money they make, or how old they are, okay?" Jessica wasn't sure why she was attempting to teach him etiquette. Maybe she owed him one, since he'd spotted the guy tailing her the day before.

"Oh, okay. Sorry, Betsy. I'm still totally in awe." He twisted the top off a bottle of beer and took a sip. "How much weight can you bench press?"

"Geez," Peter said. Betsy, who had been taking it all in, burst out laughing. Then she sat back down to drink her beer. Tommy and Jerry guffawed. Even Kim's shoulders had started to shake with laughter.

"Don't encourage him," Bernadette said, shaking her head again. She was smiling though.

"What *now*? That's not rude. People ask me that question all the time, Dude." Before anyone could say anything else, the doorbell rang.

"That must be Laura. I'll go let her in," Tommy said, turning to head down the hall to the front foyer. He paused when Betsy responded to Brien's question.

"My record's three-twenty, but I keep heavy workouts in the two-fifty range."

"Holy crap," Peter gasped. "For real?" Jessica did the math in her head, having heard somewhere that it was quite an achievement to bench press your body weight. One and a half times your body weight was pro level or something like that. *Holy crap* was right. The woman was impressive on so many fronts.

"Now who's being rude?" Brien chastised Peter. "Of course she's for real. I told you she's got powers." He was nodding his head up and down, in that bobble-head-doll-in-the-know thing he occasionally did. "It's not good to say crap, either, is it Bernadette?" Bernadette opened her mouth to speak, but the doorbell rang again.

"That has to be Laura. Will somebody let her in, please?" Bernadette asked. "The rest of you help me get out there and start dinner."

"Good idea. I'm starving," Brien added.

20 FRIDAY THE 13TH

Eric Conroy almost danced with glee. He was in a festive mood as he made his way into the boardroom, but tried to don the more constrained, professional demeanor that such an occasion demanded. His eyes scanned the room, lighting for a moment on each of the SOBs sitting there, including the two in the room who were female. He ticked off in his head what he knew about each of them that he could use against them if he hadn't already done so. Not all of them had skeletons in their closets—yet! Still, they all had vulnerabilities that could be exploited should the occasion arise.

He applied a little bit of neuro-linguistic programming, skills acquired when it was all the rage. But mostly he relied on his skilled use of the old-fashioned hustle. He prided himself on the fact he had elevated the patois of dirt-shoveling to new heights. Despite the fancy name, NLP wasn't new. Persuading or otherwise influencing others to do your bidding, without their being aware of it, were tried and true techniques that were used by old-school salesmen and con artists everywhere.

That would all be behind him with the IPO a week away. The road show, with the CEO out strutting like a presidential candidate, was moving ahead at top speed. One hundred meetings in less than a month meant plenty of opportunity for the puffed up little peacock to strut around.

Enjoy it while it lasts, Eric thought as he shook the vapid, boorish man's hand. "I hear you're doing a great job representing Pinnacle. Good for you," he said with an enormous grin on his face.

"Thanks. That is high praise, coming from you." The CEO failed to keep the sarcasm from his voice. "Where did you hear that?" He asked, as paranoia crept into his tone. Eric clenched his teeth maintaining a forced smile, as he responded.

"I have my sources, Charlie. You know that." He saw the man gulp as he gave the bumbling CEO a friendly wink. Charlie knew. This little charade of camaraderie would be over soon, too. Charles Tilly, CEO and Chairman of the Board of Pinnacle Enterprises, was one of half a dozen people in the room Eric had between a rock and a hard place.

Today, the lead underwriters were stopping by to give the board a formal update on their progress lining up buyers of Pinnacle shares to be issued. All the big boys were in on the deal, their names on the 'tombstone' published in the New York Times and Wall Street Journal. An ad taken out by the investment bankers, the tombstone provided bare bones information about the offering, along with a list of those shepherding the deal, in order of their importance. The ad also provided instructions on how to find out more about the IPO. However, by the time it appeared, with its heavy black border and dark print, it was often a done deal. Too late to get in on the IPO for most, the ad was a place to display "bragging rights" by those with an inside track. *If they only knew*, he thought. The concept of tombstone had never been more aptly applied to an ad, given the death throes imminent at Pinnacle.

He continued to make his way around the table shaking hands, asking about the family or the golf game, with no interest in the responses he got. When he reached Donnelly, he gave him a hearty greeting, slapping him on the back. That Donnelly bastard had intended to be a no show, forcing him to play a little hard ball with the man. Sure, he's in knots, given that his daughter's missing, but he owed him, big time. Besides, he wanted to tell him, *who cares?* His daughter had plans to rob Donnelly blind with the one-two punch of false allegations followed by threats to extort money from the old guy. What a loser. Extortion, now that was another matter. It was a reliable method of getting your way when persuasion failed. Sometimes the old ways still worked the best.

Donnelly was there, but he wasn't in good shape. He'd lost weight and his jowls hung loose. His eyes were bloodshot and his complexion had a sallow tone that didn't look good in contrast to the sickly gray shade of his hair. Eric wished he could tell the man to buck up. It was unfortunate he had to yank Donnelly's chain, threatening to expose his daughter's allegations to get him to show up today, but at this point, the board needed to be unified—out in full force, as the crescendo built before the IPO on the twentieth.

As Eric took his seat, he caught Donnelly's eye. *Smile, you bastard,* he thought to himself as he peered at Donnelly. When Eric smiled at the man, Donnelly did his best to emulate that smile. Eric gave him a reassuring nod. *That's more like it,* he thought, as the loathsome CEO called the meeting to order.

Two hours later, Eric whistled as he glided back to his office. Photos of bankers shaking hands with the CEO, Eric at his side, would soon be circulated worldwide. Behind them, the full board, even the distressed Donnelly, smiled at the good news. They were certain to hit the billion-dollar mark in shares, no doubt about it. The anticipated share price was already at the high end of the range originally proposed.

Who the hell came up with the idea that Friday the thirteenth was bad luck? Eric wondered. From now on, thirteen would be his lucky number. There was good news on another front, too. The Van Der Woert broad had taken a turn for the worse. Even if she lived, there was a good chance she wouldn't be much more than a vegetable. Chances were even slimmer that she'd say a word about Carr or Shannon Donnelly or anything else in the week prior to the IPO. After that, it didn't matter.

"From parasite to vegetable," he muttered as he reached the door to his office suite. His dutiful executive assistant was sitting at her desk, fielding phone calls.

"Wow, it must have been a good meeting. Word got out fast— the phone has been ringing nonstop. Do you want me to put off lunch?

"No, that won't be necessary. Go have a nice lunch. Charge it to me! I'm feeling celebratory," he said.

"That was some meeting, wasn't it?" She asked, wide-eyed. "You sure about lunch?"

"I'm sure. A free lunch once in a while is the least I can do, given all your hard work around here," he said. *You'd better enjoy it. By Christmas, you won't have a job.* He didn't flinch as that thought flitted through his mind. Nor did he let it put a damper on his upbeat mood. It was regrettable innocents like her got ground up in the marketplace. But what the hell, it's only business.

In his office, with the door closed, he let himself do a little two-step. It was all going his way. By Christmas day, he would be on a beach, lounging in a chaise, with a quarter of a billion dollars tucked away in an offshore account. Libby Van Der Woert was down for the count, after seizing in the ICU. Jessica Huntington, off in her corner, was licking her wounds. Almost a week had passed since the debacle at the top of the tram in Palm Springs. If either of those women had reported anything of significance to the police, his eyes and ears on the ground would have found out and notified him by now. He burst into a chorus of I'm dreaming of a white Christmas... *as in a snow white sandy beach white Christmas,* he thought.

21 FIELD TRIP PLAN

The Cat Pack had assembled on the back patio, with Frank Fontana at the grill. Jessica tried not to gaze too long at the dark hair curled up against the collar of his shirt; the man was always in need of a haircut. He'd caught her staring at him once already and sent her one of those smoldering smiles of his. She was still off balance from a close encounter with him minutes before. Frank had been the last to arrive. Everyone else was outside when he rang the doorbell. Frank did nothing to hide his delight at seeing her when she opened the door for him.

"So, you're out and about. I guess no one wants you back at that hospital," he teased, stepping into the foyer and shutting the door.

"You're right—especially after a near-riot by my angel heiress fans," she quipped. He tilted his head, a quizzical look on his face that she found beguiling. "I'm a star. Come on in and you'll hear all about it."

"I could have told you that," he said as he swept her up in a gentle, but possessive hug, without jarring her ribs. "You've got star quality even wearing a cast, and with that little scrape there," he said, brushing the scrape on her cheek with a kiss. Jessica giggled and felt her whole body flush. She tried to play it cool.

"Really? What about the bruise over my eye?"

"It doesn't detract from your charm," he added, placing a light kiss there, too. Jessica's heart pounded. He was still holding onto her and must have felt her heart beating like that. "You are a star, an heiress, for sure, but an angel? We'll have to see about that, won't we?" The words tickled as he spoke them, so close to her ear that his warm breath made her tingle. Just then, the patio door slid open.

"Jessica, was that the doorbell I heard?" Bernadette asked, as she bustled down the hall toward them. She took in the scene before she spoke. "Hello, Frank, you ready to do a little cookin'—outside?" He let her go, and moved a step toward Bernadette, who was smiling a crooked little smile. Jessica felt like a kid caught with her hand in the cookie jar. It didn't seem to bother Frank at all. He gave Jessica's free hand a little squeeze.

"Sure thing, put me to work," Frank beamed back at her.

"You're working pretty good already," she said. Frank burst out laughing and put an arm around Bernadette's tiny shoulders. He reached over and pulled Jessica to his side, draping his other arm around her. Jessica sighed, under Frank's spell, as the three of them walked to the back door together. What was it about the exasperating man that left her feeling lost when that hug ended? Frank was trouble—puzzling, pleasurable, but trouble.

Cookout food was the order of the day. Frank had gone straight to the grill, after greeting everyone, including Betsy Stark. He and Betsy had met once, years before at Jessica's house, when he came to pick up Kelly and Tommy. Bernadette's carne asada was sizzling, sending out the most wonderful aroma. Tofu, steeped in the same marinade used on the strips of flank steak, was sizzling on a nearby surface for Peter-the-vegan and Kim who was a vegetarian, most of the time. A grill pan full of colorful peppers and onion slices was next to that, alongside neat rows of sweet potato wedges, sprinkled with spices. Bernadette had set pans of rice and frijoles charros, cowboy beans, off to the side to keep them warm.

The weather was chilly, by desert standards, edging below sixty after sunset. Jerry, Tommy, Laura, and Kim had ventured out for a swim in the heated pool. Patio heaters were on to keep them warm when they finished swimming. For now, they were content to float around, trying not to miss a word of the story Peter March was telling about that trip home from Jessica's doctor's visit the day before. It had been Brien who alerted Peter to the fact they had picked up a tail.

"Brien stopped going on and on about the nachos he got from the hospital cafeteria and went silent for thirty seconds. He's sitting there, still. Then, out of the blue, he says, *'Yo, Peter, there's something not right about that dude back there in the pizza delivery car. I think we should prepare to take invasive maneuvers.'"*

Brien lounged in a chaise next to Peter, a cold bottle of beer in his hand, and a bowl full of chips on his lap. He was happy about the praise from Peter, and ready to embellish Peter's story, if need be. He wasn't even eating!

"All I said," Peter went on, "was *'not right—what's not right?'* I wasn't ready to ask Brien what he meant by 'invasive maneuvers,' but I looked at the car behind us."

"Yeah, when Peter asked me, I told him that car behind us might look ordinary, but was a brand-new Chevy Camaro Zl1, supercharged with a 6.2 liter V8 that cranks out 580 horsepower and about 550 pound-feet of torque. It's a sweet ride outfitted with GM's third-generation Magnetic Ride technology, a special valve-less damping and fluid system to adjust suspension firmness to match the road and driving conditions." A stunned silence followed as Brien spit out that stream of specs.

"What?" Brien asked, looking up at a round of gaping mouths. Except for Betsy, who hadn't known Brien long enough to be surprised by such a lucid spiel, and Bernadette, who had the bewildered expression on her face she often wore when Brien spoke.

"Now you know how I reacted yesterday when Brien described the car," Peter said.

"Oh yeah, and twenty-inch wheels with smokin' rims—that costs extra. Good, huh, for a pizza delivery guy?"

"Unless he delivers more than pizza," Frank commented, as he removed tofu from the grill.

"Well, I had noticed it first in the parking lot at the medical center. It didn't have that pizza delivery sign on top. So, later, when I saw it again with that Pizza Pros sign on top, I was thinking, *'Whoa, Man, what's going on?'* The most bogus thing of all: they don't even deliver pizza in this part of town." Brien-the-bobble-head was back.

"When I got over my shock at discovering Brien's latent powers of observation, I knew he had to be right."

"Dude, my powers aren't latent." Another moment of silence ensued. Both torque and latent in the vocabulary of a man who regarded the good things in life as "gnarlitious" or "bitchin," how could that be?

"There's nothing plastic about them." A sigh released them all from the fear they'd somehow misjudged the desert-dwelling surfer dude in their midst. Betsy had a puzzled look on her face, not getting it at all.

"He means latex and has that confused with Peter's reference to latent. At least, I think that's what he means. With Brien, it's sometimes a little complicated." Jessica spoke in a low voice, hoping not to offend Brien. Peter picked up the story.

"Anyway, I knew something was up, so that's when I called for reinforcements. They joined us as soon as they could, to provide you an escort, so Brien and I could apprehend the phony pizza guy. There's a sniper on the loose, so I was taking no chances by leaving you exposed, or signaling we were on to the guy too soon."

"It was kind of scary, at first," Bernadette said.

"Peter's right. If we hadn't been so sneaky and swift, that bozo would have gotten away. That car can move—zero to sixty in under four seconds," Brien assured them all.

"Fortunately, another of my guys cut him off quick, so we had him cornered in no time. Unfortunately, he wasn't our sniper, but a member of the paparazzi. He was looking to shoot you, Jessica, but with photo equipment rather than bullets."

"Lucky for you it was a roving photographer," Frank commented piling items from the grill onto platters. Bernadette took the platters he filled and lined them up on the granite surface of the outdoor cook island.

"I'm not so sure I'd say lucky. That was crafty, finding me and tagging along like that. As pushy as the autograph hounds were that had me cornered in the hospital yesterday, I'm not happy about being hunted by a reporters or snipers."

"Word's gotten around about 'that Huntington woman' causing another scene at the hospital," Laura said as she stepped out of the pool and slipped into a robe. "You're famous among the nursing staff, that's for sure."

"Infamous, is more like it. I just hope I don't have outraged nurses, with loaded hypodermics after me now. I'm glad we got back here in one piece! Two rescues in one day, Peter. So, thanks." Jessica raised the glass of sparkling water she was drinking. No wine until she finished the course of antibiotics the docs had given her.

"Hey, what about me—after all I'm Thor or Uber-Thor or whatever..." A round of puzzled expressions appeared on the faces of her friends.

Jessica spent the next few minutes filling them all in on the events at the hospital, including that Thor-Uber-Thor thing. Jessica also told them about her visit with Nora in the ICU, and Libby's latest health crisis. The revelation that Nora had given Jessica keys to Libby's car and condo caused an immediate clamor from Tommy to make a visit. Detective Hernandez had agreed that Jerry could have a look around at Shannon Donnelly's condo, with the understanding that whatever he found got turned over to him.

"All that talk about pizza delivery guys is making me super hungry," Brien said as he rose from his lounge chair and refilled his bowl with chips, pushing them to one side to make room for Bernadette's spicy, tequila-laced salsa. He snatched a couple of empanadas before sitting back down.

The empanadas, neat little packets of dough folded around cheese, meat or vegetables, were only one of the savory appetizers set out for dinner. They sat on a table alongside goat-cheese-filled dates wrapped in bacon, sautéed peppers, tossed with garlic and roasted pine nuts, and kabobs made of fresh fruit. Besides the salsa, Bernadette had prepared guacamole and chismol, a Central American take on pico de gallo, all set out in bowls. The mouth-watering accompaniments to the carne asada created a colorful display. Bernadette was waiting until the last moment to bring out warm, fresh-made tortillas from Cardenas, a local Latino grocery.

"The rest of you had better get out of the pool and dry off, before Brien wipes out the tapas," Frank said, as he stepped away from the grill. Brien eyed the table full of tapas as he crammed food into his mouth. Frank had remained quiet while Peter and Brien told the story of the events that had taken place the day before.

"You have been involved in the most incredible streak of strange situations, Jessica," Frank said, pondering the latest round of mayhem.

"Betsy and I were talking earlier about how much of my life I spend in the low probability event zone. Incredibly good *and* bad luck, I'd say." Jessica countered. She would have said more but had just taken a bite of one of Bernadette's empanadas, filled with a savory blend of acorn squash. "Good luck as in living under the same roof with one of the world's great cooks. This acorn squash empanada is amazing, Bernadette."

"Gracias. But let's get back to snooping."

"And my point is about your propensity to attract bad luck," Frank admonished.

"A certain amount of bad luck goes with the territory when you deal with troubled clients. I know that much from my own work," Betsy said. "You're in the same boat, too, Frank, right?"

"True enough. I have been in some bad situations courtesy of my work as a police officer and homicide detective. Who knew that the paparazzi could cause the trouble that jerk created for you yesterday?"

"Not just paparazzi, but fans. Don't forget I have fans now, too."

"All that makes it harder to figure out who's out to get you. The best thing you can do, until the police come up with the identity and whereabouts of that sniper, is to lie low."

"I understand, but there are things I *have* to do. Mom's expecting me to visit her in Malibu. I think it's important to find that little blue bag. Maybe something in it will validate Libby's claims about her relationship with the dead shrink. If my screwy good luck is working for us, we could also get a lead about what's happened to Shannon or who hired that sniper. While I'm out and about, on my way to Malibu, we might as well check Libby's condo and car. Presuming the blue bag exists."

"Let's hope you don't run into that red devil. That could be screwy bad luck," Bernadette said making the sign of the cross. It took another round of catch up to make sure everyone had heard about Libby's claims that Carr was in league with the devil—a red one.

"There's no reason Jerry can't go check out Libby's place. It would be better to have the police there, too. That way, if you find something of value, you don't have to worry about chain of custody later."

"True, Frank. But I'll be making that trip to the coast anyway, and I'd find it helpful to check out the place where Libby and Shannon lived in Manhattan Beach. I'm trying to get a handle on these two young women and their relationship. Maybe something will gel if I spend more time in their bizarre little world. The Manhattan Beach PD already went through there, days ago, when Shannon disappeared. They didn't find anything out of the ordinary or any evidence of foul play. So it's not a crime scene, at this point. Given the circumstances in which the whole topic of a suitcase came up, it's possible this is all a wild goose chase. I think that's why Hernandez said, 'go for it' without chewing me out first."

"Still, Libby is a suspect in what may be a murder investigation, depending on how Carr died. Have you checked with Dad and the Palm Springs PD?"

"No, but do you think the Palm Springs PD will be more willing to go on a search for a little blue suitcase based on the rant by a mentally ill young woman, suspected of kidnapping and maybe murder? When? Call Uncle Don and see what he says. My guess is his colleagues won't be any more eager to run this down than Hernandez is. But the ways of homicide detectives are mysterious, so what do I know?"

"Homicides get top priority. The contents of that suitcase could contain evidence for a motive to shoot Carr or push him off the rocks up there. I'll remind you, red devil or no red devil, there's still a gunman on the loose—a professional sniper with excellent aim." Frank was getting annoyed and annoying. So, what? She wanted a look at what was in that suitcase for herself.

"Okay, I'll admit it. I'm curious about what's in that suitcase. I have a client who gave me permission to look in the condo and car, on behalf of her incapacitated daughter who, crazy or not, *asked* me to find it. We'll wear gloves—I do <u>not</u> want to touch anything that's been in contact with Carr's bodily fluids anyway." A little shudder went through her body and she put down the rest of the uneaten empanada, having lost her appetite. "Do you really think a gunman's after me? If Libby and I were both on the hit list, I can't believe pros wouldn't have sent more than one guy to the hospital. And, if you're worried about my paparazzi and fans, I'll wear dark glasses and plain clothes, nothing flashy. I won't use my own car. I'll have Peter drive me. You'll do that, won't you, Peter?"

"Sure, we can work something out." Brien was nodding as Peter spoke, as though he had something to say about it.

"Oh, I have to go along. I need to see your mother, too." Bernadette spoke in a solemn way, but with a spark in her eyes that gave her away. She was eager to find out what was in that suitcase. "No offense, Peter and Brien, but I'd rather drive, unless you all will let me ride shotgun." Brien sat up straight.

"Uh, that's my job," Brien said. "I'm the one who needs to be in that seat. Just in case something happens and Peter needs professional help."

"You are not qualified to provide that kind of professional help, Brien. No guns," Peter admonished.

"That goes for you too, Bernadette. No guns!" Jessica added. She wasn't sure what was more terrifying, the thought of Bernadette or Brien, armed with live ammunition. That reminded her she still had her dad's gun in her purse.

"Here's an idea. You drive, but use one of our agency cars instead of the Escalade. The vehicle I have in mind protects passengers from bullets. Brien and I will follow you. When we get to the condo, I'll make sure the underground parking area is secure before you get out of the car. That ought to make you feel better, right Frank?"

"What if you find something that needs to be taken into evidence? Then what? Gloves won't prevent a smart lawyer from arguing that the evidence was tampered with, somehow, before it got to the police."

"Okay, so you come along, Frank. Get Uncle Don to put you into the proper chain of custody. You're all Riverside County law enforcement. Better yet, bring him along, too. We'll do everything by the book. I promise."

"Field trip, field trip!" Tommy chanted. "I say we all go. Why don't we check out Carr's office and condo, too?" He continued, his eyes brightening at the thought of an adventure.

"Now you want to trample those places, too, by taking the entire Cat Pack through them?" Frank was in full blown cop paranoia mode.

"The cat what?" Betsy asked with a puzzled expression on her face. In response, several members of the Cat Pack, excluding Kim, who had yet to say a word, spoke at once. "Wait a second, please. This is getting more confusing, not less. You need to appoint an official spokesperson and clue me in." Heads swiveled in unison, like cats all following the same dangling string, toward Jessica.

"That would be me." She spent the next few minutes filling Betsy in on their loosely-constructed association. Betsy got it right away. She was aware of the valley's legendary status as a playground for the much more sophisticated "Rat Pack," headed up by that other Frank.

"In response to *your* question, Frank, no I don't think we should all go traipsing through Carr's home and office. But Tommy has a good idea. Why don't we divide up—you and I can take a team to Libby's condo and car. The rest can go to Carr's office in Beverly Hills, and to his house in Pacific Palisades. Betsy had a great idea that we might learn something about Carr's silent partner by going through Carr's rolodex and his client referral system."

"What does that mean for the whole chain of custody thing?" Peter asked. "Frank can't be everywhere."

"Uncle Don can go with us, and he can be on our team," Tommy said with excitement.

"I doubt he'll agree to any of this. You know what a stickler he is. Besides, he's not even in the homicide division. He won't have anything to do with this looky-loo business." Frank was stuck in stubborn cop mode.

"It couldn't hurt to ask, could it?" That was Kim, breaking her silence to weigh in on the idea.

"Field trip, field trip, sleepover, sleepover," Tommy chanted again, stopping when several pairs of eyes focused on him. "What? We'll be in Beverly Hills. Chichi hotels, shopping, restaurants, spas... did I say shopping?"

"You'll get me into so much trouble with Father Martin. He's trying to get me to do more for my favorite charities instead of shopping."

"Are you saying I'm not a favorite charity?" Tommy's bottom lip poked out like a spoiled child. "I can't afford lunch at Spago, or a night at the Ritz Carlton, with a bottle of bubbly and a romantic couple's massage." Jerry blushed as Tommy looked at him lasciviously. Frank choked.

"The Ritz Carlton? Are you kidding?"

"Oh, okay, Frank, are you a Four Seasons fan? How about the Beverly Wilshire Hotel—we can relive the best moments from Pretty Woman. I loved that movie. Heck, you can almost spit on Rodeo Drive from the window of your hotel room. It's soooo close! We won't even have to drive to shop 'til we drop."

"Uh, I don't think it's a good idea for anybody to spit on Rodeo Drive," Brien said. "I do like that movie. Julia Roberts is still bangin'—for an older babe."

"The Beverly Wilshire is obscenely expensive, too. You don't have to shell out that kind of cash for me. Besides, if we find something, Dad and I will want to drive back to Riverside County and put it into evidence as soon as we can." At that moment, Jessica realized the decision had been made. Even Frank was in.

"Yes, we don't have to stay there, but it would be fun. That light in Jessica's eyes tells me she's ready to wave that black AMEX card around. Our angel heiress loves to play fairy godmother," Laura sighed, smiling ruefully at Jessica.

"It is a great hotel," Kim said, deadpan. "My old boss did a film shoot there that put a different spin on the Pretty Woman thing."

"Ooh, tell us," Tommy said, knowing about the "adult-themed" films Kim's former boss had made.

"No, please don't. I'd prefer not to know..." Jerry insisted. "I'll agree to let Jessica pay for an overnight, but I don't want to be flashing on anything that little creep might have done."

Jessica's head was spinning with all the chatter. Laura was right that she needed to get to work wielding that black AMEX card. But what to do first? Call Don Fontana; make hotel reservations for Saturday night, figure out how early they should leave in the morning or should they drive in tonight? How could she explain this to Father Martin? Bernadette came to the rescue.

"We need to eat before the food gets cold. Dig in, you guys. Jessica, I don't think Father Martin will mind. If you want to go to Malibu and Manhattan Beach in one day, you'll be exhausted. Staying overnight isn't a bad idea. We could stay at Hank's place in Brentwood, but I don't think he's ready to face the whole Cat Pack, do you?" She asked.

"No, I don't think he'll ever be ready for that," Jessica replied. "Frank, will you call your dad and see if he'll agree to go with us? If he says yes, it's a deal, okay?" Frank pulled out his phone and hit a button.

"Dad, have you got a minute?"

"Ask him if he'll agree to go to lunch with us at the Beverly Wilshire so we can all debrief, okay?" Frank nodded, understanding Jessica's request. Jessica did a quick count in her head, regarding the number of rooms they would need. Not more than a minute later, Frank gave her a thumbs-up. Uncle Don was in and it was go.

"Betsy, do you want to join us?" Jessica glimpsed a little flash of something pass over Peter's face—anticipation, maybe? *Hmm, Jessica* noted.

"I'd love to, but I'm doing an in-service training tomorrow."

"On a Saturday?" Peter blurted out.

"Yes, and I don't dare let my staff down or they'll be looking around for training on Law of Attraction Therapy, or some other nonsense to get continuing education credit. Not all the wackiness in my life comes from my clients. I'll take a rain check, though, and I'd love to hear all about it, if you'll call me later, Peter." That big goofy smile was back on his face as Betsy wrote her cell phone number on a business card and handed it to him.

In the meantime, Tommy whipped out his phone. In another minute, he punched in a number and handed his phone to Jessica.

"The Beverly Wilshire," he said, doing a little happy dance as she took the phone from him. Jerry rolled his eyes, at Tommy's audaciousness. "What?" Tommy asked as Jessica shushed him.

"Yes, I'd like to reserve several rooms for tomorrow night..." With that she was off and running. No need to dig out that black AMEX card because the information emblazoned on the card stood out in bold relief in her head. She had used that card so much that she'd committed the numbers to memory. In minutes, it was all arranged—a dinner reservation at Spago, too.

Betsy's words played over in Jessica's mind, "*Not all of the wackiness in my life comes from my clients.*" So true! Libby wasn't her client, but Jessica couldn't let it go. What could be stashed away in that little blue case? Could it help them find Carr's silent partner? Jessica glanced at Betsy, who was chatting with Peter like they were old friends. She thought of the conviction in Betsy's voice when she assured Jessica that Carr's associate was close. How close and did he have a hired gun waiting to take another shot at Libby or her?

In over my head, time to swim for it, she thought as she looked up. Frank stood there with a plate of food for her and a look that said it all, "Come on in, the water's fine."

22 CONDO SEARCH

On Saturday morning, Jessica awoke with anticipation thinking about the day ahead. Peter would drop off their specially-equipped, nondescript, late model car. That car would be unfamiliar to anyone tailing them, whether from the media, or on the payroll of the red devil. Peter and Brien would provide escort in another of the vehicles owned by his security company, choosing one they used for surveillance, rather than the black SUVs they preferred to use as escort vehicles.

Once they were on the road, Jessica called Detective Hernandez and let him in on their plans for the day. She didn't go into all the details about their "field trip" and "sleepover" at the Beverly Wilshire because it was too early in the morning to tangle with him if she got him riled up. She had worried needlessly. He was almost effusive in his praise for the way Jessica had planned her latest foray into sleuthing. He was grateful for the help given how shorthanded they were in Cat City. As it also turned out, he was still a homicide detective without evidence of a homicide. The body found in Cathedral Canyon was not Shannon Donnelly, but a homeless woman who was a long-time drug addict. They wouldn't know for sure what caused her death, until they got a tox screen back from the lab in another week.

"I'll owe you one after this. I'd warn you off, given that incident at the hospital, if Frank and Don hadn't been willing to go with you.

They're both good cops and should be able to keep you out of trouble."

"Well, thanks for the vote of confidence, I think."

"You'll keep me in the loop on anything you discover that might apply to Ms. Donnelly's disappearance. If you find that suitcase, you'll make sure it gets into the proper hands."

"Yes, that is the whole point behind having police officers with us, even on their day off."

"Nice of them to do that for you."

"True, but they owe *me* one for the work I did to find Kelly's killer, and they're willing to take a chance on this being a wild goose chase to get more information about Carr and Libby. And, if it's not a wild goose chase, there's the possibility that something might provide a link to whoever's behind that attempt on Libby's life."

"I'm sure I don't have to tell you to be careful and do exactly as the Fontanas tell you." This was getting old fast.

"No problem. I'll talk to you later."

The road trip to Manhattan Beach was uneventful. Sitting in that car for over two hours, even with the seat back about as far as it could go, wasn't comfortable. Jessica tried to keep apprehension from overtaking her—not just about what they might find at Libby's condo, but what awaited them later in Malibu. With GPS, none of them had trouble finding Libby's condo. When they arrived, Jessica spotted Frank's car parked at the curb near the entrance to the underground parking area. A quick call to the security team at the condo complex got them access to the area in no time.

Once inside the garage, they checked Libby's car first. Jessica used the electronic key Libby's mother had given her to unlock the doors. Peter, who had already taken pictures of the scene as soon as they identified Libby's car, snapped photos of the car's interior. Donning a pair of latex gloves, Frank opened all four doors as Peter circled the car snapping away. Jessica and Bernadette hung back, chomping at the bit to find that suitcase. But from where they stood, a few feet away, it was clear there was no suitcase in the car.

Frank bagged the few items in Libby's car. He checked the glove compartment and found nothing there, either, other than the items you'd expect to find, including a vehicle owner's manual, insurance card, registration, and a California road map. Jessica realized she'd been holding her breath as Frank searched all the pockets and compartments in the car, finding nothing in them.

"Peter, I'll pop the trunk so you can photograph that too, okay?" Jessica said, as Frank finished his search of the car's interior.

"Sure," he said, moving to the back of the car. Jessica hit a button on the electronic key fob and released the latch on the trunk. Frank stepped around to the back, too. He lifted the trunk lid and Peter took a couple of photos. More disappointment gripped Jessica. There was a bag in the back, but no blue suitcase. Instead, they found a dark green duffle bag containing a pair of yoga socks, leggings, a t-shirt, a towel, and a lightweight, rolled up mat that Frank unrolled and then re-rolled. As he looked through the items, Peter continued to document each item.

"I'm not sure what we're looking for since there's no blue suitcase in here." Frank placed the items he'd removed back inside the duffle bag. "I'll put this in my evidence container in the back of my car anyway." Frank stacked the bagged items from the car interior on top of the gym bag and picked them all up.

"Oh my God, is that a rosary?" Jessica asked.

"Yes, it's broken, but I'm pretty sure all the pieces are there."

"Bernadette's the expert on that front. Let's let her see it, okay?"

"Sure, as long as she doesn't remove it from the bag."

"Do you want me to put on those snooper gloves, first?" Bernadette asked.

"No, I don't think that's necessary. Let Peter take a couple photos, though, before you touch it." Frank took the bag containing the rosary and flattened it out for the photo. He flipped it over and had Peter take another shot. Bernadette peered at the broken string of beads for about a minute before speaking.

"There are pieces missing. It's broken right near the section holding the crucifix. See how there are three brown beads and then a silver bead, then the cross? There should be a silver bead first, then the three brown beads. The missing bead is the 'Glory Be' bead. There should also be a small medallion linking the sections together, but that's gone too." They were leaning over Bernadette's shoulder trying to see what she was talking about.

"What's up, guys?" They all jumped about a foot off the ground. Brien, who had fallen asleep riding shotgun, had joined them. A surge of pain shot through Jessica.

"Argh! Brien, don't go sneaking up on people like that," Bernadette chided him.

"Why not? I was practicing being stealthy. Guess I'm getting good at it too, huh?"

"I'm an old lady, you coulda' given me a heart attack!"

"Oh, okay, sorry. What're we doing?" Brien asked.

"*We're* letting Bernadette examine a rosary we found in Libby's car." Jessica replied.

"Wow, that's good, isn't it? Libby said you should find that, right?"

"True, but it's not clear yet what we can learn from a broken rosary. Frank, are you sure you collected all the pieces from the car?"

"I can check again, but I think so." He said. "When did Libby tell you about a rosary? Why didn't I hear about that?" Jessica explained how the rosary issue had only come up the day before when Libby had that episode in the ICU. Bernadette interrupted Jessica's conversation with Frank. She'd been peering at the broken rosary.

"There's not just something missing, but something that shouldn't be there. Mira," Bernadette said, as she pointed. They all leaned in close again. "See that smear on the shiny back of the crucifix? What does that look like to you?"

"It's hard to tell, but it could be blood, and maybe a partial fingerprint." Frank answered after another few moments. "I'll call this in to Hernandez. Somebody needs to pick up this car and go over it thoroughly if this turns out to be blood."

"That's totally spooky. How did blood get on a crucifix?" Brien asked. "Whose blood is it? Not the 'Big Kahuna's, right? Can you pick up any vibes from holding it using your *powers?*"

"Ay, Dios mìo, Brien. If by Big Kahuna you mean Jesus, the answer is no. Stop with all the questions—and the spooky stuff." Bernadette crossed herself like she was trying to ward off something evil.

"The lab will have to tell us if it's blood, and whose it is. I don't suppose Libby or her mother said anything about who owned that rosary?" Frank asked.

"No. Libby's mom didn't know why she was talking about a rosary. She doesn't think Libby's been a practicing Catholic in a long time. Libby was so insistent on the need to find it. Maybe it belonged to Shannon Donnelly and that blood is hers. Not a pleasant thought. I can't come up with a good scenario to explain a broken rosary with a bloody crucifix. Can you?"

"Let's not jump to conclusions. But, it's probably not a good thing. Maybe the lab can get something from that fingerprint." Frank sighed as he picked up the items.

"I guess we've done all we can here. It's time to go upstairs and see if that suitcase is in the condo," Jessica said, getting an anxious little tickle of doom as they stood in the low light of the parking garage.

"Give me a minute to put these items in the evidence container in my trunk. Jessica, will you lock up the car as soon as I get it all closed up again?"

"Sure." She used the key fob to lock the car and set the car alarm, still pondering the significance of that rosary. *What was it doing in Libby's car?* She wondered. The police already had DNA samples from both Libby and Shannon, so it would be straightforward to find out if the blood belonged to one of them. Jessica felt a wave of foreboding about the Donnelly's missing daughter.

"Okay, where's that key to the condo?" Frank asked. Jessica handed him the key and let him lead the way to the elevator.

"Top floor," she said, before he could ask. "Condo number four-eighty. I suppose you should have all the keys," Jessica added, handing him the key to the car and the small key to Libby's mailbox.

"Thanks, we should collect her mail and haul that back to the Sheriff's department just in case there's something in it that Dad's guys or Hernandez can use."

When they entered the condo after a silent ride in the elevator, Jessica's dark mood lifted. High ceilings and an open floor plan gave the space a bright and airy feeling. The stylish contemporary décor was in keeping with the architecture of the condo complex. Sleek marble flooring and other pricey finishes were everywhere. Upscale kitchen appliances looked brand new. Jessica guessed the two wealthy young women who lived in the place didn't cook for themselves. There was nothing in the fridge except yogurt and a variety of supplements. Built along a busy street, the complex didn't sit on the beach, but across the road from it. A corner unit, the views from a bank of windows and sliding doors were spectacular. A spacious deck provided plenty of room for entertaining or taking in the view.

"Whoa, this is awesome," Brien exclaimed. "I could totally live here. That patio is big enough to stash my surfboard and my bicycle."

"I bet it is. Libby had to be upset about losing a place like this," Peter said.

"Didn't her parents buy it for her?"

"Yes, Frank, but the taxes and homeowners fees must be several thousand a month. Even with Shannon Donnelly sharing the expenses, Libby might have been in trouble when that trust ended since she had no job."

"Well, that gives her a motive for trying to get money out of her parents, that's for sure. Money from her uncle would have come in handy too."

"That's for sure. I remember her parents talking with her about selling it and helping her downsize to something more affordable. That was right *before* Libby made those awful allegations. Mind you, they weren't talking about cutting her off when her trust ended. They were trying to come up with something that would work for her longer term, since she'd made little headway on education and a career during her probation."

"It would be hard to give up this lifestyle and settle for something less. Even scaling down might mean working for a living—not something she looked forward to, I imagine," Peter commented.

"You wouldn't think that would turn her into a raging monster toward her parents, but what do I know?" Jessica let out an exasperated sigh.

"Disturbed and unhappy women will resort to desperate measures, Jessica. Look at what happened to Kelly." Frank had a sad look on his face. Jessica reached up and touched his face.

"I get it," Jessica said. *Look at my own mother*, she thought, as she removed her hand. A wave of anxiety hit as she considered the desperate and unhappy woman waiting for her in another spot along the gorgeous So-Cal coastline. She glanced at Bernadette, who must have guessed what she was thinking.

"Sometimes they get help when they're desperate," Bernadette said in a reassuring way.

"Good point. In this case, Libby and Shannon were trying to do that when they met up with Dr. Demento. That makes me furious!"

"Well, she wasn't completely sucked in by the guy if she kept items to blackmail him. Let's see if we can find that suitcase and throw some light on what he did."

They spent the next hour going through Libby's condo. No blue suitcase could be found anywhere in the condo. Jessica was sore, although she had been on light duty, mostly watching as the others snooped. They had divided up, searching each room. Peter and Brien on one team, with Frank and Bernadette on the other. Peter had even given Brien a boost so he could check out the attic. Nothing! Jessica was about to call it quits when something Brien had said got her to thinking.

"Brien, where do you keep your surfboard? You don't have a patio—not like this one anyway."

"Even if I did, I'm on the first floor so someone could walk off with it. My apartment is small, or I'd keep it inside."

"Okay, so where?" She didn't wait for him to answer before getting up and heading into the kitchen. She'd seen a small key taped in place inside one of the drawers.

"I have a storage space at the complex, that's..." before he could finish, she interrupted him as she pulled the key free from the tape.

"Peter, can you call the security guys you spoke to when we first arrived and ask if there's a storage area available to condo owners?"

"I'm on it," he said, dialing as he spoke.

"They say yes. It's down on the same level as the parking garage. You need a key and each homeowner has an assigned compartment. The one associated with this unit is..."

"D-8," Jessica called out, holding up the key as she headed for the door.

"Bingo," Bernadette hollered. Jessica took a quick look around, making sure they were leaving Libby's lovely home the way they'd found it. Not that it was likely to be her home again, given the latest news from the ICU. Depending on what they learned about Shannon Donnelly's fate, even if Libby made it out of the ICU functional enough to live on her own, she might be moving to new accommodations, courtesy of the criminal justice system.

Energized by a surge of hope, they headed back down to the lower level. Using the directions given to Peter, they found the storage area. Frank insisted that they go back into evidence collection mode, having Peter snap photos of the area as he donned a pair of gloves. Almost as soon as the door opened, they spotted a small blue suitcase—part of a matched set stashed away in the walk-in storage area.

Peter snapped away and then Frank picked up the suitcase and set it on top of the largest piece of luggage in the set. As soon as he opened it, they all gasped.

"Eew," Jessica said.

23 A FAMILIAR FACE

Even surrounded by luxury and beauty, lunch was less pleasant than it might have been without having viewed the contents of that little blue bag. It was illuminating, however. Their group sat poolside with gorgeous blue skies overhead, tall palms swaying, and cheery sounds of resort goers. The iconic hotel held a lot of nostalgia for Jessica, not because of the Julia Roberts movie, but because she had been there many times with her mother. After Alexis divorced Hank, she and Jessica stayed at the hotel for spa treatments, shopping, and gadding about town. Often one or two of Alexis' cronies joined them for part of the day, and Jessica brought friends too. Laura was with her today, but no Kelly, no Mom.

All that history intersected, at oddly disorienting angles, with the latest calamity, courtesy of another troubled young woman hurtling toward self-annihilation. Jessica was awash in a sea of angst and dread, and put off food after getting a look at the contents of that suitcase. It did nothing to dampen Brien's appetite, so they ordered drinks and appetizers. Jessica could have used a stiff shot of whiskey or something, but couldn't because of the meds she was taking. A blast from the past hit Jessica broadside as she remembered her mother, and one or more of her friends, putting away cocktails with lunch. *Even as an adult, I'd be under the table if I tried to keep up with them,* she thought, remembering all those diamond rings flashing as they clinked glasses.

The contents of the little blue bag were what Jessica had expected, except worse. She was prepared to find a dress, like the one Monica Lewinsky had kept as a souvenir of her tryst with Clinton, but what they found was more like preparations for a mini-exhibit at a freak show. The disturbed young woman had packaged and preserved a variety of items, including underwear—his and hers, sealed in baggies labeled with dates, times, and locations. A small shock of white hair and nail clippings were in bags with stickers reading "Dr. Dick," along with the graphic details of how she had obtained them. Swabs of who knows what were sealed and marked—Jessica didn't ask Frank for details as he went through the contents of Libby's small suitcase, setting out each grotesque item for Peter to photograph. There were also several small jars containing what Jessica and Frank surmised to be a preservative. The whiff she got when they first opened that case conjured up a rush of old images from biology 101 labs: formaldehyde. What was floating in the containers required speculation that Jessica had no desire to make. She would leave that to the crime lab where Frank planned to take all the items as soon as their debriefing was over.

"I've already called Detective Hernandez and reported what we've found in the car, condo, and the storage unit. He's getting a warrant to have Libby's car impounded, presuming the spot on the rosary is blood. He's laying odds it's more likely to be Shannon Donnelly's blood than Libby's, but we'll have to wait for the lab results."

He glanced at Jessica, who was still feeling a little green around the gills as she sipped diet Coke to settle her stomach. The sips fell into a pit she recognized from previous visits to the land of 'dirt bags and the misguided women who loved them.' She included herself as one of them, having fallen for a dirt bag of her very own. She tried not to block Frank out as he ran through the list of oddities found in Libby's little bag of horrors to inform the team that had gone to Dr. Carr's home and office instead of the condo.

"That girl has watched way too many episodes of CSI," Kim said.

"Well, what has Hernandez on the move are several labeled 'Shannon Donnelly.' Some suspicious-looking items for sure—bloody tissue, several blond hairs, and a bag containing a small amount of sand and gravel. Each marked, not only with Shannon's name, but also with the phrase: 'Dr. Dick's Mercedes.' The license plate number was included, and items were dated the day after Shannon disappeared."

"Holy cow! Shannon must have met up with Carr after that fight in the parking lot. And if Libby went through his car on the date she claims, she must have seen Carr, too. Did she tell the police?" Tommy asked.

"Not a word. Mind you, she lawyered up quick once they took her in and questioned her about that last evening she spent with Shannon. I doubt Hernandez even asked Libby about Carr, since her shrink wasn't in the picture that early in the investigation. It was another day or two before they found out both women had called him the night Shannon disappeared. Carr acknowledged he received the calls, but didn't tell the police he saw either woman. What do you want to bet he picked Shannon up from the parking lot that night? Who knows what happened next?"

"He's not going to tell us. Libby may never be able to do that, either," Laura responded.

"Why didn't Libby tell me that Carr picked up Shannon if she'd figured that out? I don't get it."

"Their brains don't work like ours. Call it mental illness or bad judgment if you like, but in my experience folks who get mixed up with the Dr. Carrs of the world are concerned more about the wrong he's done to them than to others. Concern about what happened to her friend is almost an afterthought. At least Libby expressed some remorse about Shannon Donnelly's fate, although we don't know what that is yet." Frank shook his head, sadness or weariness slowed his movements.

"Well, at one point, Libby stated flat out that Shannon Donnelly is dead. I presume she knows more than she was willing to reveal during her meltdown at the top of the tram. Still, as angry as she was with Dr. Dick, you'd expect she'd be delighted to pin murder on him if she had the evidence. Why simply rat him out for sexual indiscretion?"

"Unless, no matter what she claims with the tags on those baggies, what she's doing is cleaning up after herself. All we have is her word for it that the items came from Carr's auto. The license plate number is no real proof. What if it's an effort to frame Carr?"

"That would have required more organization than Libby was capable of, don't you think?" Laura asked. "I mean, she was drunk when Shannon went missing. I could imagine Libby lashing out and killing Shannon in that condition, but frame her shrink? I doubt it."

"Hey, you know what they say, don't you? Hell hath no fury like a woman scorned. If she had it in for the dude, that could have helped her focus long enough to set him up." They all stopped talking and stared at Brien. He was trying to fish the maraschino cherry out of the bottom of his glass. As they watched, he put down the straw he'd been using and upended the glass. He got his wish as the maraschino cherry fell, along with a face full of ice.

"Brien has a point, no matter how big a fool he's making of himself," Bernadette offered. Brien, who was cleaning himself off, stopped putting errant ice cubes back into his glass and spoke.

"Give a guy a break, will you? I'm starving. If they'd brought me my nachos already, I wouldn't have had to do that." Bernadette ignored him as she picked up where she'd left off.

"Killing Shannon and making it look like her shrink did it would be a way to get back at them both. That doesn't mean she's any good at it. Anger and revenge can only get you so far—could be just far enough to get you into more trouble."

"Revenge is right up there with sex and money as a motive for murder. Maybe, you're *all* right. This could be more about cleaning up after herself, by pinning it on Carr as an afterthought, rather than a premeditated plan. She roused herself out of a coma to lead you to that suitcase, even if she didn't disclose all its contents," Frank said.

"When it comes to masterminding a murder, the narcissistic psychiatrist is a better fit," Jerry asserted. "If Libby was on to him, it would sure help explain why he was intent on killing her. Maybe you're right, Jessica, that he assumed she'd told you about Shannon's murder. That would explain why he decided to get rid of you, too."

"Your idea about the shrink being more suited to murder makes sense, I guess," Jessica said.

"About as much sense as murder ever makes," Frank said, shaking his head in bewilderment. "Once you've crossed that line and killed, there's a sordid logic for killing again to cover it up by going after you and Libby."

"Don't forget about Carr's associate, the 'red devil,' behind the effort to kill Libby before she could come out of her coma. He's got my vote as Shannon's killer, with or without Carr's help. Despite her disorganized thinking and bizarre behavior, Libby must know something. It can't just be about Carr's dirty work because he's dead, so why kill Libby?" Laura asked. The group fell silent as several servers swept down on them with appetizers and refills of their drinks.

"I can't answer that, Laura, but you must be on the right track. I guess that brings us to team two. What's your story?" Jessica asked. Now that food had appeared, she was glad to end the discussion about the suitcase and its contents.

"I've already given Frank a quick heads up so he could call it in to Hernandez. The good news is that we already have the doctor's Mercedes in impound. My guy hauled it from the tramway parking lot the day he died. Hernandez is laying the groundwork to have the forensics team go over it."

"Whoa, maybe they'll find Shannon's blood in his car. Do you think that's where Libby found that rosary?" Brien asked, cramming fries into his mouth.

"That's an excellent question. Libby left her car in Manhattan Beach, when she and Shannon went to the desert. The rosary could have been in it before that Thanksgiving weekend when Shannon disappeared. Maybe she took it from the shrink's car with all the other items, but then why not stash it in the suitcase with everything else?" Frank asked.

"It's Libby, so who knows?" Jessica responded. "She could have picked it up any time or somewhere else other than Carr's Mercedes. Stashing all that stuff she found in Carr's Mercedes does mean she went back to her condo after her Thanksgiving weekend at the La Quinta Resort. How did she get back to Manhattan Beach? If she's been back to her condo, why didn't she take her own car with her when she returned to the desert for our rendezvous at the top of Mt. San Jacinto?"

"A rental could answer both questions. Dad's guys can find that out when they put a timeline together for what Libby's been doing since Shannon disappeared. If she thought she was being followed, she might have felt safer driving a rental. Let's hope the lab learns something helpful about that rosary," Frank said.

"Too bad we can't get a report from whoever has had Libby under surveillance, huh? I'll make sure the guys investigating the trouble at Mt. San Jacinto link up with Hernandez' investigation into Donnelly's disappearance. There's not much time between the two incidents, so it makes sense to coordinate their investigations. I didn't think to ask, but if Libby used a rental car to get to that meeting at the top of the tram, she must have left it in the lot. That could be in impound, too, unless someone at the tramway didn't make the connection to Libby and had the rental agency retrieve it." Uncle Don stopped talking and typed what must have been a reminder on his cell phone.

"That's a great idea," Jessica said. "Okay, so back to your search of Carr's house and office. What did you find?" The members of team two all looked at each other.

"You'll love this," Don said, downing a little Peking duck spring roll, after dipping it in plum sauce. "There wasn't much left to find. Someone got there before us."

"No way," Brien gasped.

"Does it look as though a tornado hit it, like Laura's house did after Bedrossian's guys finished with it?" Jessica asked.

"No, if anything, it's likely to be cleaner and more orderly than it was the last time Carr was there, except a lot of stuff is missing," Uncle Don replied.

"What does that mean, missing, as in a burglary?" Jessica asked.

"In all my years as an investigator, I've never seen anything like it," Jerry said, with what might have been a note of awe in his voice. "There's no food in the fridge or the cupboards, no garbage, no mail, bills, files—drawers in his house and office emptied of their contents. Glassware, silverware, dishes, all gone, his clothes closet cleaned out. The linen closet and cupboards, too, even the bed is stripped down to the mattress. This looks more like a crime scene cleanup crew went through there rather than a crime scene. Except that instead of taking out the stuff trashed by intruders, they just took everything." Jerry stopped talking and Don picked up the story.

"They left the furniture, but had moved it around to clean the area beneath the furniture. We found the office in the same condition. Desks in the reception area and Carr's office are empty, the file cabinets too. All the bookshelves cleared out and wiped clean.

The cushions on the couches and chairs, like at Carr's house, must have been vacuumed. There's not a crumb, a coin, or a stray hair under those cushions." Don took a sip, shaking his head.

"Furniture is still there, but the electronics in the office and home are gone—no computers, phone, DVR, tape recorders, or answering machines. Carr's big flat screen television is still in his house, and his stereo equipment, but no communication devices of any kind. It's as though Carr had packed up all his personal possessions to move out and cleaned it, top to bottom. There's a faint odor of cleaning products," Don added. "Even the drains were cleaned and closed up to contain the smell of strong disinfectants used in them."

"I wish they'd left a business card, it sounds like they do a better job than the crew I use in Rancho Mirage," Bernadette said, her eyes glittering with interest. "So, what was the big idea?"

"The big idea was to sanitize the place," Peter said. "That's a 'fixer' job, not the stuff we do at our shop. Not that we haven't been asked to do it, a time or two." Both Frank and Don were scrutinizing the man. "Hey, I said we don't do that kind of work. It could have been a crime scene cleanup crew, but I'm guessing this was the work of a more *private* enterprise."

"Okay, so are you saying Carr killed Shannon at his condo or his office and someone sent in a cleanup crew?" Frank asked.

"It could be. I'm assuming someone has attempted to remove any evidence Carr, wittingly or unwittingly, left behind that could link him to Shannon or any of the women who were victims of his scheming. Small moveable items that might have stray fingerprints on them are gone. Same with his clothes and anything else that might have had traces from Shannon Donnelly or Libby Van Der Woert— supposing the hookups with both women took place at his house," Peter replied.

"Well, at least some of those trysts did occur at the doctor's house and office—if Libby's archive of precious moments is to be believed. So, what? Isn't that over doing it to go to so much trouble to cover for a dead guy? Even if Shannon Donnelly is dead and Carr's responsible, why not let the cops get all the evidence they need to peg him for it?" Jessica asked.

"Let's not forget you have his car. The police must have the clothes and other items he had with him at the hotel. Any laptop, cell phone, or tablet with him is likely to have more personal communications on it than anything in his office," Laura added.

"Your point about his car is a good one. If he killed Shannon at his condo or office, the body wasn't there. That must mean he used his car to get rid of it. Even though Libby seems to have played CSI going through his car and collecting what she regarded as evidence of some kind, I doubt she could have done as good a job as those 'fixers.' Without being able to 'sanitize' his car, why bother?"

"Well, this all goes back to the notion about a conspiracy. I'd bet money that Carr's silent partner is trying to make it hard to find a connection that leads back to him, even if Carr does get nailed for Shannon's murder. There's no rolodex, no record of referrals, or client records, like you wanted us to look for. There must have been other clients mixed up in the scam he was working with Libby and Shannon. Otherwise, why take all the files, rather than just Libby and Shannon's? The cleanup made sure whatever information Carr had squirreled away in his file cabinets, or on the hard drive of his office computer, went away before the police could subpoena his files and go through them. He had wall safes in both places and those were opened and emptied, too," Don said.

"Wow! Maybe Carr had his private stash of incriminating evidence, like Libby—something that would compromise his partner in crime. I suppose if that partner of his had ever met with Carr at his home or office, the super cleaning would make sure that there were no stray prints or trace linking that 'red devil' to Carr," Jessica added.

"I said conspiracy, but nothing about a red devil," Don retorted.

"Don't be silly, Jessica's knows it's not a red devil. A devil wouldn't leave fingerprints," Bernadette said.

"Wouldn't someone have seen something like that happening?" Tommy asked. "I've helped a lot of friends move. Packing and hauling all Carr's stuff away like that would have required a van or a truck, even though they left most of the furniture behind. It would have taken hours to do that."

"The local police are checking into it. If businesses in the area around the office have security cameras, they might have captured an image of a vehicle parked at the curb or in the alleyway behind the doc's office. I've passed that info along to the guys investigating the incident at the tramway. There are cameras in the hallways outside the doctor's office, so we might get pictures of them entering and exiting Carr's office," Don said.

"That's not likely to get you much. These are pros—my guess is you won't get a good look at them or their vehicle. If you do, it won't have much in the way of identifying information anyway. Most likely an unmarked truck or van, stolen license tags..." Frank and Don were eyeing Peter with cop-like suspicion, again.

"Sounds like you're familiar with the M.O."

"I'm familiar with such an operation, yes." Peter paused, reflective; perhaps his roots in black ops were calling him back in time.

"If they were making sure Carr didn't have secrets hidden away, why not slash the furniture and the mattresses like those guys did at Laura's house?" Tommy asked.

"They could have had a portable x-ray machine. That can be used to check for items hidden in furniture and other places, so no need to slash and smash everything. It's a much easier way to search for hiding places."

"Speaking of hiding places, that's a perfect lead-in to what we found in that otherwise squeaky-clean office. Kim found it," Don announced, after another penetrating look at Peter.

"What can I say? I worked for a sleaze bag with about a million hiding places, and I like to think I found them all while enslaved by the man. Think of me as that x-ray machine on two legs, Peter." Kim had made the rounds at Carr's home and office, looking for hidden panels and loose bits of carpet and baseboards, in cupboards and drawers, even the closets. "The guys were thorough. You could tell they'd checked the vents and light fixtures, toilet tanks, the attic—hiding places like that. It was frustrating. Nothing taped to the underside of tables, desk, bed, file cabinets, or the backs of moveable shelves. I was about to give up, but when I pulled out the desk drawers, I found it—a packet of black and white photos. Not in the drawer, but behind one of them, like it was hidden on purpose or accidentally shoved back, and kind of stuck there. Like when you have a drawer that's crammed full and stuff sort of spills over and falls down in behind the drawers." Kim let everyone know she'd finished talking by shrugging her shoulders, dropping her eyes, and resuming her lunch.

"The originals are bagged, tagged, and stowed in the evidence chest, but I shot copies for us," Jerry passed his camera to Jessica. She held it with both hands, even though one arm was held to her chest by a sling.

"Can you tell me what I'm looking at?" She asked, staring at the picture of a man in profile. There was something familiar about him. Maybe it was just that his *type* was a recognizable one. A well-coiffured man, in an expensive tailored suit, sporting a high-end watch on the arm outstretched to open the door he was about to enter.

"It's some guy about to go into Dr. Carr's office," Tommy explained. "That corridor could use some updating... chez nineties, don't you think? For what he's paying, he deserves better... was paying... deserved... okay, he's dead, I'm done."

"There's more—if you advance to the next picture in the file. That one was taken first, since you can see him head on." Jessica did as Jerry instructed. The man in the hallway, approaching the door to Dr. Carr's office looked almost straight into the camera. That odd sense of familiarity was stronger. A third picture showed him from the back, leaving with Carr and a young woman. "The time stamp on the photo says that third one was taken about twenty minutes later, Jessica."

"He seems so familiar to me. Do you think he's a celebrity?" Jessica asked.

"Let me see. If he's a celebrity, I bet I can tell you who he is." Bernadette flipped between the photos, peering at them. "No, I don't think he's a celebrity. He's not anyone I've seen in my magazines or on my shows."

"Bernadette's always up on things like that, Uncle Don," Tommy said.

"Yeah. If she doesn't recognize him, we can rule out the Hollywood crowd," Laura added, with great conviction, as she took a turn examining the photos. "That's Carr leaving with our mystery man, but who's the woman?"

"Even from the back you can tell that's an expensive suit, stylish—those little asymmetric twisty shoes she's wearing are Prada.

Her wardrobe is too office chic, and she's a blond, so, it's not Libby or Shannon," Jessica asserted after taking the camera from Laura and reviewing the photos again.

"Another woman, imagine that," Kim muttered, looking at those photos. "With guys like Carr, there are always more women."

"So, what do we make of it?" Jessica asked, that sense of recognition nagging at her—like one of those moments when an elusive word is right on the tip of your tongue.

"Carr must have had some reason to keep them. It's clear they're from the security camera footage, not just because they're black and white, but because of the angle from which they're shot, and that grainy look. It could be a client about to enter the doctor's office, but twenty minutes is a short session. A little odd for the doctor to be leaving with two clients, but what do I know—maybe couples therapy. Then why would Carr have gone to the trouble to get the photos in the first place, and why stash them away like that?" Don asked.

"The high-end clothing is too steep for the visitors to be pharmaceutical reps, but they could be business associates, rather than clients. I suppose if their business was the underhanded kind, and these are his co-conspirators, we could be back to the idea of some plan on Carr's part to blackmail them." Jessica flipped through those photos again before she handed the camera back to Jerry.

"Could be, but by themselves I can't imagine how those photos could have been of much use to him. They're completely useless to us at this point. We can speculate all we want, but that's not evidence of a crime. We'll submit them and get them on the record, though," Frank said.

"Hard to believe the crew that went through there missed them. Good work, Kim." Kim popped her head up and looked at Jessica, as a smile flitted across her face.

"Can you send me a copy, Jerry? I can't help thinking I've seen the guy somewhere before. Maybe if I stare at the photos long enough, I'll remember."

"No problem. I'll do it right now." Seconds later, a pinging signaled their arrival on her cell phone.

"Don, it's been almost a week since Carr took that fall off the mountain. Did the police get a look at his home and office before they got cleaned out?"

"Yes, they went through both places in a cursory way. They did a quick sweep looking for a suicide note, just in case that's what he was planning. They checked recording machines at his home and office to see if Libby left any message suggesting they meet, but there was nothing from her. They checked his calendars and appointment books, called his answering service, too. It's not like they had a reason to check things out as they might have done if either place was a crime scene. Preliminary checks at the house and office were part of their efforts to produce a timeline, clarifying Dr. Carr's whereabouts prior to his appearance at the top of the tram."

"Okay, so what did you find out from that?"

"Well, as far as we can tell, Carr was already out in the desert for the weekend before he made that trip up on the tramway. He visits on a regular basis and even has a favorite suite he books at one of the casino hotels. That's where he was staying the day he was killed. The homicide unit went over that room carefully. I don't know what all got checked into evidence, but I can find out. From interviews with hotel staff, Carr was a well-known womanizer and often had one with him. Investigators showed pictures of Shannon Donnelly and Libby Van Der Woert to hotel staff. They recognized them both, though nobody could say when they were last seen with Carr."

"What about phone calls? Libby acted surprised to see him, but did she invite him to meet her at the top of the tram?"

"His cell phone records show several calls that day—the last one at about twelve thirty, but it wasn't Libby," Don said.

"Who called him?" Jerry asked.

"This will add to the conspiracy theory—the number tracked to an unregistered phone. He received several calls from the same number in the previous month," Don replied.

"Cool, a burner phone," Brien said. "Someone could have been following her, so she wasn't totally paranoid. I mean, what if that's who called and snitched to Carr about where she was?"

"Very good, Brien. You may have a future in security," Peter commented.

"Yes, that would explain how Carr ended up there a little while later. I met Libby around noon and we started down that trail not long after that. If someone spotted the two of us together, that could have prompted a call to Carr. If someone told Carr that Libby and I were up at the tramway together, it could have set him off, thinking it was a secret meeting. That could have confirmed his suspicions about me, since he was already convinced I had inordinate influence over her. I guess it takes Libby off the hook for premeditated murder if she didn't lure Carr up there."

"Maybe, but this whole thing with Libby, Shannon, and Carr still has the markings of a classic love triangle, doesn't it? It might explain why the two women fought that night after a movie and dinner, and why they both called Carr that night. Could be they were fighting over him. Libby's not out of the picture yet when it comes to Shannon's disappearance. If she went off the deep end and eliminated her rival, that would have been a reason for Carr to keep her on a short leash. If he went to the police about Libby, his own extortion racket might have been exposed. He didn't want any of that to get to you, Jessica, so he might have decided the way out was to get rid of both of you up there last week."

"I hear you, Frank. This feels like we're on a merry-go-round. All of that implicates Libby and Carr in a twisted way that I can understand, but it doesn't explain why someone wants Libby dead or would go to the trouble to clean up after a dead man. Why not let the police find whatever there is to find and let Carr take the fall for an extortion racket and the death of one of his women friends?"

"Unless Carr's partner is as paranoid as he and Libby both were. This is such a strange combination of the stupidly impulsive and the maniacally conniving, maybe Dr. Dick and Libby were both loose cannons and the missing link is the guy with deep pockets calling the shots," Frank said.

"Yes, I agree with you that the person responsible for the stupidly impulsive part of that equation is lying in the ICU, or maybe in the morgue," Jessica said. "Carr made it sound like he was the one who decided it was time to toss me and Libby off the cliff, like he was taking out the garbage. That had to be opportunistic, given that Libby's impulse instigated our meeting."

"If he was trying to clean up after himself, he sure ended up creating a bigger mess," Peter offered.

"That's what stupidly impulsive gets you," Don said.

"So far, the maniacally conniving efforts haven't been much better. The thug sent after Libby screwed up, too, and a sniper had to clean that mess up, but then he got caught on film doing it. The sanitizing strategy will slow the police investigation down, but it won't end it. In fact, the cleanup efforts scream conspiracy, don't they? More mess!" Jessica shook her head.

"Yeah, just like the Cat in the Hat," Brien observed. There was a moment of puzzled silence as all turned to him. "You know how the cat sends Thing One out to clean up, and ends up making a bigger mess, so he sends out Thing Two, and cleaning up makes that mess bigger too?"

"Okay, great. Forget Libby's red devil idea. What we're looking for is the Cat in the Hat," Frank noted with sarcasm.

"Actually, Brien makes a good point. I'm sure the guy who's ordering hits and sanitizing things thinks he's smart. Maybe he is. We don't know how far he's gotten with whatever scheme he had going with Carr. Still, anybody who sees whacking somebody as a cleanup strategy has got to be 'out there,' if you know what I mean. I'm guessing he's improvising under pressure too. Whoever made those calls to the pros put them in a tough spot—demanding quick intervention without advance notice, or time to plan. That's what led to mistakes at the ICU and at Carr's office," Peter offered.

"Bad guys are never as smart as they think they are, right Frank?" Don asked.

"That's true, Dad. I suppose Peter's right though. Maniacally conniving is just another version of desperate. Carr's co-conspirator is throwing up roadblocks that will stall the investigation, but as Jessica points out, won't end it. There are more jurisdictions on the job now than ever."

"I'm guessing the guy is desperate to buy time if what you're saying is true. Buying time the way he's doing it costs a bundle, too. With those deep pockets, if he's afraid of getting caught, why not just pack up and leave?"

"Something important is holding him here," Frank replied.

"Hey, maybe he still hasn't used the ultimate, multi-purpose cleanup machine. Could be that's still in his hat," Brien said with a knowing look on his face.

"Where's that food?" Bernadette asked. "Brien will stop talking about the cat and the hat if he has something to put in his mouth. Stop chewing up that straw, Brien." He put down the straw.

Bernadette's utterance, like magic, conjured up a flurry of activity as food appeared. The rest of their lunch was much quieter. Don and Frank excused themselves as soon as they'd finished eating, hitting the road to deliver the evidence collected. After lunch, the rest of them checked into their hotel rooms, the guys hauling in luggage from the loaner car that Peter had provided to Bernadette and Jessica. Peter was accompanying them to Malibu, with Brien riding "shotgun" if he didn't pass out from the lunch he put away. The bacon topped cheeseburger he'd ordered was enough to stupefy people with normal appetites. His meal came with the option to have fries or a salad, and he ordered both.

"I'm learning from Peter to eat better," he said as he started in on the salad. Peter just shook his head as he devoured his larger salad ordered with a side of hummus and pita bread.

"If that's true, you could have ordered the edamame, or hummus, instead of the artery-clogging nachos you ate."

"I'm not ready for the mushy good stuff. I need to eat things that are crunchy, not already-been-chewed food." Kim looked at him, stopped eating the Greek salad she'd ordered, and spoke.

"Then I take it you won't be eating any more of Bernadette's guacamole or salsa. They don't crunch."

"No, no, those are okay. They go with chips and chips crunch, get it? Besides, I'm talking about *healthy* food, not Bernadette's food." Tommy snorted, almost doing a spit take. Brien realized that wasn't the right thing to say.

"Whoa, that's not what I meant. Your food's healthy, Bernadette. It's just stealthy healthy not harsh healthy." That, and the anxious look on his face, set off more chortling.

"Oh Brien, shut up, before I show you what harsh *unhealthy* looks like!" They all stopped eating and gazed, open-mouthed, at Bernadette. She put her two small fists up, moving them through the air, like she was challenging him to a fight. Brien blinked several times in a row, waiting for her to throw a punch.

"Eat your lunch. I'm just messing with you." She went back to eating the fish tacos she'd ordered.

He let out a big sigh and stuffed more salad into his mouth. The rest of them looked at each other and burst into laughter.

Jessica was pensive as she drank a cup of coffee later, alone in her room. She hoped the extra caffeine would get her through the afternoon still ahead. She pondered that lunch conversation about the culprit still on the loose... deep pockets... desperate... buying time... and if Betsy Stark was right, someone who moved in the same rarefied circles inhabited by the Van Der Woerts and the Donnellys. *Less than 'six degrees of separation,'* Betsy had said with that far-off look in her eyes. If he was the man in the photos Carr had tucked away in his desk, who was he? Could they figure it out before his desperation led him to take measures that are more drastic?

24 RED DEVIL

Jessica wanted to stay put on the sumptuous bed in her hotel room. That bed was so comfortable. Her body was objecting to the time she'd spent in cars, getting in and out of cars, sitting in stiff dining chairs, etc. All normal things to do, but not for someone who had toppled off a mountain the week before. Her whole body ached, made worse by the tension that gripped her.

As she lay there, waiting for a fresh dose of aspirin to kick in, she marveled at the havoc wreaked by that combination of Carr's impulsive stupidity and his maniacally conniving partner. Throw in Libby's special brand of troublemaking and it was surprising there wasn't more than one dead body. Carr had paid for his dirty dealings. Shannon Donnelly may have paid the price for whatever part she played in the tangled web of deceit. Add to that the carnage done to families ripped apart by Carr's cynical manipulation of the women in his care, and the toll in human terms was mounting.

What was the point of all that manipulation on Carr's part? Was it just a matter of self-gratification, easy sex, and some narcissistic ego trip? If so, why would he have had a partner? Maybe it was about the money, as manipulation morphed from sexploitation to extortion. Libby thought she was getting the money so she and Carr could run away together. Had Carr told Shannon the same thing? Was she expecting to wring money out her parents, using the false allegation gambit, and take off with Carr? Could the man have set up a competition between the two women, in which the first to score an early inheritance would win him as the prize?

"Some prize," she muttered to herself. She couldn't imagine the two women fighting over him, but women had done stranger things to get a man. Would either Libby or Shannon have come up with enough money to be able to run off to an island somewhere? If Carr got the girl, and the money, what did his mysterious partner get out of the deal? Why was a partner who already had deep pockets involved in a scheme to extort money from the parents of spoiled rich girls? A quiet rap on the door pulled her out of her rumination.

"Jessica, we should get going."

"Okay, Bernadette." Her mother was expecting them. Jessica had called to confirm, even though that had seemed an overly formal thing to do. Alexis had sounded good on the phone, but Jessica was reserving judgment until she could see for herself—presuming she could ever tell how her mother was doing. She'd missed so much for so many years.

"Do you know how to get there? I can pull up directions on my phone if you'd like."

"Nah, Peter already put the address into the GPS system so we won't get lost. He and Brien will be right behind us."

"Okay, let's go," she said, as she gave her hair a brush and added lip gloss. Most of the scrapes and bruises on her face had faded, and her right hand was no longer bandaged. Still, it was hard to feel "pulled together" with one arm in a cast and a sling. Both were part of her wardrobe for two or three more weeks.

Traffic on the way to Malibu wasn't bad by LA standards. Roads were always congested in the sprawling county with ten million residents. Early afternoon, the Pacific Coast Highway was navigable, after lunch and before rush hour. The views of the Pacific Ocean were soothing as they drove up the coast.

They had no trouble finding a spot in the limited visitor parking. Bernadette pulled into a space close to the clinic entrance and Peter pulled into a nearby space. The grounds on which the clinic sat were stunning. Fences concealed much of the facility, but the entry beckoned under a vaulted overhang. Jessica climbed out of the car, glad to be wearing a light jacket around her shoulders. A chilly breeze swirled around her as she walked toward Peter, with Bernadette following.

"Peter," she called out as she grew closer.

"Shush, shush. I just got him to sleep," Peter whispered, slipping out of the car and shutting the door with a soft click. "That guy can talk. I don't know if I'm doing the right thing encouraging him to take on a job in security. Maybe he'd be good at the interrogation side of things."

"He *can* talk, I'll grant you that. He's learned a lot already, or maybe it's just the influence you're having on him. I'm seeing aspects of Brien I haven't seen before."

"I see it too. Sometimes he even thinks *before* he says somethin'—even when his mouth's not full," Bernadette added with a wicked little smile on her face.

"Yeah, he surprises me, too, but then he goes back into surfer dude mode and blabs about UFO conspiracies, or sets out the debate about the merits of shaved ice versus a snow cone. *Did I ever think about that?* It's not like I can answer him because he's on to the next subject. Who killed JFK and was it the same person who killed Marilyn Monroe? I couldn't get a word in edgewise if I happened to give a damn about one of the topics he goes on and on about."

"I hear you. Maybe he missed his calling and should be a litigator—they talk plenty."

"Or a tour guide at Disneyland where he could talk all day long," Bernadette added.

"There must be places that would be happy to have an affable security presence, Peter. It's good you're trying to help him get a focus. He lives alone, and he works alone most of the time. Maybe he's just lonely." Peter sighed.

"You could be right. I wonder if he keeps this patter going on when he's by himself. It doesn't seem to matter much that I'm there. Does he do that when he's cleaning your pool?"

"I never noticed, but it could be. He sounds like Libby up there on Mt. San Jacinto. At least instead of red devils and dead daughters, he's muttering about something innocuous, like snow cones."

"Snow cones? Where?" Brien asked in a muffled voice.

"There's nothing wrong with his ears," Bernadette quipped. "He could listen good as a security guard if he stops talking all the time."

Brien climbed out of the car, a sleepy look on his face as he stretched.

"No snow cones. This is the Malibu rehab facility where my mom's staying."

"Not bad," Brien said. "I could totally live here." Jessica wondered about his apartment. He seemed ready to move in everywhere they went.

Nobody responded to his comment as they all moved toward the entry to the facility. The architecture was a modern take on the seaside cottage. It was hard to get the lay of the land with all the fences and trees around the complex. The low-rise-building occupied a lot of acreage on a Malibu bluff overlooking the Pacific Ocean. That made a statement in a place where it was hard to find property for sale at less than a thousand dollars per square foot. Land with beach frontage, even if you had to climb down the bluff to get to it, cost a pretty penny, too.

The entrance to the facility opened into a lobby. As soon as they stepped inside, a receptionist welcomed them warmly. Why not, if you had a family member who could afford thirty thousand dollars a week for treatment? The charming receptionist confirmed their names and appointment. She escorted Brien and Peter to a waiting area and then showed Jessica and Bernadette the way to Alexis' suite.

Their escort gave the door a light tap. Jessica felt relieved when Alexis answered the door looking composed. What was she expecting? To find her writhing in the agony of withdrawals—like Frank Sinatra in the Man with the Golden Arm. Not a chance. This was a medication-assisted detox and treatment facility with lots of services and supports.

Her mother, impeccable as always, sported pricey, but casual resort wear. Black capris and a long-sleeved boat neck silk tee worn under an unconstructed cardigan. *Cashmere*, Jessica guessed, as she rushed into the room to embrace her. As the door shut, and their escort left, Alexis returned the embrace. With the sling Jessica was wearing, it was a little awkward, but wonderful. Bernadette gave Alexis a hug too.

Alexis went into hostess mode. "Have a seat, you two. Can I get you something to drink? No cocktails, but I have bubbly water or a soda. Or I could put on water for tea—decaffeinated, herbal something or other. There's a ginger-lemon that's not bad."

"I'll take some water." Jessica felt pressured to accept something, falling into the polite mode that the hostess thing required. Why hadn't she thought to bring flowers or something for her mother? What was an appropriate gift for a friend or relative in rehab?

"Why don't you sit down and talk to Jessica and let me do that." Jessica could see her mother fighting to stay in hostess mode, but in few seconds, she yielded. Her shoulders slumped, giving up the perfect posture that went with hostess mode.

"Sure, Bernadette, if you don't mind."

"Not at all. You're supposed to be takin' it easy. I'll get us all some of that fizzy water, okay?"

"Sounds great," Alexis replied, seating herself in a club chair near Jessica.

"You look good. How are you doing?" Jessica asked. She was glamorous in dark glasses, her shoulder length light brown hair cut, colored, and styled.

"My eyes are sensitive to light and it makes my head hurt. I'm tired."

"Well, you've got a lot on your mind. Bernadette's right about taking it easy. Are you feeling sick?"

"No—not sick, just tired. Tired of being me," Alexis said, gazing out of the window at the ocean.

"Geez, what does that mean?" She asked, trying to hide the alarm that statement had set off. "I'm not tired of you! I love you—and I'm just getting to know you. The real you, not the 'Mom' you, but the *you*, you... I, I... I don't know what I'm saying."

"Oh, don't go all worrywart on me. I don't know what I'm saying either. I'm just so tired. Sad and irritable, too."

"That sounds like depression. Have you told your therapist how you feel?"

"Yes, but she feels it's too early to figure out what's going on with me. Some of what I'm going through is because of the drug withdrawals, so she says. Your mother is a tough nut to crack, Jinx.

I'm just getting to know me, so welcome to the club. Someday, when I figure out the *me*, me, I'll introduce you."

Bernadette joined them with glasses of water, and a blue bottle for refills, on a tray she found in the small, well-appointed kitchen. She handed out the glasses and then sat down.

"That's why you're here, to figure it out. You've been trying too hard for too long not to be you. I don't think it's the *real you* you're tired of, it's the phony you you're tired of being. So stop." Jessica and Alexis were both staring at the petite guru in navy trousers and a deep burgundy tunic sweater. Her head, with its short-cropped dark hair, was bowed as she took a sip of water. Jessica caught Alexis' eye, and they both burst out laughing.

"Trust Bernadette to tell it like it is," Alexis proclaimed, lifting her glass in a toast to the tiny woman, beaming at them now. "And make it all sound so easy. Here's to you, Bernadette!" They all scooted closer together to clink glasses. Jessica was rewarded with a shot of pain in the ribs. That happened ess often than it had a week ago, but it was still unpleasant when it occurred.

"To the *new you*, Mom, or the old *real you*..." she stopped, getting all tongue-tied again as they clinked their glasses. "Sorry, you know what I mean."

"Let's hope there *is* a real me—old, yes, but with some living still to do," Alexis said. Laughing again, she added, "I'm as confused as you are, Jessica, so you don't have to apologize. I owe you lots of them—apologies, I mean. I'm nowhere near that step in the twelve-step part of the program here. I received an overview, but I'm still an infidel, on the outside looking in."

"You gotta start somewhere."

"I understand that, but it feels like I've spent most of my life on the outside looking in. This isn't my first introduction to twelve-steps, although it's a new take on it here. I'm not so sure I want to go in. All that powerless before God stuff isn't inviting."

"Is it the powerless part, or the God part, that's no good?" Bernadette asked.

"Both," Alexis and Jessica said, in unison. Surprising each other and setting off another round of laughter.

"Don't tell me you're a control freak, too. Have you been in the closet all this time?"

"Oh, come on, what closet, darling? You must have noticed that I like to have things my own way." Jessica thought about it.

"I guess so—when you were around, sure."

"It's exhausting keeping it all under control—you must have figured that out by now, too, Jessica. When I couldn't do that anymore, I gave up and disappeared. I guess that's the first thing I'm sorry for, but I didn't think I was doing any good hanging around anyway. I understand the need to have control is a losing battle."

"That's because you're *not* in control. Neither am I—none of us are. All that trying and trying to have things your way, it's just a lot of huffing and puffing, so you won't be afraid because your life isn't under your control. You're right, it doesn't work." Bernadette piped up. "So you have already faced the powerlessness. You even chose a God of your own—the pills, you know?"

"Hmm," Alexis replied. "I'll have to think about that."

"I get what she's saying. For me, it's shopping. The thing I go to first for solace or comfort when I'm shook up—which is all the time these days. It's confusing, but Father Martin says an awakening soul has choices to make. Different choices than the ones I've made in the past. Not all of them easy or pleasant, but I'm trying to face up to them."

"Well, I'm no stranger to shopping as a way to take my mind off things, but what's wrong with that? You can afford it. At least it's a crutch you can choose to use or not."

"That's sort of true. I've tried to put the black AMEX card away, but I get this urge to shop. When that happens, sometimes I can say no, but other times I've got to get my fix. It's a compulsion."

"You don't have to tell me about compulsions. Isn't it strange that two control freaks like us are so easy to manipulate? With my happy pills, some of it's physical, but there's also this state of mind I crave. I know that it won't last and the path leads nowhere except to more pills. What an irony that in running from my fear of powerlessness, I end up on a path toward *more* powerlessness. How perverse is that?"

"I guess that's what an addiction is—a misdirected impulse to avoid facing up to things. Just talking about it makes me want to hit Rodeo Drive. How's that for perverse? My cross to bear, I suppose."

"Oh no, is that priest giving you the 'take up your cross' pep talk? That leaves me cold, like staring into the grave already. If life is a cross, why not run for it, straight to Rodeo Drive or to booze and happy pills?"

"I've said almost the same thing to Father Martin. It's like we're being told to mill around in a big waiting room, putting up with crap, and sticking it out."

"Well, I've heard people call Palm Springs God's waiting room, but that's a new spin on it. I get what you mean."

"If it's a new spin, it's not one I like. The odd thing is, as much as I gripe about getting sandbagged by one calamity after another, I fight and scrap to save my neck and stay alive. Go figure."

"I get what you mean. It's a lot like that old joke about the food at the fat farm. One woman says to her friend, 'The food is awful here, isn't it?' 'Yes,' her friend agrees, 'and the portions are so small.' I've already heard that one around here with all the health food regimens we're on. Life's a bitch, and then you die, but we fight, tooth and nail, to stay alive."

"That about sums it up. Father Martin's tried to get me to look at things in a different way though. Trouble brings you to a cross, as in *crossroad*—an opportunity for transformation, transcendence even, rather than a stumbling block."

"That sounds like more of that buck up, stoic stuff, with a little silver lining thrown in for good measure. Trust me, I know stoic, and I don't like it." Jessica saw something pass across her mother's face— a small shudder, too.

"What is it?"

"It's nothing. My introduction to the way of the cross came with a bunch of stiff upper lip mumbo-jumbo, that's all. There was nothing pleasant, or very holy, about it either. It seemed like just another way of hiding out, and a lot less fun than shopping or a few glasses of an exquisite chardonnay."

"Look at the three of us sitting here," Bernadette offered in a soft voice. "Even with all the troubles, we're together in this gorgeous place. The sun is shining and our bellies are full. We're sitting in a comfy room, drinking sparkling water poured out of beautiful blue bottles into crystal glasses. Don't you feel lucky to be alive, and happy to be together? Isn't that more than a little silver lining?"

Bernadette's eyes wandered from mother to daughter and back again. Jessica met Bernadette's gaze, and followed it, landing on her mother's face. In it, she saw what must have been her own expression, mirrored—a spoiled, pouty stubborn look. If she could have done so, Jessica would have folded her arms across her chest, as her mother did. With her mother's defiant gesture, Jessica's pout morphed into a smirk, and then a full-blown smile. That was infectious and her mother smiled too.

"Oh, all right. I get your point," Jessica said.

"Yeah, I suppose it could be worse. Instead of a mother who's a drug addict with early stage cervical cancer, you could have a mother who's a drug addict with terminal cancer." There was humor, but also bitterness in that statement from her mother. "Ask me the same question a year from now and maybe I'll be a better sport about it."

"You're doing fine. Bernadette's halo is glowing. As usual, she's way ahead of us. I do feel blessed to have this opportunity to go through this with you. I'm so grateful you were there with me at the hospital when I didn't know for sure where I was or what was going on. We may be powerless over a lot of what's happening in our lives, but Bernadette's right, at least we're not alone." Misty-eyed, the three of them sat there in silence, caught up in one of those moments of solidarity among loved ones struggling together. Finally, it was Alexis who broke the spell.

The three of them spent another hour talking and roaming around the complex. They visited the resort-like amenities and meeting rooms, including a gorgeous dining area where Alexis ate breakfast and lunch; at dinnertime, her mother opted to eat alone in her suite. Alexis spoke about the program, too, and impressed Jessica with how much she'd already learned about drugs, and the way they affected her mind and body, from an orientation and psycho-education classes. It was amazing, since she'd only been at the facility for seventy-two hours. This wasn't her first round of drug rehab, so maybe some of it was more a refresher than new information.

When they returned to her mother's suite, it was time to say goodbye and Jessica felt overcome by emotion. What if she and her mother never had more moments like the ones shared today? Her mother had been more open than she'd been for a long time. Not once did she go into flighty socialite mode.

"When can I come back again? I don't want to pry, but I have a lot of questions about what will happen next. Will you be able to be with us for Christmas? What about Giovanni? When do you see the doctors again?" Her eyes filled with tears as she blurted out questions. Her mother wrapped her arms around her, careful not to jar the arm or those sore ribs.

"I don't have the answers to all those questions yet. In a few days, I'll know more about how all of this will play out. We'll work something out for Christmas—presuming I'm still here and not already in the hospital. Maybe you and Bernadette can spend part of the day with me here. I've spoken to Giovanni and he'll be here by then. He'd love to see you. Have you talked to Hank? Your dad will want to spend time with you, too, since he's here in California for a change. Why don't you call him and figure out something, so when we talk later we can work around your plans with him, okay?" The tears had spilled over and slid down Jessica's cheeks. She didn't want her mother to let go, but Jessica needed to get a tissue from her purse.

"I'm sorry to be a baby. That's a great idea—Dad and I are working on a plan. Hang on while I grab a tissue, so I don't weep all over you." She patted her mother with her good hand, then turned and reached for the purse she'd left on the coffee table. She grabbed it by the wrong strap and dumped a lot of the contents onto the plush carpeting. The three of them looked down.

Alexis gasped.

"A gun! What are you doing with a gun in your purse? Isn't that Hank's gun?"

"Uh, yes, I can explain. Sort of..." Jessica said.

"I'm the one who has some 'splainin' to do—the gun was my idea. I had it with me the other day when we were chased by the paparazzi. I gave it to Jessica, and she forgot to give it back after we knew it was paparazzi and not a sniper."

Alexis' mouth opened like she was about to speak. Instead, she bent down and picked up the gun.

"I guess this goes back to you then, Bernadette. You shouldn't be carrying around any extra weight, Jessica." Alexis handed the gun to Bernadette, who stuffed it into her bag. Alexis picked up the other items on the floor, including Jessica's cell phone. She stopped for a moment and peered at the image that had popped up on Jessica's phone—the one Jerry had sent Jessica at lunch of the man lurking outside Carr's office.

"That's an odd picture of the man. Does your firm have some business with him now that this IPO thing is going on?" She handed the phone back to Jessica, who had gotten her bag situated on her good shoulder, so she had a hand free.

"IPO thing—what do you mean? Who are you talking about?"

"Eric Conroy. That's his picture on your phone."

"Eric Conroy, do I know him?"

"Darling, he was at Hank's gala back in July, remember? I was surprised you hadn't already met when he introduced himself to you. The man's quite the 'influencer' as they say in the social networking circles these days. That's just another way of saying wheeler dealer, as far as I can tell, but he's a rather charming fellow. How could you forget him with that goatee and shock of red hair?"

"I need to sit down." Jessica felt faint. She took another look at the photos of the man on her cell phone. The memory of the well-dressed, redheaded man she'd met that night at the gala returned. Their encounter had been brief, but she hadn't regarded him as charming. In fact, there had been something disconcerting about him. At the time, she thought it might have been the striking resemblance he bore to the Heisenberg character on Breaking Bad, except for that red hair. On his arm was a young woman, closer to her age, so maybe twenty years his junior. His date for the evening had been introduced as an up and coming member of some PR firm. A big one; Paul's firm dealt with them regularly. Pinnacle, yeah, that was it. It wasn't his devilish goatee, but something in his eyes that had made Jessica uncomfortable when they were introduced. Perhaps her powers of repression were working better than she thought. *Less than six degrees of separation...* Betsy Stark's words came to mind.

"There is a red devil, Bernadette." Bernadette sucked in a big gulp of air and sat down too.

25 BLOND WEARS PRADA

Jessica was a woman possessed when she returned to the hotel. Dinner was at eight, so she had two hours before she needed to get ready. She took out her laptop and went to work. What she had learned heightened her sense that Eric Conroy was the red devil Libby had referred to, and Carr's silent partner.

A lot of public information about Eric Conroy came up with a Google search. That was not at all surprising for a man well-versed in techniques to garner and shape media attention. A high-ranking executive, in an elite marketing and public relations firm, gaining attention was his forte. Despite his devilish goatee, the media portrayed him as a benevolent figure. He could be found at important events throughout the Southland. That included charity galas, political fundraisers—for both sides—red carpets, ribbon cutting ceremonies, press conferences, name it, and he was there.

There was nothing sinister in any of the online information, nor was there anything revealing about his personal life. No mention, anywhere, of family, past or current, or of women. The man knew how to spend money, obvious from snapshots of Conroy handing over the keys for pricey cars to valets at swanky restaurants, bidding on items at silent auctions, playing golf or skiing at exclusive resorts, and hosting a party aboard his boat. No, not a boat, but a yacht. To be sure, a modest model by mega-yacht standards, but the *Sweet Retreat*, was an expensive toy. He was always well-dressed, as he had been in those grainy photos taken outside Carr's office.

The media had documented his rise through the ranks at Pinnacle. There was nothing sinister about that, either. Speculators regarded Eric Conroy, second in command, as a likely successor to the top man at the firm. A brief bio on the firm's website focused on the positions he'd held since they hired him at Pinnacle years earlier. While still in his late thirties, Conroy made partner, the youngest member of the firm ever to achieve that status. Pinnacle's rise into the ranks of the top twenty-five public relations and marketing firms in the nation, was, in part, attributed to him. When he became Executive Vice President, the company and the press credited him with having enhanced the firm's international presence. *Okay, so he can afford all the toys, clothing, and amenities,* she thought. Why get mixed up with a two-bit hustler like Carr and his extortion racket?

The big news about the firm meant Conroy would soon have even more money. Alexis' reference to an IPO was correct. An Initial Public Offering meant selling shares of Pinnacle to investors. That process was underway; the IPO was imminent. Her search of old articles in online business news outlets revealed the idea had been under discussion for some time, with a lot of debate. Earlier this year, the debate ended, however, and the company filed an S-1, a document that she knew well.

The S-1 was a term bandied about by Jim and his pals when shepherding new ventures or cleaning up after old ones massacred during the great recession. IPOs are the holy grail of startups—the point at which the high-tech equivalent of a garage band becomes a pop sensation. Not everyone wants to become the next big thing. So maybe that was the reason for doom and gloom on the faces of some board members in earlier photos she uncovered.

Jessica pulled up the S-1 for Pinnacle, the official term for the forms filed with the SEC announcing the proposal to take the company public. The three lead underwriters taking the issue public were household names. The roadshow, where big names in high finance took the wannabe pop stars on tour, was already well underway. Out and about singing the praises of Pinnacle, they were lining up investors. At the helm was the current CEO, speaking with confidence about the firm and its future. All the news leaked to the press was good. Apart from those well-placed leaks, it was all polished, professional, and squeaky clean. What did she expect to find?

Trouble, that's what. Anyone willing to get mixed up with the unscrupulous Dr. Carr, and the troubled women associated with him, would surely have had problems before. Had other young women like Libby directed those "red devil" epithets, or something like them, at Eric Conroy? There were plenty of images of the dapper executive at events with women—some of them renowned. Not one of them appeared unhappy in photos taken with him. Nor was there any evidence, even in scandal rags, of any woman hell-bent on embarrassing him, like Jim Harper's lovely bride was wont to do. In a public interest piece about his participation in a charity event where they auctioned off a night out with him, he was characterized as one of SoCal's most eligible bachelors. No one ever hinted that he was a womanizer or a playboy. If she believed the PR, the man was a loner, married to his job. She did not. Carr had come up clean, too.

"He's a ruthless, unprincipled psychopath, willing to pay someone to kill Libby!" Jessica sputtered to herself, getting more worked up with each word. "Stop! Calm down," she ordered aloud. Unjust authority and betrayal by those in whom you have placed your trust, personally or professionally, were triggers for a fast ride into the panic zone. She didn't need that now.

That ardor and small things Jessica unearthed online, kept her on the hunt. In one photo, the existing CEO clasped Conroy's hand after a board meeting earlier in the year. Both men were smiling, but the tension in their jaws was easy to read.

"That must have been a bumpy meeting," she said, as she read the news story that accompanied the photo.

The good news for Pinnacle just keeps coming...
Reuters, July 15, 2013

Pinnacle announced that net fees in 2012 topped two hundred million dollars for the first time. The firm credited much of that growth to new offices opened in Asia and the Middle East, brainchild of Executive Vice President, Eric Conroy. The award-winning firm, identified by Advertising Age as one of its A-List Agencies for three years in a row, recently moved into the top five on several rankings of firms in relation to their industry-based performance. Information about the company's financial robustness and recent performance is part of the firm's disclosure that they hope to get even bigger. Pinnacle announced a proposal to follow the lead of several of their most successful competitors. After months of speculation and some debate, the board voted today to take Pinnacle public. No one at the firm has said how much capital they hope to generate from such a venture, but analysts say that an IPO could raise more than a billion dollars. The move should support more rapid expansion into global markets, spurring continued growth in earnings.

"A billion dollars," she gasped reading the story again. *Why aren't the boys beaming?* Money like that would have had her ex, and his cronies, high-fiving each other. Well, more likely, in the world of bespoke suits and three hundred-dollar ties, they would have been pouring top dollar single malts and breaking out the hand-rolled Havanas. Maybe some high-fives too, off camera.

Jessica peered at that photo and a tingle ran through her. There in the background, sitting at the table of sober-looking board members, was Ned Donnelly, Shannon's father. He was grim-faced. Was he upset about what had gone on at that meeting, or a stricken man, dealing with problems of his own? It had been taken *before* his daughter's disappearance, so that couldn't be the cause of his misery. Was she already in Carr's care at the time, and did his troubles have anything to do with Carr and Conroy's scheming?

Jessica took another look at news coverage of the Donnelly investigation. Donnelly looked disturbed in July, but not devastated as he did now. Since Thanksgiving weekend, when Shannon went missing, the press had dogged him about his daughter. He'd made a point of appearing in public; at first, stating that he was cooperating with the police. He made an appeal for his daughter to return home, if she could do so, and offered a substantial reward to anyone with information about her whereabouts.

As the investigation dragged on, he had disappeared from sight. After last week's events at the top of the tram, reporters had linked Libby Van Der Woert and Shannon Donnelly. *They must be after him again*, she thought. Given her own recent encounter with paparazzi, and angel heiress fans, Jessica could understand Donnelly's decision to withdraw. Still, maybe he would be willing to talk about his daughter, his role at Pinnacle, and his association with Conroy. If she were his lawyer, she would advise him to keep his mouth shut about anything having to do with his daughter, especially if he was dealing with horrendous allegations of abuse, like Libby's parents.

Maybe Hernandez had already learned more about Donnelly's trouble with his daughter before she disappeared. Detective Hernandez had given Jessica his private cell number after that last round of phone tag when she tried to reach him about that meeting with Libby. He picked up on the first ring.

"No, not yet. It's only been two days since we talked. Now, we've got all that stuff you collected to go through. What's the rush with Donnelly?"

"If he doesn't refer you to his lawyer when you ask those questions about his daughter, ask him about Eric Conroy while you're at it. Tell me how Donnelly reacts," Jessica had said.

"Eric Conroy? Who's that?"

"I'm sure he's Libby's red devil, Detective."

"Oh no, we're not going down that path with your favorite escapee from looneyville, are we?"

"You do know it's not a good thing to refer to people with mental health problems as escapees from looneyville, right?"

"Save all that for the shrinks. In my book, crazy is as crazy does. It's my job to figure out whodunit, not why. I'll take that back. Motive matters, but all that who-shot-John crap about mitigating circumstances—that's for you and your lawyer cronies to deal with. So, what's up with this Eric Conroy character?"

"Frank and Don Fontana told you about all the items retrieved from our search of Libby's condo, car, and storage area. I don't know if they mentioned the items found in Dr. Carr's office."

"The main thing I heard was Carr's house and office got a good cleaning. That means whoever caused all the trouble at the hospital is still at it. Somebody's making an awful lot of effort to muck with the investigation into Carr's life. They mentioned something about a couple black and white shots of some guy."

"Yes, and it's Eric Conroy in those photos. I didn't recognize him right away. You know me and kismet, though. I stumbled upon someone who saw one of the photos on my phone, and reminded me I'd met the man."

"Stop with the kismet stuff already. That drives *me* crazy. The cleanup crew missed a few photos, so what?"

"Eric Conroy is in Carr's hallway and at the door of Carr's office—reaching for the door handle and about to go inside. Then, a few minutes later they're leaving together, all chummy. They look like images taken from a surveillance camera in that hallway outside

Carr's office. Jerry Reynolds is trying to figure out how Carr got hold of them."

"So? Some guy you met before was seeing a shrink, big deal. Carr must have had male clients, in addition to all the screwed-up Beverly Hills girls' club members."

"Sure, but why have those photos of the guy? I doubt Carr kept photographic records of everyone in his care. And detective, I'll bet they don't all look like red devils. That's hard to see in the black and white photos we found, but go check out photos on the Internet. It'll be easier to get what I'm saying. With a little goatee and bright red hair, I can see how Libby could have come up with that red devil name for Conroy."

"That's a stretch, Jessica, to make red hair and a goatee the basis for suspecting Conroy was Carr's co-conspirator. Heck, we don't even know, what scheme Carr had going involving Libby Van Der Woert, Shannon Donnelly, or anybody else. You're the one who said we might all be wasting our time looking for this Donnelly woman if she's taken off with some new boyfriend, or maybe she's whiling away the hours in a spa retreat somewhere. We don't have a body."

"Yes, but someone tried to kill Libby and did a damn good job sanitizing Carr's home and office. Why do that, unless there's something to hide by destroying evidence? Conroy has the resources to pay for pros to take Libby out and clean Carr's house and office like that."

"What's your point?"

"Someone must have a good reason to spend that kind of money to shut Libby up and to hinder an investigation into Carr's activities, Detective."

"We're going around in circles. I already told you we don't have a motive for any of this."

"If Eric Conroy is behind this, I'll give you one—about a billion of them, in fact."

"Okay, go on. I'm listening."

"Conroy is a big shot at a PR firm here in Los Angeles. Pinnacle Enterprises is a high-profile company with a big deal in play. An initial public offering that stands to net the firm a billion dollars, or more, if all goes as planned." Detective Hernandez let go a low whistle.

"Big deal is an understatement, in my world, anyway—maybe not in yours."

"It's not chump change in my world either. For folks used to raising money through IPOs, it's the requisite amount you'd expect to generate for the big-name investment banks to make it worth their while. They take seven percent of any deal, so it has to be big. And from what I've read, all the big boys are involved. Right now, they're in the middle of what they call the roadshow. That's dozens of meetings across the country with investors to line up subscribers before the IPO that's set for Friday, December 20th."

"That's less than a week away."

"Yes, it's a timeline that would pressure an upscale lowlife, like Conroy, to take drastic action—like silencing Libby, fast. She's grabbed the headlines at a sensitive moment for the deal of a lifetime. I'm not sure what his connection is to Carr yet, but complications from the likes of Libby Van Der Woert are the last thing he wants at a time like this. His share of a billion dollars is more than enough to cover the costs of cleanup—killing Libby and sanitizing Carr's house and office *is* chump change."

"I agree. He'd do just about anything to keep a deal like that on track. To be that close to a billion dollars is a hell of a motive. I'll need more than that, though, to make him a person of interest in my investigation into the Donnelly woman's disappearance, much more to consider him a suspect. Even linking him to Carr might not get us far. Unless we can tie him directly to Donnelly's disappearance, there's not much I can do. He's not implicated in Carr's death, so the Palm Springs PD doesn't have a reason to question him either. The whole point of hiring pros is to keep all of this at arm's length."

"I hear you. I'll put Jerry and others from my investigative team on Conroy's track—digging into his background to see if we find any shady dealings or links to Carr. The SEC and the investment banks have checked out Pinnacle, but I want to have a look at the company's financials. That's difficult to do because the company is privately held. I'll see what Kim can do about that. Before you get off the phone and mumble under your breath about my impulsive nature leading me to jump to conclusions about Conroy, here's an interesting coincidence for you. Who do you imagine is a board member of Pinnacle?"

"Not Ned Donnelly?"

"Yep, I don't see why that matters yet, but it feels like it does. That's a little too much kismet even for me. Donnelly's daughter was seeing Carr, so now we have this degrees-of-separation thing going... Carr connected to Donnelly through his daughter and Conroy connected to Donnelly through Pinnacle. What could have brought the three of them together?"

"Okay, so we're back where we were when we started this conversation. I may not have a reason to pull Conroy into a room for a chat, but I will have another one with Ned Donnelly. Maybe if I ask the right questions, he can shed some light on this. I'll see if he's been holding out on me about what his daughter was up to in the months before she disappeared, and I'll do a little probing about Carr and Conroy."

"The man doesn't look well, so go easy."

"Good grief, what do you think I'll do, shine a bright light in his eyes and give him the third degree?"

"No, it's just that you can get carried away."

"The only time I get *carried away* is when some amateur sleuth is sticking her nose into things that are better handled by the police. A calamity magnet like you, willing to let kismet, hunches, and impulses guide you is enough to put any self-respecting police officer on edge. I'm sure I don't have to tell you that, if you're right about Conroy, he's a ruthless, money-grubbing cutthroat. I doubt he'd think twice about paying his pros a little more to take out a busybody who threatens to impede his billion-dollar deal. You gotta spend money to make money, you know. And Jessica, one of his hired hands has excellent aim."

"You're singing to the choir. I am intimately familiar with what ruthless men who lust after money and mega deals can do."

"Email me those photos, since you snagged a copy. I want to see for myself if the guy in that hallway is Eric Conroy."

Jessica ended the call and emailed the photos. She hoped Hernandez could have that follow-up conversation with Ned Donnelly soon. Did he and his wife have any inkling that there was something more than a patient-client relationship between their daughter and the psychiatrist? Was Donnelly aware of any connection between Carr and Conroy? Depending on the answers to those questions, they might get a step or two closer to verifying the identity of the maniacally conniving counterpart to the stupidly impulsive Dr. Carr.

She had a few more minutes, so she tried to refocus, looking for another angle. What about Pinnacle? Who could give her a glimpse of what was going on behind the scenes at Pinnacle? What had all the "debate" been about before the announcement to pursue an IPO? She tried to recall the name of the young woman who had accompanied Conroy at that tribute to Hank at the end of July. Eric Conroy had been a happy man that night, so perhaps the troubles at Pinnacle were already behind him by then. When Jessica emailed those photos to Detective Hernandez, she flashed on a memory of the handbag carried by the fashionable blond with Conroy at the Never Built gala for Hank.

"Prada," Jessica whispered, just like the woman in that photo taken outside Carr's office. Maybe it was the same woman. Conroy had introduced her as a colleague at Pinnacle, the woman's name and position eluded Jessica, but when she went through the directory on the Pinnacle website, it didn't take long before she hit upon a name that sounded familiar. Carla Fergusson, Executive Assistant to the Chief Financial Officer of Pinnacle. In another few seconds, she had a face to go with the name.

"Got you," Jessica said. She had the right woman. Carla Fergusson was as attractive as she remembered. Medium height and build, with flawless skin, blond hair, and deep set brown eyes, she exuded confidence. Although their meeting had been a brief one, she had struck Jessica as pleasant and more likable than her companion, Eric Conroy. From the website, Jessica learned that Carla Fergusson didn't answer directly to Conroy, but to the company's Chief Financial Officer. There had been nothing in the research on Conroy to link him to the woman. Still, there had been a familiarity between them that seemed more natural and relaxed than one might expect for people who only met around a conference table.

Jessica felt the contours of a plan forming. It might not be a great one. None of the police officers in her life would condone it, but they wouldn't be there for dinner to object. Some of her Cat Pack friends might not like it either. She couldn't drive, so she needed help. Maybe someone would come up with a better plan, after she filled them in on the latest turn of events at dinner. She'd already suggested they stay put at the hotel tomorrow night, too, and drive back to the desert on Monday. She didn't say what time on Monday. Their dinner reservation at Spago was for eight o'clock. They had a lot to talk about. More than that, Jessica learned, they had celebrating to do. The evening would be a late one. She could never have guessed how late.

26 AN OLD FRIEND

After Jessica and Bernadette left, Alexis felt energized, more upbeat than she had in ages. Maybe she could do this. The cool breeze swirled around her as she gazed at the blue waters of the Pacific. The sound of the waves was soothing, rather than annoying as it had been earlier in the day. She almost went to the lovely dining room for dinner. Rumor had it that a handsome, young actor had joined them all in rehab, and might put in an appearance at dinnertime. What intrigued her most was the stir he might create. Although the day had been pleasant, it had also been tiring, so she let her order for dinner to be served on her private patio stand. She pushed the simple, but perfectly prepared food, around on her plate.

Even with the meds they were giving her, she recognized the withdrawal symptoms. It wasn't just her lack of appetite. Twitchy feelings, mild nausea, and bouts of "chicken skin," as Bernadette would call her goose bumps bothered her, off and on. In the background, for the moment, was that sense of dread that overwhelmed her at other times. An unshakable feeling of impending doom was one reason she took so many lovely, mind-numbing drugs. Call it angst, the old ennui, depression or anxiety; that didn't make it any easier to bear.

Whatever it was, the waves came and went in her life as they pleased. Their visits were not as regular as the sonorous pounding of the sea below. True, she was in her first week of detox, awaiting the news she was clean enough to undergo treatment for cancer, but that wasn't the only reason for her current uneasiness. The little scene with Jessica about Eric Conroy troubled her as it replayed in her mind. She didn't like the pallor her daughter's skin had taken on when Jessica understood who that man in the photos was. Why all the drama because of that poor troubled woman's rambling about a red devil?

Eric Conroy had struck Alexis as just one more aspirant, working to join the one percent. Based on what she knew of him, he had succeeded. That IPO, creating so much buzz, would cement his position at the top of the heap, along with the other partners at the firm. The money from that bonanza would trickle down—not out into the world at large, but to many others at the firm who held private shares in the company. Even an IPO, split too many ways, wouldn't raise the bar for everyone on the payroll at Pinnacle. The trickle was a trickle by the time it got down to middle management. Eric Conroy would do well, though.

What was the big deal about that? Alexis had seen the man several times over the years. He wasn't her type, but struck her as amiable enough. Why did he have such an impact on her daughter? Who in her network had introduced her to him and when?

Her memory was a little jumbled, so it took more effort than in the past to ferret out information like that. It wasn't just aging, but another "gift" of detox and the toll drug use had been taking on her mind as well as her body. The breezy smile of that woman with Eric Conroy, at the Never Built event for Hank, came back to her. Alexis had been a little surprised by his companion. There used to be another woman in his life. In another half second, it all came back to her.

Sally Winchester was a delicate blond, a little older than Jessica was. She didn't mix with Alexis and her cohort of cronies, but her mother did. It had been at one of Dottie Winchester's parties that Alexis first met Eric Conroy.

He'd been dressed to the nines, bowing jauntily as Sally embraced her mother. He had struck Alexis as rather debonair and she'd said as much to Dottie. They watched Eric and Sally as they circled the room for the ritual exchange of air kisses and greetings. Then Dottie spoke.

"Men aren't always what they seem. You should know that by now." The abruptness of her tone had shocked her. Dottie was a rather nonjudgmental woman, more reticent than many of her other friends to dish the dirt. Perhaps, it was a mother's disdain for the man about to snatch her daughter away from her. Alexis had tried to make light of it.

"Not son-in-law material, I take it. I get it. I have doubts about my son-in-law; trust me. Eric Conroy's Executive Vice President of Pinnacle, according to Sally, and the next in line as CEO. Doesn't he get considerable scrutiny?"

"Scrutiny, my ass. Eric Conroy's a legend in his own mind and he's put that CEO idea into Sally's head. He thinks she can influence me, but it won't work. If I have anything to do with it, and I do, he'll never be CEO of Pinnacle, nor will he be my son-in-law." Another couple had sauntered toward them at that point, and Dottie went back to playing gracious hostess.

Alexis had let it go and never brought it up again. She'd heard, not long ago, that Dorothy Winchester resigned her position on the board of Pinnacle earlier in the year. She hadn't given it much thought, but had attributed the decision to illness or aging. Until now, she'd forgotten all about Dottie's comments regarding Eric Conroy, a man Alexis hardly knew and cared nothing about.

Maybe she should mention all of this to Jessica, since the man had evoked such concern. Dorothy or Sally Winchester might have something useful to say about him. Dottie hadn't referred to Eric Conroy as a red devil, like Libby Van Der Woert, but Dottie had registered strong objections to him. If he was still on Jessica's radar the next time she visited, Alexis would have her call the Winchester women. The uneasiness dogging her increased as she focused on those recollections of Eric Conroy. A sudden scraping sound startled her.

"Who's there?" She asked.

"Is that you Alexis? It's me. Claire. You want to come over for a drink?" Her neighbor's head appeared from around the corner of the dividing wall that made their patios private.

"Sure. I'll probably float away, given how much liquid I drink. Not good when I'm trying to sleep and have to get up to use the bathroom. What the heck? It'll just take me a second to grab a warm sweater, okay?"

"That's a great idea. I'll do the same. You want to share my dessert? It looks delicious, but I'm not that hungry."

"I haven't eaten mine yet; I'll bring it with me. I bet it's the same." The berry crumble thing looked good. She dashed into her bedroom and pulled on a bulky cardigan. Alexis' loquacious socialite routine wasn't all fake. People were among her favorite distractions, up to a point. She found them interesting, as long as she could keep the subjects light, on topics that didn't require that she divulge personal information or, God forbid, feelings.

Claire was quite an interesting woman. Oxycontin had become her new best friend after a skiing accident had left her with a lot of back pain. Like Alexis, Claire had traveled widely, so it would be great to compare notes about the places they had visited.

Does she have children? Alexis wondered. *Were they as likely as Jessica was to get mixed up in mysterious, even dangerous, circumstances?* Those questions sent a chill through Alexis that had nothing to do with the cool evening air in Malibu.

"I'm calling Jessica, before she gets on the wrong side of Eric Conroy," Alexis declared, as she hit the speed dial on her cell phone. After three or four rings, the phone went to voice mail.

"Jessica, it's Mom. I thought of someone you should speak to about Eric Conroy. Call me, please, before you do anything more about him. Love you!" She ended the call, grabbed her dessert, and headed next door. She stopped as she crossed the threshold and stepped out onto her patio, stunned to realize that she had gone all day without thinking about those pills in the lining of the bag in her room. The next time Jessica visited, that bag was going home with her. *Why hadn't Jessica picked up that phone?*

27 TROUBLE AT TIFFANYS

Jessica sat in the back of a police car that was parked on Rodeo Drive, in front of Tiffany's. Darkness had fallen, and the shops had closed, but the legendary shopping mecca was lit up like a red-carpet event was underway. The lighting was courtesy of Beverly Hills' finest—cops *and* rescue squad vehicles. Bernadette sat beside her. Her other friends were standing around, being interviewed, or waiting to be interviewed, by the officers at the scene. Except for Peter, who was being tended by EMTs. Jessica had already given her statement—short and to the point, considering how quick trouble had come and gone.

"How can this be happening to us, Bernadette?"

"I believe you about that trouble magnet idea of yours. It's okay. Try to relax. We'll be done here soon. Then, we can all go back to the hotel and have dinner. Brien must be about ready to make a run for it. He was already putting the pressure on to get out of Tiffany's so we wouldn't lose our reservation at Spago. That was over an hour ago."

Jessica tried to relax, as Bernadette suggested. She rested her head on the seat, closing her eyes. The images came rushing in on her. Their little group had stopped at Tiffany's on the way to Spago for dinner. The trip to Tiffany's had been Tommy's idea. When Jessica made that round of phone calls asking everyone to consider staying over at the hotel for another night, Tommy whooped with delight.

"Woohoo! I'll stay here as long as you want. Jerry won't mind, either. We're uh, celebrating, and, uh, we might be late for dinner." Those last few words rushed out of his mouth.

"Okay, Tommy, what's up?" There was a tone of excitement in his voice that she recognized from all the years she'd known him.

"We're going to Tiffany's in a few minutes. Thank goodness, they're open 'til seven tonight... we're looking for rings!"

"Tommy, sweetie, does that mean what I think it means?"

"Yes—we're getting engaged! Can you believe it? I'm in love. We're in love." He was breaking down as he spoke, overcome by emotion and Jessica felt herself tearing up. Just when you thought rot had overtaken the world in which you live, something wonderful happened. True love was a rare event, so why not celebrate like mad when it happened? She was smiling ear-to-ear; a cloud lifted from her. *Love lifts you up,* she thought, remembering those words first spoken to her by Bernadette, years ago and repeated many times since.

"I'm overjoyed. Can we meet you there and see what you two picked out? I mean, it's okay, right? You're ready to make this public, yes?"

"Oh hell, yes! If I could get on Eye on the Desert, I'd let Patrick Evans break the news to all my friends."

"Don't do that, you might get a fan following—I'm not sure you two want that, do you? I wish we could skip all the dark stuff tonight, altogether, and just celebrate. But I need to share what I found out today and get input from the rest of you."

"Maybe you're right about not needing to make a media splash. Don't worry about dark stuff, though—I'm on cloud nine, or ten or whatever. Nothing will get to me, tonight."

"You deserve all the happiness in the world. Head on over to Tiffany's and I'll call everyone and spread the word. We won't get there until right before closing time, to give you a little privacy. Then, we'll all walk on over to Spago for dinner at eight, okay?"

"Sounds great, I'll go tell Jerry. He's making himself look gorgeous—like he needs to work at that. I am so lucky that he loves me!" There was wonder in that breathless statement.

"Yes, you are lucky. You know what?"

"What?"

"I love you, too," she said.

"Aw, that's another reason I'm so lucky. What would I have done if you hadn't loved me all these years? After Kelly... without you, I... would have been lost, like she was." Tommy choked up.

"Don't think about that tonight. We're doing what we can to rid the world of sickos who prey on lost young women. Love is still the best antidote to all that sorrow—and you've found that. Let's get this party started, okay?"

"Okay, my dream date is all ready to go. See you in a little while."

The wheels in her head were turning. First, she called everybody and asked that they meet in the lobby so they could walk over to Tiffany's together. She didn't tell them why—just that they should get ready for a big surprise. Next, she called the store to make sure the rings got charged to her and not to the lovebirds. A small price to pay for the hope those few words from Tommy had brought her. She also made sure the shop would accommodate them if things weren't all wrapped up by seven on the dot. That was not a problem. Last, she ordered little gifts for each of them, to mark the occasion—pendant necklaces with hearts for the women and key rings for the men. Each would be engraved with Bernadette's words "love lifts you up."

When they arrived at Tiffany's and figured out what was going on, everyone's mood was ebullient. Tommy and Jerry had narrowed down their choices to three. With a little feedback from the Cat Pack, they made their final selections—two sleek bands of white gold, each with a single diamond. By the time they all walked out of the shop, it was seven thirty and apart from Brien's concern about getting to Spago by eight, no one worried about a thing.

"It was all so wonderful. I don't get how life can change, in a split second, do you?" Jessica snapped her fingers.

"I know it happens, Jessica," Bernadette replied. She did, too, having lost the love of her life at a young age. Bernadette knew well that life could be one way one day, and different the next. Remembering that moment while sitting in the police car, Jessica shut her eyes as though she could shield herself from the memory of what had happened next.

They'd all stood outside Tiffany's, thanking the security guard as he let them out of doors he'd locked at closing time. Jessica hadn't noticed, but Peter had gone into security mode when they hit the street. He called out "Gun! Back, inside the store, now!" The guard didn't hesitate, and held the door open for them.

As Peter called out, he jumped in front of Jessica, pulling her a step closer to the doorway. They all scrambled to follow his orders. He was the last to retreat, still scanning the street as he backed through the doorway.

"It all happened so fast," Jessica sighed, recalling an all-too-familiar sound—gunfire! As Peter took that last step through the doorway, he was hit. The impact, along with his own efforts to get inside, propelled him backward, and he fell hard onto the floor. As the door to Tiffany's shut, a second bullet struck and pinged off the overhang that sheltered the store entryway. The security guard had pulled a gun from his holster, and someone triggered a silent alarm. The police must have responded instantly, perhaps fearing a robbery was underway at the legendary jewelry store, as sirens could be heard in a matter of seconds.

The guard also called in medical help for Peter—not sure where the bullet hit, Jessica ventured to have a look, her heart pounding as she bent over Peter. He was lying motionless on the floor, his eyes closed. There had been an awful crack when the huge man struck the floor.

"No blood," Jessica remembered saying, right before letting out a yelp. Several other Cat Pack members echoed with yelps of their own. Almost in unison, they jumped back, startled because Peter's eyes had popped open, and he sat up rubbing the back of his head.

"Whoa, it's like seeing a dead body sit up in a morgue—like in a zombie or a vampire movie." Brien said. "Awesome—are you okay, Bro?"

"I'm not dead and I'm not your bro. Yes, I'm okay. Thanks for asking."

"But you got shot, Dude." Brien persisted.

"Yeah, that's too bad. Messed up the leather, I'll have to get it fixed," Peter said, looking at the front of his jacket. "Kevlar worked, though. It stopped the bullet, but it knocked me on my behind."

"Uh, Peter that wasn't your behind that made that cracking sound when you hit the floor," Brien said.

"You'd better stay put until the EMTs get here and check you out," the security guard admonished Peter, placing his weapon back in its holster. In almost the same instant, there was a pounding on the door; the first responders had arrived.

Once it had become clear there was no robbery in progress, the store had gone back to closing for the night. Police fanned out and searched the area for a shooter. EMTs moved Peter to the back of a rescue vehicle while they checked him out. He would have a nasty bump on his head, but other than that, he was unharmed. They'd all joined Peter as a police officer took his statement.

"My guess is the shooter had you in mind as the target, Jessica," Peter had said.

"You think it's the sniper that's been on the loose?" Bernadette asked.

"That was no sniper," Peter told them and the police. "A sniper wouldn't have waved a handgun around like that for me to see. And a sniper would have aimed higher." As Peter told the police, he'd spotted a figure standing across the street, "wearing a baseball cap and in dark, baggy clothes—sweats. Short, maybe five-five, maybe too small to be a man."

"Are you saying it was a woman?" A police officer asked.

"Was she an enormously pregnant, platinum blond?" Jessica had asked. The only woman Jessica could imagine gunning for her was Cassie Harper. It wouldn't be the first time their paths had crossed on Rodeo Drive.

"I don't think the clothes were baggy enough to hide an enormously pregnant woman. Cassie's taller than that, too. I could be wrong about it being a woman, but that bullet is from a low caliber handgun—a girlie gun. Whoever did this was out of here quick, too. It doesn't sound like your ex-husband's wife is in any shape to make a getaway like that shooter was able to do." The officer was staring, like he was trying to figure out what to write down.

"Hang on," he said. "I'll call in the description you just gave me." He stepped away for a moment while they continued to stand, mulling over events.

"Even if it wasn't her, you might be in Cassie's cross hairs now though. When this gets out, she'll hate you even more for upstaging her again... and on holy ground, Rodeo Drive," Laura had said, trying to lighten the mood.

"Great, that's just what I need. Two angry women trying to shoot me," she said.

"What if it's one of those fans of yours turned stalker?" Tommy asked. He was moving into prankster mode. They all headed in that direction as stress from the strange turn of events took hold.

"Let's not forget that the sniper is still out there," Kim added. They all looked at Kim, trying to figure out why she brought that up. "So maybe three shooters after you... I'm just sayin'," she added, giving her shoulders a little shrug.

"Tommy, I'm sorry about this. I feel horrible about ruining your wonderful evening—missing our reservation at Spago and oh yeah, putting your life at risk from a stray bullet."

"Please don't say you're sorry. First, this is not your fault. Second, we can do Spago another time, and third, this has to be one of the most memorable engagement events on record. Am I right, Jerry?"

"You'll get no argument from me about any of that. This is one for the grandkids," Jerry smiled as he reached out and put his arm around Tommy's shoulders. Tommy turned to mush, right before Jessica's eyes.

"Uh, let's not forget we haven't had dinner yet. There's still time to celebrate, right?" That was Brien making sure they all kept their priorities—in other words, his stomach—right. "Officer, how long is it going to take to wrap this up? We're hungry." The police officer, who had rejoined them, just stared at Brien for a few seconds, shook his head, and went back to making notes.

"Once I'm done with Mr. March, here, I'll let each of you tell your story for the record. Then you can go. It doesn't sound like we have much to go on here. Maybe we'll pick up somebody in the area, thanks to that description, but I wouldn't count on it. Keep an eye on your friend here, who just happens to be wearing Kevlar. Just in case that bump on the head turns out to be worse than it seems now." He eyed the motley little band with wariness. "I'm not sure what you all are mixed up in, but I think it's time to back off."

That's a record, Jessica thought. A police warning to back off, issued like a citation, in under fifteen minutes. "Thanks officer, we'll take that under advisement," she had responded.

"Sounds like lawyer lingo, Ms. Huntington, is it?" He asked, checking the list of names he'd made. Before she could respond, he went on. "Huntington, Jessica Huntington, why does that name sound so familiar?" Then it hit him. "You're the angel heiress, right?" He asked, shaking his head again. "Wait 'til the guys hear about this. You're next."

Jessica had little to tell the officer about what had happened that night. When he asked who might have it in for her, about her buddy in Kevlar, and their comments that it might not be *"the sniper"* who targeted her that night, she was too tired to explain it all. She suggested if he wanted to know more, that he speak to officers in another of the jurisdictions involved, referring him to George Hernandez and both Fontanas.

Later, when he dropped them at the hotel, he spoke to Jessica. "We may have more questions for you all, after we check with the Cathedral City PD, the Palm Springs PD, and the Riverside County Sheriff's department." He shook his head again, took the business card Jessica handed him, and helped her out of the back of the police car, as she struggled with one arm in a sling. "You are one lucky lady, Jessica Huntington," was the last thing he said to her. *The next person who tells me how lucky I am is in for a dose of bad luck—of my making,* she thought as she joined her friends in the lobby. That's all she wanted to hear—another cop telling her how lucky she was. *Enough already! It's almost as annoying as being told to back off,* she thought, as she thanked the man for the ride. The police officer had insisted they be driven to the hotel even though they were only a couple of blocks away. As he had pulled up at the hotel entrance, Jessica checked the time, using her smart phone. It was after nine o'clock. She'd received phone calls during the melee and had voice mail messages, several of them from her mother.

"Oh no," she said, after listening to the voice mails. Her mom had become more anxious with each call. Jessica stopped in the lobby to call her. She decided to keep the latest bad news to herself. "Sorry,

Mom, I had the phone off for a while. It's been a wild night. Tommy and Jerry are getting married." Her friends were standing a short distance away, waiting for her. When she finished her call, they all moved toward the hotel restaurant that was still open for dinner.

"Okay, well, I planned to tell you this over dinner, but Mom has helped us figure out who Libby's red devil might be. His name is Eric Conroy. He has, or had, a woman friend we need to talk to about him. She might just be the key to figuring out this whole scheme. I had a plan I wanted to run by you about who to talk to next, but Sally Winchester has just gone to the top of my to-be-interviewed list." Laura stopped in her tracks.

"Well, that will be hard to do. She's dead." They all stood there for a moment before Brien went into fearless leader mode.

"We need food. Follow me," he said, making a beeline for the restaurant.

28 MORE WOMEN

Saturday evening, before the debacle on Rodeo Drive, Jessica had decided that she would visit Pinnacle. She planned to track down Carla Fergusson in person Monday morning. She'd make an appointment with the woman if she could get one. If that didn't work, she intended to lie in wait and confront her if she spotted her, at lunch, or at the end of the day. Basically, Jessica's strategy was to stalk the Fergusson woman until she agreed to speak to her. Cornering her, while the pressure was on with the impending IPO, felt like the best chance to find out what was going on.

As exhausted as they were, there was a palpable sense of anticipation in their little group as they sat down for their belated dinner. Seated in the posh restaurant at the Beverly Wilshire hotel, late on a Sunday night, there wasn't much of a crowd. Thankfully, for Brien's sake, they ordered food right away—getting bread and crudité into Brien's hands before he passed out. The staff served champagne right away too, and they toasted Tommy and Jerry's engagement as well as their good fortune that no one was seriously hurt.

"To Kevlar," Peter offered, after they'd said cheers to Tommy and Jerry. Jessica, throwing caution to the wind, raised her own sparkling crystal glass of bubbly. Then Peter turned to Laura and Jessica. "Okay, what gives, you two?"

"First things first, I guess. As I said before we sat down, thanks to Mom, I now know who the guy is in that photo taken outside

Carr's office. I'm also sure he's Libby's red devil and Carr's co-conspirator." With that statement, she passed around her phone. Front and center was a full-color picture of Eric Conroy, pulled off the web, the goatee and shock of red hair on display. Murmurs and gasps circled the table as they passed the photo around. Jessica explained how her mother had found the black and white photo of Eric Conroy on her phone and immediately recognized him.

"Conroy has deep pockets, about to get even deeper if all goes as planned." There were more gasps as she filled them in on the man's connection to Pinnacle, the IPO set to launch, and the amount of money at stake. All eyes were on her, too, when she revealed that Ned Donnelly was on Pinnacle's board.

"That's a ton of money," Tommy said.

"He must be under pressure with that timeline hanging over him," Peter added.

"Yeah, all he needs is some yahoo, like Libby or Shannon, stirring up trouble with the deal of a lifetime in progress. Guys like him don't want to take any chances with mouthy young women." Kim looked angry as she said those words. A moment of silence passed as Kelly's presence seemed to hover over them. Appetizers and another bottle of champagne broke the spell.

"I've already shared this information with Detective Hernandez, who will have another conversation with Ned Donnelly. Here's the best I can do, for now, to connect the dots. I have a hunch that Shannon Donnelly was giving her parents the same grief Libby's been doling out—allegations made about her father, or another family member. Ned Donnelly looks grim months before his daughter disappears. He's one of several unhappy campers in the background at Pinnacle board meetings where Conroy is basking in the limelight." Jessica nibbled on a bread stick to ease a mild sensation of nausea brought on by stress, hunger, and lowlifes.

"Maybe Shannon was after money, or Carr's love, but extortion can pressure people into doing many things—like getting you to vote a certain way at board meetings. Or, it might be enough to get you to resign, if you're unwilling to cast your vote his way. What helped me get this far along in my thinking is another bit of information from Mom. She called me while we were in Tiffany's and again when we were tied up afterward. When I called her back a few minutes ago, she said she remembered where she met Conroy. He was involved with Dorothy Winchester's daughter, Sally. Surprise, surprise, Dottie Winchester, served on Pinnacle's board of directors for years, resigning not long *before* that IPO vote took place. Fortunate for Conroy since Mom says Dottie didn't approve of the man—not in a leadership role at Pinnacle and not as a prospective son-in-law. Mom suggested I speak to Sally Winchester, if I had concerns about him. That won't happen though, will it Laura?" She glanced at Laura, uneasy to hear what she had to say about another dead daughter.

"No, it won't," Laura replied. "When you were in the hospital you mentioned, in passing, that there might be more women tied to Carr. That got me thinking. Carr spent a lot of time out in the desert with troubled young women in tow. Given his medical credentials, I wondered if he'd ever admitted patients to the hospital. So, I checked with a friend in medical records and asked her to check. Then, Kim, when you said that with men like Carr there are always more women, I decided to call my friend and see if she had found anything. What she discovered is that Libby Van Der Woert was admitted to the hospital weeks ago when she *accidentally* took more medication than prescribed. Carr was the admitting physician. They pumped Libby's stomach, kept her around until the next morning, and then released her into his care."

"Okay, that's news—not the least bit un-Libby-like, however," Jessica said.

"True, but before that, there was another, similar situation—an accidental overdose. Unlike Libby, at the time of her admission, Sally Winchester was unconscious. She never recovered consciousness and died the next morning. It was Carr who called an ambulance and asked to have her admitted. He claimed Sally had called him, complaining she didn't feel well, and he was concerned that she might have taken too many pills or something like that. My friend remembers the incident well because there was an inquest to determine if the death was an accidental overdose or a suicide. Sally Winchester had a lot of drugs in her system at the time of her death. Besides the ones prescribed for her by Carr, she took medication for congestive heart failure. Her weakened heart, the overdose, drug interactions, or all the above, contributed to a radical drop in blood pressure. That triggered a massive stroke that killed her. So, officially, stroke was ruled the cause of death, and an accidental overdose the manner of death. Sally was young, just thirty-three years old, another reason my friend remembers the incident so well." They all lapsed into silence once again. Tired and hungry, they spent the next few minutes finishing their appetizers. They must have looked glum, because several of their servers stopped to ask if everything was okay, and could they get them anything else before their main courses arrived. Brien asked for more bread, but the others only did what they could to be polite and smile in response to the servers' inquiries. Once their meals arrived, a few minutes later, Jessica could finally speak again.

"Yet another sad story involving Carr. It makes me sick," she sputtered. "Maybe her daughter's death is what led to Dottie Winchester's resignation. That sleaze, Conroy, is mixed up in this, I just know it. I wonder how close that vote was that won Conroy the deal of a lifetime. Sally Winchester might have had plenty to tell us about her ambitious suitor. Too bad she's dead."

"Her mother's not dead," Bernadette said. "She might have plenty to say about Conroy too—she worked with him and must know what went on between him and her daughter. Get Alexis to call her and let's go see her," Bernadette said. "I'll drive."

"Oh no you won't," Peter said. "Not with someone taking pot shots at Jessica. If Dorothy Winchester agrees to speak to you tomorrow, Brien and I will drive. I mean drive, as in you and Jessica sit in the back seat," Peter said, trying not to look at the enormous steak Brien was devouring. "Speaking of things that make you sick. What is that, about three pounds of raw beef, Brien?"

"Two pounds, rare, Man, just the way I like it. Shotgun!" Brien said, to claim his favorite seat, before plunging his knife back into the Porterhouse steak meant for two.

"Why do you think I said they would be sitting in the back?" Peter asked, averting his eyes again from the massacre underway on Brien's plate.

"Oh, yeah, okay," he shrugged.

"It feels like it must be about two a.m., but it's not even ten yet. I'll step out and call Mom. If she feels okay about calling Dottie Winchester, I'll ask her to see if she's willing to talk to us." When Jessica returned, her food looked delicious. Her appetite was back. "All set, guys. Mom got Dottie on the phone and called me back right away. Dottie is more than willing to have a conversation. She's been trying to convince people for years that Conroy is no good. We're all set for tomorrow after lunch—at her place near Pasadena."

"Wow, that's amazing. Go Alexis," Tommy said.

"Maybe she'll give you something that will get the police to investigate Conroy," Jerry added.

"Maybe, but I have another angle to pursue, too! I've also discovered who the woman is in that photo with Carr and Conroy, taken outside Carr's office."

"You've been busy," Kim commented.

"What can I say? I'm motivated. And, if we figure this out, we won't have to be dodging bullets from shooters—amateurs or professionals. Here's the scoop on the blond in that photo with a penchant for Prada," she said, and then filled them in on her plan to confront Carla Fergusson at Pinnacle on Monday morning.

"Could you do that, Peter? You know, stick around and play bodyguard on Monday?"

"Sure, I can. It's good to be the boss," he replied, in a better mood now that his roasted vegetables, quinoa, and other well-prepared vegan choices from the menu had put him in a culinary-induced happy place.

"I'm the boss of my pool business, too, so I'll have a talk with myself and figure out how to make it work," Brien said, smiling. They were all giving him the "are you serious" kind of scrutiny. Brien flicked his head so the shock of blond hair, which had fallen into his eyes, moved back into place. The smile he wore was a reminder that he was a good-looking guy. Jessica caught Kim lingering on that smile before she shook her head and went back to eating.

"Uh, just in case you were wondering, that was a joke. I have to call a friend of mine to sub for me, but I don't have to talk to myself before I do that."

"What can the rest of us do while you're meeting with the little old lady in Pasadena and trying to corner the woman in Prada?" Tommy asked. "Jerry and I have already fixed our schedules, so Monday's clear."

"Well, since you asked... I can't believe Conroy hasn't been in trouble before. So, digging into his background, would be great, if you two will do that while we're in Pasadena. Kim, I also want anything you can find in the way of financial data about Pinnacle.

Like the stuff you uncovered about your old boss's enterprising ways." They all nodded in agreement.

"Laura, do you have any connections with staff in medical facilities, here, in LA, like the hospital at UCLA or Cedars-Sinai? It might be worth checking to see if Carr's been entangled in similar incidents involving distraught young women admitted to ERs for accidental overdoses in Beverly Hills."

"I can ask, but it might take me a while to figure it out."

"No problem. We could all use some spa time in the morning, don't you think? So, how does it sound if we spend the morning getting the stress massaged out of us, go to the terrific brunch they serve here, and leave the snooping to the afternoon?" That brought on another round of toasts as they finished their dinners.

"What's for dessert?" Brien asked, minutes later, as servers swept in to remove their plates. Dessert menus appeared.

"Wow, there are surprises on this—even vegan goodies," Peter proclaimed, looking almost as eager as Brien was.

"Speaking of surprises," Tommy said as he handed Jessica his phone.

Angel Heiress Targeted by Unknown Assailant on Rodeo Drive, the banner headline read, accompanied by a photo of police and rescue vehicles parked outside Tiffany's.

"Great, I'm in the news again. Just what I need," Jessica moaned, handing the phone back to Tommy. "Maybe we should hire paparazzi to find out what this Conroy character is up to. They're really on the ball!"

"Uh, sorry, that's not what I wanted you to see... it's this." Tommy handed the phone back to her and she read the headline out loud.

Hollywood's Blond Bombshell Goes into Labor at Upscale Bistro, Sparks Fly!

"Yes! Thank you, Cassie. Another diversion from the limelight, courtesy of Jim's beloved. Woohoo!" Jessica announced, picking up her champagne glass.

"I have to say, the woman's timing is impeccable," Laura added. "No way was she going to let the angel heiress monopolize the headlines."

"And talk about an ironclad alibi," Jerry added. "She couldn't have been your shooter tonight, that's for sure."

"To life! Even with Cassie-the-worm-hearted as your mother," Jessica said.

"To perfect timing, and all the paparazzi and fans she could ever want!" Laura added.

Dinner, and maybe the champagne, had done wonders for their spirits. Jessica felt back in control, hoping it was more than just the buzz from wielding that black AMEX card as she'd been doing the past couple of days. She flashed for a moment on that earlier conversation with Bernadette and her mother. Here she was again, masterminding an extravaganza, in the middle of an investigation into muck and mire, all courtesy of well-dressed men cast as winners and milling about in hoity-toity circles. It couldn't keep that sinking feeling away, completely, but oohs and aahs over desserts kept the volume low on the questions that dogged her.

29 KIERKEGAARD SNAPS

"What can I say? It wasn't me," Kirk groused.

"Don't get annoyed with me, Kierkegaard. I'm the guy who sends you money, remember? When, and if, you do a job the right way, that is," Conroy said, chomping on a cigar. He'd lit it to celebrate the fact that this was the last Sunday he would ever spend as a chump working for Pinnacle. By next Sunday, LA would be a fading memory. Not a pleasant one, at this point.

"Don't call me that. Nobody calls me that," Kirk snapped.

"Set off an existential crisis, did I?" Eric laughed, intending to be nasty. "Let me remind you I'm also the guy who can make or break you—not just your reputation, but your legs." *Or your neck*, he thought. The man on the other end of the phone took a deep breath, but he sounded no less annoyed when he spoke again.

"You said keep an eye on her, so that's what I've been doing. If I had shot at her, do you think I would have missed?"

"If you didn't do it, who did?"

"I don't know. You said keep tabs on her, not babysit. She has a bodyguard of her own to do that. I hear he took a bullet for her. He was wearing a Kevlar undershirt or something, so he's okay. Just say the word and I'll take a shot. Is that what you want?"

"No, no, don't do that. What I want is to slide into Friday, nice and quiet. I guess whoever took that shot at her did us a favor, eh? That ought to get Jessica Huntington to cool it. Good grief, it's only been a week since Libby Van Der Woert shoved her off a mountaintop. What is she doing here, in LA, anyway?"

"From what I can tell, partying with friends. They all checked in for the weekend at the Beverly Wilshire and hit Tiffany's tonight. Some reporter said the visit to Tiffany's had something to do with an engagement ring. Huntington and her friend, a family housekeeper or something like that, visited a clinic in Malibu this afternoon before she met up with friends at Tiffany's," Kirk replied.

"A Malibu clinic—as in rehab? Is she looking to check herself in?" Eric asked.

"Yes, as in rehab. Transformations, a high-end place that caters to celebrities. I'm sure you must have heard of it. I can find out why she made that visit if you want me to. Does it matter?"

"No, I guess not. I still want you to keep an eye on her."

"Will do," he said before he terminated the call. Eric was taken aback.

"You are pushing it, my friend," he muttered, staring at the blank cell phone screen. "No more business from me, that's for sure." He relit his cigar and took a few puffs. It didn't matter. Soon, he wouldn't need to work with Kierkegaard Kunzel, or anyone like him, ever again. That thought lifted his mood. Friday loomed with the pot of gold at the end of the rainbow. What if he had to put up with a few more dustups, who cares?

"Who names a kid Kierkegaard, anyway? No wonder he ended up as a cranky gun for hire," he snorted, in between puffs on his cigar.

Still, it nagged at him that the Huntington woman was in LA, had dodged a bullet from an unknown assailant, and had garnered more news coverage. Who else had the busybody in their scope? Was she involved in some drug-related case? Could be she'd picked up the wrong client at that cushy rehab resort or stepped over the line trying to be helpful. "It would be just like her. She comes from a long line of snooty do-gooders. Not my problem. Hope she gets what she deserves." He took a big swig of the cognac he'd poured for himself.

The previous night, both the current *and* former Mrs. Harpers had been on screen, side-by-side, on every site that catered to the entertainment industry. They'd rebroadcast the story this morning of the Tiffany's incident, but it was already yesterday's news. Cassie

Carlysle-Harper, or whatever her name was, sure was a looker: tall, blond, and built. At least until she blew up like a blimp. She'd stolen the headlines.

He had to hand it to the Hollywood star. The woman knew how to draw attention. Not all of it good, but then, "there's no such thing as bad publicity, is there?" Eric asked, speaking aloud in his empty office. "No one could afford the kind of coverage she's getting from this. Well, maybe I could, once those Pinnacle shares are sold on Friday," he chortled. He poured himself more cognac, and sat down to finish his cigar, watching the footage being rebroadcast.

The latest scene featuring the tantrum-prone star relegated the trouble at Tiffany's to page two. Just like that! A proclamation had gone out, through all La-La land: Cassie Carlysle had gone into labor. Diva-style, at a trendy restaurant where she, and the buffoon she wed in the past year, had gone for a late dinner. "With Huntington *and* Carlysle as notches on his belt, that guy must have something. I don't see it," Eric muttered as he stared at a reporter interviewing restaurant staff. He didn't need to hear it all again, even though parts of it were funny.

Less than an hour after that scene on Rodeo Drive featuring the previous Mrs. Harper, the new Mrs. Harper countered with that photo op of her own. The pregnant woman had been ornery since her arrival at the restaurant. She ordered items and then sent them back when they didn't meet with her approval. Known to have a temper and already facing assault charges, she hadn't struck anyone or raised her voice. But when her water broke, she panicked. Panicky wasn't much better, or very different, from angry, apparently. There weren't any cameras in the house, at that point, but diners whipped out smart phones and jumpy images made their way to television screens everywhere. He chuckled as those clips reappeared.

Cassie Carlysle was holding her belly, howling like a werewolf or something. The "suit" she'd married, James Harper, tried to calm her down when the cheeky broad hauled off and slapped him—right in the face. Eric guffawed out loud. He wouldn't have laughed if a woman hit him, or shrieked at him, like that. No matter how blond and well-endowed, he would have put her in her place.

"You loser, she's cussing like a sailor and threatening to kill you! All you do is stand there and take it. Oh no, look out, look out!" He said, as a clip featured the wailing woman taking swings at restaurant staff trying to help her. Food was flying and patrons were scrambling. "Help her get the hell out of that restaurant! You could sure use my services to put the right spin on this disaster," he said, shaking his head. "Sorry to say, I won't be around to help you. Salud!" He raised his glass with that salute and hit the off button on the TV just as the network reran footage of the EMTs joining the circus. The press was on their heels.

"Hear this," he announced, making a vow as he refilled his glass. "My future won't be dictated by a troublesome female. You will all stay out of my way, if you know what's good for you," Eric downed the second drink he'd poured. He didn't much care what Libby Van Der Woert had on Carr or what Jessica Huntington was up to. Let them try to throw a monkey wrench into his plans. He was no James Harper, gaping, slack-jawed, at a woman who didn't know when enough was enough. He knew exactly what to do with uppity women, especially when they became too much trouble.

30 WICKED WOMEN

"At one point she was screaming, 'Jim, you blankety-blank-blank, touch me and I'll kill you.' There are brief glimpses of her face, but she could do it—kill him, I mean. Jim is toast," Tommy announced to the group seated around a table at Sunday brunch.

"Oh no Man, not another dead husband," Brien said, hanging on every word Tommy spoke.

"It couldn't happen to a nicer guy," Laura commented, with a smirk on her face. Everyone at the table gawked at Laura, astounded that those words came from her. It had been less than six months since her husband was murdered. "Hey, Jim's a jerk. So is she. In this case, it might be a mercy killing, not even murder." Laura shrugged as she took a delicate bite from a strip of bacon.

"She has assault charges pending, so Jim could be in more trouble than he knows. Not my problem! What was she doing out on the town in her condition, anyway?" Jessica asked.

"Where I come from, you work until the last minute and have that baby wherever you are. You city girls got it good. For my mother and her friends, it wasn't a fancy restaurant like that. A baby will get here whether you're cleaning the fish, hanging laundry, or feeding the chickens."

"Point taken, but even on a good day, this woman is a beast. They ought to have her in seclusion or restrained, and under an armed guard in her condition! At least they got her out of there, so the whole world didn't have to witness that succubus give birth."

"It's like the Blair Witch Project, Beverly Hills style, with all those dark, jumpy video clips. Spooky," Brien said, doing his man-in-the-know head bobble. Jessica hadn't seen the movie, but those scary scenes, with eerily-lighted selfies, and a lot of heavy breathing came to mind from the movie promos, so maybe.

"I'm not sure I get that 'suck a bus' part, though." A puzzled puppy dog expression had replaced that man-in-the-know look on Brien's face.

"I'll explain it to you later," Peter offered.

"Thanks, Dude." Brien dove back into the stack of Challah French toast on his plate, satisfied with that promise from Peter. The brunch, like their spa visit and everything else at the Beverly Wilshire, was first rate and Brien was making the most of it.

"The witch part of Blair Witch Project sounds about right," Kim acknowledged.

"Yeah, she put curses on everyone in that restaurant before the EMTs arrived a few minutes after the chaos began. That was on top of curses directed at Jim. Just in case you didn't recognize him in the blurry, smart phone video clips being tweeted out, her vicious voiceovers make sure you know who her baby daddy is. 'James Harper, you jerk, you did this. I'll make you pay!' Followed by a string of expletives and growling. Grrr!" Tommy said, mimicking her nasty tone of voice and the growl that followed.

"Whoa, that *is* wicked," Brien said with great conviction.

"If he doesn't start divorce proceedings before the end of the year, I'll be astonished," Jerry added.

"Some people will put up with lots of abuse. Besides, Jim will look like an even bigger jerk than he does now if he files for divorce from his wife who just gave birth. He's screwed until next year, at least."

"You're right, Kim. When she leaves the hospital carrying her little bundle of joy, all the world will coo at her. Jim's in for months, maybe years, of this. If he files for divorce, can you imagine that? The custody battle will be epic," Laura said. "He'll wish he was a dead husband." Everyone stared at her again as she stabbed a chunk of melon on her plate.

"What? What did I say now? You don't think Jim will kill *her*, do you?"

"I doubt anybody will kill anybody. Some divorce lawyers stand to make a fortune if they go in that direction," Jessica said, sighing. "And yes, there's likely to be one hell of a custody battle. With Cassie and Jim as parents, it could be the first one, ever, that's about who's forced to end up with the baby. I can't imagine either one of them wanting to be a parent."

"Sì, pobre bambino," Bernadette said with sadness.

"Poor baby is right. If the child is anything like her mother, the rest of us will be sorry too. Just look at how much grief one Cassie, Libby, or Margarit can cause." Laura said in a woeful way. Despite her seeming glibness about murder, the memory of the wretched Margarit still caused pain.

"You don't believe in the whole tabla rasa thing?" Peter asked.

"Yo, Peter, are you speaking Spanish now too... ta-bla ra-sa?" Brien enunciated each syllable. "What's that?"

"Latin, Brien, and tabla rasa means when you're born, your mind is a blank slate, ready for whatever life writes on it," Peter added.

"Blank slate, oh, okay," Brien repeated, with a stare to match.

"Some slates are blanker than others," Kim muttered under her breath. Peter just shook his head.

"What? Uh, okay," Brien said, trying to figure out what the murmurs meant. "You'll tell me later, right?"

"Sure," Peter said and went to work eating the food on his plate.

"I don't know about Cassie or Margarit, but Libby's situation sure makes a case for genes though. She's lived about as close to a charmed life as you can get. Her parents love her, have given her everything, and they've gone to professionals for help since she was a kid. She's like a throwback to her grandmother, according to Nora. And, yes, poor baby is right, Bernadette. That child will have nature *and* nurture working against it. I can't imagine anyone spending a childhood with Cassie Carlysle-Harper and ending up whole. Was it a boy or a girl?"

"Girl," Tommy said. "If it's about genes, she's doomed."

"Well, I wouldn't go that far. Heck, I still have hope for Libby if she recovers from that last round of seizures. She's capable of feeling something close to remorse, based on what I heard up there on Mt. San Jacinto before Carr showed up. Carr's a whole different animal—*was* a whole different animal. His associate, Eric Conroy, must be too. That was a cold, calculating decision to pay someone to go into the ICU and kill Libby. A guy like that has to be stopped." Jessica was emphatic as she spoke. *What would it take to stop Eric Conroy?* She wondered.

"It is odd how these people find each other, isn't it? Not just Cassie and Jim, but Libby and Shannon and Dr. Dick, and, now, Conroy seems to have had his hooks into another doomed woman," Jerry commented.

"Two of them, possibly. It's not just Sally Winchester who seems to have become involved with Conroy. Let's not forget the Prada-loving co-worker who showed up on his arm at my dad's gala back in July. These guys can be compelling when they want to be. I can testify to that. I fell for the ever-creepier James Harper, before Cassie did."

"At the risk of sounding like one of our detective friends, are you sure it's such a good idea to meet with Carla Fergusson? If she's under Conroy's spell, then asking probing questions about her beau's business activities could tick her off. You love in-your-face confrontations with evil masterminds, and you may well get one. I don't see why Carla Fergusson won't set you up with Conroy." Laura was obviously worried.

"Here's the thing. Back in July, I got the same vibe from Carla Ferguson that I got from you, Kim, the first time we met." Jessica smiled at Kim as she spoke. "No Saraswati tattoo, but Carla was angry that night at my dad's gala when I ran into her in the ladies room. She was in there removing a spot from the fabulous dress she wore and muttering under her breath when I stepped out of the stall. 'Men,' she said, 'sloppy devils, even at a black-tie affair!' I urged her to send the guy a bill for ruining that gorgeous dress. 'Not when the devil is your boss's boss, and a real charmer,' she said, sounding angry and sarcastic, you know? Not words spoken by a woman infatuated with Conroy. Anyway, she stepped back into accommodating colleague mode fast. 'I do deserve a raise. My congratulations to your father, it's a great event.' Then, she dashed out of there, back to Conroy's side. When I saw her later, she was all smiles, touching the man, all flirty-like. Maybe she's conflicted about him. Who knows what it takes to see a guy like that for what he is and get away from him. Maybe she's at that point, or could be, with a nudge."

"Well, in my case," Kim said, "I found the creep of my life because I was young and dumb and desperate for attention—anything that seemed like someone gave a damn was hard to resist. He was a troll, out there looking for lost girls and boys like me. What shocks me is that money didn't protect these women from predators like Carr and Conroy. When I first met Mr. P. and the doc, I was just grateful to have food and clean place to sleep. That wasn't how Kelly fell into their clutches, was it?" Kim asked looking at Tommy.

"No, I'm not sure what put my sister onto the doomed-girl-track. She not only had food and a place to sleep, but friends and family who loved her—it just wasn't enough," he replied. Heaviness descended upon them. Jessica hurtled toward despair.

"You don't have to understand it to stop it," Bernadette said. "Right is right and wrong is wrong. You stop it, when you can, before anyone else gets hurt. I'm going with you to check out this Carla Fergusson person. That red devil won't try any of his funny business with two of us in the room—even if she tells him about your visit."

"Let's hope so. I'm in no condition for another Lucy and Ethel situation," Jessica worried aloud.

"Peter will be there, too. You won't be going into the lion's den alone this time. The Cat Pack will have your back," Tommy said, making hissing sounds and clawing the air. It would have set Frank on edge if he had been there. Her decision to meet with Carla would have done that, too.

"And me," Brien said, shoving one last bite of food in his mouth.

"You ready to roll, Peter?" Jessica asked, surprised to find she missed Frank. Not the prospect of being chewed out, or the worried look he would have had on his face. There was a kind of comfort she found in his presence. *I guess I like the strong, not-so-silent-type,* she thought, as she let out a little sigh. Not enough to call him and tell him what she was up to, though.

"Sure, let's go see if Dottie Winchester has the key to nailing this Conroy creep. If that's the case, you won't need a meeting with Carla

Fergusson or anyone else after today. I won't rest easy until he's nabbed, and can no longer afford the services of a sniper, or whatever other hired help he has working for him," Peter said, marching toward the exit. As they headed to the car, Jessica's phone pinged. She stopped to look at it.

"It's a text message from Detective Hernandez."

31 A MOTHER SPEAKS

The Winchester estate sat on a hill in a community Jessica knew well. The city of San Marino, home to the Huntington library, was a familiar part of family lore. Henry Huntington, her father's namesake, had built a mansion there, early in the twentieth century. Great-great-uncle Henry, or something like that, played an instrumental role in California history. The Huntington name was everywhere in San Marino, as it was elsewhere in the state.

The city, with its tree-lined streets, expansive residences, lavish greenery, parks, and gardens was picturesque, often featured in Hollywood movies. Dottie Winchester lived in a Georgian Revival masterpiece, sitting at the highest point on one of those lush, shady streets. A member of the household staff welcomed Bernadette and Jessica. Not a butler, but Dottie's fortyish personal secretary, Andrea Jessop. Jessica had spoken to her that morning to confirm their appointment. Brien and Peter planned to wait in the car. Peter was intent on keeping an eye out for anyone monitoring their whereabouts. As soon as they arrived, Andrea put in a call to their own security team, which showed up in minutes to chat with Peter and Brien. So far, Brien had been on his best behavior, mimicking Peter's demeanor, and not saying a word. Jessica had another of those surges of hope that Brien was not just good-hearted, but teachable. He couldn't be a wannabe surfer and pool boy his entire life.

Andrea, in pearls and a twin sweater set, worn with gray woolen slacks, looked every bit the gentlewoman assistant to the matron awaiting them. She had welcomed them all into a gracious formal entryway, adorned with marble floors and a stunning arrangement of fresh flowers atop a vintage console. Once Peter and Brien connected with the security team, Andrea asked Bernadette and Jessica to follow her down a hallway. Then they passed through an exquisitely detailed living room, with classic symmetrical lines, elaborate crown molding, and a massive fireplace. Original art hung on the walls, and an antique tapestry hung above the fireplace.

Andrea swept through to a dining room that could seat twenty or more. She opened a set of tall French doors leading outdoors to patios affording a view of the pool and gardens beyond. Seated in a wheelchair, at a patio table, was the matriarch they had come to visit.

Jessica almost didn't recognize Dottie Winchester. They had met a few times, but the woman she remembered had been formidable. Taller than her mother, Dorothy Winchester had been a striking figure. The person who stood to greet them was tall, but frail and a little bent. Gone was the dark hair that Jessica recalled. Stylishly cut, Dottie's hair was gray, almost white. Her eyes still shone brightly, but with less confidence and determination than had resided in them the last time they met.

"Welcome, Jessica, it's wonderful to see you again. It's been years, hasn't it, since we saw each other?"

"Yes, I'm sorry to say that's true. I was in the Palo Alto area for a decade and didn't get back here to LA often. I'm afraid I lost track of my family's friends once Mom and Dad were out of the country so much of the time," Jessica said.

"Well, there's nothing to be sorry about. You grew up and started a life of your own. That requires focus, doesn't it?" She eyed Jessica's sling, but said nothing. She seemed to tire and sat again.

"Let me give you a hand," Bernadette said, with an ease and familiarity that surprised Jessica. She took one of Dottie's arms as Andrea rushed to take the other. The two women eased Dottie back into her seat.

"Bernadette, I am so glad to see you. I'm supposed to thank you for your latest contribution to the scholarship fund this year in Guillermo's name at UCLA. Much appreciated. That's old news, though. It's been a while for us, too, hasn't it? Look at what I have with me." She reached into a pocket on the wheelchair and pulled out a beaded rosary.

"Bernadette was so kind when Harry passed away," she said, directing her comments to Jessica. "A tower of strength, but I suppose you know that already. How remarkable her life has been, even after the tragic loss of Guillermo."

"Yes, I've counted on her kindness and strength my whole life, a lot lately." Jessica could tell the praise was getting to Bernadette, who was eager to change the subject.

"I'm sorry about Sally. I didn't know you lost her, too," Bernadette said softly.

"We kept it all hush-hush, since we weren't certain what had happened. After an inquest ruled her death a terrible accident, I just withdrew. I haven't been well, and I haven't wanted to see anyone... I'm sorry."

"There's no reason to apologize. Trouble's a hard thing to share. When it involves someone we love so much, it's even harder," Bernadette said.

"It was quite a shock. More so than Harry's passing, since she was so young. I was more and more in the dark about her life. We weren't even speaking when she died. I knew she was in trouble, but what could I do? I've thought about the last year before she died, and I still haven't come up with anything else I might have done."

"Won't you sit down," Andrea said. She was so quiet that Jessica had almost forgotten she was there. "If you'll excuse me for a minute, I'll go see what's holding up the tea."

"Thank you, Andrea, where are my manners? Andrea has been a blessing through this whole ordeal. If I hadn't been able to rely on her, I don't know what might have happened. She's like you, Bernadette, a rock." Dottie smiled at Andrea, who returned a brief smile before dashing off.

"We're glad you're willing to talk to us," Jessica said.

"When Alexis said you had some concerns about Eric Conroy, I didn't hesitate. Sally was always a fragile girl; I blamed myself for that. I was overbearing, but I found her temerity hard to take. Still, she was sweet, smart, and a talented writer and poet. She grew into such a lovely young woman. I believed she had a chance for a happy future, although a writer's life is not an easy one—even with the patronage my friends and I could offer her." Dottie paused, staring out over the fountains and lavish pool, to the pastoral view of well-tended gardens.

"When she went out with Eric and they became engaged, I was hopeful, at first. I didn't like him much, but I thought her love might bring out the good in him. Within weeks, the pressure started. It was subtle in the beginning. Eric used the time he spent here to figure out which way I was leaning on some issue that had come up at a Pinnacle board meeting. I didn't object to his inquiries, although I would have preferred that he be more direct. I didn't object, either, to the fact that the man was ambitious and in a hurry to get ahead. The manipulative way he went about it rubbed me the wrong way. Not just manipulation, but distortions of the truth, misrepresenting the positions of others on the board, creating the illusion he had more support than he did for an issue. I knew he was hustling me, Jessica, and I didn't like it. He wanted the top job at Pinnacle and he wanted to take the company public. I had doubts about both matters."

Sounds issued from behind them and the French doors opened. A member of the household staff wheeled out a little cart with tea, chocolate-dipped strawberries, diminutive sandwiches, and a lovely assortment of tarts. Andrea made sure the doors were open wide enough for the cart to pass. Once the staff member had served them, Andrea dismissed her.

"I'll take it from here. Thanks!" The young server left, and Andrea seated herself with tea and treats of her own.

"Now, where was I?" Dottie asked. "Oh yes, Eric turning up the pressure. When he didn't get his way, hustling me by himself, he enlisted Sally to make his case. That just made me even more convinced that he was an unprincipled man and not leadership material. When I objected to that tactic, my relationship with Sally took a turn for the worse. I didn't understand how bad things could get." She glanced at Andrea before going on. "Only Andrea, our lawyers, and a few family members know what happened next."

"It's okay, we won't tell anyone," Bernadette said.

"If I thought it would help stop that despicable monster, I wouldn't mind one bit. He's as slippery as an eel," Dottie said, taking a sip of her tea. Andrea fidgeted in her chair, perhaps worried about Dottie, or upset because she knew what was coming.

"What happened?" Jessica asked.

"He broke it off with Sally, supposedly because I didn't approve of him and he didn't want to come between her and her family. She became hysterical and blamed me for ruining her life. She claimed I just didn't want her to be happy, and didn't like the man because I couldn't control him, like I did her. It was quite the scene. The next day, she moved out. I wasn't sure that was a bad thing, except that it happened under such acrimonious circumstances. When she told me, a few weeks later, that she was seeing a psychiatrist, I felt relieved. Moving out on her own, in her thirties, and getting into treatment made me think that the whole mess with Eric might turn out for the best."

"Let me guess. Sally was seeing Dr. Richard Carr, right?" Andrea turned to look at Jessica as Dottie exclaimed.

"Why yes! How could you know that?"

"He's part of my latest troubles," Jessica responded, raising the arm in the sling a little. "I imagine you've heard about the debacle at the top of the Palm Springs tramway." Andrea shook her head, no, before Dottie could speak.

"No, I haven't. I don't get out much, nor do I keep up with the news. It's just too depressing most of the time. What did I miss?" She looked at Jessica and at Andrea, who averted her eyes.

"We were afraid it would upset you," Andrea said, almost in a whisper. "Dr. Carr's dead. He died last week. I'm sure Jessica can give you more details, since she was with him." There was something odd in the way she spoke that last sentence, perhaps mistrust in her voice, maybe even resentment.

"I'm sorry to bring this up if you felt the need to keep it from Dottie. I hope you don't find this upsetting, but, yes, Carr is dead. He, another thirty-something female client of his, and I all took a tumble off the mountain last week. His client and I made it. He didn't."

"Well, I'm not sure why you thought that would upset me, Andrea. Dr. Carr turned my daughter against her father. It doesn't surprise me he met with an early, ugly death." A whoosh escaped from Jessica's lips. There it was—same guy, same M.O., and tied to Conroy. "I suspected he was in cahoots with Eric, given the way this all unfolded, but I had no way to prove it. Do you?"

"Not yet, but we're working on it. Did Sally meet Carr through Eric?"

"I'm not sure. That's what I figured when Sally said she wanted me to resign from Pinnacle's board, *or else*. The trouble that had started weeks before finally made horrible sense. By then, it was too late for Harry. My husband wasn't well, and after being accused of raping his daughter when she was a toddler, life was more than he could bear. He went downhill fast." As Dottie spoke, she clenched her fist, and angry tears flowed. Both Andrea and Bernadette handed her tissues. Too small a gesture of support, given the enormity of the burden those words conveyed.

"I'm so sorry. I doubt it will surprise you, or make you feel any better, to learn that Sally wasn't the only young woman led down that road by Carr. And I'm betting Conroy was Carr's secret partner in at least one more situation involving Pinnacle."

"Another board member?" Dottie asked.

"I think so, but we're still in the process of putting all the pieces together," Jessica replied. Dottie was quiet for a moment. Then she looked up, her eyes wide, as though it had all become clear.

"Ned Donnelly, right? That poor man, I knew something was up, but with all the trouble here at home, I didn't even take the time to ask him what. Now, I can see it—the same sad desperation in his face that Harry wore, followed by Ned's unexpected cheerleading for Eric, and a surge of enthusiasm for taking Pinnacle public. I didn't get it. Now I do. Who knows how many others he had in his pocket by then? Can't you go to Ned and get him to tell you what's going on? Before it's too late. His daughter must be at risk like Sally." Andrea looked down and squirmed in her seat. She didn't make eye contact as Dottie shot off a series of questions, becoming more agitated with each one. "What is it? What else have you concealed? Is Shannon Donnelly dead?"

"We're not sure, Dottie. She's missing and the police are looking for her. That's all we know, for now," Bernadette said, reaching out to place a hand over Dottie's clasped hands. Andrea lifted her eyes to meet Dottie's gaze.

"We thought we were doing the right thing—keeping trouble from you. Since you stopped following the news, why bring it up?"

"We—what do you mean by we?" Dottie demanded.

"Did I say we? I meant me. It was my decision to keep all of this from you. I, I, uh, I consulted with Dr. Wooldridge, but he deferred to me. I'm sorry."

"Wooldridge and I will talk about this later. From now on, don't shield me. I'm not a child, and I still have my wits about me. I'll face whatever I have to face, especially if it involves my friends and family. Have I made myself clear?" Andrea glanced up and nodded. For a split second, her eyes darted Jessica's way. She was angry and fearful. Did she think Dottie would fire her?

"Dottie, I can understand why you're disappointed in Andrea, but it sounds like she's been doing her best to decide whether to draw your attention to these disturbing events. None of it happened too long ago. Shannon Donnelly disappeared Thanksgiving weekend. The investigation into her disappearance is still underway. The young woman with me up on Mt. San Jacinto last weekend said some things that make it sound like Shannon is dead. She's not a reliable source, however, and for the moment, at least, the police can't question her further."

"I guess I'd better pay attention to the news again. Maybe if I act more like my old self, I'll be treated that way. Alexis is a fortunate woman that her daughter is still in one piece. She deserves a break, given all she's dealing with. At least she's back in rehab," Dottie sighed.

"I'm surprised she didn't hide her current troubles from you. She's not big on sharing bad news." Jessica felt uncomfortable saying those words.

"She wouldn't hide that from her old pill-popping, drinking buddy, who's stayed on the wagon despite the tragedy of the past couple years," Dottie said, sipping her tea. Jessica must not have hidden her shock.

"Why do you think I'm serving you tea, dear, rather than some delightful vintage from our wine cellar?" She took another sip. "It has been a struggle. The doctors don't help, either. It's almost a reflex to offer consolation in pill form. I'm sure that didn't make your decision any easier did it, Andrea? You've had to watch me struggle." They all sat in silence for a few minutes. The blue skies and the splendor of their elegant surroundings soothed, but didn't assuage the anguish that sat there with them.

"So how are you going to get this guy?" Dottie asked. "He needs to be put away for a very long time."

"I'm not sure yet. I came here hoping to find a way to connect Carr, Conroy, and extortion. That's all much clearer now. Using Carr's extortion scheme to get his way at Pinnacle ties the two men together. Conroy's slick, though, so proving that a conspiracy existed between the two men is tough. Did Eric contact you and ask you to resign?"

"No, Sally was the bearer of the threat. The 'or else' part came a few weeks after the initial onslaught of accusations. She showed up here one day, unannounced. Against my better judgment and advice from our lawyer, I let her into the house. There was another round of accusations that her father had been abusing her for years. I asked why she hadn't come to me when it all happened. She went into some mumbo-jumbo about repressed memory. That it was my fault, too, since I was always too busy to listen, and she was afraid to tell me. All these different reasons jumbled up and spilled out in an incoherent way. I suspected she was on drugs of some kind, but if I'd accused her of that, the conversation would have ended right then and there. Instead, I told her I was ready to listen. That must have shocked the hell out of her, or it wasn't in the script. That's when she went ballistic and threatened to go public with her story. Sally said the only way out was for me to give her one last chance at happiness. Resign from the board. Her last words—the last time I ever spoke to my daughter, she screamed at me. 'Resign or I'll ruin your life, like you've tried to ruin mine! Father will pay, too, for your stubbornness. This is one fight you will not win, Mother.' It wasn't her threats that caused me to resign, although that part about her father got to me. It was more the realization that I hated being on that board, anyway. Pinnacle had asked too much for too long. So, I stepped down. The rest, as they say, is history. Two months later, Sally was dead, and the fix was in on the IPO. I presume he's got the CEO thing wrapped up too, but no one will talk about succession, with an IPO in the making."

"I hate to ask you to think about this anymore, but was there anything odd about the circumstances surrounding Sally's death?"

"Other than the fact that, as I suspected, she was taking a bunch of drugs prescribed by Carr, no. She'd been on antidepressants before, but never all the other drugs. It wasn't the Xanax and Ambien that killed her though. Some combination of antidepressant and an anti-psychotic drug were at high levels in her system. It was all a horrible accident, according to investigators. I wondered why she was alone. Where was the love of her life? Why did she call her psychiatrist and not Eric when she realized she'd taken the wrong pills if that's what happened?"

"No one's asked Eric any of those questions, have they?"

"Oh hell, no! There wasn't any reason to question anybody about anything, once they ruled Sally's death an accidental overdose. My husband and my daughter are dead because of him. Not only is he going to get away with it, but he's also about to profit from it. That's just wrong."

"I won't let him get away with it. There has to be a way to stop him."

"You can count on my prayers and anything else I can do." With that, Dottie picked up the rosary lying on the table near her plate. The message from Detective Hernandez flashed through Jessica's mind, at the sight of those beads.

Blood on the rosary NOT a match to Libby or Shannon's blood type, the message had read.

"Did Sally have one of those?" Jessica asked, pointing at the rosary.

"She did, yes. One reason I had hope things would work out, after she left home, was that she had rekindled her faith. Father Caverly mentioned how happy he was that Sally had scheduled an appointment with him. He assumed I knew all about it. I was too embarrassed to tell him otherwise, or to ask later why she had made that appointment. What if she had gone to him with those accusations about Harry? It was all I could do to face the man after that. Why do you ask?"

"This is a stretch. We found a rosary—part of one, anyway. It was in a car belonging to Libby Van Der Woert. She's the young woman in the ICU who fell off Mt. San Jacinto with Dr. Carr and me. Libby thought the rosary was important. The word she used was 'key,' the 'rosary is the key,' or something like that." Dottie sucked in a little gulp of air.

"Like this one, maybe?" She asked. Dottie took off a silver chain she had around her neck. On that chain was a tiny key. "This key was clasped in Sally's hand when she died. Not the rosary, but a medal and a couple bits of chain from a rosary were in her hand, too. The items were given to me along with her clothes after the autopsy. I decided to wear the key, along with Harry's wedding ring, on this chain around my neck. A silly old woman's attempt to keep her lost family close," Dottie said, her voice breaking, as tears fell.

"Maybe it's what Libby meant," Jessica said softly, as a chill ran through her. *Not another suitcase*, she thought. "Do you have any idea what the key is for? Why would it have been with that rosary?"

"I have no clue why it would have been with the rosary. It had this little loop on it, like it had been attached to a link in the rosary. That's how I got the idea to put it on my chain. It reminds me of the keys that went to the diaries Sally kept. She'd taken them with her when she moved. After she died, I cleaned out her condo and brought them back, along with other small mementos. That included pictures of me and her father. Not a picture anywhere of her fiancé, but her abusive parents, yes. I've thought about reading the diaries, but I just couldn't bring myself to read hateful things about her father or me. I don't understand how it's related to the rosary. You might ask Father Caverly. Maybe she said something to him about it." Dottie dabbed at her eyes. The anger that had energized her earlier had gone now and she faded into a shadow-of-her-former-self right before Jessica's eyes.

"I'm going to go take a nap. You're welcome to go through that box of diaries—take them with you, and the key. Come upstairs with Andrea and me. She'll show you where they are. Bernadette, you should come along, too. Jessica's not in any shape to carry that box. There must be twenty of them, one for each year of her life since she was ten or twelve." With that, their tea party had come to a sad and abrupt end.

They walked with Dottie and Andrea through an enormous kitchen, to an elevator that took them upstairs. Jessica and Bernadette said goodbye to Dottie. Minutes later, Andrea accompanied them back downstairs, and out to the car where Peter and Brien waited. Brien rushed to get that box from Bernadette and loaded it into the back of the car. Neither he nor Peter asked questions, taking their cue from the somber expressions the three women wore on their faces. *Please, let there be something in those diaries that will bring Conroy to justice,* Jessica thought, as she waved to Andrea.

When they settled into the car and buckled up, Peter turned around to head out of the driveway. Jessica looked back at the enormous estate. A woman watched from an upstairs window.

"Peter, uh, what did you think of Andrea?"

"Too tall," he said. "Not the shooter on Rodeo Drive."

"Yeah, okay, that's what I thought. Something's not right about her, though," Jessica said.

"Tell him about the key. We found a key and that medal missing from the rosary in Libby's car, didn't we?"

"Yes, we did. Detective Hernandez needs to check the blood on the crucifix to see if it's a match to Sally Winchester's. Her blood type should be on file at the hospital where she died."

"He should have the DNA results soon, too. That's why I put Sally's hair brush in the box with the diaries, Jessica. You can give it to Jerry to take to Hernandez tomorrow afternoon."

"That's primo snooping," Brien said. "Do you think that Andrea person saw you? She's stealthy."

"Thanks. I don't think she saw me do it," Bernadette said. "I can be stealthy, too, when I need to be."

"Are you talking about the woman in the upstairs window, Brien? You could tell it was Andrea?"

"Yes, and she wasn't just watching us leave. She was on her phone, too," Brien said.

"Want to place bets on who she's calling?" Peter asked. A sinking feeling stole over Jessica. The likelihood that it was Eric Conroy made her sick.

"Whoever she was calling it can't be good. Do you think Dottie's in any danger?"

"I don't think Dottie's the one Andrea's calling about," Peter said, making eye contact with Jessica as he peered at her in the rearview mirror. "But I can talk to her security guys and get them to check on her if you'd like."

"Do it, will you, please?" Jessica leaned back against the seat while Peter issued commands to the system in the car. He called and expressed his concerns to Dottie's security team who assured him they would take care of it. They'd place someone in the house with her until further notice from Peter.

Would that be enough to keep Conroy from killing someone else while the clock ticked down the days until that IPO launch? Jessica wondered.

"Let's see what Carla Fergusson has to say. We need hard evidence. Maybe she's got it if there's nothing in Sally's diaries. If Carla will meet with me," she added. *And she doesn't just get on a phone, like Andrea Jessop, and invite Eric to our meeting,* she thought as she leaned back against the seat for the ride back to the hotel.

32 WHAT DIARIES?

"Calm down. Hysteria won't help. Tell me what's happened."
Conroy paced as he listened to the woman speaking on the other end
of the phone. Hard to believe a spinster like her could have such a
checkered past. You just never could tell, could you? Lucky for him,
though, that she, like so many other mousy, milk-toast types had
secrets to hide. He had needed eyes and ears on the ground, inside
that house when Sally had become an iffy resource.

"Two women were here, asking Dottie a bunch of questions
about Sally. They know about you and Carr, too. They had a key, and
they took Sally's diaries. Who are they? What is going on?"

"Diaries? What diaries?" Eric asked, almost shouting. "Why is
this the first time I'm hearing about them?"

"Why is this the first time I'm hearing about extortion? Dead
women, too, Eric! What have you dragged me into? You said all I was
supposed to do was give you updates about what was going on here
between Dottie and Sally. Then it was updates about Dottie's
condition and any plans she had to inquire into Sally's death. I didn't
bargain for getting mixed up in extortion, even though that's what
you've been doing to me. Missing women—maybe murdered—is just
too much! I want no part of it."

"You weren't in a position to bargain about anything.
Remember? You still aren't. Besides, I've paid you well. Go ahead
and squawk about extortion if you want to. Once they peek at your

bank account and see money going in, not out, that'll be the end of it. You're mixed up in plenty, though, whether you want to be or not. Now, take a deep breath, settle down, and do what you're being paid to do and give me information."

For the next ten minutes, he listened. He kept silent, but broke the pencil he was fiddling with when Jessica Huntington's name came up. That she had made a connection between him and Carr disturbed him. That she *and* the cops were zeroing in on the link to him and Pinnacle, was worse. Still, it didn't sound like she had tangible evidence of any wrongdoing. The women who might have evidence weren't talking—two dead, the third not long for this world, given the reports from the ICU out in the desert. Eric cursed that idiot Carr, once more, for getting involved with the daffy skirts he was treating. When told to get rid of her, Carr had not hesitated to silence Shannon Donnelly. His ruthlessness had been surprising. Carr had come in handy before that, too, managing Sally, Eric's own foray into the land of daffy skirts. When he got involved with Sally Winchester, he hadn't realized how difficult she would be to control until it was too late.

"Tell me about those diaries and the key," he commanded.

"What's there to tell? Sally kept diaries—a whole box full of them. One for each year—childish stuff, for the most part. I read through them once they turned up here."

"Okay, so what's in there about me and Carr?"

"You were her one true love. She loved your eyes and the red hair, her very own Prince Harry. She wasn't keen on the goatee. That had to go after you two got married." Andrea laughed when she spoke the next line. "According to Sally, you were the start of her new life—the old one ended. Boy, did she get that right, prophetic even, given she was dead a few months later."

"What are you laughing about, you dried up old hag?" Eric asked. He felt the need to defend Sally. She had been a lovely thing. It wasn't her fault her mother kept her sheltered, naïve, and pent up in that gilded cage they called a home. Heck, if things had gone in a different direction, he might even have married her. She would have been a good wife for a CEO. Too bad for him the CEO option didn't happen. And too bad for her that she had a change of heart and became a liability rather than an asset. Not even the good doctor could keep her in line. *What is it about uppity women?* He wondered.

"If you're done insulting me, I'll hang up now," Andrea sniffed, incensed.

Spoken in true schoolmarm fashion, he noted.

"I don't get it—are you telling me there was nothing in there about our break up, or seeing Carr for treatment?"

"She was whining about Dottie's disapproval and how misunderstood you were, but no, nothing about a break up. That would have been this year, though, right? The diaries ended last year."

"There's no diary for this year? Is that what you're saying?"

"Yes, that's what I just said." A note of uneasiness had entered her voice. "I presumed that her last few lines about a new life starting with you ended the 'dear diary' era."

"Oh, you *presumed*, did you? Well, what about that key Dottie was wearing?"

"I didn't know about that key until today. Dottie never said a word about it."

"Were there keys with the other diaries, Andrea?"

"Yes," she said, in a low voice.

"Was one of them missing a key?"

"No. Sally kept a whole set of keys in a jewelry box. Each one tagged with the year. One key for each diary," Andrea replied, wariness in her voice now.

"Okay, so where did the key come from that Dottie wore around her neck?"

"Apparently, it was among the personal effects Sally had with her at the time of her uh, her um, death." Wariness had been replaced by a tone of out-and-out stress as she answered that question.

"Here's what you're going to do, Andrea. Go upstairs and search every inch of Sally's room. Look through everything Dottie brought back from her condo, too. Make sure if there's another diary that you get it before someone else does. Got it?"

"Sure, I'll do my best. I can't be too obvious about it or Dottie and the staff will ask questions. I can go through Sally's room while Dottie's napping. Going through all of Sally's things in storage will have to wait. I can do that after the staff has left and Dottie's asleep for the night."

"Do not wait. Dismiss the staff. Give them the rest of the day off, whatever it takes to get rid of them. Knock that old lady out cold for a few hours and get it done."

"I can't dismiss the staff, Eric. After that visit from Jessica Huntington, security put a man inside. The best I can do is try to get out to the storage in the garage once it gets dark. There's no guarantee I can do that, but I'll try."

"Trying won't cut it. If you don't get back to me by morning, I'll take matters into my own hands. You don't want me to do that, do you?" He didn't wait for a response. As soon as he ended the call, he entered another number. He had a new job for Kirk.

33 A TIPSTER

When Jessica returned to the hotel Sunday afternoon, she zipped through those diaries. The first thing she discovered was that the key didn't go with any of the diaries she had. Second, someone had gone through those diaries before her. Otherwise, why were some unlocked while others weren't? Not Dottie, since she said she couldn't bear to read them. And, Dottie would have realized the diary that went with the key she wore around her neck was missing. Jessica's first choice as the culprit was Andrea Jessop. She could guess about Andrea's interest in reading through the diaries if she was doing Conroy's bidding, but Jessica wanted to quiz her about it. What was in it for Dottie's dutiful assistant? That meant another visit to San Marino, so she could push Andrea for answers. That visit would have to take a backseat to two others, however. Visits with Carla Fergusson and Father Caverly were next on the to-be-interviewed list.

Reading those diaries felt voyeuristic, a feeling made worse by the knowledge that their author was dead. They revealed little of value to her investigation, except to confirm that Sally Winchester had been an easy mark for a con artist like Conroy. Though in her thirties, the woman had an almost childlike view of men, and a teenaged, rebellious nature toward her parents. Sally poured out her heart about how her mother so misunderstood Eric, and vowed not to let Dottie come between them. She was head over heels in love with him and it was easy to imagine that she would have done anything for him. A break up would have been devastating, and she would have been putty in the hands of an unscrupulous psychiatrist like Dr. Richard Carr.

The real trouble had begun this year when, according to her mother, Sally's life had turned upside down. Too bad, since the last diary had ended on such an upbeat note. As 2012 ended, Sally was convinced her new life had just begun and the next year would be the best. Her account of what happened after that was missing.

Where was the 2013 diary that went with that key? Why did she have the key with her, but no diary? If that diary had been at the hotel the night she died, it would have been among the personal effects returned to Dottie. Where had Carr been the night he called the rescue squad? Perhaps he was in her room that night, found the diary, and took it with him. If so, why? Had the rosary broken during a struggle, cutting Sally's hand and leaving that smear of blood on the crucifix? Was someone after that key? If so, then why was it left behind with Sally's body?

Detective Hernandez was looking for a match to the blood and the partial print. Now they knew the remnants of that rosary belonged to yet another troubled woman in Dr. Carr's care. Were there more women? Had one of them fired that shot on Rodeo Drive? Why? How did Libby get the broken rosary months after Sally's death? So many pieces to a puzzle; her mind was reeling. The solution was tantalizingly close; but close wouldn't get justice for the lives trashed by Carr and Conroy, nor would it stop whatever carnage was yet to come.

Hope quieted her torment. Carla Fergusson might have the answers if Jessica had read her right that night in July. Was she a defiant young woman, ready to share her story about the charming psychopath running amok at Pinnacle? She intended to find out.

Trying to unravel the dirty secrets behind Carr's manipulation of women wasn't Jessica's only line of investigation. With Bernadette posing as her client and a potential investor, Jessica would ask Carla Fergusson general questions about Pinnacle. What were their goals for the future, earnings potential, further expansion, who would be at the helm, etc., etc., etc.? She also would inquire about the climate in the boardroom, slipping in a question about Dottie Winchester's resignation. Asked tactfully, those questions, too, might pass as nothing more than a potential investor's due diligence. Jessica wanted to see Carla Fergusson's face as she posed questions about the process that led up to Conroy's deal of a lifetime.

That wasn't all. She planned to use those questions to work around to even tougher ones. Kim had unearthed Pinnacle financial documents, without saying how she found them, which revealed discrepancies between the materials filed with the SEC and earlier company documents. Jessica had listened to her ex and his cronies' whining and chortling about corporate misbehavior long enough to recognize several odd things. Such as a long-term account still on Pinnacle's books, doing business with a company that had been a household name, but hadn't made it through the Great Recession. Not good. How many other accounts might also be tied to defunct companies?

There was also a mysterious drop-off in debts, from one year to the next, on Pinnacle's books. Drop-off wasn't quite the correct term. If she was reading the materials right, it was as if by magic, corporate liabilities morphed into assets. Much of the hocus pocus was courtesy of their expanded international profile. Pinnacle's corporate wheeling and dealing slid from one part of the world to another.

The sudden appearance of off-balance sheet entities is what set off alarms for her. *Shades of Enron*, she thought. As far as she could tell, debt incurred from expanding Pinnacle's overseas offices one year turned up bundled, securitized, and sold a year or two later, by an off-book entity—a Pinnacle subsidiary that dealt in investment products. Perhaps she was missing something; after all, the SEC had been all over Pinnacle's balance sheets before the IPO. Still, the whole point of off-book entities for Enron-like gambits was to *remove* items from the balance sheets. If you worked in corporate finance at Pinnacle, like Carla Fergusson, it might be something you'd stumble upon. She would start with a few questions and see where all of this took her with the Fergusson woman.

The other important thing on her "to do" list was a visit with Father Caverly. She hoped he might divulge the nature, if not the specific content, of the discussions with Sally prior to her death. Did she share anything about the accusations made against her father or about her relationships with her parents, Conroy, or Carr? Did she raise any red flags about Carr, Conroy, or Pinnacle and the circumstances surrounding her mother's resignation? Was Sally drugged up and deluded or a willing party to extortion to help the man of her dreams take his rightful place at the helm of the flagship PR firm? Did her disclosures to the priest signal remorse, a possible precursor to a series of confessions to authorities?

Her skin crawled as she recalled the ruthless way in which Carr had reacted to Libby's change of heart. Had Sally Winchester come to a similar turning point? If so, did she overdose accidentally, or did she have a little help from Carr, Conroy, or one of Conroy's hired hands? Jerry was checking to see if he could find any evidence that Carr or Conroy had been out there in the desert when Sally Winchester died. If Sally had called Carr for help, as he claimed at the inquest, maybe he did more than just call 911 on her behalf.

The complexity of the case and the chaos of the previous week were getting to Jessica. Angst and weariness warred with her compulsion to put things right. Maybe it was an urge for justice or a need for the scales of good and bad to be put into balance—an offshoot of her inner control freak. She would be so glad to see this year end, now only a couple of weeks away. She planned to have a memorable celebration to mark the occasion. If they could nab Conroy, the slithering snake, there would be even more to celebrate. Her cell phone rang, startling her, and she whooped with alarm.

"Hi, Frank," she said, recognizing the hunky detective's cell phone number. She tried to calm her racing heart.

"Is that all you have to say?" *Uh-oh, make that testy, hunky detective,* she thought.

"I take it you saw that news item about Tiffany's, right?"

"Dad saw it and called me to ask what happened. He tried to call you himself, several times today. Dad's more than a little put out about it." *Like father, like son,* she thought. She was too tired to wrangle with Frank, though. Several ways to ring out the old year and ring in the new one with the man popped into her head. Maybe it was time to end her "no men" vow, along with the year.

"I'm sorry. I had the phone off most of the day while I was talking with an old friend about Carr and Conroy. I turned it back on a few minutes ago and didn't even check for missed calls or voice mails." She leaned back on the pillow, trying not to get irritated by Frank's tone. She'd learned that he had a hard time expressing his concern for her in a soft way. At first, anyway, since her apology flipped a switch.

"We were both worried, that's all. You sound tired. Can you tell me what's going on?"

"Sure, it might help me to go through it all. We're brimming over with information, but don't have the missing links to put it all together." She started with the events at Tiffany's. Then she filled him in on what she had learned from Dottie Winchester and her suspicions about Andrea Jessop. The diaries, the tiny key, and plans to speak to Father Caverly all tumbled out. She ran through the issues she had uncovered about Pinnacle without mentioning the fact that she intended to track down Carla Fergusson and have a chat.

"I'll see if I can find out what progress they've made about the shooting at Tiffany's. That's not good, even with an amateur shooting, rather than a pro. You already know that, right?"

"Yes, I get it. I've wracked my brain trying to figure out who else I could have ticked off enough to shoot me. Could Dr. Dick have another girlfriend on the loose who blames me for shoving him off the mountain?"

"Who knows? It could be, or maybe the crazed fan idea is right. Does it matter? All the signs are pointing to the fact you've reached the 'cool it' point in all of this. As if you weren't already there a week ago when you came within an inch or two of losing your life," he said, with exasperation growing as he spoke.

"I understand that. It's just that we're so close to getting this guy. I can feel it," she said.

"That's what has me worried sick. If you can feel it, maybe he can too." Frank let out a sigh and took a deep breath. "I have news about Pinnacle that ought to make it easier for you to take a step back. Please don't repeat this. I have it on good authority that you're not alone in raising concerns about Pinnacle's books. Someone called in a tip that set off an investigation. It's a matter for the FBI, so I can't get details about how far along they are but something's up. You need to keep this between us, for now."

"Wow, that's great. Is there any tie-in to Carr and what's been going on with the dead and missing women left in his and Conway's wake?"

"That's a good question. If they get this guy, Conroy, on a financial crime, maybe the conspiracy with Carr will become evident."

"How about any information about where the tip came from?" That image of Carla Fergusson floated into her head.

"Not a clue about that, either. You've stepped into the middle of another mess, for sure, and this one may be above both our pay grades."

"Fell into it is more like it, don't you think? It sounds like I'm on the verge of getting chewed out by federal cops any second now, too. That would be a first."

"They might not be as charming as I am when they pay you a visit. I'm having a wave of regret about not being able to deliver my latest warning in person. On the other hand, just the thought of those lovely green eyes makes it hard for me to be as tough on you as I should be, so better to hear it from me on the phone. Ah, what am I going to do about you?" She was back to thinking about plenty he could do, but that wasn't the point.

"Tell your dad I'm sorry to worry you both. We have a couple loose ends to wrap up tomorrow and then it's back to the desert for all of us. I promise." As she hung up the phone, she considered his advice. Why not end her pursuit of loose ends, sleep in tomorrow morning, and hit the spa before driving back to Rancho Mirage? Shopping sounded good, too. Tommy could use some things for his trousseau—did gay men have those? She looked at the time on her cell phone. Who was she kidding? No way was she going to back off so close to the finish line. Her palm itched as she held the phone, wondering what was still open on Rodeo Drive. What was she going to wear to Pinnacle for that meeting with Carla Fergusson? What would Bernadette wear?

She got up and hit the hotel phone line for the concierge. Maybe it was dicey to make the schlepp to Rodeo Drive, so why not let them come to her? In minutes, the hotel staff had it all arranged—samples in her size and Bernadette's, from several designers, and a stylist to meet with them, including Tommy and Jerry, who could pick out items for themselves. Tommy and Jerry had decided they wanted to take a South Seas honeymoon cruise and now they'd have the wardrobe to do it.

Over dinner at Spago, she and Bernadette shared what they'd learned from Dottie Winchester with the rest of her Cat Pack pals, including the key and missing diary. She also provided a quick summary of what she found, or thought she'd found, in all that paper about Pinnacle. She also mentioned the brief conversation with Frank, leaving out the part about the other investigation underway into Pinnacle. That retelling of all the intriguing leads uncovered, was enough to set her on the trail again.

She wanted Conroy to pay for what he'd done to the Donnelly family and the Winchesters, but that wasn't likely to be of much concern to the feds. What difference did it make to the FBI if a louse like Conroy trampled the heart of a young woman on his way to becoming CEO of a billion-dollar company? Trampling hearts was no federal crime. Jessica set out her plans for the next day: meetings with Carla Fergusson, Father Caverly, and a follow up with Andrea Jessop.

"Why don't you let us follow up with the priest?" Tommy asked. He couldn't hide his happiness about the time spent with the stylist and dinner at the famed eatery. "We can do that while you're meeting with that Fergusson person and Andrea Jessop. Then we can all meet up for lunch and report in before we drive back to the desert. I vote we come back here for lunch with Wolfgang." He had a sublime expression on his face. Since Wolfgang Puck had shown up, in person, at the restaurant. Tommy was still agog.

"Sure, Tommy, why not?" She sighed. "Since I won't know what's happening at Pinnacle until I try to make an appointment, I doubt I could have gotten all that done tomorrow, anyway. Until I have a time set to meet with Carla Fergusson, the rest of my day will be on hold. So, yes, let's go ahead and plan to meet for lunch. Maybe by lunchtime, this whole mess will be over. Wouldn't that be great?" She allowed herself to bask in the glow of that possibility as she sat with her friends.

34 A MUTINY

At eight Monday morning, she called, asking to meet with Carla Fergusson. As planned, Jessica claimed she and a client were interested in investing in Pinnacle once it went public and had a few questions about the company. As she pointed out to Carla Fergusson's assistant, her client had a substantial investment to make once shares became available on the secondary market. The assistant put Jessica on hold, but was back in an instant and told her Ms. Fergusson had a cancelled meeting and would put them in that slot if they could get to her office by ten. If not, they could arrange a meeting for later in the week. She took the ten o'clock appointment, ended the call, and spoke to Bernadette, who stood nearby in Jessica's hotel room.

"My weird luck's working for us today. Pinnacle is in an accommodating posture with that IPO hanging out there, I guess."

"Why not? They want that stock price to go up. Do you think Carla Fergusson recognized your name?" Bernadette asked.

"Could be, but I barely remembered her from that encounter at Dad's gala. If she recognized my name because we met at the gala, that could be a good thing. It could explain why she was so willing to meet on such short notice." Of course, it could also be a bad thing if she recognized Jessica's name and was accommodating her request on Conroy's behalf. The meeting at Carla Fergusson's place of business was on the record, and their arrival would occur in full view of colleagues, so this was no furtive back-alley tete-a-tete. Still, anticipation loomed as Bernadette helped make Jessica presentable.

That was easier than it might have been because of their session with the stylist the day before. The stylist had brought her a stunning Versace silk pantsuit in taupe. The sleeves were wide enough to fit over the cast, but not by much. Jessica wasn't ready to wear heels, so she chose a comfortable pair of flats. Sore ribs and the broken arm in a sling remained as the last vestiges of the Mt. San Jacinto incident. That is if you didn't count the intermittent dreams of falling or dangling by a thread, trussed up in climbing gear, or at other times, stark naked.

By nine, they were ready for what should be a thirty or forty-minute drive to Pinnacle. Bernadette was elegant in a Chanel suit with classic lines, but a deeper rose color than the famous suit worn by Jackie Kennedy. Low heels and pearls completed the ensemble. The stylist had called in help for their hair and nails, so they both had chichi "dos" and perfect nails for the occasion. Jessica was still letting her hair grow out, but it was trimmed and the blond highlights were now covered by a glossy brown shade.

"Wow! You two look great!" Brien exclaimed. "You look super rich Bernadette." As he spoke, he opened the door so they could climb into the back seat of the car. Peter waited behind the wheel.

"Thanks. What makes you think I'm *not* rich?" A baffled look swept over his face. As he climbed into the front seat, he answered her.

"Uh, if you were rich, you'd be retired on a beach in Boca or somewhere, right?" Bernadette just smiled and shrugged.

"You do both fit the part—except for that sling."

"If anyone asks, I'll blame it on a skiing accident," she said. Fat chance that would work, with all that angel heiress nonsense floating around. No one who knew about it would have to ask her what happened.

"I hope no one asks me questions. I don't know much about investing, although your dad has tried to help me out over the years."

"That's why you have a legal representative with you. Jessica will do the talking," Peter said, as he pulled away from the hotel entrance.

"Whoa, that's like rich people, too. You two have this wired, don't you?"

"I sure hope so," Jessica replied. She grew quiet as they drove through traffic, heading downtown to the Pinnacle building. They arrived with plenty of time to spare, so went with Peter to park in the garage attached to the building. The lobby area of the Pinnacle building was what you might expect for a PR firm that served members of the power elite. It was replete with gleaming marble, brass fixtures, ambient lighting, and banks of elevators. Security guards were everywhere, wearing blazers and slacks.

"What do they think we'd steal?" Bernadette whispered.

"Clients, or more likely, photos or confidential information about clients. You know how sneaky and resourceful paparazzi or fans can be," Jessica said as they approached the no-nonsense guard seated at an information desk with a sign asking them to check in. An employee of the firm was signing in ahead of them. The security guy had a build as solid as the marble desk he sat behind. "This is about monitoring the comings and goings of employees, too. All present and accounted for, and if you're let go, you're escorted out of here, on the spot. No chance for you to take proprietary information or client files with you," she whispered to Bernadette.

"May I help you?" the guard asked when it was their turn. Jessica gave him their names. He looked at her and then scanned Peter and Brien, who were standing behind her. "They can wait in the lounge," he said, motioning with his head toward a luxurious waiting area. She could tell Peter didn't like it, but he knew better than to challenge the rules used by security-minded companies. Especially companies, like Pinnacle, that dealt with the high and mighty. On cue, a distinguished-looking gentleman, star of stage and screen, swept into the lobby with his entourage and she heard Bernadette draw in a breath as she recognized him. In seconds, a squadron of security team members and individuals wearing Pinnacle name badges, stepped from a nearby elevator and surrounded him.

"We've got him, Scott, thanks," a woman called out, along with a code number. Scott, the guard signing them in, scanned a page in front of him and wrote down the code or a name or something. Then he checked the time and wrote that down.

"Not everyone has to wait to check in," Bernadette said.

"No, I guess there's a VIP service. Not for his team, though," she said, nodding toward two oversized men who had come into the lobby with the celeb. They headed to the area where Brien and Peter waited.

"Put this on, please, and turn it in here before you leave, Ms. Huntington. I'll call to have someone from Ms. Fergusson's office escort you upstairs."

"Thanks, Scott," she said. "See you in a little while." Bernadette clipped her badge to her jacket, and then reached over and helped Jessica put hers on. She'd tried, but struggled with one arm in a sling. When they looked up, a well-dressed young woman had appeared in front of them. *That was fast*, Jessica thought.

"I'm Donna, Carla Fergusson's assistant. Will you follow me please?" Moments later, they were on the elevator. When it didn't stop at Carla Fergusson's floor, Jessica looked at Bernadette. Bernadette knew it, too. Something was up.

The elevator finally came to a stop and the doors opened. They stepped out into a lavish waiting area with startling views of the city below. Without a word, the assistant stepped back into the elevator and disappeared. The red devil, himself, held out his hand in welcome.

"What a pleasure to see you again. We met at that gala for your father in July, right, Jessica? May I call you Jessica—and Bernadette, yes?" Eric Conroy was polite enough, friendly even, but didn't wait for either of them to reply to the questions he asked. There was stress in the set of his jaw, just like in that picture where he was shaking hands with the CEO. Jessica suspected that, despite what he said, it was not a pleasure to see her again.

When they entered the large office, Carla Fergusson was already there. She didn't even feign pleasure at seeing Jessica when Eric introduced them. "You remember Jessica Huntington, don't you Carla?"

"How could I forget? You've been in the news a lot." Somehow, the way those words came out gave her the shivers. Like maybe Carla Fergusson was hoping to see Jessica's name in the news again soon but in the obit section of the LA Times. "Given all that's been going on, it's hard to believe that investing in Pinnacle is so important to you. That's why I called Eric. I was sure you and your client would prefer to get the answers to your questions straight from the horse's mouth, so-to-speak." She smiled. Not a friendly smile.

A "humph" erupted from Bernadette, as they sat down next to Carla Fergusson and across from Eric Conroy. Jessica was too apprehensive to figure out exactly what Bernadette said in Spanish, but made out the words "horse's ass," or something like that.

"Can we get you a drink or shall we get down to business?" Conroy asked, still standing behind his desk in the posh office. Jessica wasn't interested in a drink, but she could use a few more minutes to evaluate the situation. Despite the surprise at seeing Conroy when they stepped out of the elevator, she still wasn't that worried. The Cat Pack discussion about the fact that she and Bernadette weren't going it alone echoed with reassurance. If she and Bernadette didn't turn up in an hour, Peter would get antsy. He would ask questions and, if that didn't work, he'd have authorities upstairs in no time.

"A drink would be great," she said, examining the expensive digs. It was good to be Executive Vice President at Pinnacle, except for the way he clenched and unclenched his jaw every so often. *The CEO's office must be something to behold,* she thought, taking in the opulence in which the second-in-command ruled. She glanced at Carla Fergusson, who was even tenser than Conroy; on pins and needles.

"What'll it be?" He asked, pulling out an expensive bottle of cognac from a cabinet nearby.

"Early in the day for me—even for an exquisite forty-year-old bottle like that. Coffee would be great. Do you have a cup handy?" She asked.

"Of course, how do you want it?"

"Black," she replied, in her mind adding, *and piping hot, just in case you do something impolite.*

"How about you, Bernadette?" He asked, as he motioned Carla to fetch coffee from a commercial version of a single cup brewer system.

"I'll have the same, Mr. Conroy," she responded.

"On one condition," he said.

"What's that?"

"You call me Eric. You'll soon be part of the Pinnacle family," he said.

"Sure, Eric. Why not?"

As Carla made coffee, Eric poured himself a glass of the cognac and sat down. The bottle came with him.

"It's five o'clock somewhere, am I right?" He asked, sipping the tawny-colored elixir. Jessica nodded. She couldn't argue with that. The tension between them was getting to her and she wondered if it showed.

"So what questions can I answer for you?" *What the hell*, Jessica, thought, *why not lay it all on the table?* Before she could speak, though, two things happened. First, Carla set a cup of coffee down on the table next to her chair. Then a cell phone rang. Jessica reached into her purse and pulled her phone out, but it wasn't hers that had rung.

"Excuse me, please. I need to take this," Conroy said, picking up his cell phone. "Kierkegaard, what can I do for you?" He was buoyant, expecting good news. "What do you mean? That's your name, isn't it?" He chortled, giving Jessica a little wink, as if she were in on his little joke. At the expense of whoever was on the other end of that phone, so it seemed. "What? What are you saying?" Jumping to his feet, Conroy blanched as he listened to what Kirk had to say. Carla, who was making a second cup of coffee for Bernadette, turned and stared. Conroy was as white as a sheet.

"What is it?" He didn't respond. Instead, he stepped out of his office, shutting the door behind him. The three women looked up a minute later as the man's voice rose loud enough that they could hear him speaking in the next room. Not that they could make out what he was saying. Carla handed a cup of coffee to Bernadette, her hand trembling a little. Then she sat down, literally on the edge of her seat.

When Conroy returned, chewing his bottom lip, his face was suffused with rage. He glanced at Jessica. A cold, hard look was in his eyes that had become dark round saucers in his florid face. "Did you do this?" He scanned Jessica's face with care.

"Do what?" She responded, perplexed as a dozen scenarios raced through her mind.

"Someone ratted us out to the feds. Was it you?" He asked, peering at her as his face flushed deeper with anger.

"No, it wasn't me," she replied, still gripping the cell phone she'd taken from her purse.

He paused, and then gazed at Carla as if he might ask her the same question. The woman was a stone statue, perched on her chair. He shook his head. When his eyes returned to Jessica, he spoke again.

"Apparently, we have unwanted visitors on their way here. I suppose if you had known about this, there wouldn't have been any reason for your meddling today, right? They've already arrived at Dottie Winchester's estate, speaking of meddlesome women." That got Carla's attention.

"Do the authorities have Andrea?" She asked.

"No. Maybe she's the one who tipped them off. Kirk tells me Andrea was nowhere to be seen when the authorities arrived."

"Who's Kirk? Why would the feds be *there*?" Carla asked, her eyes pinning him to the spot. "Andrea said Jessica took Sally's diaries and there wasn't anything in them about you or Pinnacle." Jessica and Bernadette snapped to attention. That uneasy feeling she had about Andrea hit Jessica like a kick in the gut. Her hopes that Carla had been the whistleblower to the feds were dashed. Bernadette reached out and picked up that cup of hot coffee. Jessica shut off the sound and slid her cell phone into the sling. Then she picked up her own cup of coffee.

"Who knows what they're looking for? Dottie was on the board here for a long time. Maybe, her resignation puts her on the list of go-to people, and they think she has documents or knows something about Pinnacle. Or, maybe they think Sally had something important in all her stuff stored at Dottie's house. There's a bunch of hyenas at my house, too, besides the ones stuck in traffic just down the street. Heave-ho, it's time to shove off. Launch Plan B, now! Send the orders," Conroy said, downing the remaining cognac in his glass. Carla was searching for something on her cell phone. She hit a button, presumably sending a text message relaying those orders about Plan B.

With that, Conroy moved into action. He opened a safe, hidden by a painting hanging on the wall behind him. Pulling a leather portfolio from the safe, he unzipped it. In his haste, items fell from it. That included money and identification documents that he scooped up, putting a packet of cash into his suit pocket as he shoved items back into the portfolio.

"Here, just in case we're in a hurry later." He tossed what looked like a passport to Carla, along with another neatly wrapped stack of bills.

"How are we going to get out of here, if the building will be crawling with federal agents any minute?" Carla was standing now, poised to run.

"You're right. We need a distraction, don't we?" He eyed Jessica. No way was she going to be his distraction. If he took one step toward her, hot coffee was going into his face. Quick as lightning, he stuffed papers from his safe and desk into a trash can that he picked up. He set the can up on a shelf, right under the ventilation duct. Picking up the bottle sitting on his desk, he poured the rest of the ninety-proof cognac over the papers. Then he took several cigars from a box and stuffed them in a pocket. Then, he dumped the rest into the trash can, lit a cigar, and tossed it in, too. The contents caught fire and smoke curled up toward the vent. At the same time, he hit a button, and an alarm wailed. The office was filling with smoke, although the ventilation system was sucking away at it. Flames leapt from the can. Conroy tossed in raffia and dried plants from a nearby flower arrangement. More flames sparked and noxious smoke rose.

"Down the back stairs now, let's go!" Jessica was about to let out a sigh of relief, thinking he would leave them behind. That was fine. She and Bernadette could have that fire out as soon as he left. If not, security, the rescue squad, and police authorities, maybe even the feds, would be there in a matter of minutes.

Suddenly, from a pocket in his suit coat, a gun appeared. "You two, move, both of you." She was about to heave that cup of coffee at him when the sprinkler above her released a deluge. Carla reached out, grabbing her arm and pulling her, not toward the doorway leading to the outer office, but in the opposite direction. A panel in the back wall of Conroy's office slid open, revealing a set of stairs. Jessica glanced over her shoulder as she turned to follow Carla. Conroy was pushing Bernadette ahead of him, pointing that gun right at her. *Not again*, she thought, as they headed down those stairs, going somewhere she didn't want to go, at the behest of a well-dressed thug.

While making their way down twelve flights of stairs, to an underground parking garage, Jessica pondered the events of the last few moments reviewing Conroy's words: *'heave-ho,' 'shove off,' 'launch plan B,' passports and money...* She knew where they were heading if they could run the gauntlet of police and get away. The feds would seal off Pinnacle's parking garage, so they might not even get out of the garage.

When they got down to the parking garage level, they didn't stop, but kept going. Down another two levels, to a door that led from the stairwell to an underground tunnel. It was an old maintenance tunnel, thankfully, rather than the sewer system. They walked through those tunnels for a few minutes, turning several times, before exiting through a set of doors, leading into another stairwell. An even more rickety set of stairs than those leading from Conroy's office, awaited them. After climbing two flights, they passed through a door that Conroy struggled to open. That led into what looked like an abandoned parking garage. Hard to believe such a thing existed in a megacity desperate for room to park cars. With that little walk in the warm tunnels, Jessica felt less soggy, although her new suit was a goner and her hair was hanging in her eyes. Bernadette was in much better shape. Standing off to the left and moving out of the way quickly, she'd missed the worst of the downpour that had drenched Jessica.

An older model Mercedes sedan sat off to the side of the decrepit garage. Conroy motioned for them to move to the car and get into the back. He took both of their purses and handed them to Carla. She climbed into the driver's seat as he got into the passenger seat, still holding the gun.

"Lock them in," he ordered. Carla clicked the child locks, so that they had no way to escape from the back seat. He waved the gun at them.

"No monkey business, you two, and I'll let you go. Let's just hope, for your sake, this doesn't become a hostage situation." He smiled a cruel smile. Who was he kidding? This *was* a hostage situation. Jessica plotted to get that purse back. In the meantime, she would do what she could. When Conroy shifted in his seat, facing forward, Jessica nudged Bernadette. Opening the sling, a little, she let Bernadette glimpse her cell phone secreted there. With the sound off, she had felt it buzz a couple of times. Peter could track them using the GPS in her cell phone, but she hoped she could text him their destination. Minutes later, she got her chance.

They arrived at the exit from the poorly lit garage. A padlocked chain-link gate and bright orange traffic cones blocked their way. "Hang on," Conroy said, jumping from his seat and pulling a key to the padlock from his pants pocket.

"This guy thinks of everything, doesn't he, Carla?" Bernadette asked, leaning forward a little. Jessica slid the phone out as Bernadette kept talking. "Can we get a little air back here? Maybe you could turn on the air conditioning or open the windows. It's stuffy. I'm sweating, and my heart's still pounding after all those stairs. Even going down them is hard for an old lady like me. I don't want to pass out on you..."

While Bernadette rattled on, Carla fidgeted with the air conditioning. Conroy had that chain unlocked and was pulling it out of the way. As he moved the orange cones, Jessica slid her phone out and typed one word: **MARINA.** When the text was on its way to Peter, she slid the phone back into the sling. Then she patted Bernadette on the shoulder. Bernadette settled back against her seat as Eric opened the door and climbed in.

"That's much better, gracias."

"What's much better?" Conroy asked, as he fastened his seat belt.

"We've got the AC on. It was stuffy in the back seat." He shrugged as Carla pulled forward, out of the garage, and merged with traffic on the road. As far as Jessica could tell, their little detour underground had taken them several blocks from Pinnacle. Carla drove with care, leaving downtown LA behind. She didn't get on the freeway, but stuck with side streets until she got to Santa Monica Boulevard, heading west toward the ocean. The *Sweet Retreat*, anchored in Marina Del Rey, wasn't far away. Twenty minutes, maybe, for Peter to pick them up, via GPS, or to run down the information on Eric Conroy's yacht, or both. She glanced sideways at Bernadette. Her lips were moving as she prayed. Rosary beads, the beautiful crystal beads her beloved Guillermo had given her before he disappeared, were in her fingers. *God, please listen to her. This is on me, not her, so mercy, please?*

As soon as they turned onto Santa Monica Boulevard, Conroy called ahead to the crew of the *Sweet Retreat*. "This is Eric. I'll be there in twenty minutes, and I expect you to be ready to head out, got it?" He'd just ended the call when his phone rang.

"Yeah, Kirk, I know, I know. We got out of there just in time. Thanks for the heads up." He paused, listening to Kirk. "I'll send it to you. You know I'm good for it. I won't even ding you, either, for not getting the job done." That must have set Kirk off because Conroy held the phone away from his ear. He let Kirk go on for another minute or two, said goodbye, and ended the call. His phone rang several more times before they arrived at the marina, but he didn't pick it up again.

Not too many places could provide anchorage for a hundred-foot yacht, like The *Sweet Retreat*. It was easy to spot. When Carla parked the Mercedes, Conroy had the gun out again, motioning for them to get out. *This is ridiculous*, Jessica thought.

"I'm not sure what you have in mind, but you don't need us— not both of us, anyway. Let Bernadette stay put here in the car. Lock her in the back seat, and she won't be able to get out." While they were talking, Bernadette scooted forward, reached into the front seat and picked up both of their purses.

He was chewing the bottom of his lip again, perhaps considering what she said. "Get out, both of you. When we're at sea, we'll put you in a dinghy and you can paddle your way back. It's the least I can do, as much trouble as you've caused me, according to that idiot Carr, anyway." He waited for Jessica to join Bernadette. She helped Jessica put the strap of her shoulder bag over her head, cross-body style.

"Move it," Conroy barked. He motioned toward the dock. The *Sweet Retreat* sat in deep water at the end of a long, narrow floating walkway that wobbled as they trudged to the yacht. They had to walk single file, with Carla in the lead and Eric bringing up the rear. On either side were smaller boats moored along the way. Jessica could glimpse parallel walkways on either side, too. She hoped she might spot Peter and, for a second, thought she saw a figure off to her left. When they arrived at the yacht, Conroy stepped ahead of them and onto a gangplank for boarding the yacht. That's when Plan B went overboard, so to speak.

"Put that gun away. This is a mutiny," Andrea Jessop said, laughing as she and a crew member on board the yacht peered down at him. Each held guns of their own—big guns. When he hesitated, Carla got into the act.

"I'd listen to the 'dried up old hag,' if I were you." She was holding a gun on the man now, too.

"What the...?" Before he could finish, a bullet zinged past them. They all hit the ground. Eric's gun flew away, landing in the water with a splash. Jessica's ribs were screaming as she landed with a thud on the bag she wore. As soon as she could see straight, she looked around for cover. At the same time, she tried to figure out who had fired that shot. On a parallel walkway, she could see the figure of a young woman, in a baggy shirt and sweat pants.

"Dick's dead, and it's all your fault!" Shannon Donnelly cried out, her hands shaking with rage or some other intense emotion. She had a gun aimed right at Jessica. Conroy, egoist that he was, didn't get it. He assumed she was talking to him.

"What are you talking about? I had nothing to do with Carr's death. It was Dick's idea to take you out too, so don't blame me for that either." He was getting back up on his knees, from the prone position he had taken when Shannon fired that shot. "How come you're still alive?" Jessica wondered about that, too, as she motioned Bernadette to scoot back, putting a boat in a slip to their left in between her and Shannon. Bernadette did that, but also pointed at Jessica's bag.

"Liar, liar," Shannon said, firing wildly. This time she *was* shooting at Conroy, with no more success than she had when shooting at Jessica. He let out a grunt as he did a belly flop, flattening himself out on the walkway. That set the walkway to bobbing again. Jessica was getting seasick, as she scooted backwards toward Bernadette. "He said you were a liar. So did Libby, you red devil. Dick wouldn't kill me. We were in love." More bullets flew, hitting the water and pinging off the side of the yacht.

"Son of a!!" Conroy shrieked. He grabbed at his leg as he scrambled toward Carla. Wrestling her gun free, he punched her hard in the face. She rolled off the walkway into the water. Andrea, without regard for gunfire, slid over the side of the yacht and pulled Carla's head up out of the water. The two bobbed alongside the walkway.

In the distance, Jessica could hear sirens wailing. The beating blades of a helicopter could be heard, closing in on their position. Help would get here too late for Shannon, though, if she didn't do something, quick. Jessica reached into her purse and removed her father's gun. She'd taken it back from Bernadette after they left Malibu.

Eric Conroy was up on his knees. Crying and screaming, Shannon was pulling the trigger, but had no more bullets in her gun. Eric took aim. Propping herself up on her cast, Jessica steadied her right hand, aimed at Conroy's backside and fired. She may have hit him, but it was hard to tell. Another shot came from that crew member up on deck who had taken cover from the salvo of bullets fired by Shannon, but was now back on his feet. He shot at Conroy maybe a split second after Jessica fired her gun. The blast that killed Conroy, though, came from a sniper rifle held by a man wearing a baseball cap and sunglasses.

"Nobody calls me Kierkegaard," he had shouted before taking that shot. With that, he tipped his hat and tore off in a speedboat. Conroy lay still. Shannon sank to her knees, immobilized by emotion, not gunfire, because Conroy hadn't fired the gun he held. Sirens could be heard everywhere, close now. The helicopter that was almost overhead veered away to follow the sniper. In minutes, Peter was storming toward them, followed by Brien and an army of officers from various jurisdictions. Police and EMTs pounded down the walkway toward Shannon too.

"Hang on, Ethel!" Jessica hollered, as that walkway bounced.

"You too, Lucy," Bernadette replied.

EPILOGUE

Jessica rode a rollercoaster of emotions as she sat on the patio in Rancho Mirage. The bucolic setting lulled her, filling her with gratitude as she gazed at happy golfers at play. Mountains provided a picture-perfect backdrop to the manicured golf course. A gentle breeze caused palms to sway and carried laughter with it. That she and Bernadette were safe, unharmed by Conroy's malice or the barrage of bullets that took his life was reason for gladness. Still the confusion and terror she'd experienced lingered. The depths of depravity and stupidity represented by that confrontation at the *Sweet Retreat* was hard to believe! "A ship of fools," she muttered, counting herself among the fools.

It had been a week since that showdown. Authorities were still sorting out all that had gone on that day, and all that had led up to that dramatic end to Eric Conroy's life. Various jurisdictions were tugging at different threads tangled up in Carr and Conroy's web of deceit, hoping to catalog the crimes and understand their schemes. Understand was the wrong word. *Could you ever do that?* Jessica wondered. *Understand the harm visited on the world by ruthless men in positions of power?*

"Earth to Jessica," Tommy said, waving from the swimming pool as he spoke. "Do you want to do this or not?" The Cat Pack, assembled on the sprawling patio, was there to debrief. And eat, of course. Caterers were preparing their meal in the home's roomy kitchen while they sat around with drinks, talking. She'd already revisited the events that occurred at Pinnacle and the marina. The media, drawn by gunfire and police, arrived in droves once word got out that the angel heiress was in trouble again. They broadcast parts of the story again and again.

"Sure, where should we begin?"

"How about we start with Sally Winchester? Tommy and I have information about that diary," Jerry said as he floated in the pool on a lounger.

"Yes, I suppose it makes as much sense as anything to start with Sally Winchester," Jessica sighed. "So far, she seems to be the only dead daughter, despite our fears that Shannon was dead and that Libby might not make it. It's awful that she was the victim of a ruthless collaboration between Carr and Conroy. A match made somewhere other than heaven. Each had his own scheme running when the two found each other. As we figured, Carr was using young women to extort money from his clients' parents by alleging child sexual abuse based on recovered memories. Conroy put a new twist on that scheme by using Carr's extortion methods to control board members at Pinnacle. That included Ned Donnelly, Dorothy Winchester, and several others. The IPO wasn't Conroy's only strategy to profit from his position at Pinnacle. Another gambit involved a longer con—skimming money from Pinnacle, falsifying financial documents, and hiding money offshore."

"It's too bad we may never know how big a scheme Carr ran on his own, and in league with that red devil Conroy. A lot of his missing files are back, retrieved from the case records management service Carr used. That was a great idea, Betsy, to look to see if he had used a service like that after Conroy had Carr's home and office cleaned out," Jerry commented. Betsy smiled as she sat next to Peter.

"Yeah, that *was* a good one. Who even knew such a service existed?" Peter was smiling now, too.

"Glad I could help." Betsy took the praise in stride, but Jessica saw her wink at Peter, causing his smile to widen. *Cat Pack investigations and matchmaking services*, Jessica thought, gazing at the newest twosome to emerge among her friends. She tried not to look at Frank in a moment of weakness created by Peter and Betsy's flirting. Frank was in swimming trunks and had thrown a shirt on when he climbed out of the pool. It was open, exposing a well-muscled chest. His hair, still wet and unruly, glistened. *Shoot,* Jessica said to herself. She was looking at him and he caught her. *Where was I?* She wondered, as she tore her eyes from his.

"The Beverly Hills PD is trying to figure out how to make those records available to families that want to sue for malpractice. I'm not sure how much luck they'll have filing claims against Carr's insurance company now that he's dead. Once the story got out about the false allegations and extortion racket Carr had going, the outcry began. When the moneyed raise a ruckus, the justice system takes notice, so who knows? There are more Libbys and Shannons, so maybe more dead daughters like Sally Winchester too, but I hope not. The police are picking up where you left off, Laura, checking on admissions to ERs in the LA area with Dr. Richard Carr as the admitting physician. I suppose that will dredge up horrific issues for families who lost someone to an overdose in his care. Hopefully, they'll come forward, too. At least there won't be any more—not from Carr or Conroy's dirty dealing anyway." Disgust must have registered on her face.

"That's something. You can't track down every desperado in couture," Tommy quipped. He was being playful, but this had stressed them all out. Jerry got them back on track.

"Getting back to Sally Winchester, tell us what was in that diary we retrieved from Father Caverly. You got a look at it before turning it over to the feds. We know Sally gave that diary to Father Caverly a few days before she died. Why?"

"She had figured out, by then, that Carr and Conroy were in cahoots and planning to rip off investors with that IPO. Sally was angry and confused after Conroy ended their relationship, but she wasn't sure what to do. For some unknown reason, she still had feelings for that dirt bag. She was in deep, that's for sure—first love and all that. The diary is one of the most disturbing things I've ever read. Sally was on cloud nine when the year began and then she plummeted into her own private hell. She admits Conroy put her up to extorting her parents—not for money, but to get Dottie to resign." Jessica paused and caught her breath.

"Anyway, that rage Sally directed at her parents all collapsed into a pool of despair once Conroy dumped her. She didn't say she was contemplating suicide, but that overdose was an accident waiting to happen. Still, Sally did the right thing and called in that tip to the feds about Pinnacle. One of the last entries in her diary was about making amends for what she'd done to her family by saving other families from that disastrous IPO. It also sounds like she had, or planned to have, a confrontation with Conroy. She wanted him to turn himself in to the authorities. If that confrontation took place the night she died, she might have had a little help with that overdose."

"What happened the night Sally died is another mystery we won't be able to completely clear up. Thanks to Jerry, we know *both* Carr and Conroy were with her that night. Hotel surveillance footage puts them on the premises at different times, with Carr the last to leave. That was after he called 911. Too little, too late, but was it an error in judgment or did he delay calling for help intentionally? Who knows?" Frank shook his head, taking a sip from the beer he held.

"That fits with what Shannon told Detective Hernandez and other authorities. It's a miracle she survived. Maybe Carr had feelings for her. More likely, she was just lucky Carr died up there on that mountain before he cashed in big on his share of the take from the IPO. The money Shannon would get if her parents turned over control of her trust fund to her would have been chump change compared to the payday Carr hoped to get from the Pinnacle IPO. Who knows what he would have done once Conroy paid him off? Shannon was hell-bent on getting that money from her parents, and as diabolical as Libby in her quest," Jessica said.

"Yeah, but no better equipped than Sally Winchester or Libby Van Der Woert when she came up against those scumbags," Kim added. "My guess is Carr would have done away with her too, if he'd survived his effort to get rid of you and Libby."

"It could be. Libby and Shannon were both creating trouble for Carr. The last round started at their condo in Manhattan Beach when Shannon brought that broken rosary to Libby. Shaken, she told Libby she'd overheard Conroy and Carr quarrelling. Conroy didn't know that Carr had hidden Shannon in another room when Conroy barged in to chew Dr. Dick out about getting involved with daffy skirts like Libby. That infuriated the shrink, who reminded Conroy he'd had a daffy skirt problem of his own. They fought about what had happened to Sally. Carr claimed he'd saved Conroy's neck by cleaning up after him that night Sally died. Apparently, that included picking up that broken rosary, straightening up so it didn't look like Sally had fought with anyone, and then calling 911. He even accused Conroy of giving Sally too many pills or the wrong pills. Conroy countered by blaming the psychiatrist for giving Sally too many of the wrong pills.

After Conroy cooled off and left, Shannon caught Carr with that broken rosary. He'd picked it up all right, but kept it; maybe to use against Conroy if he needed a little leverage of his own. Anyway, Shannon took it, but she wasn't sure what to do with it, and can't remember how it ended up in Libby's car. The blood on the crucifix is Sally's, and the partial print's a match to Conroy."

"Why did Shannon take it?" Kim asked. "I know what I would have intended to do with dope like that on a weasel like Conroy, who must have ripped that rosary out of Sally's hand. These Beverly Hills chicks are hard to figure out."

"You're right. I bet she was trying to protect her head-shrinker boyfriend, thinking he was in trouble about Sally," Bernadette commented from the chaise in which she sat. She was drinking something stronger than beer—a frosty Margarita that Tommy had whipped up for them.

"It could be, but Shannon says she felt confused since the two men had blamed each other for killing Sally. In addition to accusing Conroy of giving Sally the pills that killed her, he also told Conroy that if he'd called 911 that night before he left the hotel, Sally would still be alive. So, Shannon could have been trying to nail Conroy. What a frigging waste," Jessica groused, taking a swig of her Margarita.

"I don't think Shannon or Libby could clear their heads enough to go to the police—at least not until Libby called me up to Mt. San Jacinto. Running off to the desert was Shannon's idea. The dispute between Carr and Conroy had created a crisis. The two women got themselves so worked up about that fight Shannon overheard that they ran for it. Once they got to the La Quinta Resort, they bickered. Shannon says the thing that bothered Libby most about the whole mess was that Shannon had been in Carr's house when she eavesdropped and then took that rosary. Libby was enraged to find out Carr was sleeping with them both. That night in Cathedral City, they fought over him. When they got back to Shannon's car after dinner and wine, their fighting got physical. Shannon got a nose bleed. They both called Carr, as we already know. They didn't ask him anything about Sally, but demanded that he choose between them. Instead, he played them both—told Libby to get a cab and go back to the La Quinta Resort. He picked up Shannon and ran the 'you're the love of my life' routine on her. After that, he stashed

Shannon in a condo out here in the desert, knocked her out with drugs, and she didn't see him until the next day. Carr must have paid Libby a visit to cool her down—maybe that's when she cleaned out his Mercedes and added more lovely items to her little blue suitcase a few days later when she went back to Manhattan Beach. I'm not sure how Libby got the idea Shannon was dead, but maybe it was the timing of her disappearance, the stuff she found in his car, or just wishful thinking."

"Whoa, that Carr dude was busy," Brien said. "Somebody was following Libby, who was that?"

"That's a great question. Carr had his hands full juggling Conroy and those two women—and who knows what else? He must have hired someone to keep tabs on her. Maybe Conroy suggested it after the confrontation he and Carr had about his involvement with troubled women." She replied.

"We know Carr checked into a hotel the weekend he died. He got that call on his cell phone around twelve thirty, later traced to a burner phone, so the hired hand idea makes sense. That must be how he learned that Libby and Jessica were together up there. Shannon seemed like she was doing what Carr had told her to do—staying out of sight—until Carr fell and broke his neck. That's what killed him, not the gunshot. Anyway, after he died, she made it her business to stalk you, Jessica," Frank said.

"Shannon was about as far off the deep end over Carr as Sally had been about Conroy. I gather that's why she was trailing me, and took those shots at us on Rodeo Drive, trying to make me pay for his death."

"She's got skills if she could keep up with you, Jessica," Peter said. "Even Brien didn't spot her."

"I wasn't looking for Shannon, Man. Why didn't you see her, Uber-Thor?"

"You guys were on the lookout for a skilled sniper, not a nondescript thirty-something woman in baggy sweats and a hoodie or a baseball cap. Besides, we all thought she was dead."

"Well, she won't get to use her skills—for a while anyway," Kim said.

"Yeah, she's likely to do some prison time for the list of misdeeds to her credit. Although a good lawyer might make a diminished capacity claim stick," Jessica said.

"In her case, that could be right," Betsy said.

"A lot of what she's done makes no sense, like shooting at you when she had the red devil in her sights at the marina," Laura added.

"To Shannon, I must have seemed like a bigger devil than Conroy. Shannon says she thought I ruined everything. She got it into her head that I called Carr that day and lured him up there to kill him. Maybe she was with him when he got that call, and he was fuming about me being up there with Libby. Put two and two together, but had the math all wrong. You're right, Laura, that it makes no sense—she makes no sense."

"None of these women do, starting with Sally Winchester," Kim said.

"Sally's diary reads like a gothic romance novel, that's for sure. Suspenseful, too, knowing what was going on as she agreed to go against her family to help the first man who ever showed her so much attention. He was her first lover, too. There's a heartbreaking apology to her mother for using her father as fodder in Conroy's plotting at Pinnacle. After Sally started treatment with Carr, and he loaded her up on drugs, she went downhill fast. Still, she was lucid enough to put a lot of the pieces together about the fraud going on at Pinnacle. She gave that diary to Father Caverly for safekeeping because it contained information about a safe deposit box. That's where she placed the evidence gathered about Pinnacle before she called the feds. I hope some of what she wrote brings Dottie consolation if she can bring herself to read it."

"Yes, let's hope so. This has been terrible for Dottie, even now that both those maleantes are dead. Lucky for her, she's so tough. She has to find a new assistant now, too."

"Andrea Jessop and Carla Fergusson are singing at the top of their lungs," Frank added. "The feds arrested Carla Fergusson's boss, Pinnacle's Chief Financial Officer. He colluded with Conroy to raid the coffers at Pinnacle, cook the books, and stash money in offshore accounts. Carla helped them implement their plans. That's how she knew enough to go rogue on Conroy. Plan A was to steal hundreds of millions from that IPO. Plan B was to make do with the tens of millions the culprits had already squirreled away. The yacht was part of the getaway strategy in either case. Conroy must have had no clue the two women he'd enlisted to help him had come up with a plan of their own. Andrea kept him in the loop about developments in the Winchester household—even before Sally moved out. Conroy had Andrea over a barrel, blackmailing her about an arrest that had occurred years before. The police never charged her, and she had the arrest expunged from her record. Expunged doesn't mean gone, however. He threatened to tell Dottie Winchester unless she cooperated."

"Does that mean the feds had figured out Andrea was in cahoots with Conroy?" Jessica asked.

"Yes, the feds launched that raid on half a dozen locations all at once that morning when you and Bernadette went to meet with Carla—without telling me. That included the Winchester estate where they were after Andrea and the records Sally used to expose the fraud at Pinnacle. They didn't know about the safe deposit box until you all recovered that diary from Father Caverly. They would have picked Andrea up too, but she wasn't in the house. Conroy had ordered her to find Sally's missing diary by morning, or else. It turns out, Kirk was the 'or else.' He was at the Winchester Estate looking for Andrea. If she didn't give him that diary, Conroy ordered Kirk to get rid of her. Kirk was lurking when the feds moved in. He found out enough about the operation that morning to call Conroy with that heads up, while you were sitting in his office. Anyway, Andrea was out in a storage area searching for the diary when the feds moved in. She slipped out before the authorities located her, got a text message from Carla about Plan B, and headed to the marina in a cab."

"Andrea had some secrets of her own, besides the ones she was keeping from Dottie," Bernadette said.

"That's for sure. Jessica was right about Carla's anger and defiance toward Conroy. She and Andrea had hooked up months earlier and planned that mutiny. If Shannon hadn't shown up and started shooting, there's a good chance Andrea and Carla would have killed Conroy and fled by the time the feds got to the marina. Carla claims they would have let you and Bernadette go, Jessica. Maybe, but you two weren't part of the plan any more than Shannon was. Nor could they have known you'd get a message to Peter with the inside track on their escape route."

"Well, I figured the feds had the yacht on their list of locations to hit that day, too, at some point. I'm grateful Peter got help there quick though. Carla must have information the feds can use to recover the money stashed in offshore accounts, right?"

"Yes, she's using that to negotiate with the feds for leniency for herself and her gal pal."

"Okay, so my head is spinning. I must have missed something. How did Shannon end up at that marina?" Laura asked.

"Kismet! As much as that grates on Detective Hernandez, it's as good an explanation as any. Shannon took a wrong turn that turned out right. She followed us from the desert to Beverly Hills and was loitering around the Beverly Wilshire. That's how she knew she could find us at Tiffany's. She overheard us talking about going back to Dottie Winchester's estate for another conversation with Andrea. Her plan was to get there ahead of us and wait for me to show up so she could shoot me," Jessica said, shuddering.

"That was stupid," Brien said. "Why didn't she just shoot you in the lobby?"

"I don't know, but I imagine it had something to do with wanting to get away with murder. If I get a chance, I'll ask her," Jessica said.

"If she'd made a move on you in the lobby of the Beverly Wilshire, I like to think I could have stopped her. Where was I when she was close enough to hear our conversation?"

"I don't know that either, Peter. I'll put it on the list of questions for my next interview with Shannon, which I hope happens—never! By the time Shannon got to Dottie's, the raid was underway. She was trying to get out of there when she spotted Andrea making her escape. You won't believe this, but Shannon's the one who gave Andrea a lift to a cab stand in downtown San Marino. While she was in the car with Shannon, Andrea called Carla and left a message. Something like, 'Carla, I'm on my way to the marina. I'll be ready when you and Conroy get there with Jessica Huntington.' All Shannon had to do was follow that cab."

"Okay, well that answers my first question," Laura said. "Last question, I promise. What's with the sniper?"

"I can answer that one," Frank replied. "The helicopter tracked him down and the police cornered him. They had him surrounded, so he surrendered. He's playing let's make a deal, too, so who knows what will happen to him? They may give him life in prison, in exchange for information about members of 'la crème de la crud' who have hired him over the years. Not just Conroy, but other people with the money to pay Kirk, as he prefers to be called, to do their dirty work. He sure made it obvious when he shot reminded Conroy he did not like being called Kierkegaard! Conroy was trying to stiff him too, refusing to pay for that botched attempt on Libby's life, so he had more than one reason to shoot Conroy. Kirk also claims he couldn't just stand there and watch Conroy shoot an unarmed woman. Shannon had a gun but was out of bullets and Conroy had a gun pointed right at her."

"That's why I took a shot at him. It sounds like I missed him, though," Jessica said.

"It's okay, that sniper got him. Kirk won't be shooting at you or anyone else since the cops got him now, too." Bernadette was trying to look on the bright side, as usual. Jessica still wasn't feeling great about the fact that she had fired a gun at a human being—even one as loathsome as Eric Conroy.

"Thank God this is almost over. I will be so glad when this year comes to an end. We're having a New Year's Eve party, and at twelve-o-one, I will burn the 2013 calendar. What gives? Are all these people mentally ill, or just miserable, evil people?"

"Some of the trouble is due to mental illness. But as I've said to you before, most people with mental health problems are more likely to be victims of crime and violence than perpetrators. It's human nature; good and evil playing out around us."

"You sound like Father Martin," Jessica said.

"Could be, but have you heard the Cherokee story of the Two Wolves? My Cahuilla great-grandmother told me the story when I was very young."

"I could use a *good* story after this bad one. Tell us, okay?" Brien asked.

"According to legend, an old Cherokee is teaching his grandson about life," Betsy began.

'A fight is going on inside me,' he said to the boy. 'It is a terrible fight and it is between two wolves. One is evil – he is anger, envy, sorrow, regret, greed,

arrogance, self-pity, guilt, resentment, inferiority, lies, false pride, superiority, and ego.'

He continued, 'The other is good – he is joy, peace, love, hope, serenity, humility, kindness, benevolence, empathy, generosity, truth, compassion, and faith. The same fight is going on inside you – and inside every other person, too.'

The grandson thought about it for a minute and then asked his grandfather, 'Which wolf will win?'

The old Cherokee simply replied, 'The one you feed.'

The troubled daughters of Beverly Hills seem to have been feeding the wrong wolf," Betsy said.

"That *was* a good story, Betsy. You're right about those 90210 girls," Bernadette said. "That Dr. Dick and the red devil, too. If you have another story like that, don't tell it yet. I need to check on our dinner, but I'll be right back." Bernadette scurried into the house, calling out to the caterers as she entered.

Jessica was about to speak when her cell phone rang. She recognized the phone number belonging to her ex but took the call anyway. "Speaking of wolves," she said. "Hello, Jim."

"Jessica, it's Jim."

"Yes, I know, that's why I said hello Jim," she rolled her eyes.

"Oh yeah, I'm sorry. I, I think... I've made a horrible mistake and I'm in trouble," Jim said in the weirdest tone of voice she had ever heard him use. She wasn't sure if he was crying or on the verge of tears. Or maybe he'd had one too many Margaritas; his speech sounded slurred. Her mind was racing, trying to figure out if this was a personal call or a professional one.

"What kind of trouble?" She asked. All eyes were on her. Before he could reply, the screen door slid open with a crack and Bernadette flew out onto the patio.

"Jessica, Giovanni just called. It's Alexis, they've taken her to UCLA medical center in an ambulance. Giovanni says she's asking for you. We need to get there as soon as possible. Frank, do you have your cop light to put on the top of your car?" Frank, already on his feet, was buttoning his shirt and pulling on a pair of sweat pants he had worn over his trunks. Jessica was trying to process what was going on when she heard Jim's voice, calling to her as if from a great distance.

"Jim, I've got a situation here—it's Mom. Something's happened and we've got to get to LA right away. I'll get back with you once we're on the road, okay?" She couldn't hear what he was saying, his response was muffled. "Jim, are you all right? You didn't take anything, did you?" She wasn't sure why she'd even asked that question. Maybe because she was worried that's what her mother had done. He didn't answer. "Jim, are you there? Where are you?" She asked several more times before she got an address from him. Frank was on the phone to a dispatcher with 911 asking for help to be sent to that address.

"Go, you guys, go," Laura urged them. "We'll take care of things here."

"Thanks," Jessica said as she, Bernadette, and Frank dashed to his car.

The year isn't over yet, Jessica thought, as she got into Frank's car and called Giovanni.

~~~~~

Thank you for reading *A DEAD DAUGHTER*. I'd love to get your feedback about the book, so please, please, please leave me a review on Amazon and Goodreads!

Sign up at http://www.desertcitiesmystery.com for news, recipes, excerpts from works in progress, book features, and other blog posts.

Jessica Huntington is back in the fourth Desert Cities Mystery, *A Dead Mother* @ http://bit.ly/deadmothr.

Jessica's ex-husband, James Harper, and her mother, Alexis, are in big trouble in A Dead Mother. Family dysfunction, infidelity, murder, and mayhem—what else can you expect from members of the rich and famous who move in Jessica Huntington's circles? An arraignment in court goes off the rails after Jim Harper's Bel Air mansion is trashed and a man is left fighting for his life. Jessica's love life almost veers off track, too, as she struggles to balance job, family, sleuthing, and her attraction to Attorney Paul Worthington and Detective Frank Fontana. When the body of a prominent member of the Palm Desert community is found dead on the side of the road, Jessica gives up hope that this year will be better than the last. It's a three-ring-circus of calamities as Jessica and her friends get pulled into another whirlwind whodunit. There are plenty of well-heeled heels to choose from among the suspects with murderous motives: love, lust, lucre, and loathing.

I hope you'll check out the books in the two other cozy mystery series I write.

The Corsario Cove Cozy Mystery series available on all eBook platforms. This series features Brien Williams the land-locked surfer dude, turned pool boy, turned security guard in humorous most excellent adventures. He's not alone. As it turns out, Kim Reed, is the woman of his dreams. Who knew? Follow the adventures of Gidget and Moondoggie as they set out on a life together. Available in Paperback and on your favorite eBook platform.

Cowabunga Christmas! Corsario Cove Cozy Mystery #1 http://books2read.com/u/mdKPlX

Gnarly New Year! Corsario Cove Cozy Mystery #2 http://books2read.com/u/b6Q7x6

Heinous Habits! Corsario Cove Cozy Mystery #3 available as an eBook until Sept. 30, 2017 in the SUMMER WHODUNNITS box set @ http://books2read.com/u/brgNv7 As a standalone Oct 1st.

Radical Regatta! Corsario Cove Cozy Mystery #4 Coming Soon!

Why not try out the novellas in the Georgie Shaw Cozy Mystery Series? Meet Georgie Shaw who works for a Disneyesque entertainment empire. When there's a murder at Marvelous Marley World, the handsome detective, Jack Wheeler, steps in to investigate.

Whodunit? Who's out to frame Georgie for the murder? Read Murder at Catmmando Mountain. Meet Georgie, Jack, and Georgie's big-mouth Siamese cat, Miles—as in Miles Davis. There's more than murder and mayhem in this series—a second chance at love, too, for Jack and Georgie. The first three mysteries are available in a box set http://bit.ly/Shawboxset

Find the entire series on AMAZON at http://bit.ly/shawcozy

Before you go.... Bernadette and Jessica have a few recipes from the delicious Cat Pack get-togethers. Yum!

RECIPES

Spaghetti with Salsa Di Pomodoro
Serves 6

Ingredients
4 tablespoons (1/2 stick) plus 1 tablespoon unsalted butter
2 carrots, finely chopped
1 small celery stalk, finely chopped
1 small yellow onion, finely chopped
2 lbs. fresh plum tomatoes, peeled, seeded and chopped, or 1 can (28 oz.) chopped plum tomatoes, drained
1 teaspoon sea salt [plus 2 tablespoons for water to cook pasta]
1/8 teaspoon freshly ground pepper
1 lb. spaghetti
10 fresh basil leaves, chopped
4 garlic cloves, chopped fine
1/2 cup grated Parmigiano-Reggiano cheese, plus more for serving

Preparation
In a large sauté pan over medium heat, melt 4 tablespoons of butter. Add the garlic, carrots, celery, and onion and cook, stirring frequently, until the onion has softened and the carrots and celery are tender, about 15 minutes.
Add the tomatoes, 1 teaspoon salt and pepper and cook until the sauce begins to bubble. Reduce the heat to low and cook, stirring occasionally, until the sauce has thickened, about 20 minutes. Season with salt and pepper.

While the sauce simmers, cook pasta in a large pot of boiling salted water, stirring occasionally, until al dente according to the package instructions. Drain, reserving 1/2 cup pasta cooking liquid.

Add the drained pasta to the sauce in the pan, stir and toss over low heat until well coated with the sauce, adjusting the consistency with some of the cooking water if needed. Add the basil and the remaining 1 tablespoon butter and toss to distribute evenly. Remove from the heat, add the 1/2 cup cheese and toss again. Transfer to a warmed serving bowl and serve immediately, passing additional cheese at the table.

Snapper Veracruz
Serves 4

Ingredients
4 7-9 ounce Snapper fillets
2 tablespoons lime juice
2 tablespoons olive oil
1/2 cup of finely chopped, white onion
4 garlic cloves, finely chopped
1 can (28 ounces) crushed tomatoes or 1 1/2 pound of tomatoes, finely chopped
1 small bunch of flat parsley, finely chopped (about 1/2 cup)
2 fresh branches of thyme
2 bay leaves
1 teaspoon Mexican oregano
1/2 cup Manzanilla [Pimiento Stuffed] Green Olive, whole or sliced
2 tablespoons small capers, rinsed
4 pickled jalapenos peppers, thinly sliced
1/4 cup dry white wine
Salt and pepper to taste

Preparation
Sprinkle filets with salt and place in a shallow pan. Cut limes in half and squeeze juice all over filets. Place lime halves in pan, cover, and marinate in refrigerator for 1 hour.

Heat oil in a large sauté pan over medium-low heat. Add onions and cook until golden, about 10 minutes. Stir in garlic, and cook for 1 minute.

Add tomatoes (break up if canned); cook for 10 minutes. Add olives, capers, jalapeños, jalapeño juice, parsley, rosemary, marjoram, oregano, and bay leaves. Season with salt and pepper; cook over low heat for 20 minutes.

Add filets and marinade, cover, and cook, turning once, for 4 minutes per side. Discard bay leaves and limes. Serve immediately with rice and tortillas or with tiny roasted potatoes and steamed carrots in a mango salsa.

Bagna Cauda
Serves 4

Ingredients
12 garlic cloves
1 cup extra virgin olive oil
3.5 ounces anchovies in oil
1/4 cup of cold butter

Preparation
Peel the garlic cloves, then mince 4 to 5 of them and finely slice the rest.

Place all the garlic, the olive oil, and anchovies in a small saucepan and place over VERY LOW HEAT.

Cook gently for about 20 minutes, or until the garlic is soft and fragrant but do not let the garlic brown or fry. Keep your eye on it and stir occasionally to check that there's no danger of browning the garlic.

Just before removing from heat, stir through the butter. Serve hot with raw or cooked vegetables cut into sticks or wedges for dipping. You can store in the refrigerator for a few days maximum.

Artichoke Gratinata
Serves 4-6

Ingredients
3 tablespoons olive oil
1 garlic clove, minced
1 pound frozen artichoke hearts, thawed
2 tablespoons chopped fresh parsley leaves
3/4 teaspoon salt
1/4 teaspoon freshly ground black pepper
1/8 teaspoon red pepper flakes
1/2 cup chicken broth
1/4 cup Marsala wine
2 tablespoons butter
1/3 cup plain bread crumbs
1/3 cup grated Parmesan

Preparation
Preheat the oven to 450 degrees F. Warm the olive oil in a heavy bottom skillet over medium-high heat. Add the garlic and cook for 1 minute. Add the artichoke hearts, parsley, salt, pepper, and red pepper flakes and cook until the artichoke hearts are starting to brown at the edges, about 3 minutes. Add the chicken broth and wine and simmer for 3 minutes. Transfer the artichoke mixture to a 2-quart baking dish. Melt the butter in the same skillet used to cook the artichokes. In a small bowl, mix the melted butter with the bread crumbs. Stir in the Parmesan and top the artichokes with the bread crumbs. Bake until the top is golden, about 10 minutes.

Carne Asada with a la Bernadette
Serves 8-10

Ingredients
3 pounds flank steak
Marinade
3/4 cup fresh squeezed orange juice
1/2 cup lemon juice
1/3 cup lime juice
1/2 cup soy sauce
4 ounces Reposado Tequila
4 garlic cloves, minced
1/2 large onion, sliced
1 finely chopped canned chipotle pepper
2 fresh jalapeno peppers, seeded
1/2 cup olive oil
1 tablespoon mild chili powder
1 tablespoon cumin
1 tablespoon paprika
1 tablespoon dried whole oregano
1 teaspoon ground black pepper
1 bunch fresh cilantro, chopped
Salt to taste

Preparation
Combine all marinade ingredients in a bowl. Whisk together until well-blended. Reserve one cup marinade, cover and refrigerate to be used after meat is cooked.

Place the flank steak between two heavy plastic freezer bags on a flat surface. Pound with the soft side of a meal mallet until 1/4 inch thick. After pounding, poke meat all over with a fork.

Place meat in a large dish and pour marinade over it. Allow to marinate for 24 hours.

To cook, preheat outdoor grill to medium high heat, and lightly oil the grate. Remove meat from marinade and place on grill, discarding used marinade. Grill until desired doneness—about 5 minutes on each side for medium rare.

Remove meat from grill and slice across the grain. Pour the one cup of reserved marinade [you can let this sit out while meat is cooking to reach room temperature] over the hot meat and serve immediately.

To serve, place two small warmed tortillas on top of each other. Add desired amount of meat. Top with tomatillo sauce, pico de gallo, avocado, cotija cheese, onions, and cilantro. Garnish with a wedge of lime, to be squeezed over taco before eating.

ABOUT THE AUTHOR

Anna Celeste Burke is an award-winning, USA Today bestselling author who enjoys *snooping into life's mysteries with fun, fiction, and food— California style!*

A few words for you from Anna...

Life is an extravaganza! Figuring out how to hang tough and make the most of the wild ride is the challenge. On my way to Oahu, to join the rock musician and high school drop-out, I had married in Tijuana, I was nabbed as a runaway. Eventually, the police let me go, but the rock band broke up.

Our next stop: Disney World, where we "worked for the Mouse" as chefs, courtesy of Walt Disney World University Chef's School. More education landed us in academia at The Ohio State University. For decades, I researched, wrote, and taught about many gloriously nerdy topics.

Retired now, I'm still married to the same, sweet, guy and live with him near Palm Springs, California. I write mysteries set in sunny California! The Jessica Huntington Desert Cities Mystery series set here in the Coachella Valley and the Corsario Cove Cozy Mystery Series set in California's Central Coast, The Georgie Shaw Mystery series set in the OC, and coming soon, The Misadventures of Betsy Stark also set here in the desert. Won't you join me? Please join me at:

http://www.desertcitiesmystery.com.

CPSIA information can be obtained
at www.ICGtesting.com
Printed in the USA
LVHW08s2148101018
593201LV00033B/704/P

9 781508 620372